OUR HOSPITAL

ALSO BY SAMUEL SHEM

NOVELS

The Healing Quartet

The House of God

Mount Misery

Man's 4th Best Hospital

Our Hospital

• • •

The Spirit of the Place

Fine

At the Heart of the Universe

The Buddha's Wife:
The Path of Awakening Together
(with Janet Surrey)

PLAYS

Bill W. and Dr. Bob
(with Janet Surrey)

Napoleon's Dinner

Room for One Woman

NONFICTION

We Have to Talk:
Healing Dialogues Between Women and Men
(with Janet Surrey)

Fiction as Resistance

OUR HOSPITAL

SAMUEL SHEM

BERKLEY
NEW YORK

BERKLEY
An imprint of Penguin Random House LLC
penguinrandomhouse.com

Library of Congress Cataloging-in-Publication Data

Names: Shem, Samuel, author.
Title: Our hospital / Samuel Shem.
Description: New York: Berkley, [2023]
Identifiers: LCCN 2023013967 (print) | LCCN 2023013968 (ebook) |
ISBN 9780593439319 (hardcover) | ISBN 9780593439326 (ebook)
Subjects: LCSH: Physicians—Fiction. | Nurses—Fiction. | COVID-19
(Disease)—Fiction. | LCGFT: Medical fiction. | Humorous fiction. | Novels.
Classification: LCC PS3569.H39374 O87 2023 (print) | LCC PS3569.H39374 (ebook) |
DDC 813/.54—dc23/eng/20230324
LC record available at https://lccn.loc.gov/2023013967
LC ebook record available at https://lccn.loc.gov/2023013968

Printed in the United States of America
1st Printing

Book design by Kristin del Rosario

To Janet and Katie

With thanks to the doctors:
Denis Noble, Walter Micky, David Heber, and "Eat My Dust"

With gratitude to
New York University Grossman School of Medicine—
which gives me time to learn, teach, and write.

And wordsmiths:
Rosemary Ahern, Tracy Bernstein, Robin Straus

"My house shall be called
a house of prayer,
but you have made it
a den of thieves."

—MATTHEW 21:13
(NEW KING JAMES VERSION)

CONTENTS

OUR HOSPITAL

THE FIRST WAVE

FLYING BLIND

1

Dr. Roy G. Basch was dead tired. It was past midnight and he had been driving north for over an hour on the New York State Thruway, from Montefiore Hospital in the deep Bronx to his new house in Columbia, New York, the town where he had been born and raised, 128 miles north of Manhattan. The house was a grand 1854 classic sitting high up on Mount Merino overlooking the Hudson and the Catskills. Columbia, to its inhabitants, was known as a town of breakage. If something could break—especially something to do with town government or weather forecasts—it would. But Roy had been assured that the house was now breakage-free.

He and his wife, Berry, had been living in Costa Rica on a mountain above Carmona, Nandayure. A paradise, yes. But with the coronavirus rampant in America, they decided to move closer to their daughter, Spring, who was working and living with a long-term boyfriend in New York City. When Roy was asked to help out at the hospital in Columbia, they had taken a trip back home and, falling in love with the town, they found and bought their dream house.

Going home. For good. In all ways.

Two more hours to go. He was drinking coffee but, strangely, the caffeine didn't seem to be working. The initial jolt had been fine, then vanished. His eyelids were getting heavy and scratchy, and he couldn't stop yawning. *Weird.* He cranked down the windows and let in the cold air to help him stay awake.

It had been a long day. He'd gotten up early at their daughter's condo on the now-chic Upper Upper West Side—not far from the George Washington Bridge, where his immigrant grandfather Samuel Fuchs, a metalworker, had toiled. A rare photo showed Sam hundreds of feet above the Hudson, with an acetylene torch and no safety harness. In his spare time he'd made, out of copper, elegant Sumerian wine vases, all curves and shine, copied from the Museum of Natural History.

Tough, that generation.

That afternoon at Montefiore Hospital, Roy had given a Surgical Grand Rounds, a talk to a packed house of 300 doctors, nurses, and others, on "Staying Human in Medicine: The Danger of Isolation and the Healing Power of Good Connection." At dinner that night at the NYC Sailing Club, he'd drunk too much wine with eight of the top Montefiore surgeons. Awareness had recently heightened of this novel coronavirus out of China that was spreading rapidly. The main precaution recommended by the CDC was not to shake hands but to bump elbows.

A few days before the Montefiore gig, he'd also done one at Downstate Medical School in Brooklyn. He was in demand as a speaker because he had become a celebrity, the real live doctor who was the model for the hero of the classic "internship" novel called *The House of God*, and its sequels, *Mount Misery* and *Man's 4th Best Hospital*. Now he was exhausted. Hence his torpor behind the wheel.

Finally, with relief, he turned off the thruway at the Catskill exit. He passed the Catskill Country Club. In his boyhood, the private golf course near his home in Columbia did not admit Jews. But Catskill

Country Club, a public course a half hour across the river, did. Finally there it was—the Rip Van Winkle Bridge across the Hudson River.

God I loved my summer job as toll taker on the bridge during high school and Harvard, with my snappy uniform and gun in the drawer that had never been fired since it was put there in 1939. Looking up at Olana, the grand palace on top of the hill built by the painter Frederic Church.

He turned left along Mount Merino and then right into the long driveway of the new house. He got out of the car, dragged himself into the house. The sharp, tart scent of fresh paint was a joy, snapping him awake for a moment. The renovation was finally complete. He called Berry, still at Spring's apartment.

"I'm home, hon," he said.

"Thank God."

"Long day. Love you, g'night."

"Love you too, sleep tight."

It was almost two a.m., but he was now so tired he felt jazzed. He dragged himself up the 1875 grand staircase, the creaking a comfort. He poured himself a shot of George Dickle sipping whisky and lay back almost horizontal on the new leather-scented couch and watched the news, all bad. After a few minutes he clicked it off and sat up.

He was so tired he slouched back in the couch. And then tried again to get on his feet.

On your feet yay and a sudden blow a sense draining to steady falling forward fell facedownonfloor . . .

———

Berry called his cell phone at six in the morning, no answer. She left a message. At seven, nothing. Another message. She steeled herself and called Dr. Amy Rose, the intensivist in charge of the Kush Kare Hospital emergency room and ICU, and left a message to call. Nothing.

Panicking, she called Amy's uncle Orville Rose, their dear friend and forever doctor for the town, who knew *everything*. Almost 75, Orville was old enough to be up early. He picked up on the second ring.

"I'm frantic," she said to Orville, telling him the details. "Somebody's got to go over there. There's a spare key under the back door mat."

"I'm on my way," said Orvy.

At Roy's house, Orville put on a mask and gloves and went in, shouting for Roy. No answer. Worrisome. He walked through the rooms and finally found Roy sprawled facedown on the oak floor, in a significant puddle of blood. Orville tried to turn him over—*whoa!*—dead or unconscious bodies are *heavy*! He tried again, but no way. Roy groaned, awoke. He needed help to roll over, dazed and bloody. Orville did a quick assessment. The blood was from a gash in his forehead and temple, clotted—hours old. A fall on his face—there had been no time to prevent a direct facedown hit—could be heart arrhythmia—transient, now in normal sinus; breathing okay. No signs of stroke. Feels feverish. Been drinking—George Dickle. Kind of obese. Disoriented, mumbling. Probably drunk. *Please don't let it be a stroke!*

Orville called Lebowsky Ambulance and Taxidermy to take Roy to the hospital, then called Berry.

"Clearly he fell, fell on his face."

"But why? He never has fallen that way, never. Why?"

"Dunno, but we'll find out."

Roy was now fully awake, in normal sinus rhythm. Angry that he was being taken to the hospital.

Orville knew Roy well; the Jewish community in Columbia was small and tight, and he'd helped Roy into medicine—as he did a generation later with his niece Amy.

At the start of Covid, when the emergency doctors at Kush Kare realized how dangerous it was to stay and take care of patients at

Kush Kare, many of them quit. Those who remained were now *really* stressed. Orville knew Roy was back in New York and had asked if he would help, and if he knew any doctor friends who might come to help as well. Roy said he would be glad to, and he brought in two other former interns of the House of God: Eat My Dust Eddie and Hyper Hooper. Both were recently retired in California, and bored. They jumped at the chance to work with Roy again and had already arrived at Kush Kare. Roy was supposed to join them after the event at Montefiore.

"So I passed out, from exhaustion," Roy said, lying on a stretcher in Emergency. "Big deal. As I told you in detail, it was a long day, and I was dead tired. For some reason I blacked out and fell."

"What was the last thing you recall?" Amy said. She was in full anti-Covid garb, covering every part of her body.

"Finishing my drink—just one—maybe two—of bourbon. So I fell down. So what?"

"So clearly you didn't try to break your fall," said Amy. "That's not normal. Your heart might've stopped, couldn't pump the blood up to your head—" She looked at the cardiac monitor. "EKG just now is showing runs of atrial fibrillation." She pointed the temperature gun at his forehead. "A hundred and one—fever. Blood pressure low."

"So? If you do an EKG, *everybody* my age has something—often runs of atrial fib."

"I am your doctor now, Roy. Me and Orvy," said Amy. "As you know, 'if a doctor tries to treat himself, he has a fool for a patient.' Okay?" He nodded. "I have to work you up completely. Starting with chest films."

"For what?"

"Covid."

Roy looked startled. "There's no sign of it. No breathing problems."

"It's becoming clear that all kinds of symptoms could be Covid."

7

She saw his face go white. "Roy, honey, we're just finding out how easy it is to catch this. And spending all that time without a face mask in big crowds, right?"

He nodded. "The only restriction the hospitals made is 'No shaking hands.'"

"So you were exposed for hours?"

He sighed. "Why do you think I fainted?"

"Either the atrial fib, or, most likely, orthostatic hypotension, fainting. You fell without putting your hands down to break the fall. It's one of the first protection reflexes a baby has—if they sense they're about to be dropped, out go the arms to protect themselves. What's it called? The *Moro reflex*? If you didn't extend your arms, that means you were out before you hit the floor. Our Covid expert here, Dr. Dandona, has had two other patients with your symptoms. He thinks that Covid can damage peripheral small blood vessels, and so the blood pools in the legs. And with your heart straining, the blood didn't get to the brain."

A cold, damp shiver went through Roy. "Oh God."

"There's no test for the virus yet," she said. "But clinically I think you've got it. You're in good shape but, frankly, your weight is a risk factor—I just read a paper showing that Covid thrives on fat. The fever might vanish in a few days, but it's all new territory in medicine, this virus. Nobody knows bubkes. We're flying blind. I'm going to have to admit you, to watch you carefully."

Roy let this sink in, his face still blanched. "One more thing?"

"Sure, hon."

"I'm scared of being in the hospital for any length of time. They're dangerous, especially in spreading pathogens. And from what I've heard about the Kush management? Death! So can I arrange it to stay at home—at least until we see if it's going to get worse or not?"

"Roy, Roy!" she said, shaking her head. "There are things we can only work up with you right here, under observation. With this virus, things can change in a split second. This hospital, especially with the new team—me and the great nurses and Hooper and Eddie—is really the safest place around."

"Okay. But let's make it as quick as possible. I want to get to work with my guys here. I got them here, and I don't want to let them down."

2

It was a hard May 2020.

Kush Kare Hospital in Columbia, New York, was the flagship of Kush Kare Private Equity Inc., a for-profit chain of hospitals across America. A for-profit that was listed on a lot of lucrative trading routes. Clearly its workings were murky—maybe not equity at all. A clever goulash of nonprofit and big-time profit.

It was on the same site as the very first hospital in Columbia, called Whale City Infirmary, founded just after the Civil War. A grand charitable mission: to care for each and every wounded, even the rare Confederate soldier who wound up there. And it was totally free.

With the rise of Covid, the hospital was a zoo: frazzled doctors, nurses, techs, labs, cleaners. And patients stacked up lying on stretchers in hallways, coughing, crying—and dying. Dr. Amy Rose was nine hours into her six-to-six shift, and it seemed like 20. She could not go on.

She went on.

She was chief of both Emergency and the ICU, the Intensive Care Unit. Her official title was "intensivist," one of the ones who run *toward* the danger. She had done just that for a month in the bone-dry Har Har Somali refugee camp, but she had never seen anything quite like this.

No doctor, she thought, had ever seen anything quite like this. Even after two months, they were flying blind. Risking. One patient might look healthy, only to die suddenly. Another might look sick as hell, and make it. Being a virus, Covid had no curative treatment. They didn't even know what would *help. But we docs like leaning out over the tips of our skis. It's exciting and terrifying at the same time.*

The hard thing for Amy was ensuring she had no exposed skin. For 12 hours a day she was sealed head to toe in plastic PPE, personal protective equipment. It was stifling. The pants and gown and mask and protective N95 face shield and gloves made each of her senses blur and rebel; her fingers felt fuzzy and far away, like she was a spacewoman out on a moonwalk. Real life seemed more virtual than Zoom. It was nearly impossible to feel connected to a patient, or to fellow health-care workers.

Now there was no touch, no contact of any kind. Except eyes. They almost never went into a patient's room. She felt like a leper. When a physical intervention was strictly necessary, several space-suited docs and nurses went in. Otherwise, all patient information and care were addressed from outside, either on screens or with robots controlled by toggles on handheld joysticks. The rooms were sealed off, with negative pressure airflow. Bad air sucked out, good air pumped in.

The only other time someone (let's face it, usually a nurse, not a doctor) entered the patient's room was, with a surgical-gloved hand, to hold the hand of someone dying alone; if possible, holding up an "I"-phone or laptop so that family members could be "with" their loved one.

Amy knew scientific studies demonstrated that a crucial element of healing is experiencing a feeling of connection with the health-care provider. Eye contact, touch, voice, facial expressions of all kinds, are key. Without good connection, mortality and morbidity go up. Isolation is death. Connections heal.

Of these the only one that remained was eye contact. Years ago, Amy had spent a few months working in Casablanca. The women's jellabas covered all but their eyes. And what eyes they were! Not just the dramatic makeup, but the dramatic way they used their eyes, taking in and sending back all kinds of strong emotions.

In the hospital, she thought now, the distance they had to maintain was necessary, but damn sad. And *hot*. No way to cool off. No way to pee unless you had time for a major undertaking! Just the physical exertion of donning, and doffing, the protective plastic cocoon was hellish. *How can I make it 'til six?* she thought for at least the tenth time that day. *Gotta make it—and then get out fast.* The high point of the day was dinner back at the house with her uncle Orville, aunt Miranda, and cousin Eleanor. And, of course, Ben, the dog.

The only sounds were the *bleep-bleeps* of the mechanical warnings going off—often in error. The loneliest sound was not hearing unmuffled human sound. Eerie, suffering silence.

She and the other doctors and nurses each wore their photo IDs on their chests.

Even if it might not help patients, it helps us remember who we are.

On first meeting Amy, you'd be taken with her smarts and vitality and—with her patients especially—her ready kindness. The glint in her blue eyes that enticed, "Hey, let's talk and talk, and laugh as we do." Her auburn hair had, over the years, gone all the way from ponytail to shaved and back, depending. The threadlike scar from the edge of an eyebrow to an ear, from shrapnel in the Somali refugee camp, was less disfiguring than sobering, even attractive. Like a veteran wearing a patch over an eye.

Amy was in charge. All the members of Amy's team—even the prickly ones—were each other's saviors. In the foxhole together.

"Ready?" she asked Leatrice Shumpsky, the head nurse, who was assisting just in case.

"Ready." Shump was a gem, a smart, tough young grandmother, a Columbian through and through. She seemed to know everyone in town, their histories and their stories. Whenever she chanced upon a friend coming into Emergency, or worse, a member of her high school class, she took it hard, and deaths, well, deaths were a grand sorrow.

Amy had come to see her as a cool, sharp-humored Catholic saint who had eaten the right wafers and said "No, thanks" to the nutty ones. Her ordinary Saint Mary's Church compassion held firm in the face of the ever more conservative Evangelical churches sprouting in surrounding rural Kinderhook County. She was RC-tough, full of curses and jokes galore, and chief ER nurse on the day shift.

As Shump put it, "Somebody has to fight all this crazy, and it might as well be me."

Amy hitched up her resolve, said out loud, "Be kind, kid," and walked with Shump into the room to intubate Mary Platt, 43, only a few years older than Amy herself. She had the classic signs and symptoms of Covid—including, on her chest X-ray, those glassy dots in the lobes of both lungs. Mother of four. Secretary in the office of Whale City Real Estate. Healthy but for one dire risk factor: grade 3 mitral valve disease. For the past few hours the team had tried everything, but on 100 percent nasal oxygen, her blood oxygen saturation rate kept falling—it was now below 70 percent. The lungs couldn't aerate the blood anymore. The sparkly shreds of Covid got in the way.

Now she was wide-eyed with fear, laboring to breathe. Without oxygen, her exhausted chest muscles were getting tired—on the verge of giving out. You could almost see that leaky mitral valve creaking, regurgitating blood back out the wrong way on every beat. She was starting to die—and Covid, for some reason not yet known, could kill fast, shockingly fast. A person melts to blood.

"Mary, as we talked about before," Amy said, "we need to put a breathing tube in, put you on a respirator in Intensive Care to breathe for you. We spoke to your husband just now. Ventilation is necessary. Okay?"

Tears ran down Mary's cheeks. She nodded her agreement.

What Amy didn't say was that of patients put on a ventilator, 80 percent never get off. That's why before doing the procedure, Amy always tried to set up a video conference with the patient's family—it could be the last time they spoke. Mary's condition had worsened abruptly. The aide had prepped her for the endotracheal tube.

Amy put a hand on her arm and squeezed reassurance. She said—making sure to use the "we"—"We'll be *with* you the whole time, taking the best care of you we can, together. Got it?"

Mary gave a weak smile and nodded.

"Okay, now we're going to give you some medicine to make you sleepy."

Amy flashed on a month she'd spent during the bad epidemics in Cape Town, South Africa, where doctors routinely "turned positive" for HIV and drug-resistant tuberculosis. Once, in the emergency room, she watched a young woman doctor intubating a man infected to the gills with these two contagious diseases. As she put the tube down his trachea, the man suddenly blasted out cough after cough all over the doctor, who hadn't gotten out of the way. Amy never found out what happened to her.

Okay, kid, she said to herself, *all brains on deck. This is where you can die. Unless you're poised to jump out of the way, if this patient does 'the Cape Town maneuver,' showering you with a million Covid-19 viruses, next week they'll be intubating you.*

Focus. Pray. Who to? Who cares.

Amy took a deep breath. The procedure was called RSI—Rapid Sequence Intubation—a series of steps designed to intubate the patient quickly without them breathing—while minimizing the risk of their coughing. Amy was so tired, she repeated the four steps in her head, even though she could probably do them in her sleep: (1) knock the patient out; (2) when the patient is briefly paralyzed, hurry up and pray like hell that I can get the endotracheal tube in before they suffocate; (3) jam a metal laryngoscope down their throat to lift their head by the jaw and try to get a good look at the vocal cords; (4) stuff the plastic trach tube through those vocal cords and into their lungs, secure it, and then hook it up to breathe for them.

The ventilator would do nothing to cure Mary, of course. All it did was buy time to figure out what the hell to do next. This new killer coronavirus—Jesus, had it only been here six weeks?—was crazy unpredictable. The only real treatment? Keep the body going and let it heal itself. And pray like hell for a treatment protocol.

A second doctor was always there to help if needed at an intubation. In this case his name was Dr. Binni Prabhat, Indian-born and raised in prosperous Kerala, Oxford-educated, so he had a sexy accent. He was a couple of years younger than Amy, slender, with a regal nose, alert brown eyes, and almost comic ears. He laughed a lot, and she had never seen him angry, even in the most enraging emergency moments. Married and divorced twice, first to an Indian PhD in economics, second to an American hairstylist. His slight figure and cared-for, pressed clothes suggested gentleness. Binni had done his American residency in emergency medicine at Montefiore Hospital in the Bronx. Its Emergency Ward was the second busiest in America, serving the vast basin of the poor. There he became expert in gunshot wounds and savage disease and death, and when she'd come back home a few months ago, they bonded over the craziness of caring for people in the worst places in the world. And over their outrage at how American health care neglected so many.

Binni had followed several of his "mates" from New York City up to the relative calm of Columbia, and he could bring his NIH research on Covid, most of it done on computers. Kush Kare, getting some of the stipend, allowed it. She admired his unending calm. In the roughest times, the saddest times, calm.

"I don't *do* calm much," she had confessed. "I don't get it."

"I do *seem* to, my friend. If things get tense, especially if I'm told to do something regarding a patient's care that I don't believe in, I merely say 'Fine, fine'—and do nothing."

"But don't people find out, eventually?"

He smiled and shook his head no, in a loose, rolling manner.

"Tell me," she said. "I need to learn how you do it. Tell me quick!"

"By using ahimsa."

"Nonviolence?"

"That is not the proper translation. Better is 'creative love.'" He smiled. "Never fight back into the face. In those predicaments, I tell myself, 'Go for ahimsa. And never go in alone.'"

"I wish I could learn that!"

"Yes yes, Amy, I shall welcome being deft in teaching you the creative love."

She smiled, and he smiled back.

"And I'll be deft in learning," she said. "Creative love. Deal?"

"Even in this hellish pandemic, from our hearts."

The intubation of Mary went smoothly. She was admitted to the ICU. A life saved? Odds not. But she was young, and had a loving family. They'd champion her cause.

———

Columbians were being battered by the first wave of the virus.

For two months, since mid-March, Covid-19 had raged through New York City and spread fast throughout the state. All through rural Kinderhook County and the town of Columbia, the war was growing fiercer by the day. Finally, New York City was beating down the virus with a simple, proven, three-pronged scientific directive: test, mask, and shelter at home (called social distancing).

But Kush Kare was getting killed. Most of the city of Columbia tried hard to follow the directions to protect themselves and others. But many of the farmers, truck drivers, and others living out in the rural parts of the county rejected the science, embracing the lie that the virus wasn't deadly. They believed their beloved President, who said it was "all a hoax." This deep split was a festering nidus of infection, fueling the detonating pandemic.

Worse, when the danger of dealing with Covid became apparent in late March, almost all the older, mostly white doctors gave their legally required four-week notice to quit Kush: they would officially flee in late April. Last week all four emergency doctors left. All over the USA, the only reasons good doctors would take a job in a Kush Kare hospital was either to stay in their community or for money. But most senior doctors didn't want to die for, or in, Kush Kare.

And so, for the past month Amy had tried to recruit doctors to start right away. But nobody wanted to work there. Finally she asked her uncle Orville Rose, now semiretired, if he knew any doctors who might join in.

"I'll try," he'd said.

The very next day he called back. Emergency was too loud to hear him. "Hang on," she said, "I'll get to a quiet place." She went into the on-call room. "Go ahead."

"I've got three great docs. You know one of 'em, and he knows you. Born and bred right here in Columbia. Guess who."

She tried to focus, riffling through who it might be. A blank. And then: "Not Roy Basch?"

"Bingo. And not only him, but two of his best doctor friends, Eat My Dust Eddie and Hyper Hooper."

"Unreal!"

"Very real. All of them think they can start in about three weeks—late April."

"How the hell did you do this so fast?"

"One thing I've learned about our small town, dear, is y'gotta look ahead for potential breakage. I figured this crash would happen at KK, so I've been working on it for a while."

"You knew this would happen?"

"Soon as I saw the Covid comin', the rest was easy. Roy called his closest pals. They'd gotten bored in retirement—their children grown, gone—and they like action. If Roy calls, they come."

"You're a genius."

"We got lucky."

And so Eat My Dust and Hyper Hooper had shown up on April 20, about two weeks ago. They'd left their families at home in California—Hyper in Southern, Eat in San Francisco.

———

Roy had spent nine days in the hospital with intensive care. In addition to high fever and low oxygen, he had heart arrhythmias—finally treated by propranolol. In the worst 12 hours, in his delirium he vividly pictured the virus tiptoeing toward the aperture of the lungs, peeking down in, and then saying, "Nah, let's not kill him." And that was the start of getting better. If it gets into the lungs, that's the death edge. A matter of pure luck.

At home, he was having a rough time: no energy, none at all; his body in bed all lead. Hardly able to get up out of bed and stay awake without naps, feeling groggy; low blood pressure and depressed.

Everything a chore. The precautions! All food and drink meticulously wiped down with Clorox wipes—everything from boxes of crackers to chicken to all produce; not only Cloroxed but sitting overnight in the fresh air. All letters and packages got Cloroxed—and only after that can we open them. The whole damn house smells and tastes like an operating room!

Luckily he hadn't given it to Berry or Spring. Berry was now always behind a mask and gown that Amy had gotten from the hospital. She came by as much as she could to check on him, but it was lonely in this big house, and scary.

He isolated himself, and talked to himself about his recurring fear.

You are losing your sharp mind, your memory is crappy. You're losing your wits and your ability to write. In the mirror, now, a gaunt face—like The Scream. *As if you've aged, and suddenly you're old.* A proto-gomer. Terrifying. He was scared of not getting his mind back to normal, and lasting damage to multiple organs. For arrhythmia or pericarditis, the treatment was propranolol, but for fatigue and mental dullness? There was no treatment. *Except, as Orvy always said, "The tincture of time."*

———

Even with the arrival of sharp-humored Eat My Dust Eddie, who actually *wanted* the night shift—"To take care of a few delicate matters of equity—not in the social arena, but in the financial"—Amy's shift did not often end promptly at six. She was *responsible*. Sure enough, at half past six there was a run of really sick patients. She texted Orville to go ahead with dinner without her.

In the maelstrom of disease this evening, one patient stood out. Bob Bate Jr. At 21 and five-six, Bob was close to 300 pounds. Many of our Columbians are overweight, tanked up with cholesterol and lipids. Obesity didn't run in Junior's family, it raced.

His father, Bobby Bate Sr., of Bakery, Fresh Bait and Tackle, had died a year ago of, well, fat—hell for doctors to treat the damage it wreaks on every system of the body. No match for insulin. Junior had taken over the store, selling bait while consuming whole baking sheets of buttery pastries. He presented with cough, fever, and atrial fibrillation, and a chest X-ray showed Covid. Yet in the waiting room he refused to obey the mask rule, screaming it was "tyranny."

A rule is a rule. Butchy Lee Ervin, Security, wheeled him out to the parking lot and left him.

Eat My Dust Eddie could care less that someone like Bobby had left the hospital. But legally he needed to get him to sign an AMA— Against Medical Advice—discharge form.

Eddie as the witness, and Butchy for protection, went out to the parking lot.

"Y'got Covid," Eddie said. "You wanna die? Fine with me. Sign here."

"Covid is fake news. You doctors just do it for the money."

"Sign here."

Bobby paused. "What else could it be?"

"Nothing else. Not fake. Here, sign."

"I'd rather die!"

"Now you're talkin', kid," said Eat My Dust, "now you are *talkin'*!" He turned to Butchy Lee. "Do what you want with him, Butchy, he's history." He snapped up the form and turned away.

"Hey, wait! Is it a painful death?"

"Ah, nuthin' much," Eddie said over his shoulder. "Just slow suffocation, drowning in your own blood."

"Wait wait! Wheel me back in."

With the help of two burly orderlies and one kind, weight-lifting housekeeper, Amy and Eddie managed to get him onto the examining table and started to put in big fat IV lines.

Suddenly Junior's oxygen plummeted. Cardiac arrest. The team converged, lasered in on saving him.

In the midst of the resuscitation, Amy noticed, standing on the other side of the glass, a tall, wispy young man with a narrow face and oiled black hair. Wearing a dark, well-tailored business suit with a narrow red tie and a KK-logo mask. On his chest was a sparkly badge. He beckoned Amy to come out.

Amy waved him away and went back to saving Junior.

It was frustrating. With drugs and shocks they got him out of atrial fib, but then he'd click back into a fatal ventricular tachycardia.

They'd shock him again—he'd go back to normal sinus for a few minutes, and then v tach again, over and over. The team was losing him. Amy went another step, slipping a pacemaker into the heart—which worked briefly, then atrial fib and v tach prevailed. They had tried everything. Nothing had worked. Amy called off the resuscitation.

A kid dying is always hard. Many of them, the docs and nurses and orderlies, had kids that age, and many more were patrons of the store, hooked on the Bakery, Fresh Bait and Tackle Thursday Specials. Leatrice offered a whispered Our Father.

For a long moment the team stood there in silence staring at the mess on the floor—bloody syringes, vials, tubes, and IVs, the floor crisscrossed with bloody footprints, and in a corner the bright purple jumpsuit they'd cut off Junior and his forlorn red baseball cap. Depressed and exhausted, they started to file out.

Immediately, two men from Kush Kleaning started mopping up the blood and trash.

Still waiting was the willowy young KK man whom Amy had never seen before.

"Hi," he said in a cheery tone, as if the carnage he had just watched happen had not happened in reality but in a top-rated new doctor drama, say, *Hospital Hunks in Hell.*

Pointing to his badge, he said, "Kenneth S. Miller Jr., director, Kare 4 Safety. I have to inform you that there are, like, *two* dangerous safety violations. Luckily they are easy fixes."

Amy and the team faced him in tight silence, their rage palpable.

All except Eddie, who, covered in blood, moved to slip by him.

"Please don't leave. It'll just take a sec." Miller read from his "I"-phone. "Number one, it is not safe to put slogans on the walls, and not with Scotch tape." He pointed the phone toward the bloody alcove behind them. "To be in compliance, that slogan has to come down."

The team turned around to look. It was one of the famous "Laws of the House of God":

AT A CARDIAC ARREST
THE FIRST THING TO DO
IS TO TAKE YOUR OWN PULSE

They turned back to Kenneth S. Miller Jr.

Silence.

It seemed palpably possible that someone on the team was going to commit an additional safety violation by strangling Kenneth with his or her bare hands. The odds were on Eddie.

Leatrice Shumpsky jumped in, trying hard to save Kenneth's psyche or even life. "Are you saying, dear, that the *slogan* is unsafe, or the Scotch tape?"

"Yes! Both are unsafe. A first warning is, like, a *warning*, but—"

"What's the second 'dangerous safety violation'?" Amy asked pleasantly.

"At the nurses' station, the nurses are, like, drinking beverages from bottles and leaving them open to the air. Open pop bottles or other bottles are, like, unsafe."

Slowly Eddie pushed his way past Amy. If you were on Eddie's team, he'd die for you like he did for his buddies in the rice paddies of his war. If you were on the opposing team, look out. His balding head shined red-gray in the bright lights, his beard shined scarlet. His protective gear was covered in blood, wet and glistening.

Eddie walked slowly to Kenneth S. Miller, who had to back up and back up more and couldn't get out of the way but eventually found himself against a wall in a corner, between a pile of bedpans and a wheelchair containing a senior citizen name-tagged Roz Cohen gesturing and crying, "Go avay go avay go avay!"

Slowly Eddie raised his bloody gloves toward Kenneth's throat.

Kenneth's eyes got wide. He clutched his "I"-phone in front of his face, waving it back and forth as if to hex a monster.

They stood there silently for what seemed a long time.

Willowy young Miller Jr. started to shake, scared to death.

Eddie smiled. "Did I *touch* you?"

Silence.

"Answer!" Eddie barked.

"No!"

"And you feel nice and *safe* right now? Kush Kare safe?"

Miller hesitated. A tough question.

Eat My Dust leaned down over him and put his tanned, chiseled, and lined-with-pain face about an inch from Miller's. Slowly, enunciating each word, he said, "I did not hear you answer. To repeat: You feel nice and *safe* right now?"

"Y . . . y . . . yes, I feel safe right now."

"Good. Be careful down here, Mr., um . . ." He checked his badge. "Kenneth S. Miller Jr. It's emergency here 24/7, full of crazy people who are very very *very* . . . hungry."

3

Amy didn't get back to the big Victorian house downtown on the Courthouse Square until almost ten.

Orville, his wife, Miranda, and their daughter, Eleanor, lived in the lower two floors. Amy had a private entrance in back leading up to the third-floor apartment, which had been—in the 1870s—the servants' quarters. Orville and Miranda were in a high-risk group: both over 70. In addition, Miranda had had polio when she was a child, a severe case that had left her with damaged musculature of one leg, and a limp. At her age she was at risk for a post-polio syndrome, often focused in the lungs. She could well be immunosuppressed. Very dangerous.

Eleanor was 28. When the pandemic hit she had been going for her PhD studying humpback whales in breeding grounds off the Ecuador coast near the Galápagos. Calling her parents from Quito, she said, "I'm coming home to keep you from dying." Ever since quarantining with them, she had been meticulous in protecting them. And, it would turn out, meticulous in everything else.

Amy was equally fanatical about not bringing Covid home. Her transition back to the apartment was a scrupulous, life-or-death ritual. Entering her designated back door, she stepped into the original mud room at the base of the stairs that twirled up three flights. In the mud room was the "dirty" area; the whole top-floor apartment was the "clean" area. She took off her shoes and *all clothing* and put them into the mud-room "dirty" hamper. Naked but for "clean" clogs, she climbed up, and showered, keeping the space "clean." Since it was a respiratory virus, her separation of dirty and clean areas was probably overkill, but it made her feel better. She also ensured that no virus survived on her "dirty" clothes before they went into the washer: each day she had a different, dedicated group of clothes that she sprayed down with hydrogen peroxide and then left to sit for a total of five days to ensure they had not been contaminated. After enough clothing had been through this process, she could wash it without worrying too much. This ultra-protocol allowed her to move without fear anywhere downstairs where the three others lived.

———

Orville Rose sat with Ben in the kitchen, the man at the table, the huge black Newfoundland on the floor. Miranda was asleep, and Eleanor was holed up in her room, probably texting and meticulously drawing pencil portraits of animals taken from photos of pets her friends were sending her, then sending them back as gifts.

The man and his dog had heard Amy come in, and Orvy was keeping the salmon and broccoli warm and the beer cold. He had been sitting there obsessing, trying to recall the name of the astonishing New Orleans pianist with the huge hands and fingers who was a regular on Colbert's show—the best satire in America. Orville was trying all different ways to recall his name, not giving in to his "I"-phone for the answer. He was stuck on the idea that it started with a "D"—something like "Datso"—or maybe not. Amy would know, but for him it was a fight to the death to recall it without asking her.

25

At 74, having seen early dementia in his patients, some with a rapid decline, how could he not wonder if he himself was losing it? Was it just normal aging or the hellish Big A? Lately he was getting damn frustrated with his body—bumping into things, stumbles and spills and slamming a door on a finger as he reached back to close it behind him—and his memory: not being able to find his keys or credit cards or a scheduled appointment or where he'd put the will or the toothpaste or remember whether he'd fed the dog already that day. The social distancing was dulling him down and jacking up his fear. His Zoom patients, many of them even older than he, reflected his own worry, but normalized it too—except for the ones whose "normal" turned into not recognizing their spouse or kids anymore. Names were hardest. He could google Colbert, but as a matter of pride, and potential proof of sound mind, he didn't.

He always stayed up until Amy returned. She was his shining light and closest relative: the only child of his difficult older sister, Penny, and Milt the real estate shyster. Orvy was Amy's beloved uncle. Practicing medicine in New Jersey, he got divorced and joined Doctors Without Borders, showing up in hellholes and romances all over the world. When he was 39 and had fallen deeply in love with Celestina Polo in Italy, his widowed mother, Selma, had died suddenly. But to get his half of the family fortune he had to live in her house—this house—for a year and 13 days continuously. This he did, joining old Dr. Bill Starbuck and becoming a doctor for the Columbians. In his youth, the town had been an anti-Semitic, dangerous place. Orville never knew when another attack would come. He had come back against his will and started doctoring the town, hating it.

But later he realized that while he had come back to heal the town, the town healed him. When Bill died, he took over. Orville met Miranda, and they had Eleanor.

Eight years or so ago, Amy's parents took their dream vacation up the Yukon. It ended prematurely when their small plane crashed, killing both of them. Amy inherited everything, which freed her from relying on doctoring for money. Now Orvy, Miranda, and Eleanor—and Cray, the son of Miranda's short-lived first marriage—were all the family Amy had. Cray, a lawyer, was married to an Italian artist and lived in Rome.

Uncle Orville had led Amy out of her stifling family, showing her a whole new world. When Amy was in high school, he had done for her what Bill had done for him. He took her along on his rounds, showed her the joys—and sorrows—of small-town doctoring. A blessing. And like all blessings, it was mutual.

Now, as often happens in old men, as he was waiting alone for Amy in the sleeping house, memories of his life with her kept him company. Floating in tonight was the day she was born, attended by Bill Starbuck.

All seemed normal to Orville, but all of a sudden Bill said, *Somethin's wrong, I'm goin' in. Total hysterectomy.*

When Amy was delivered, Bill handed her to Orville. That first moment of her life was with him. Her face all wrinkled and red like a little old lady, the baby kept looking into his eyes. Quietly, merely *looked*. And he looked back. His heart twisted on its spindle like a ripe fruit on a tree of ribs, and he, childless, fell in love. He never forgot the feel of that eye contact. It was the beginning of their special bond. *I was imprinted on you*, Amy would say, growing up with the story, *like a little duckling*. When Bill finished, he came out bloodied as a butcher and motioned Orvy to walk him out into the Columbia Memorial Hospital parking lot. Bill expertly snapped a Camel out of the pack and lit it, blowing out those two spirals of dragon fire through his nostrils, relieved. *Paper-thin*, he said, holding up his index finger and thumb close together. *The wall of that uterus was paper-thin. Never saw a thinner, more porous uterus. On the edge of rupturin'. Don't know how that baby ever made it to term in that paper bag of a womb. Reckon it's a miracle.* Orville asked how he knew to go in.

Didn't, Bill said. *I got lucky. That's the damn thing about doctorin', you're always makin' a hundred percent of the decision on fifty percent of the data.*

From that time on, Orville and Bill called Amy "the Miracle." Growing up, Amy would use Orville—a self-described "sixties radical stuck in a conservative town"—as a buffer against what she felt was a boring, deadening religious upbringing.

I imprinted on you, Uncle O, she wrote when she got into Stanford Medical School. *How could I* not *become a doctor? And when I graduate, I'll change my last name from "Plotkin" to "Rose."*

Now, with her coming back and taking over most of the practice, the generations had come around. "Paper-thin"? No wonder she had specialized in obstetrics.

Tonight, maybe because he was feeling old and vulnerable and she was risking her life daily to care for the Columbians, a pile of memories came back—maybe *that* was it, he thought, *maybe the force of these memories is crowding out the missing name of that pianist. Try again. Was it Hurt? His beloved Mississippi John Hurt? Nope. C'mon, brain, keep trying!*

Suddenly Ben, in dog years the same age as Orvy, hauled his mighty 90 pounds up onto his massive black paws and, tongue lolling, tail wagging, walked to the kitchen door.

Orville, who was criticized constantly by Miranda and Amy for his hearing loss, had heard nothing. Ben had become his hearing-ear dog.

And there she was. What a lift! He worried, her being so late—all those hours being in the eye of the contagion. She loved Colbert too, and would know the bandleader's name—but no, he wouldn't ask her, wouldn't admit that he couldn't recall something so familiar yet *again.* He paused, she was going upstairs—and then bingo! *Batiste! His name is Jon Batiste! In the nick of time! Take* that, *Alzheimer's.* He smiled.

"Hi, Unc," Amy said, bending down and giving him a kiss on his bald head, which, thanks to her ritual shower, was safe. "Sorry I'm late."

"I'll get the salmon."

Amy still saw on first glance the younger man who, after all, had walked her out of her stifling only-child teens. In his baldness she saw the chestnut hair mixed with gray at the sides, and his mustache and short beard as well. The tanned face, fine lips, and finally eyes, the enduring and sparkling blue of, say, the Mediterranean. His laughter was unchanged—he had taught her that: "You can always tell a person by their laugh."

But he doesn't laugh all that much, now, she thought. *Could it be his hearing loss?*

Both were tired, and as she ate they spoke quietly of their day. Orvy knew, or had heard of, most of the patients Amy had seen. His patients on Zoom were mostly seniors, although their children and grandchildren were a part of his now virtual practice as well. Amy had taken over his physical office on Fifth Street, seeing patients under strict antivirus commandments—which did not go over well with some Columbians. But no mask, no doctor visit.

Orville usually knew the families of the day's emergency admissions. As he'd said to her about being a doctor in a small town: "The only person who really knows the truth about what's going on around here is me. I get to lift up the lid, peek in, and see past the bullshit."

For Amy, his aging was difficult. She'd say something, and he'd say, "*Whatwhat?!*" It seemed to be getting worse. Two years ago he had gone to the hearing clinic out in Austerlitz. Tests confirmed he had normal age-related hearing loss, especially of the high frequencies, which made it hard to hear women. The (female) audiologist said that adjusting to a hearing aid takes a lot of effort: "It's a job. *It's like having another job.*" That did it. Orville said to her, "*Another* job? Are you nuts? I've already got one giant job—you think I'd take on

another? I'm outta here." Ever since, he was adamantly against hearing aids, referring to her for some reason as "the Rhino Lady."
He asked everyone to try harder, look at him when speaking, and he
would study a book on "Lip Reading for Dummies." People in the
family faced a conversation with him with trepidation.

Saddened by his plight, feeling a rush of fatigue, Amy focused on
her dinner and just listened.

"Do you remember," he was saying, for some reason, "when I first
came back to Columbia, that day we borrowed Henry Schooner's
BMW motorcycle and went up to Olana?"

"Sure," she said loudly. "Your fortieth birthday, my first motorcycle ride. It was amazing!"

"A perfect moment, a late summer evening, yeah. We were lying
on our backs on the grass looking over the Rip Van Winkle Bridge
and the Hudson. I told you that when I was six I was outdoors lying
on my back like that and clouds were passing above me and I had a
vision—*There's something else. Something else that is whole, of which I
am just a part?*" She nodded. "I ran back home and told Selma. She
said, 'Sorry, Orville, but there's nothing else but this.' I was crushed.
But right then I thought I was *worth* something, because I was part
of that something else. And I decided I wouldn't listen to her—I
learned not to listen. And that was the reason I had to leave town,
because if I stayed here, I'd die."

"I remember, yes."

"Good. And do you remember what you said?"

Amy closed her eyes, seeing it again. "Kind of. I asked you . . .
something like, 'Do you think that Grandma Selma's vision died
here too?'"

"Yes, dear. At sixteen? To have such *seichle*?"

"Which means what?"

"Wisdom. You were amazing. You are amazing."

"Right now I feel more wiped out than amazing."

"Whatwhat??"

Enunciate. Loud. *"Right now I feel more wiped out than amazing."*

"Sorry."

"No no, it's good, great even." She looked into his eyes and, again telling herself *up the volume and be crisp and clear*, she reached over and took his hand and said, "Orvy, I love you more than I love any other person on earth, and I'm so glad to be with you, *just so glad*!"

Orville choked up. Tried for a moment to stop it, but all at once he was crying, hard, sobbing, shoulders shaking.

Amy was crying too, and they started to embrace but the salmon was in the way and they had to maneuver past it—laughing through their sadness of age and time and love.

4

The next morning, as Amy, masked, stepped out of the house to poop and pee Ben, the chimes of the Presbyterian church rang out 14.

Sleepy, she didn't know what the real time was, but she knew that the one time it was not was 14.

She glanced at her Fitbit: 05:34.

Columbia was a town known for breakage.

For as long as she could remember, at public events when things were supposed to work, they often broke. Microphones would give out just after someone said, "Testing, testing." On Memorial Days in the Columbia cemetery, just as the Gettysburg Address began, the viewing stand would collapse. The town newspaper, the *Columbia Crier*, seemed to celebrate great breakage. The editor herself, Lisa Cohen, had written such recent headlines as:

Scabies Infests Health Department
Bomb Meant for Gopher Torches Barn
$4.4M Sewer Project on Table

Native Columbians had a deep sense that you couldn't count on things working, not only in the physical world, but in the cerebral.

Amy was good physically and cerebrally. Her challenge was different: dealing with suffering—of her patients and herself. Dealing with the spirit. Not a word that core Columbians used. She herself had not made much progress in spirit. But having practiced medicine and surgery all over the world, and with her 40th birthday looming, she felt she had earned a certain clarity about what was real.

Staring at Ben's huge lavender-red tongue lolling and drooling out of his mouth like a freshly caught king salmon, she smiled. Ahh, to be a dog. To be him. A short life, but good.

She had arrived back in Columbia four months ago on New Year's Day, to join Orville as "town doctor." He had tried to sell his practice. No buyers. None. Miranda, his wife, said it had hurt him badly.

His little office at Washington and Fifth Street was said to have been the first in town, even before the Nantucket Quakers landed here in 1780 and built their utopia. Orville had always been on staff at Whale City Memorial Hospital. But his was the last independent medical office left standing in all of Kinderhook County.

A few years ago Whale City Memorial was bought by a private equity fund—based nowhere, with a goal of nothing but money. Private equity investment was almost risk-free: *the borrowed debt was on the hospital, not on the buyers.* Columbia became the home franchise of many that composed a chain of for-profit hospitals all over America called "Kush Kare." The CEO, a Wall Street guy named Jason Kush, had built a humongous third or fourth home out in Kinderhook County, complete with a helicopter pad, in what for hundreds of years had been the idyllic WASP hamlet of Spook Rock. Recently a sign had gone up at the entrance to the village:

RICH LIVES MATTER

Orville had always said, about being a doctor, "I don't do this for money; and I've got to be my own boss."

But to be able to admit patients to the hospital, he was forced to sign up with Kush Kare on salary. In the meeting, Orvy started describing his practice but didn't get far before the chief business officer running the meeting said, "Yes, yes. But it's all about the money. Let's do the numbers." The cash was calculated by the national Kush metric of Orville's productivity. Money and legalese were king. The contract plus nondisclosure agreement with KK was 34 pages.

Years ago, after Amy finished medical training at Stanford, she came home and spent time as Orville's partner, and at first loved it. But it didn't last. While it was heavenly to be with Orvy, something about the practice paled. Not exciting enough. Back in California she got into an on-and-off romance with a former med classmate, Bernie Shapiro, outdoorsman and shrink. Nearing 40, she wanted a child. He was "neutral" to this but turned out to have no viable sperm. She wanted to get a sperm donor or adopt; he didn't. Like Orvy, she started off around the world.

Last autumn Orvy had called her in California, told her he was thinking of slowing down, and would she like to come back, work with him, and take over whenever she wanted.

"If not . . . ," he said, a hitch in his voice. Silence. "If not," he went on, his voice still wobbly, "I'll just sell it. Or, if no one wants to buy it, I'll just close it down for good."

Something didn't sound right. Older than his 74 years, older than when she'd last seen him, last year. *Tentative.*

Sure enough, later that night she got a call from Miranda. He was having "aging" issues, she said, feeling "worn-out."

"You'd better come, dear."

Stunned, she had flown back the next day.

———

Amy's morning addiction was coffee and breakfast with *Morning Joe* on MSNBC. The show was a rarity: TV as close to real as possible. But by now all media had been sucked down into the maw of the President. Joe and Mika and their team were astute and fearless, real old-time journalists. But Amy loathed TV commercials, especially the phony drug ads, each one curing every disease easily and promptly—and then ending direly, with a disclaimer:

"WARNING *zylophuxyou* may cause sudden death, *in which case call your doctor.*"

To kill the commercials, she taped every *Morning Joe* in advance and fast-forwarded through the commercials, starting right at six. It was heaven.

Each weekday morning she was riveted to the President talking bubble bath. And so now, with her coffee and Iggy's sliced French loaf and olive oil, she tuned in to the tube.

The Rose Garden.

Reporter: "Mr. President, with the United States about to reach a total of one hundred thousand deaths, would you have done anything differently?"

"Nothing, no. I take no responsibility at all. I give myself a ten out of ten. I wear it as a badge of honor. Of honor. A badge of. Strong. It will all disappear. Like magic. Before you know it. We're winning. Disappear it will all very soon. The virus is a hoax."

"You shithead!" Amy screamed.

It was the start of her two-minute rage. Her *daily* two-minute rage.

"But, sir," another reporter went on, "a study from epidemiologists analyzing the pandemic concluded that, if you had just begun *any* preventive policies *just two weeks earlier* in March, you would have saved the lives of thirty-seven thousand Americans."

"Fake news. And *you're* fake news too. Next?"

"AAAAaaaaahhh! You moron! You . . . you *paraquat!*"

———

As usual outside the office there was a line down the block: patients waiting to see Amy. To do so, they had to not only wear masks but stay six feet apart in line, as indicated by painted dots on the sidewalk. Her office was on the ground floor of a small house on Washington Street, the main street running east from the Hudson River straight uphill, passing the hospital, and ending at the reservoir and cemetery. The cross streets were named Front Street (the Quakers didn't believe in designating a First Street, because God came first), and then Second through Eighth. The office was just down from the corner of Fifth and Washington.

Washington Street itself going east from the river uphill to the cemetery was safe. But the cross streets going north from Washington, below Fifth Street, after dark were dangerous, a land of violence and drugs. Gunplay. Horrific abuse. Murders. Above Fifth was okay, safe night and day. The city was bounded by the river on one side and on all the other sides by a rural county spotted with odd hamlets. So its tax base was capped. It was always broke.

The tradition of the practice, ever since Bill Starbuck took over after coming back from World War II and continuing when Orville took over from him in 1984, was not to have scheduled appointments. You just went into the small waiting room, where you took notice of who was sitting there ahead of you, and waited your turn. A kind of rapid cognitive test. The sane helped the crazy. There was no receptionist. When Dr. Amy opened the In door, you got up and walked into the small office. When she was finished, you went out a different way, through the Out door into a dim hallway, leading straight back out to the street. Often on that short walk, Amy's hand was on your shoulder: warm in winter, cool in summer.

The office had once been the oak-paneled living room—with the examining room behind a curtain. Over the fireplace was a 14-point buck, tilted a little, and on the wall was a framed photo of a man in a cowboy hat and scowl, his handlebar mustache drooping down, his arms crossed over his chest, and a revolver clasped in one hand, pointing up past his ear, with the caption in pitted bronze: "Josiah Macy, Columbian Doctor, 1834–1861."

He had died in a gunfight, caught in a patient's wife's bed. In the corner was a massive old safe like what you see in the saloon in cowboy movies. Behind a curtain was the examining room and table with metal stirrups.

All of this—the 14-point buck, the lascivious gunslinger, the saloon safe, the stirrups—all made it seem that you were getting doctored in a frontier town of the Wild West.

The scarred desk and swivel chair had been there forever. Orville had told Amy that by the end of his decades sitting in the doctor's chair he felt that his butt had expanded to fill out the template of Bill Starbuck's fat butt—perhaps as Bill had filled out the butt of the doc before him.

Behind Amy's desk and chair were two embossed wooden signs. From Bill Starbuck:

YES SMOKING

And from Orville Rose:

NOT REALLY

After a mostly routine morning of caring for Columbians, in walked a familiar elderly couple, Mrs. Crystal Scomparza, of the Bash Bish Falls Scomparzas, way out in Copake in the foothills of the Berkshires near the Massachusetts line. A former accountant, she was married to the long-retired, clever, and corrupt Columbia mayor Americo Scomparza. He was now scrunched down into one side of the chair beside her, blank-eyed, silent, and still. He had terrible chronic kidney disease. Orville had been keeping him alive; now he looked bad. Amy was on alert. Covid plus renal failure is a death sentence.

"He thinks he's got the Covid," Crystal said. "I found out yesterday, when he was pretty communicative. He insisted on treating it himself."

"How did he treat it himself?"

"Like an *idiot*." She sighed. "He followed the President's treatment. Yesterday I caught him drinking a bottle of bleach. Actually, *two* bottles, Lysol and Clorox the both. I screamed at him and grabbed the bottles, but he was saying, 'The Big Mac says it's a disinfectant, knocks out the virus in a minute.'"

"The Big Mac?"

"Our affectionate moniker. He says it knocks it out in a minute, cleans out the lungs fast. So this idiot husband a' mine rigs up a UV light that he'd ordered from Amazon because the President said, 'It shines through the skin into the lungs and it's a cleaning of the lungs and—'"

"Crystal, didn't I tell you *not to believe anything medical* coming out of that man's mouth?"

"Yes, you did, and *I myself* didn't. It's him. He's been drinking the bleach in secret. I threw out all the bottles. But I'm so worried, Amy." She shook her head, dabbing her eyes with a hankie. "This morning he seemed a little better—I mean not really but I settled him in front of the TV and went out for a walk. I came back and found him acting pretty demented—I mean *more* demented. He was arguing with people who weren't, like, *there*. But he *seemed* better after he drank the Lysol. *Better* today, definitely."

Amy stared at Americo, a small 78-year-old man looking 98. As a girl she'd known him as an energetic, take-charge mayor. Now he was slumped, bald head down, gasping, mumbling—something about "four whores" or "some mores."

"This is *better*?" Amy had gotten up from her chair at "Lysol" and was taking vital signs, opening up two buttons on America's shirt to expose Scruffy's Rhomboid Space, where you can put your stethoscope bell on the patient and slither it around to examine almost all the organs in the belly and chest—without ever having to undress the patient. Heart rate in normal sinus, but tachycardia at 140, with runs of aberrant beats and then a dead stop: *one thousand one, one thousand two, three*—and then back into NSR. Breathing was shallow, bowel sounds like a straining Amtrak local—and rebound pain in the appendix site. The only urgent finding was cardiac—what sounded like an elongated QT interval in the beat of the heart. *Deadly.*

"*Definitely* better," Crystal said. "He seemed to be coming out of drinking the Lysol okay—and Clorox too—but when I came back after my walk today I caught him at the fish tank finishing drinking something *else*—and he got worse right away and before he collapsed like this I got him into the Caddy and came here."

"He drank the water from the fish tank too?"

"Well, not the water . . ."

"Hurry! What?"

"Remember Big Mac's going on and on about a miracle drug for malaria that works like a charm on the virus—"

"Oh God, not hydroxychloroquine?"

"That's it! Big Mac said a *lot* of people are taking it, a *lot* of people say it's miraculous—"

Amy knew that the elongated QT cardiac finding was why the drug had not been approved for Covid. In recent studies, it caused sudden death. She called Scomparza Ambulance and Taxidermy, a block away on Fourth. They'd be there *stat.*

"But where'd he get the pills—not the fish tank—"

"I asked him that myself. He just mumbled—'Not pills.' Then I saw on the floor an empty bottle of fish tank *cleaner*. He saw it on Fox. That it's *an ingredient of.* So he drank the whole bottle, and here we are and—"

Packy Scomparza and Joe Lebowski rushed in, loaded America cheerily onto a stretcher like a candidate for embalming, and without breakage were gone.

———

Almost all Amy's patients that day had come to "rule out Covid." Luckily it was a light morning. A lot of Columbians knew that it was a risk to go out—even into her private little office.

There was great loyalty to Orville. He was much beloved for being "a good doc." A relic. Never put a computer between him and his patient. He just sat there rocking in Starbuck's chair that had molded to his body and *looked his patients in the eye.* For years he hadn't even billed insurance—"I didn't become a doc to do data entry." People paid what they could. The New Yorkers paid a lot, which covered for those who paid a little, or none. When one of his patients was in the hospital, the Kush "billing drones" would fight the war across the computer screen against the "insurance drones." It was all about money. *Payment.* Kush would bill the highest amount of money; insurance would the pay the least money. Both sides lied like crooks. And with both sides lying like crooks, both made out like bandits.

Amy followed Orville and Starbuck's lead: no laptop between her and her patients, and pay what you can. Luckily, she had money. She had read somewhere—Tolstoy? the great Dr. Chekhov?—that "money is the new slavery." For her, it was the new freedom. And her giving back, all over the world.

Amy attracted Columbia's mix of recent immigrants. The town, under the new Black mayor with support of the liberal New Yorkers, was even a "sanctuary city." This enraged the President's local base.

Orville's was the only doctor's office, besides the hospital, within walking distance of the poor people of color from down below Fifth, including those in Bliss Towers, which was public housing. "Bliss," ironically, was the name of a philanthropic doctor who lived out in Taconic and raised Black Angus cattle, and who had financed most of it himself.

All of the poor, and the "artistic" and "liberal" refugee New Yorkers, wore masks. Masks were really hard to find, thus often homemade—in the Black community, in colors and patterns of Africa, some lettered with "Black Lives Matter."

But the MAGA-faithful man, woman, and child refused to wear masks.

Amy refused to see them.

"What about my rights? This is America, a free country. It's my choice. *Freedom's* choice."

"My freedom isn't only for *my own* benefit," she'd say for the hundredth time, "it's the freedom to help *other* people. Like you. My freedom is to take care of *others*. To treat the greater good."

They rarely gave in, even in great distress. If they were really sick, she buffed and turfed them up the street to Kush Kare—which in any case mandated masks.

In four months as Columbia's doctor, she'd often had her heart torn open by the suffering. Especially of the poor, many of them Black or immigrant families. Now almost all had lost their jobs.

They were trapped in a horrific dilemma. Either keep safe sheltering in place and not be able to feed your family or pay your bills, or risk Covid by slogging away at your minimum-wage job like working at grocery stores or picking up garbage or all kinds of cleaning and unskilled work. Or really dangerous jobs, like the death-trap meatpacking arm of the giant Beef Schweitzer Food Solutions LLC. Housed in a big-box building a 20-minute bus ride out of town, it was known to be a cesspool of virus. When the usual workers got sick, the jobs were easily filled. Bad pay, but enough to eat and pay the rent.

So the choice was stark, a matter of life or death. *Job* or death. But what if the job *meant* death? A miserable death, on a ventilator. No in-hospital contact with loved ones, not even on your deathbed. *Food* or death? Most had children, and who of us would not have taken the risk, for them? The other most dangerous job was nurses' aide at Sundown Haven Nursing Home. It was crawling with Covid.

———

"My wife Jenny's out in Sundown, and she's real sick," said Robert Van Ness, glancing at the empty patient chair beside him, as if Jenny were there sitting beside him in the other patient chair. "I'm scared to death she's going to die."

He was Amy's last patient of the morning, and she was "desperately" needed at the hospital.

But this comes first.

Amy had heard Orville talk about Robert, a high school basketball teammate. Often the "walk-in" with a patient tells a doctor everything. Alongside the 75-year-old man, who was almost a foot taller, she felt like a midget. And she felt a—what was it?—yes, a *presence.* He used a cane, probably arthritis and injury from a life of hard work and sports. His large worker's hand in hers had felt rough, with keloid scars from lacerations. He sat down, at first slowly, and then the last part heavily. Wringing his hands together. Arthritis? Worry about his wife? Above the mask his eyes were pained. She sensed deep suffering. *Van Ness*, she knew, came from some Dutch patroon given land inland from the river sometime after Henry Hudson—thinking he was sailing up to "the Furious Overfall" to China—docked here in 1628.

Amy knew the family. Robert had been a great Bluehawk High

School athlete. After going to Siena College on a basketball scholarship, Robert had come back to town and organized the Youth Health and Fitness Team of the '60s, and stayed on for decades. Orville had always told her that if you want help doctoring the Black community—or *any* part of the crazy quilt of races and creeds now in Columbia, "call Robert."

"Tell me about it, Robert," she said.

"Not that long ago, after a fall, she went into the nursing home out in Omi. We were told it was temporary—physical therapy, doctor visits. This morning I get a call. Lot of my friends' children are workin' there. One of 'em takes care of her, Hazel Brown, an' she says Jenny's got a fever and is breathin' hard, and says she can't taste her food. Can you help? Do some kind of test?"

"There are no tests yet, but I'll call 'em up." She picked up the phone.

Robert sat stoically in silence, waiting quietly but for his hands rubbing together in a sad, slow dance. His athlete's body was still big, but fallen: skin losing elasticity, muscle melting to fat. Tendons and ligaments losing pliancy, drying out—because they have no real direct blood supply, and old vessels get more clogged. His wrinkles, brow, and hands were a record of all his years of service to youngsters, and long being a leader in the fractured community.

Amy put the phone down. "Okay, Robert. I talked to the boss. Yes, Jenny does have symptoms now—she's feverish and coughing. I told them to get her to the hospital right away."

"So y'think we can get her into the hospital tomorrow?"

Amy realized he hadn't understood. "No, Robert. *Today.*"

He looked startled. "Really?"

"Really."

He stared at her, eyes wide.

"I'll call the hospital and let them know I'll be taking care of her, starting this afternoon. You might not get to be with her much, because we don't want you catching it."

He teared up. She handed him a box of tissues. He took one, a frail bright-white piece of paper in his big hand.

"I know how you and Orville are real good friends, Robert."

He looked into her eyes and then started to cry, not easily but like men do, fighting it until the fear of losing the dear woman who loved him more than any other for more than any time might die, might be *gone*. That old torn body clenched, then shuddered hard, and he was weeping, crying his heart out.

Tears came to her eyes too—the first in a long time with a patient.

Amy passed him the whole box of tissues. He took a few. Composed himself.

"Doc, you are real kind, like Orville always was—is—to me. I love that guy." He smiled. "Did he ever tell you why he and I—are still such good friends?" She shook her head. "Well, he bein' Jewish, was gettin' beaten up by the Italians. And he was a great basketball player, first sophomore to make the varsity—and we had great teams with us three Black stars. He was a great shooter! One day he came to practice with a broken thumb. Turns out the Italians had broken it. 'How long they been doin' this?' I asked. 'A lot.' So I look at Chick Chick and Butchy Lee, and they nod, and I say, 'Well, *they ain't gonna beat you up no mo'*.'" Robert smiled. "And they never touched him again. The Italians were tough, but not as tough as us Blacks. Back then, everybody was scared of us."

With joints crackling one by one up his spine, Robert raised himself to his six-four height and nodded to Amy as he walked out.

Leaving behind a sense of gratitude, shared.

Gratitude tends to do that.

5

The census was rising. Walking from her car to the entrance, Amy had seen a makeshift tent with spillover of patients. At this sight she sensed, as so often in her travels, the precarious care doctors and nurses could offer in a fraying, cheapskate system of care.

For-profit Kush Kare was expert at fake. It spent millions trumpeting its image—two "K's" rampant above a scroll reading **WE KARE**. Millions of dollars were paid for ads that ran on TV and the dread 'net. Stars were paid off to give false testimonials, ads to offer fakery: "Lowest cost to you in your health care" and "Enroll in our 'K-Klub' and earn points with each admission, so that on your next admission you can upgrade room and board, with concierge medicine 24/7." KK kame—oops—came across in video media as being "a five-star hospital, the best in American history." Fake news.

Amy had only been there two hours but she was just plain tired. The PPE felt like a straitjacket. She and Binni and big Eddie were flat out, as was the heavenly messenger, Leatrice Shumpsky. Each was holding the others up barely, sometimes physically, and with spirit. All seemed just plain *down*.

But Hyper Hooper, a veteran of the House of God, had arrived. Leaving his wife, kids, and grandkids back in LA.

He was the most hyper doc anyone had ever seen. "Short and solid," he'd say, "like the old Jews—built low to the ground, for speed!" He had delicate hands and long fingers, and an almost elegant swan's neck. Below his black hair and bald spot, his face was square, but always in gear, in a slight smile, which in an instant, and often, was a laugh. His Ashkenazi nose linked him to his parents, concentration camp survivors who—get this!—had met in a relocation camp and somehow conceived Hyper. Those light eyes were often wide in awe— like a kid who never grew up, looking for toys—no, *expecting* toys. Born into trauma, he saw doctoring as relief, a way to live on the edge and have fun. In fact, his research at UCLA Med was big fun. His credo? "Better medical care is better nutrition." His research at UCLA proved that the world's main carcinogen was body fat.

"Fat fat fat!" he'd cry out to docs and patients alike. "Ninety-six percent of Covid deaths have fat as a comorbidity!"

After leaving Man's 4th, Hyper researched, with Western drug trials, ancient plant remedies in China, and struck gold. He distilled the essence of red rice yeast. Proved that it lowered cholesterol and other killer lipids comprising the Great American Diet of fat: the sizzle of meat and drizzle of butter. His Refined Red Rice Yeast pills decreased cholesterol without the crippling side effects of Big Pharma drugs like Lipitor, which could melt your muscles into noodles. His Fat-Blasting groups and books really worked. He cared ferociously about both science and helping people to live. A genius, running on indigenous steroids. His good-byes were always the same: "Stay hyper, it's the best defense."

As dire as any medical issue was, he damn well would see it through to some good resolve, or not. And see it three steps ahead. When he was on call, he was totally *there*. Even if he'd been blasted at work, looking like crap, he would hit the afterburner, with his credo, "Up a notch, no *mishegas*."

And what a teammate he was! When he was with the team, he was really with them. And when not, not. Hyper never seemed tired or irritable. An optimist. Like a kid facing into a stable full of shit, figuring that this meant there must be a pony in there somewhere. He didn't walk up stairs, he ran. Didn't sit in chairs, but rocked. His first act at Kush Kare was to donate new black-mesh-and-ratchet rocker chairs for the doctors' on-call room. His mind worked so fast that he didn't seem to be thinking at all, and often got the solution faster than anyone else.

Despite a good six hours of sleep, Amy felt worn-out already, and went into the doctors' on-call room, the sole sanctuary—bunk beds, tables, and the new chairs, male and female changing rooms, showers, bathrooms. Junk food.

Hyper, despite having been up on night call for 24 hours straight, looked like, well, like he always looked, clear hazel eyes sparkling, mind sharp, ready to lean into *more* chaotic medicine. And, rare for even good docs, he "played well with others"—Hyper and Shump had bonded at once, a lovefest.

"Hyper," Shump had said, "just needs crib rails."

He reported to Amy what had gone on. It had been a Hyper night—pitch-perfect. Just plain good doctoring.

"My last admission was your patient," he was saying to Amy, "ex-mayor Americo. After I went over his whole chart and talked to his wife—a sweetheart—I just about killed myself leaching out the fish tank cleaner that was killing him and put him on dialysis to save a kidney or two. He has great insurance, so he got one of the last open beds—which, if the world was just, we could use better for just about anyone else. I hear he was a *goniff*—a thief—right?"

"Very."

"Shit," he said. "Why do these shits survive? And why do the just plain good people die—"

Bing bing bing. A human voice, excited: *Prone Team Prone Team. Cubical 12, Cube 12.*

Hooper, still gowned up, grabbed his headgear and left. Amy took longer.

The Covid was amazing in its pattern of throwing accepted rules of treatment to the winds. A new study about "proning" showed that keeping the patient prone on his or her belly instead of on the back increased the ability of the lungs to reach higher oxygen blood saturation and aided survival.

Amy and the team had walked through the difficult maneuver and had been waiting for a suitable candidate. There were two issues that made proning difficult: first, almost all the patients who did best on proning were fat—no one knew why; second, it was fiendishly difficult to turn a patient over on his or her bulging stomach safely without dislodging the spaghetti of lines and tubes, including the endotracheal tube and IV lines and catheters for urine and sensors or even cardiac pacemakers, and the machines that were monitoring it all, in real time, and usually *stat.* The team had walked through a practice proning. It did not go well. They prayed that their first proning patient would be thin.

The Columbian odds were against that, and sure enough, the patient fit the profile. The whole emergency team came to help. The patient was Jerry Gorman, the king of Columbia's garbage/incinerator service. Over the years his lungs had inhaled a ton of burning ash and—like the rest of the town—a lot of cement dust from the Universal Atlas and Lone Star plants. On rainy nights when the cement dust was fierce, it coated everything including car windshields. Water couldn't dissolve it. We Columbians kept gallons of vinegar in our entryways to dissolve it, which—on really bad days—left the whole town smelling like a green salad gone bad. Columbian lungs were compromised. Jerry Gorman had been admitted earlier that morning with a precarious blood oxygen of 66.

On his back, he was hooked up six ways from Sunday, with external IV lines, tubes, wires, and chrome supports for all of these—including an endotracheal tube to keep a ready airway, just in case.

Now his oxygen saturation had suddenly plunged to 50—which would mean sudden death.

The team faced their first proning. Proning under pressure. It was life or death—and that fact made everyone energized and focused. And so it was no accident that though they'd never done it before, each recalled the part he or she would be asked to play. Time slowed, fear fell, everybody was recalling, and clear.

The main thing for flipping the patient onto his stomach was to secure all the lines, and to do it fast. Any delay in oxygen could be fatal.

Eat My Dust Eddie had trained in surgery, and sutured lines in place, sometimes into the flesh, sometimes to cloth. Hyper delicately swiveled the endotracheal tube into a holder that was secured to Jerry's face, to keep it in place. If this is done haphazardly, and there's no air? Dead patient.

Amy removed the cardiac monitoring leads from Jerry's front, while Shump placed padded adhesive dressings over all the pressure points—chin, shoulders, elbows, crests of the hips.

"Ready to flip?" Amy shouted. "Lifting team get ready."

Up stepped Butchy Lee and Chick Chick from Transport, and also a bulky CNA—clinical nurse assistant—named Simon Talbott. Each said, "Ready."

"He weighs a ton, so we go slow," Amy said. "We flip on three. One. Two. Three!"

Slowly, each one lifted—but the sudden dead weight startled

them all and he began falling back down. But then each adjusted, hoisting slowly, grunting, inch by inch, with Amy following the rotation of each part of the body, holding on to leads or tubes and especially checking the endotracheal tube to make sure all were still connected—because, if not, poor Jerry could suddenly die. They did it. Jerry was flipped facedown.

Shump quickly put the monitoring leads on Jerry's blotchy back; Hyper adjusted the endotrach tube. The cacophony of *bleeps* and *whooshes* and *plucks* started up again.

A cheer from the team.

"We're now proners!" said Talbott the CNA.

"Prone to prone!" Hyper answered. "That's us!"

"Anybody gotta hernia?" called out Eddie. "I'm lookin' for surgical work. A chance to cut is a chance to cure."

Amy and Hyper walked back to the on-call room, sat, and cracked bottles of root beer.

A knock at the door.

"Enter to grow in wisdom," Hooper called out.

"Hi, guys!" Kenneth S. Miller Jr. Same suit, same Kare 4 Safety button. "Can I have two secs?"

"Are you *serious*?" Hooper said, looking at him sternly. "Two secs is *nuthin'*. Take two minutes. I'll start the clock." He picked up his "I"-phone. "Annnd . . . *GO!*"

"*Going!* Thanks, Dr. Rose, for taking down the 'Take Your Own Pulse' thingee."

"Not me, I hadn't noticed it was down."

"Someone told me you did it and—"

"I resent that," Amy said. "I would never destroy hospital property, and—"

"Anyhoo it was taken down. But now there are *two other problems*. One is, is that it's *back*. Same place."

"You're joking me."

"Not. Did you put it back?"

"As I said, it is not my job description to take things down from walls. *Or* put 'em back up. Clearly we need better Kush Security—"

"One minute to go!" Hooper called out.

"Butbut*but* there's a new problem, a worse problem."

"Oh no!" said Amy. "I hope it's not serious."

"Like, *very.*"

"Shall I get out my scalpel?" Hooper asked.

"*Stop interrupting me!* The two minutes is mine and it's almost—"

"—*it's almost up!* But I'll extend it, if you have the time?"

"I have the time." He composed himself. "A new slogan has been put up in Kush Kare—*twice*!" He consulted his "I"-phone.

PUT THE HUMAN BACK
IN HEALTH CARE

He stared at them. "What the hell does *that* mean?"

Amy and Hooper looked at each other and shrugged their shoulders.

"One copy is in the waiting room, big and high up so it can't be reached without a ladder. The second is *even higher up*! On the hospital façade."

"Really? *Higher up?*"

"*Very.*"

"I hope they didn't put it up that high with unsafe Scotch tape," Amy said.

"Worse. They are both riveted into the walls. With *rivets*? Like, professionally?"

Hooper's phone rang, playing the Beatles' "Let It Be." "Time's up, Kenneth Miller Jr. sweetie. Thanks for the update and—oh my God but *surely*—nah, couldn't be . . ."

"What?" said Kenneth. Hooper said nothing. "Whatwhat*what*?!"

"You aren't insinuating that we *physicians* would have anything to do with that, right?"

"I wouldn't? You were, like, at the scene of the crime and it's making people *angry* and—"

"Now, *that*," said Hooper, "makes *me* really angry. Implicating *us*?"

"Who else?"

"Must be *somebody* else, right? We're docs, we don't desecrate, we amputate, and cree-ate. We don't abuse hospitals, we 'man' them. Let us know when it's fixed. You're dismissed."

Kenneth paused, seemed to think. Puffing out his pigeon chest, he said, "I have just about had it with you. I will be taking this to the next level up."

"Good! Love it!" said Hooper. "Boy power. You go, child!"

Scowling, Miller left. They both smiled.

"Hey, Hyper," Amy said, "can I ask you something?"

Rocking in his chair, he said, "Go for it."

"We've got a lot in common. How 'bout sometime we get to talk? Maybe get Indian or Chinese takeout when we're both off?"

He stopped rocking. His eyes widened in surprise. "I thought you'd never ask. I mean, I'm too intense for a lotta people. I get screened out?" He laughed, nervously, and said, "Love to."

During her shift, Amy kept on looking for Jenny, the wife of Robert Van Ness. Finally she arrived from the nursing home—with three others having symptoms of corona.

Amy examined her. High fever, cough, gasping for air—an emergency. She sent out tests and started treatment: oxygen, checking airway, locating a precious ventilator. But because Jenny and the others had Medicare/Medicaid—the lowest-paying insurance—the chief of billing did not want to give away a precious bed. Luckily, by now

Amy had power: no one else could lead the Covid team. The chief of cash caved.

Then came the hard part. The moment she dreaded.

Robert and Jenny were in the hallway of Emergency. They had gotten lucky—in all the hospital there was only one last ventilator, and she was getting it. She was severely oxygen deprived—by finger gauge, 61. Gasping, trying like hell to get air into her lungs, and trying like *more* hell to get it out. Smothering. "I can't breathe!" is the worst way to die.

"I can't breathe! . . . I . . . can't . . . breathe!"

"Jenny dear," Amy said, "you need to be put on a ventilator, a machine to breathe for you. I'll take you in, okay?"

She nodded.

Now the moment. The worst part of the job—to tell the husband or wife or children or parent that their loved one will be sedated so she won't fight the ventilator and that they won't be able to communicate with her, or visit her in person, as long as she is on it.

Jenny seemed to understand, and she turned to Robert.

"What are you tellin' us, Doc?" he asked.

Jenny looked into his eyes, squeezed his hand.

They looked at each other steadily, and quiet except for her gasping. Jenny saw him understand.

But Amy had to say it out loud.

"Robert, she will be in isolation, nobody can go into or out of her room. And so . . . well . . . this, right now, may be the last time you'll be able to talk with her . . . in person. For a while."

Tears poured out, running down his cheeks. With his free hand he tried to wave it all away. He was trembling, unable to speak. He looked down, away.

"I'll leave you two alone for a few minutes. You understand?"

Head down, shuddering with tears, he shook his head back and forth slowly. Not to say "no," but to show he couldn't bear this.

She left them, to find the last ventilator.
Alone in the bathroom, she cried, a little.
The damn tears cloud the plastic.

————————

Just before she was off shift she got a *stat* text to go up to the top floor, the Henry and Nelda Jo Schooner Suite. Henry was born and raised in a broken home down in a bad inlet of the river. He made it big in real estate and had been our congressman for decades. Although he now lived out in Spook Rock, he was a force—a great benefactor for all things Columbian.

Every KK Hospital had a suite on the top floor, always named after a multimillion-dollar investor, 10-million-dollar minimum. The suite was the home of the local office of KK LLC, used for official hospital and KK board meetings and gala events, mostly fundraising. Recently, most of it had been turned into a special, private hospital ward. None of the intensivists had yet seen it.

Stat? She was desperately tired, needed sleep.

But as she had done her whole doctor life, when it seemed that she couldn't do another minute, let alone another hard patient, she did. In fact, in a furious and crazed renunciation of her exhaustion, she decided that since she'd gotten no exercise for *days*, she—a serious runner—would not take the elevator but run up the six flights of stairs.

She made it to three and her lungs gave out and she felt like she was going to die. Dizzy, about to faint. Chest heaving, sweat running down inside the protective plastic and down the rest of her body . . . and she slid down onto the floor. *I've caught the corona I can't get air and I'm gonna die!*

She ripped off the helmet and took heavy gulps. Sweet air! Sweetie teensy air molecules.

After a few seconds she started to breathe easy, feel clear.

What the hell had happened? And then she got it. What a jerk. After five hours of never getting out of your gear and now running upstairs? You're sucking in your own CO_2, back into your lungs, instead of oxygen. Literally running on fumes.

She walked slowly up to the top-floor landing, She noticed the surveillance cameras and put her helmet back on.

RESTRICTED ACCESS
RING BELL.

The door buzzed her in and clanked shut behind her like a jail cell, and she was astonished.

The whole top floor, all glass windows looking eastward toward the Berkshires, and westward down over the little town and river and then the high undulating peaks of the Catskills. She was facing a desk. A woman in a business suit, donning a silky black mask. Name plate? "Natasha O'Brien, RN, MBA/HBS." Amy had never seen her before.

Natasha stood and closed a thick book and came around the desk and put it down. *What's she reading? Resurrection?* Tolstoy?

"I know, I know," she said, following Amy's gaze. "Not much action here. Tolstoy makes the day go a *lot* faster. This was his last novel— don't know what I'll do without him."

"*Natasha.* Got it," Amy said. She took off her N95. "Look, I'm totally exhausted and off shift and almost passed out climbing the stairs, so I hope this is not a long meeting?"

"Oh my God!" said Natasha, appalled. As if training a dog she said, with utter firmness: "*Sit. Down. Here.*" She gestured Amy to a leather couch. It smelled new.

Amy sat down heavily and it felt heavenly.

"Now. Can I help? A drink, carbo, veggie, steak? We have a full kitchen up here."

"No, thanks. All I need is to go home ASAP. To sleep. What's up?"

"Dr. Rose, wow!" she said. "You look green. I am *obliged* to get you something to rehydrate and make sure your blood sugar is okay. Tree-fresh-squeezed orange juice and a glass of bottled water? I recommend Gerolsteiner. Smallest bubbles of any."

Amy nodded. Natasha left—Amy heard a grinding sound, an automatic slicer and juicer machine—and was back in maybe 30 seconds. The orange juice was, well, tree-fresh, yes. And yes, the bubbles *were* teensy. *Ahhh.*

"Bullet points," Natasha said.

Amy blurrily sensed that this woman—narrow face, alert blue eyes, clipped blond hair, and strangely plump lips—was fiercely confident, and "good with people."

"Why did I invite you up here for the first time, after four months? Because you are the leader of our Covid team, and you are, frankly, the most remarkable doctor we have here, and I just wanted to say hello." She smiled, a smile that seemed real. "I'm an RN and did an MBA at HBS. I administrate this ward. We might in fact ask to use your expertise at some point for our special patients. Are you ready for, say, a ten-minute tour?"

"Ten max. Let's do it."

They had opened up the whole top floor, creating a KK Hotel for the family of the patient to stay in, with their own private express elevator and "Business Center with Board Room." Natasha said that the patient and family could also enter from the roof, flying in and landing on the helicopter pad above. Most of it was state-of-the-art. A hi-tech operating theater with the capacity for robotic surgery no matter where in the world the patient—or surgeon—was. A full lab, everything. A full wardrobe of hard-to-find PPE, N95 face masks, and face shields. A large bedroom for a doctor on call. But the most remarkable sight?

Two ventilators. Not beaten-up, breakage-prone, overused ventilators like those down below, no. Pristine ventilators, shrink-wrapped in plastic. *Gorgeous* ventilators. There was also a small workout room, whirlpool, and sauna. TVs and those Bloomberg terminals used only by professional traders.

"Except," Natasha said, "no laptops or phones allowed in the Mindfulness Sanctum Sanctorum." She glanced at her Fitbit and announced, "Goodgood. We're just shy of our ten minutes. Any questions?"

"Yes, two. One, who are the patients? Two, who takes care of them?"

"The *patients* are high-value, high-impact individuals who have invested generously in the Kush Kare Private Equity Fund. The *care* is provided by the patients' dedicated concierge physicians, always available. From anywhere." She smiled warmly. "And we are inviting you to be one of them."

"You want me to sign up for a particular patient?"

"Oh gosh no! We will be getting patients here from all over the world—and given your remarkable career—your expertise in disease in all parts of the globe—well, you would be a high-value acquisition. You see, each Kush Kare Hospital all over America chooses one local doctor, as a crucial, lead clinical stakeholder, and here in Columbia you are it. The retainer, remunerations, and perks are, well, *wonderful.*"

"I'll consider it." Amy got up. "If and when my brain starts working again."

Natasha walked her to the door, both hands outstretched like guard rails against a crash.

At the door, facing Amy, Natasha said, "Oh, and by the way, I can help you deal with that infant Kenneth Miller Jr. His idiot rich father is on the Kush Board, and idiot rich son needs simpleton job." She smiled.

"Got it, Amy said. "And thanks."

6

"Close your eyes," Amy said to Orville.

"*What?*" Orville replied. "What'd you say?"

Miranda looked at Amy and shook her head in dismay.

"Close your eyes!" Amy said loudly. "Do *not* open them 'til I tell you. On pain of death."

Grumbling, he closed his eyes.

Three weeks later, noon on Memorial Day, which had rushed in as early as it could that fatal year, the 25th of May. As if to get this year of carnage done and buried. On the front porch, Orville, Miranda, Eleanor, Amy, and Ben were sitting around the breakfast table.

"Keep your eyes shut," Amy said to him. "No matter what I do, do *not* open them." He nodded. She gestured toward the driveway. A masked young woman pranced in quietly on running shoes. Without hesitating she went to Orville, and with practiced skill she slipped two hearing aids into his ears. And pranced away, back to the edge of the driveway.

"Hey!" he shouted "What the hell are you—"

"*Listen* to me!" Amy snapped. "I'm going to—"

Putting his hands to his temples, he cried out, "Don't *shout* at me! Jesus!"

Amy, Miranda, and Eleanor looked at each other. Amy went on, in a normal voice, "I was not shouting. I was, and am, talking to you at my usual level that you have not been able to hear. Repeat after me: 'I got Stacy—an audiologist—to get your data from the Rhino Lady, get hearing aids, and put them in.' Repeat."

"'I got Stacy—an audiologist—to get your data from the Rhino Lady, get hearing aids, and put them in. Repeat.'"

Silence. More silence.

"Oh my God!" he cried. "I hear you perfectly! And I don't feel anything in my ears!"

"Take off your blindfold."

His eyes were wide, astonished. He sat there, looking around, listening. "Amazing. All the mush is gone, like I don't have to clear my throat and—" He paused. "Birds! I'm hearing birds!"

With a thumbs-up, Stacy jumped around in joy, waved, and bounced off.

"Yes!" Miranda said. "Birds are high-frequency—you have the common high-frequency loss. You hadn't been hearing women's and children's voices, or anybody whispering—right?"

Orville nodded.

"Well, you're gonna hear it all now," said Miranda. "Especially *me*! No more asking me 'What? What'd you say?' a hundred times a day! No more divorce."

Orville smiled, nodded, looked around. He sensed that even his *sight* was better, seeing with clarity how Miranda's bright red hair was laced with gray, skin that redhead's cream color and freckled, and her two gems, her bright green eyes. *How gorgeous she is, and how caring.*

"Damn it, Miranda," he said, "why were you so against my gettin' these things all these years?"

She threw her glass of sparkling water at him.

"Dear one," he said, mopping it up and then taking her hand. "I'm . . . really sorry."

She smiled, nodded.

He reached out his hands to her and Eleanor. "It's like . . . like outside life has just kicked in!"

Amy and Eleanor had become great running pals. It was an outlet for Amy's pent-up stress, after hours of respiratory metrics and highly charged talks with families. Eleanor, who had grown up painfully shy, talked better while running than face-to-face. They left the group for a fast five-miler. But after only ten minutes, at the perimeter of the old New York State Training School for Girls, Amy got a *stat* call.

A woman in labor, on a farm way out in Taconic, the southernmost part of the county. In labor 12 hours. Baby stuck. All are panicking. The midwife is out of town, no one covering. The husband was told to call an ambulance to drive all the way down to Northern Duchess County Hospital—costing a fortune and taking an hour—said no. And then he got abusive.

Kush Kare had no obstetrics. President Jason Kush himself had canceled all obstetrics in all of its franchise hospitals across America, overheard saying, "Delivering babies is a loser. A fiscal loser. And Kushes aren't losers. We don't need the malpractice risk or the crappy reimbursement."

And so to have their babies, Columbians had to drive at least 40 miles upriver to Albany Medical. Some died, bleeding out on the shoulder of old Route 9.

Amy rarely did house calls, but for a compromised delivery, she went.

Back at the house, she made her apologies, sad to leave, said she'd be back for the fireworks. *Such a little family left. There won't be a lot more of these gatherings. Face it, it's precious. Precarious.*

———

Driving out, she was tense—it sounded like it could be big trouble. Baby death, mother death, the worst.

But as these things go, the divinity—perhaps sensing the upcoming ugliness—cut her a break, of beauty.

In her new Subaru she was soon driving through the just plain wonder, rolling hills and valleys with the Berkshires in the background, old bridges over splashing shaded streams and sometimes glades, and 100-year-old trees—her friends the trees. She had always loved trees more than any others of Mother Nature—copper beeches with their leaves looking, in the sunlight, like, well, copper, and rare chestnuts and stands of white birch that had been dying out but not here, no. And water. Kinderhook County was rippled with waters— coming down from the Taconic Range in waterfalls to the west, the streams from the north that wandered here and there happily and noisily until, courting their master, the down-facing gravity, into the ruling Hudson. The vast corporate farms were there, having flattened the land, but also, in the tortuous stream-etched woodlands, there still were family farms, often out of sight up a tree-lined road, and often just a wooden sign and an ancient Airstream trailer or a rusted modern version, with a propane tank, a TV antenna, and a dog.

Ahh, for those wanderings alone out here. On her 16th birthday Orvy bought her a used Fiat, and she began her adventures. In high school on her wanderings alone—or on doctoring calls with Orvy starting in high school and then after medical school for all those months—they'd explored almost all of this. Seen, with "good-doctor" eyes, the suffering of the people trying to live off the land—either because they'd fled to it, or because it was a centuries-old family farm demanding that they take care of it. She had been surprised by the hardscrabble poverty, the farmers barely making it. But that was nothing compared to now.

The house was remote, in disrepair. The yard was scattered with junk, but for a recent attempt at a wooden porch, with two aluminum folding chairs and an old barrel for a table. A dog of mixed pedigree—hopeful golden, or hellish beagle—was tied with a frayed rope to a doghouse, growling and barking. Another small house was nearby, with a single rocking chair and a small table.

She put on her mask.

A young man rushed out of the doorway, frantic. He was blond-haired and baby-faced, as if not yet able to shave, anywhere from 19 to 30, thin as a sapling, cigarette in his hand. He wore a white T-shirt that read—in sparkles—"Dad 2 B."

"Thanks for comin', Doc. Name's Royal. Alice is in big trouble. Come quick."

"Put your mask on first."

"What?"

"I can't come near either of you—your wife or you—unless you wear masks."

"Aw, Doc, c'mon. This is *an emergency*. And besides, we don't have any masks."

"I've got plenty." She opened her bag and took out several.

"I dunno . . ." He pondered this. The dog barked, as if it too was being told to put on a mask.

"Why not?"

A scream of pain came from inside, then silence.

"Alice needs you, Doc, right away."

"A mask, or you stay out here. It's the rule."

Another scream.

"How 'bout I can be the exception."

"No exceptions." Silence. "Why won't you wear a mask?"

"It's a hoax! A fucking hoax to run people like me over and leave us in the dirt. Look at this—" He gestured at the cluttered yard, the old truck. "*I'm goin' nowhere fast.* But the President is standing up for me. It's the principle! My hard-fought cherished freedoms!"

"Okay, okay, I get you. I'll attend to Alice, but listen carefully: you do *not* come inside the house when I'm in there, or I'll leave."

"She needs her husband's support."

"Wear a mask, you can support. Yes or no. Quick!"

"Shit." He thought it over carefully. The screaming continued. "Nope. I ain't no traitor."

"Good. Do *not* come in. I'm going to put on my protective suit." *Great. I'm going into a nest of Covid.*

She went back to the car and got out gown and gloves and N95 mask with the OR light and booties. Again, the enemy was heat, and soon would also be CO_2 exhaust, clouding common sense and diligence.

In the trip through the living room and kitchen Amy was appalled at the mess and scatter, open cans of both human and dog food, dirty dishes in the sink, tools on the table—a ratchet wrench and a hacksaw. But the bedroom had been worked on, decluttered, things neat and clean.

Propped up on pillows was a girl—at best 20. Her pajama top was drenched.

"Hello, Alice. I'm Dr. Amy. Sorry I have to use this gear."

"You have to. I myself try to follow— I can't get masks but I sewed a few. One good thing is I never have had fever or other symptoms."

"Lucky you. Here, put this mask on. And I'll leave some more masks for you. How long have you been in labor?"

"Since last night. Waters broke then. Sorry the place's such a mess. God bless you for coming, missing Memorial Day. Sorry about *these* fireworks. You're the answer to my prayers."

"What happened?" She attached the fetal monitor, for the mother's contractions—normal—and the baby's heartbeat—skipping beats, with runs of tachycardia, as if to catch up. Worrisome. In distress. *Have to hurry. Slow down thinking. Hurry.*

"She's stuck," Alice said. "I'm trying to breathe like they say on the 'net, and, like, not panic. But it's wicked hard. I don't care about how much it hurts, Doctor, I just fear for my baby. I never been through this before." She grimaced in pain. "Where's Royal?"

"Without a mask, he can't come in. I won't risk it. You should insist on it. Anyway he doesn't need to see this, right?"

"Yeah. He's got a weak stomach. He likes to think he's tough, but he's a pup—*owww*!"

Amy had put on a blood pressure cardiac module and had an IV ready to go. She examined her quickly—all normal but the delivery. The head of the baby had crowned, visible but "stuck," hadn't gone any farther despite strong contractions.

Thank God she's young. Why won't it move? Usually, it's the head that's the problem—and I could do an episiotomy to give it room, but here, after thousands of deliveries, some in hovels or outdoors under the stars—that doesn't seem to be what's going on. Something else is holding it back. She focused her headlamp, looked more closely. Aha! It wasn't the head, it was the shoulders. She could feel the outlines of both shoulders impacted against the inner wall of uterus. Jammed. Like trying to push a plastic hanger out through the cervical neck. *Have to try to get fingers of both hands in there, slide them down on either side of the head, feel what, exactly, is getting in the way. Luckily I've got small hands—ob-gyn hands. Now. Gently, ease in along the side of the head— and then the other side. Aha. Yes. Both shoulders are too broad to squeeze through. This means the two clavicles—the thin bone from the breastbone to each shoulder—are jammed up on both sides of the neck. If I were in a hospital, the baby would be out by now, a C-section. But now, Plan B. Learned it in a rotation in the Navajo. Break the two clavicles. Sounds ugly but works every time. Go.*

She took a deep, concentrating breath. Let it out slowly.

Left side clavicle. One finger on the shoulder end, one on the breast-bone end. Bring both fingers toward each other steadily, compressing the bone. Feel the pop as the clavicle breaks in half at the center. Other side. One finger on one end, one on the other. Bring together, pop.

Amy withdrew her hands and placed them on either side of the head so that when it started to move she could gently guide it and the shoulders out, preventing a vaginal tear. She waited.

It's just mechanics. It will work. Damn it, work.

One one thousand, two one thousand . . .

The head started to move, then move faster. She helped it out. Noticing the two clavicles, one on each side, folded just enough to get through.

The baby wailed. The mother screamed. Release. Joy.

"It's a girl," Amy said, cleaning the baby off. "I'll check her out and give her to you in a minute."

"How's it going?" Royal, at the doorway to the bedroom.

"Get out of here!" shouted Amy.

"But—"

"Stay away. Go out on the porch, near the door!"

He withdrew to the front door.

She examined the baby. "Your baby's okay."

"Thank God!" Alice cried.

Royal returned, drawn by Alice's exclamation. "She may have a couple of small bones that are bruised or broken, but they'll heal perfectly, quickly," said Amy. "Mother and baby will need hospital care for a couple of days, mostly observation. I'll call a doctor friend at Duchess Hospital who will take care of you and the baby, and put you in touch with a great obstetrics nurse who can walk you through being a first-time mother. I'll call an ambulance. Do you have insurance? Medicaid?"

Royal shook his head no.

"Okay, here's the deal: the first baby—and the ambulance—is on me. The second has to be on Medicaid. Deal?"

"Ain't that the government, because if so . . ." He caught himself. "Deal."

"Good. Here—some masks. Both of you have to wear them. Have to wash hands, a lot!" Amy glanced at the front door, where Royal was smoking. "After all this, do you want your wife and baby to die?"

"No!"

"Well, to keep them *alive*?"

She waited until he acknowledged this, with a nod.

"You have to wear a mask when you're around them. And don't touch them unless you wash your hands first. On your word of honor: yes or no?"

He looked down, and then up again.

"*C'mon*, son. Wash your hands, and then step up to see and hold your beautiful baby?"

A slight nod.

"And comfort your wife. Your baby girl and her mother need you. *To be a dad*. Okay?"

"Okay."

Before she left he'd washed his hands and, masked, was walking into the room to their baby.

In the car, she let out the kind of breath that feels like you haven't been breathing for a while. But then an old feeling blasted her—a fist in the gut. A chill, a sense of falling, failing—*no, not me who failed. But Bernie, damn him!* He didn't want a baby. A child. A family. Now my time is running out. *Where's mine?*

7

Amy was yearning to get back to the family but got paged. Holidays are carnage for hospitals. Columbian breakages were high—firecrackers, homemade celebratory bombs and ammo. Drunken Columbians exploding while lighting fuses, throwing lit firecrackers at each other, or slipping them underneath skirts, shirts, blouses, and one death so far by holding the fuse of a canister bomb *just that little bit too long in the mouth* to blow off a little too much of a face.

The Emergency Ward was full of "rule out Covid"—despite there being no reliable tests. The waiting room was almost full. Some were huddled up with chills—on a 90-degree evening—some sweating buckets. Choruses of coughs. One carrot-haired kid slumped over sleeping, waiting for his turn.

To make things worse, there was an overflow of relatives and friends of those waiting to be seen, spilling out onto the tarmac circle outside. It seemed to be a mixture of those partying and those in dread—for their beloved family members who were patients.

Blasts of firecrackers and cherry bombs punctuated the humid summer night.

Once inside, Amy was swamped. From two stretchers in a hall-way to the several patients in the beds of Emergency, she clicked into another realm, one of *I am in charge. Do what I say. Stat.*

Even Binni Prabhat looked overwhelmed and scattered.

I came to this hospital in its final year being run by the city of Columbia, he had told Amy, before they sold off to Kush. I immediately handed in my resignation. In two minutes I had a call from Jason Kush, the President. He wanted me to be chief of emergency with a goal of, quote, "Making Kush a Five Star Best in Show. You will have total autonomy." The pay was more than I ever dreamed, as a clinical research-focused doctor. And then—unbelievable, really—Kush promised I could keep up my lab work here—three rooms in the basement and a research assistant. At Einstein, I had a lab, working on human stem cells, I harvest them from pregnant mothers, and I was researching how to transfuse them to fight various diseases, especially for those patients with low immunity. And so when the Covid arose, I naturally thought to try infusions of the stem cells to fight off the virus. In my meeting with Kush he said, "There's a difference between not-for-profit research and for-profit. For-profit has no publish-or-perish crap. The private sector always wins. I'll treat you with care, compassion, and handsome stock options."

Now Amy hardly recognized Binni. Behind his faceguard he was frantic. Eyes wild, teeth clenched, flitting quickly this way and that, one patient after another from a line of stretchers backed up in the corridor, seeing if he could triage them out—called "Meet 'em and street 'em"—and then rushing back to the nurses' station to see what was piled up next. A lock of his lush black hair, usually combed meticulously, was flopping here and there against the plexiglass shield, and he was distractedly whipping his head this way and that to try to keep it away from his eyes. Like all doctors at some time or other, right now he was "losing it."

"Hey, Binni!" she shouted, rushing to him. "Your hair needs some attention."

"What doesn't?" he said, looking away toward a patient's scream.

Facing him, she took him by both arms and squeezed so he couldn't move. "Look at me." He did. "*I am here. I will help.* We're gonna be okay, and if not, *that's* okay—because we're doing our best, *together.*" Still he struggled, but she held on, eye to eye. Firmly, she said, "*Calm!*" A reminder and an order. "*Deft*, remember? If so, *smile.*" She squeezed his hands.

He took a deep breath, held it as long as he could. Exhaled. Smiled thinly, nodded, squeezed back.

To staunch the bleeding—that of the *docs*—Eddie was staying longer than his shift, and Hooper was on his way in.

For all his gruff stuff, Eddie was a heart-of-gold doc. He had medico mojo and knew how to connect and direct anyone from his years in his cancer practice in California. Standing at the nurses' station, he was hanging up the phone. Amy and Binni joined the nurses gathered there as Eddie exclaimed, "Get a load of this!"

"Mike Fiddler is the patriarch of a bunch of basket weavers out in Copake—they make and sell these incredible baskets. He has terrible heart disease and asthma—runs in the family. I've got him on both drugs. So today he decides his heart is giving out and he's had enough, he's ready to die, takes to bed. Big family, on vigil, praying. So I get a call just now from his wife. 'He won't die. He can't breathe good 'n' can't talk, but he will *not* die. Five days. Truth be, we're gettin' *fractious*. What do we do?' I tell her to put the phone on speaker. What I hear is *wheezing*, heavy *wheezing*. 'Mike,' I yell, 'it's not your heart, it's your *asthma*. Take your asthma pill, okay? You're *not* dying.' So Mike asks, 'What if . . . *wheeze* . . . that don't . . . *wheeze* . . . work?' And I go, 'Call me if you die, buddy, okay? Go for it!'"

Binni, Amy, and the nurses were wide-eyed.

"What's with you guys? Don't you know the delivery of medical care when you hear it?"

Their laughter was just what they needed.

They jumped back in together, triaging and treating.

Mostly it was triage—sorting emergencies, based on patient history and oxygen saturation number—in the Binni Prabhat Classification System: "Mild, medium, or hot—like a curry. "Hot" meant the lungs were compromised. Has the virus tiptoed up to the lungs and tiptoed back, or fallen in? If in, intubate, ventilate, pray. The lung is the great equalizer; everyone has one.

At the nursing station was a new sign:

THIS IS GOD.
DO NOT CATCH COVID.
I'M FLAT-OUT TOO.

Amy threw herself into work. At one point she asked about the two admissions she had been following: Mayor Scomparza and Jenny Van Ness, Robert's wife from the nursing home.

Ex-mayor Scomparza had done great on dialysis and had been discharged that morning, with admonitions to go to the clinic called KK in KK: Kidney Kare in Kush Kare, twice a week (and ordered to forgo Lysol or Clorox or shine UV light up his ass or drink fish tank cleaner).

Jenny was still alive, able to tolerate periods of breathing by herself, but then relapsing. She might still make it, and might not. The "visits" with Robert and her family when she was off the ventilator—from outside her room looking in and talking on the "I"-phone—were okay, but with each intubation the torment returned.

As the day faded, there was even more of a rush. When Amy was presented with the Holsapple family—husband, wife, teenage daughter, all with low oxygen—she didn't see how she could go on. But following them in was Nurse Leatrice! Amy asked, "What are you doing here?"

"They've been our next-door neighbors since I was a little girl. No problem. I'll get changed."

Finally, at seven, God spoke—"Thou shalt not stay at Kush Kare tonight"—and Amy could leave. Binni was off duty as well. The men's changing room was closed for cleaning—not of the men, but of the room.

"Damn!" Binni said, "*now* what? I've had it, quite had it. I can't wait one more minute to get out of here. Damn."

"C'mon," Amy said, "use the women's. Nothing about a naked body matters anymore."

It was empty. Exhaustion hit them. They fumbled each other out of the PPE—a meticulous stripping to stop viral spread and then throwing it away safely and suddenly they were naked but for their underwear—her black bra and panties, his white boxers.

"Oh my God!" said Binni. Suddenly he was shivering—in the hot, close room, shivering?

"Yeah?" She diagnosed his shivering as a rush of sympathetic adrenaline—how sweet!

"I . . . I have never seen you this way—all of you, even your face and neck and hair and . . ."

"And?"

"You are gorgeous! You are a handsome woman and your, uh, lingerie is, well, I mean, makes you so enticing and exciting! Oh my, I'm sorry."

Amy smiled. "And you—so handsome too, so cute! In the masks and all, and now in this light, I can really *see* you! The black curls to your hair, your alert soft eyes? And the way your lips purse—dimpling up—like they're smiling at the ends?" He blushed. "You are one . . . handsome . . . dude. Dangerous."

"The virus?"

"That too. I was thinking dangerous attraction to you . . ."

"Oh my!" he said, blinking.

"Under all those protections, you're so, I don't know, delicate, and I could die to look at that cute belly—oops, I shouldn't have said that."

"You are the most beautiful woman I've ever seen in . . . in all of medicine. I would love to take you in my arms, and I would stay taken, just holding you, touching you for a long time."

They stood there, eyes caressing bodies.

"What's it been now, five months?" Amy said. "For five months all I've seen naked are damaged bodies in extremis—no, not quite. The only male I've seen naked is my great love, Ben."

His face fell. "Oh, I see, well then—"

She burst out laughing. Seeing his dismay, she couldn't stop. In her bra and panties, big letting-go laughter. She waved her hand "no, no." "Ben is . . ." Belly laugh. "My dog!"

"Thank God!"

They got dressed and walked through the ER, out.

She said, "So, another day in the slaughterhouse."

"And wouldn't you know it, dear Amy? I am a vegetarian."

That "dear" felt good. *Really* good. She smiled. "Any bad breakages today?"

"Nothing serious, no." He paused. "Frankly, Amy, I am more scared of walking home in the dark of night than I was all day on duty."

"What? Why?"

"The hatred of the downstreet whites. It's worse lately. North Front Street has gotten to be a dodgy part of town—except for where I live, the row of condos overlooking the river. The people of color in Bliss housings are friendly, respectful. But parts of the North Side, in run-down houses, are scary—drugs and guns—like what we fled New York to get away from! With the Memorial Day holiday, I'm fearful to walk alone in darkness. So . . ." He struggled. "Could you drive me home?"

"Sure." As they walked out together, the young man with carrot hair who had been slouched over, sleeping, in the waiting room was still in that same posture. Amy's sixth sense went wild. She stopped, putting on gloves and a mask. Lifted up his chin, and let go. Flaccid. Dead.

"Did you know him?" she asked.

"No, never saw him."

They went back to Leatrice, asked about the boy. She looked at the list.

"Yes, Dr. Rowe saw him. He wrote 'Symptoms of Covid. Oxygen 90. Not urgent. Can wait.'" She sighed. "I'll take care of this. Get out of here."

"Amazing," Amy said to Binni as they walked out toward her car in the doctor's locked lot, "this is the second sudden death I've seen—they come in looking okay, and bang—dead."

"Yes. This virus is getting quite agile. One can't diagnosis it by the 'look.'"

Just then, a shiny black four-door pickup truck came fast toward them, then turned sharply into the circle in front of the hospital and, honking, tires screeching, went around, and then around again, still honking. Two long aerials, one on each side of the windshield, held pennants:

MY VACCINE IS JESUS
DON'T TREAD ON ME

She drove him downtown. From Third Street down to Front, no one was out walking alone. Streetlights were blown out, rubbish strewn, and a couple of bars were open. People were sitting out on their stoops, waiting for the fireworks. No masks. Just north of this was a row of brand-new upscale condos on the escarpment, overlooking the Hudson and the Catskills.

"Right here, this condo is mine." He turned to her. "Oh, what an evening. Is there any possible way that we can see each other, you know, normally?"

"I don't see how, but I want to, too."

He took her hand, gently, and looked into her eyes.

She kissed him, gently, a chaste kiss.

He kissed her back, gently, then exited the car.

As she drove home to join in celebrating a Memorial Day dinner picnic on the porch and then to watch the fireworks, she was flushed with hope. How just plain nice it was, to feel, to be, for a moment to find herself at—what?—yes, at the level of love.

8

An hour later Miranda, Orville, Amy, and Ben were sitting on the front porch, watching Eleanor in the front yard practicing flying her drone in the Courthouse Square.

It was the first time she'd unpacked the four-footed flying machine since using it off the coast of Ecuador to observe whale behavior without influencing it. This was the key to her PhD at Duke, studying the effect of the unregulated tourist industry of whale-watching boats on the whale breeding grounds. None of the family had ever seen a drone up close. Zooming fast this way and that, up, down, sideways, *all* ways—totally controlled by this one human. Eleanor had Miranda's red hair and creamy skin, but brown eyes and Orville's height. He had taught her to run and they had run together—and from early on she had been graceful, strong.

Now she was totally in control of this poor little drone. Amazed calls from the porch echoed off the granite face of the Courthouse.

What a great thing for her, this adventure, Orville thought. Even with her being obsessive, in ways they'd not noticed when she was away at Duke. When she came back to live with them a month ago,

Miranda and Amy and he had been startled by how meticulous she was, in all things, especially the environmental thrust of literally everything—including three different kinds of compost and waste-sorting into special containers, which Orville could never understand: why did paper napkins go into the green compost bin rather than in the blue one that took cardboard and newspaper?

"Dad, you are *not* getting this right!" she would say, trying once again to explain.

He tried, and failed. She was alert. Sometimes she would send Orvy a photo of the innards of a garbage can, pointing out the flagrant errors between "trash" and "recycle."

Now she guided the cute drone right over their heads on the porch, its whirring like a whining "hello," and set it down gently on its four chicken-like feet. Everyone applauded. She, still modest, blushed, but bowed. It was hot and muggy. She reached for a large bottle of Pellegrino sparkling water—but then she noticed another bottle one-third empty. She stopped. Stared at the two bottles. Looked at Orville. Shook her head slowly.

"Oooo-kay, El," Orvy said, bracing himself. "What did I do now?"

"You opened another bottle before you finished the first."

Orville clenched his teeth and looked to Miranda, then Amy—who both broke out laughing.

"I'll take care of it," Eleanor said. She poured one bottle into the other, making a whole bottle. She filled her glass amid silence. "Look, you know I like things neat, and earth-friendly, right?"

"Yes, dear," Miranda said, "but it seems like it's been turned up a notch since we last saw you."

"You can't work close to whales—especially when they're mothering their babies and you see them tangled in nets, trying to protect them from the poisons—it's the worst! Plastic kills! They starve to death—and the babies, abandoned, die too. It's the first time I've been that close to them, and it broke my heart. Going green here is the least we can do."

"You haven't talked to us about this," said Miranda.

"Well, now I am."

"We're in, El," said Orville. "Just tell us how we do it."

"Great. It's not easy, but I'll get the data. I'll write it all out and post it." She smiled. "It's not just for me, it works for you two already."

"How does it work for us?" Orvy asked.

"I wash all the dishes, and look at all the new stuff I've ordered from Amazon to make your life easy. The whole kitchen is new, arranged in perfect order, right? I even order your coffee every two weeks—your favorites, Peet's decaf French for Dad, Italian for Mom, both 'fine-grind'?" She paused. "And huge bags of Ben's food too."

"You're a miracle, dear, "Miranda said. "A round of applause."

"Thanks," Eleanor said, assessing the empty plates, bottles, strewn napkins. Her oval face scrunched up, her brown eyes narrowing. She twirled a lock of red hair on an index finger. "Um, is it okay if I clear?" Nods all around. She quickly made a tower of plates and started back into the house, but then stopped as she passed behind Orville. Balancing her load, she bent over him and kissed his bald head. "Dad," she said, "I'm *really* glad you got hearing aids."

Orvy was startled—it was so un-Eleanor. Nodding, he said, "Me too, El, me really too."

She went in. Sounds of dishes and utensils clashing.

Orville and Amy and Miranda and Ben looked at each other. And all burst out laughing, even, he let it be known and in his own way, Ben.

Eleanor came back. Smiling, satisfied. "And with my workouts and running, and your aches and pains, there's another great thing about living in this house now."

"What's that, El?" Orvy asked.

"You're never that far away from a bottle of Advil."

A black limo with darkened windows pulled up. Spotless, its high polish reflecting the slivers of streetlights. The limo parked in front of the porch. Out of the front seat came a crisp-white-shirted driver, holding a phone, checking out the security. He opened the passenger door. Out stepped a chunky man in a dark suit, white shirt gaily open at the neck. Aviator sunglasses. His signature hair was stunning—bright white, full and combed, a traditional part to one side. He looked good and strong. More—he looked *sure*. But not as sure as he did in his frequent interviews on TV.

"Henry?" said Orville.

"Happy Memorial Day, my friend. And all best wishes from Nelda Jo." He and his driver put on their masks—matching US flags. He gave the masks a thumbs-up!

The family Rose put on their various masks as well.

"Brought some chilled champagne," Henry said, nodding to his man, who took out a cooler and fluted glasses. He came up and pretended to shake hands, making people laugh. "Good t'see ya all again, Amy, Miranda, Eleanor, Ben—and my best friend in Columbia, the man I admired—*still* admire, now more than ever—my old friend the good doctor Orville Rose."

Henry Schooner's Victorian was 134 paces directly across the Courthouse Square. The porch light was a golden yellow, lighting up the warm underbelly of the porch roof. Orville had spent a lot of time, over the years, staring at that golden bulb, that underbelly, that house. Henry grew up as the only child of a single mother living in the Furgery, a tattered settlement of shad fishermen on a polluted inlet of the Hudson.

He and Orville were in the same high school class, Henry a bully—and Orville his main target, for being three things that Henry was not: a Jew, a varsity athlete, and smart. Schooner was expelled in his senior year. He joined the Navy, went to Vietnam, came back to

Columbia as a Purple Heart hero, and married to a rich and dazzling Oklahoma blonde. He and Nelda Jo had two kids, and in 1984 created a then-novel business: the Columbia Health Club and Spa. It went national. He sold out for a ton of money and went into real estate at just the right time, the boom of New Yorkers buying into the county. Three decades ago he had won the 19th District congressional seat as a Republican, and joined the Committee on Defense, working himself up to the lucrative and powerful position of chairman. He was a rarity: known for making hard deals without pocketing hard cash.

Whenever Orvy saw Schooner, a memory of physical abuse popped up—*still*. But 30 years ago, when Orville came back to Columbia and became town doctor, Henry and he had become friends. Schooner was the main benefactor of city and county. His golden light across the park was always on, a beacon welcoming you to "drop in anytime." Amy and Miranda knew all this, about their "friendship."

Amy saw, above Schooner's mask, in his light blue eyes and shocking white hair, an animal wariness and power. She recalled Orville saying to her once as they watched him on TV, "Be careful, Ame. After you shake his hand, make sure you count your fingers."

But given the other Republican House and Senate members, Schooner was at the top in moral courage—often voting with Democrats. He kept saying he might just run for President—after all, he was known all over the Empire State by the greatest American accolade: "*A real nice guy.*" And he had that rare pixie dust—he looked more real on TV than in reality.

There were a couple of spare chairs on the porch, and Orvy moved them a few feet away, saying, "We're practicing social distancing, Henry."

"And thank *God* we do!" Henry said, nodding, as if every foot of distance was gold. He smiled broadly as he took off his dark suit jacket and handed it to his man, then rolled up his white shirtsleeves.

He didn't just *sit* but somehow *settled* happily, as if saying, "Here is a man who knows how to settle happily into chairs for satisfying long visits."

"Can't stay long," he said, "but after almost seventy-five years in the same town and the same friendship, it's . . ." He fumbled in a pocket and came out with a bright white handkerchief—a handkerchief, *in this era?*—and under his mask blew his nose.

He sighed, composed himself.

"Today I flew from DC into Albany, home for this great holiday—Nelda Jo and our kids and grandkids celebrate out at our spread in Spook Rock. Short and sweet. Just a couple of gunshots and taps and we're done. But then I recalled that your whole family would be here today and after throwing the switch for the fireworks I just *had* to drop in. I mean, how many people do you love"—he paused, seemingly choked up—"*that you met in grade school?*"

Another teary pause, wipe, blowing of nose.

"I never told you, Orvy, that you—and your mom, and our dear buddy Clive—were incredibly important in my life, overcoming the forces of single-mom poverty, and forgiving my transgressions that made me what I am today."

His masked and gloved man had distributed the flute glasses of champagne.

"A toast! To the good—no, the *great* Dr. Orville Rose and family!"

Orville caught Amy's eye, and both lifted eyebrows and smiled.

"My seventy-fifth is comin' up soon! Yours too! Let's hope you can come out to Spook Rock for it. Looks like you great docs are finally gettin' this darn virus under control. Y'can almost hear it calling 'Uncle!' Amazing, you physicians, what you've done! Can't wait to get this economy moving. Gotta open it all soon. Health, jobs, freedom."

Mentioning all this brought strained silence.

Orville and Amy stiffened. They saw that Schooner sensed the stiffening. All tacitly agreed: *Do not go there.*

Miranda handed him and his man slices of warm apple pie and vanilla ice cream.

Schooner seemed lifted to a heavenly realm of pure *thanks!* and carefully ate each crumb. Soon, seeming sated, he said, "Gotta go. Nelda Jo sends love." He got up—teetered—and plopped back down heavily.

With an arm from his driver, on the second time, he made it. When he did get up, everyone was pulled to get up too.

Amy felt she had gotten a doctor's glimpse of the real Schooner. The body is flabby. A lot of rich food and booze. But a mind as sharp as a tack, honed by a white-hot calculation, on all things.

"Yeah, I gotta get back to work on good government, this great republic we've been given. Day in, day out, down there in Washington, I'm a resister, would you believe it? I gotta resist the idiocy of our party's knuckle-draggers and . . ." He considered, paused. Then, in a stentorian voice he went on, ". . . *and resist going down into the weeds of crazy!*"

As he left, he asked Amy to walk him down the steps. At a social distance, he said, "Heard you had a good talk with Natasha the nurse in the private pavilion. If you ever need any help at the hospital—*any* help—just call." He presented his card, holding it with a thumb and forefinger on each side, saying, "My personal direct line." His man escorted him to his limo.

On the porch, silence. No one wanted to say anything about Schooner. After a while, the silence softened.

"I was thinking," Orvy said finally. "This little family—with Cray—each of us is trying to better the world. Miranda won't tell you, but she's writing a great history of the Columbian hero and scoundrel General William Scott Worth and—"

"Don't! Please!" Miranda said. She was always secretive about her writing, didn't want to jinx it. It was a deeply rooted trait, keeping secrets. As a girl in Florida, after she caught polio, she kept her shrunken leg secret under long pants. She knew that keeping secrets had a big downside, but still she struggled with it.

"I'm sorry, hon," Orville said. "I shouldn't have done that, but I mean I feel so thankful, grateful, to you for, well . . . everything! I mean life's so chancy now, a flicker of a butterfly's wing one way or the other and none of us would be here. And loving you—and El and Amy and *Ben*—the key has been the key—"

Ben, hearing his name and trying to get a pat on the head, had lurched against Orville, his tail slapping Miranda, almost tipping both over. Shouts stopped him. Sensitive, head down with hurt, he started plodding off in banishment. "Aww, Ben," Orvy said, "I'm sorry. C'mere!" Joyously he did.

"What I meant to say, Miranda," Orville went on, "is that I'm sorry I put you in the spotlight."

"Oh, it's fine. An old pattern. I *should* share more. Maybe I will."

"That'd be great, Mom. I never know what you're writing."

"I'm glad you do share so much, what you're up to. I mean, except for boyfriends—"

"*Mo*-om. Don't go there!"

"All in all," Orville said, "we're all good. And what I was going to say is, is that my heart is bursting with how lucky we all are."

"Unless," Amy said, "you just jinxed us so that—"

Explosions—fireworks, fracturing the tolerant black sky. And a deeper silence, for all the noise. Most of the Columbia crowd would be watching from Parade Hill, the high escarpment above the Hudson. In lulls the clunky brass band of Evans Pumper Number 9 was playing old favorites red-meat patriotic music—the proud echoes off the courthouse façade declaring that the USA was *kind of*, well, *intact*, despite everything.

The grand finale was followed by silence, the reassuring kind after a racket. A stillness.

"Wow! That was *loud*!" Orville said happily. "Crashing!" He looked at Amy, cherishing her being back, being *here. All of us here.*

A long silence. No one wanted to break it.

Finally Miranda said quietly, "Someone once told me that this kind of silence, at this time of night, means that there are angels passing overhead."

"Yes!" Orville said happily. "Y'know what? Given what's going on in this place, this country, world, I hereby declare that all those present are members of the Family Rose Resistance Brigade."

Laughter.

"I mean it. What's going on now, this virus—and this viral President—is *bad*, and can turn worse, turn on a dime. Even *Schooner* knows it. It's dangerous, depressing. But being so bad is how things change, crying out for the good." He looked to each, holding each for a moment. "This is hope. This is what hope *is*. This is how hope manifests, to change. Something else will have to happen. *Stick together.*"

"Got it," said Amy, even though she didn't entirely. "Do I hear an 'amen'?"

———

The next day at work, as if our town had been privy to what Orville had said about hope and change, the dread Kush Kare seemed to have come alive with good medicine.

All day, no deaths!

At six at night, change of shift, there tiptoed into Emergency the faint sounds of singing.

Amy was walking out with Binni and others, Eddie and Hyper following. As the singing wafted into Emergency, most of the night shift followed. Outside, there was clapping and shouts and singing of the chorus of "New York, New York."

Who? What?

Maybe 50 or so Columbians, all masked up, were serenading their medics. The conductor was Freeman Bell, the piano teacher—prostate cancer, stage 4, on radiation, and in pain, Amy knew—he was smiling and waving and singing in a healthy tenor with his Episcopal church chorus.

The doctors and nurses and orderlies and ambulance drivers and undertakers stopped, came closer, surprised and overwhelmed. Other ordinary Columbians were arriving, singing and clapping, sending notes of gratitude to all.

They know how bad it is, Amy thought, *and they know how hard we try.*

She looked at Binni, whose eyes were shiny with tears—and her eyes welled too.

More and more Columbians joined in and went on to "God Bless America" and "The Star-Spangled Banner" with its weird ending in a question, and "Take Me Out to the Ball Game" even though the game had been canceled, and then Reverend Chester Hughes and Lady Brown Jackson, soloist of the Black AME Zion chorale, sang "Amazing Grace."

The crowd hushed, then joined in until there were so many singing that the song itself seemed to have gotten its lungs healthy too, and by chance or fate was now positioned so that the concave brick face of the hospital focused the notes and voices and bounced them back over the heads of the crowd and hustled down Washington Street with "legs," so that they might even have been heard at the river, and the facing mountains.

All with no breakage, none. Healing.

A FALSE SENSE

9

Hiroshima Day, August 6. The 75th birthday of the day they dropped the atom bomb.

It was Orville Rose's birthday as well.

Amy had prepared meticulously to get to the celebration before six o'clock sharp, when the Zoom to Italy would begin with Miranda's son, Cray, and his inherited Italian family, hunkered down in a grand family villa between Milan and Lago d'Orta. Leaving time for decontamination, she had to leave the hospital at four thirty, tops. She still wasn't sure if Binni could get there on time. One of his bad traits was his trouble committing totally to social endeavors. And he was always late.

"It's the Indian way," he'd said to her that morning, rolling his head this way and that in an Indian way.

"This is not India, okay? For better or worse, this is America. Get with it."

But more and more lately she found herself thinking of him, at odd breaks at work or before going to bed, or even when waking up.

He was brilliant, and somehow both familiar and exotic, and there was a sureness about him, or a kindness. Given his two divorces, she was leery of getting too involved, but she had never before seen such a—what?—a gentle man. Except, of course, Orville. He had a 12-year-old daughter, Razina, living with his ex. He and she were very close, but he didn't dare to have her visit, because of Covid. They Zoomed often.

Binni's house had a deck facing west over the river and on up up and more up to the high edge of the crashing Catskills. Whenever she stayed over, often after making love, they'd sit and talk—that gentle talk after good sex. Binni had introduced Razina on Zoom. The screen made it easy to get to know each other.

Recently, after hanging up on Raz and looking out over the grand expanse, Amy said, "I'd give up almost everything, even now, for a girl like yours."

"Do you want to talk about it?" Binni said.

"Not much to talk of. It didn't happen. I had the total workup, they found a few little things that they tried to fix. And then there was nothing else to try. Weird. And then it was a diagnosis of 'older eggs.'"

"I am very sorry, dear."

She turned to face him. His face had changed remarkably, his lower lip pushed out and trembling. Tears were in his eyes. And she too felt like crying, not so much for her infertility, but for his sadness for her. They held each other's gaze for what seemed a long time, until a softening, and a hug. *He has suffered in love too, and a lot.* His being hurt, and the resultant vulnerability, made him even more attractive. *A plaguetime of opening up, yes, for both of us. Gingerly.*

Being so fatigued at work, having a kind, brilliant man was a life preserver thrown to her. They—and only they—understood the daily hell and—sometimes—the daily sorrow. He was a kind man. And able to laugh amid the hell. *All I really want to do is to be a simple person in a good family. I've never had it, for my own. Can I have it now? Can any doctor have it?*

────────

After a national lull in Covid, as if it were catching its own breath, it came on much worse.

It was a hellish summer, in news and in medicine. The policemen murdering George Floyd, the Black Lives Matter demonstrations all over the country, the crackdown on the demonstrators, and the President urging his faithful to fight the virus by marching to "liberate Michigan, Minnesota, etc.," to liberate the whole nation really by not wearing masks and carrying military-grade assault rifles loaded with ammo into statehouses.

There had been a burst of copycat "Liberate Columbia" parades, complete with pickup trucks with banners, assault rifles, and Confederate flags, honking and shouting, driving up to the cemetery and down to the river a few times—a ride of about five minutes—but Columbians paid little attention and the parades succumbed to breakages and that was that.

In response to massive BLM marches all over the country, and with a huge turnout in Washington, D.C., streets were sealed off and resisters beaten up by unlabeled soldiers. At night thugs on horses galloped into the humans, tear gas bombs exploded, and helicopters hovered low in blinding argon lights, blasting out jolts of ungodly sound that pierced brains like another kind of bullets.

Under the weight of the vast suspicious underbelly of our country, of the Midwest and South from Florida to Arizona, and up to Idaho and Minnesota, many great Americans took no anti-Covid precautions. They threw down their skimpy masks and picked up their fat guns and marched into their statehouses to claim their freedom to be infected.

Delighted, the virus munched up the humans.

———

That morning, after their dawn walk around the Courthouse Park, Amy and Ben sat on the couch and watched *Morning Joe*. The President was proclaiming that he had won the war on the "Chineeese Kung Flu, and now let's all loosen up and get out there and have a great summer. Let's all MAGA!"

"Murderer!" Amy shouted at the TV. "You're the scum of the earth!"

Her two-minute rage got so loud that Ben, usually doggedly impartial, broke out and howled.

Morning Joe quoted Dr. Fauci saying that American deaths from Covid had reached 200,000. This jibed with what Amy was seeing in the hospital. Many people's attention span had run out, and rather than following the guidelines, they'd gone back to doing whatever the hell they wanted. The trajectory of contagion had shot up like a rocket.

If there was one enduring quality of the town, it was the spirit of the place. Miranda, as official Columbian historian, had looked at the town from its founding in 1609 to the present and discovered that when Columbians were asked by their leaders to pay more taxes for the general good, such as increased police for the safety of all, they said no. And breakage reigned.

But Amy and her team persevered.

She found herself thinking how, during the first wave, she and her team had been fresh, challenged, learning exponentially, scared, yes, but excited and in new territory, working flat out together. The team of intensivists had set the tone for other health-care workers, leaning out over the edge of their understanding, not knowing what they were doing, but doing it together.

But now she and her team were tired. Often fractious. No treatments had been shown to be of benefit. They had seen enough to be bone-cold scared of what was coming next.

But why—except for the President telling everybody to go out and have summer fun—why did they face such a horrific second wave? Answer? *The holidays.*

Holidays are jet fuel for pandemics, and there were far too many in the summer. Memorial Day, Father's Day, Flag Day (whatever that was), July Fourth.

And events like the Sturgis, South Dakota, population 7,020, Motorcycle Rally, which attracted 500,000 unmasked bikers from all over the country, who wandered this way and that and sat down in crowded bars and then went back home and spread the virus like their bike exhaust, seeding the fertile heartland with swaths of virus from the Great Lakes to the Gulf of Mexico, and from the Smokies to the Rockies—a nationwide Covid virus franchise.

The President was everywhere on TV and Twitter, reassuring Americans that what was happening was not happening. It broke your heart to see so many millions that believed him.

———

Kush Kare was bleeding money. Mainly because of the contagion of Covid. The hospital was in an epidemic of not making money. The state had mandated the cancellation of "jackpot" treatments—high-paying, mainly *elective* surgeries that could wait. Surgeries such as gall bladder removal, hernia repair, hip and knee replacements. These surgeries, which could wait for some future time, were called by the Kush Fiscal Team "high-cash-volume health-care insurance pay-ments." The volume of high-cash-volume payments had been turned down so low they were inaudible.

But! While the hospital industry was bleeding money because of not doing big-money operations, the health insurance industry was raking in money, by *continuing to collect the usual monthly insurance premiums.* Insurance companies had lots of this nice green money coming in, and had little money trickling out in payments. Insurance was soon making *billions* in profit. It was a huge bonus for health-care insurance companies not to pay out money for health care. Ful-filling their highest goal: multimillion-dollar executive bonuses. Insurance stocks soared.

In all the mess of this, things got clear: Insurance's reason to exist? *Money.*

Medicine's reason to exist? *Quality. Quality of care for human beings. And postponing a cancer surgery is not quality of care.*

In hospitals there was a fierce War across the Screen: on one side of the screen, you had hospitals billing the insurance companies the *maximum* for the patients' care; on the other side, insurance companies paying the *minimum* for the patients' care.

The stock of Kush Kare was starting to wobble.

And so KK scheduled a video address entitled "Thanks!" It was not only sent to every one of their tens of thousands of employees across the nation, but in fact it was read out loud by the top person: founder, majority investor, chairman of the board. It was the first time that Amy, Hyper Hooper, and Eat My Dust had heard President Kush's voice.

And what a voice! *The* Voice! Clear, calm, considerate, compassionate—a basket of reassurance that could not help but bring up images of your beloved uncle Mortie. And yet, and yet, in all the kindness, there was a kind of firmness, like Uncle Mortie when he told you to stop your shenanigans and behave—*right now*—behave or real bad shit would happen. All in all, a strong, powerful man at the top. The fact that he wasn't on camera—that he was read-ing the text that was scrolling on-screen—made it even more power-ful. Like a modern Wizard of Oz.

"Sincere thanks for your superb sacrifices. Things are going well. We could not have done it without every single one of you work-ing miracles. Unfortunately, 'every single one of you' is no longer fiscally possible and therefore we are making layoffs of fiscally non-high-throughput nonessential workers, many of whom have risked their lives during the pandemic. Laid off are nurse assistants, transportation, orderlies, and other groups (see attachments). Be well and thanks."

There was no mention of a long-standing and beloved KK Columbia doctor, the lone psychiatrist at our hospital, a rumpled old *mensch* named Moonbloom. His specialty was suicide prevention, which didn't generate much revenue for the hospital. He had quit and they did not hire a replacement.

Obstetrics had long been closed—low revenue, and horrendous malpractice payouts when things went bad.

Amy and the other doctors and nurses had tried to contact the administrators about the dire layoffs, which were compromising good care. They got nowhere. Every administrator was working from home, most in Spook Rock, a town that had been swallowed by the rich. The managers said they were the wrong person to talk to and suggested going "higher up." The senior managers said the same. This was repeated higher and higher, through junior vice presidents and senior, until Amy got the home number of the highest up, J. Kush, President and CEO. She was told that he would be glad to talk to her and alas he was tied up traveling to his fleet of KKs and would get back to her when he was, well, untied up. *Not.* From then on, whenever she called he was traveling but would get back to her.

None of the KK Columbia administrators had announced that they would *not* be coming in to the hospital anymore. But one night under cover of dark they had all just left. Since the doctors had never met the administrators in person, for a long time Amy and the team thought they were still working in their offices. Or possibly, rumor had it, up on the top floor below the bull's-eye helicopter pad, the suite Amy had visited once, where she found Nurse Natasha reading Tolstoy.

But then, one day, in the middle of the hellish first wave, the whole hospital staff had seemed much more relaxed and efficient and nobody could figure out why. There were no big hassles, no pressures, a lot less tension. A welcome change. But why? A real puzzle.

At team meeting Eat My Dust had cried out, "Hey hey hey! *The bosses don't come in here in person anymore*, to mess with our patients and slow us down and piss everybody off! Volume is down, baby, down!"

On the other hand, given Kush Kare's main mission to stop bleeding money, they were not ordering enough N95 masks, and new well-fitting gowns and other necessities were again in short supply. Hoarding once again appeared. This meant that working in the hospital went back to being as dangerous as in the first weeks, six months ago, before anyone knew what the hell they were doing.

Worst of all, the stress of the second punch of the pandemic, exacerbated by the indifference of the administration to the impact all this was having on the hospital staff, led to some nurses leaving. Kush Kare paid poorly, but it was the only hospital for miles around and plenty of locals had wanted to work close to home. Now, however, nurses left because they were no longer feeling safe from the virus—and worried about infecting their partners and kids at home.

And suddenly "Travel Nurse USA" firms sprung up all over America, placing nurses in other parts of America, mostly in the Midwest. It was enticing. Higher pay for less work. For instance, in the Intensive Care Unit it was standard for nurses to have two patients for a shift—which at first was KK's standard. But during Covid surges they were taking five or six patients at a time. Almost impossible. Travel nurses were making up to 6,000 dollars per week, 2,000 dollars per shift. Way more than, twice as much as, what they were getting paid at home.

There was no way that KK would compete. National studies found that safe staffing was one nurse for every four patients. Kush Kare had gone to one for six and now occasionally one for eight. Heading toward a deadly ten. It got impossible. As the first two nurses said good-bye—teary, and guilty—they said they were no longer willing to put up with the lack of support, respect, and, yes, fair wages from our hospital's administrators.

————

It was now three thirty in the afternoon, an hour before Amy would have to leave for Orville's party.

Her last patient of the day was Bill Morris, her mailman. Because in repeated tests he could not breathe by himself, he was being taken off the ventilator to die. His extended Irish family wanted to be there on Zoom, and she wanted to be there with them. Amy had fashioned a tight connection with them all—the best possible through pixels. These days had made Zooming so essential that it often seemed more comforting than real life.

There was a new night-shift doctor, an intensivist nicknamed Dr. Sev, and this would be his first solo night; for some reason he had requested nights. A short, bearded, and brush-cut "numbers" man, he was a math genius whose nickname came from his Princeton thesis on the number 789. He was awkward and shy—just about as non-intensive as a human could be, but with two high-value specialties: computers and renal disease. Way back when Roy Basch and the others were interns in the House of God, and Sev was a medical student, they had all fallen in love with the Fat Man, their savior, a medical resident. Years later, when the Fat Man got a chance to start an outpatient clinic leaning up against Man's 4th Best Hospital, Sev—by then a renal doctor—showed up to do computers for the team, saving the day. Afterward, shy guy Sev had made a fortune in a biotech company based in Albany, 34 miles up the road from Columbia—and bought a mansion in Spook Rock and retired there with his mother, his wife, and his five children.

A few weeks ago, when he heard that Roy Basch, Hyper Hooper, and Eat My Dust Eddie were joining Amy's team, he signed up too. Kush Kare was delighted because many of the Covid patients had comorbid kidney damage, requiring dialysis—which was a last lonely cash cow; unlike elective surgery, it continued during the plague.

This afternoon, Amy was orienting him. He'd rarely worked hands-on in an ICU, and he was a novice in Covid. His relationship with the digital machines would make that part of it easy, but Sev was not known for his relational savvy, or his tact. The human part would be tense, but he was all they could find for night work.

"This virus is tricky," Amy said, briefing him quickly before she had to go back to help Bill die. Nurse Surrey was already in the room, where she could see Amy. She had turned off the ventilator and was titrating his breathing with the usual end-of-life cocktail.

"Last week," Amy said, "I admitted two patients, a twenty-three-year-old healthy-looking guy, and an eighty-six-year-old man who looked terrible—and guess who died, and who made it?" Sev's eyes got larger.

"Yeah."

"It's not logical."

"It's horrible."

Sev considered this. Then he said, "And so, with a Covid patient, when do you give up?"

"Never!" Amy blurted out, startling Sev.

Amy's anger surprised her. But in a few minutes, one of her favorite people—Bill, her cheerful postman who had come through the worst weather, even a blizzard, like a saint—would die on Zoom.

"Sorry," she said. "This stuff is tough. You never get used to it— thank God." She took a deep breath. "Transitioning to comfort care doesn't mean we're giving up. It means we're accepting that I, the doctor, can't fix the patient. I can't bring them back to a life they would find acceptable. So we—not I, but *with his family*—change the focus of care from trying to make him better to making sure he's comfortable, accepting that the disease that made him sick will result in his death. Giving comfort care is not giving up. It's stepping out of the way of the process killing the patient, focusing on the comfort. I'm still *caring for him*, for *them* . . . maybe sometimes too much, because the suffering can be too much for me—but with a different focus."

Sev was speechless, his eyes wide.

"Sorry, Sev," she said. "Look. It took me a long time to understand this—with a lot of botches along the way. Decades of deaths all over the world. What I've *seen* . . . ?" She stopped, knowing that if she started that horror film, it would still—still?!—stab her in the heart.

"No, no . . . I . . ." Sev stammered. "That was . . . was . . ." Sev had tears in his eyes, and looked away, searching for a Kleenex, not finding one.

Clearly he hadn't yet gotten used to not being able to get to a Kleenex when clad in the PPE. Amy knew how to deal with crying in PPE, but now wasn't the time. She waited.

"The word 'caring' . . . ," he said. "That was so . . . *kind*. I wish I could understand these kinds of things—I mean, these kinds of kind things. I'm . . . more head than heart." He looked down, away, clearly ashamed.

"Hey!" she said loudly.

He turned back to her, his eyes still down.

"C'mon, Doc, give me some eye contact." He did. "I don't believe that for a second, Sev. We learn from death. We learn from suffering *with* others. *Compassion*." She glanced at the nurse, outside of Bill's room, pointing to her watch, then holding up five fingers, the minutes until the final Zoom between Bill and his family would begin.

She turned to go. But the shy little guy looked so puzzled, so crestfallen, that she hesitated.

Give him something.

"One thing I've learned?" He nodded. "We live with doubt. Bad doubt. I still don't know if I made the right decision about the timing of my intubating him. Should I have tubed him sooner? We learned from the first wave that maybe we were tubing them too early. Should I have waited longer? Would it have made any difference? I don't know. But what I *do* know, Sev, is that for him and his family, my best wasn't good enough. And neither was it good enough for the three others who died this week in the same manner, the same lonely, antiseptic, online death. The only solace I find is the relationship, the rapport I'm able to establish with their families. Most all of them know the town doctor, Orville Rose, and a few even knew Bill Starbuck, before Orvy. Listening to the history of these docs and this town, well, it's a gift. And *that's* the proven therapeutic, here, as we work to treat the patient and the family. On day one I tell them we're a team. *I'm the expert on medicine, and they're the expert on the patient, and our medical care will be a team effort.* I call the families every day, and I make sure that I learn one new thing about the patient—Bill worked as a shoeshine boy in New Orleans and claimed that he'd once got a hundred-dollar bill from Fats Domino. And I'm as open about myself with the families if they ask about me. Connection makes the families part of the team. And so at the end, *mostly*, when death arrives, they know we've done all we could. This helps with their guilt, for not being able to be with their loved ones."

Nurse Surrey was gesturing at her to come. Amy signaled okay.

"I have no idea when this pandemic will end," she said. "Someday I'll have to process all this. The lives lost, the pain and suffering. And y'know what's the worst?"

"The deaths?"

"No. I'm . . . I'm, let's say, *familiar* with death. I've come to terms with it. Well, maybe. But coming to terms with the suffering? Manmade suffering? No." She paused. "Sorry to hit you so hard on your first night. I'm on call, Sev, if you need me."

Back into the room with Bill Morris, mailman. *Her* mailman. The kind of guy who recently showed up at Orvy's house at ten at night with a special delivery letter to Dr. Amy Rose but no address beyond "Columbia NY 12534." He had stood there in his mask and gloves and said, "Sorry to come by so late, Doc, but I was worried this might be real important, life and death." He left.

The return address had jolted her. Her chronic California flame— Bernie Shapiro, whom she was supposed to wed until she finally ended it. She ripped the unopened envelope to shreds.

Bill was a veteran of Afghanistan. Back home, grateful to be alive, he always seemed to walk his route happily—even the dogs liked him.

But recently there had been another postman on his route.

Bill showed up in Emergency with sudden fever, cough, flattened by fatigue, gasping terribly. His numbers were bad. Amy had flashed on a small study from the first wave that said early intubation might be worse for survival. But Bill looked in extremis—chest radiology showed a lung full of those strange ground-glass hives of virus. A judgment call. She had a quick talk with Binni, and with Orville. Both said ventilate.

Amy had brought his wife into the room, told them both that Bill couldn't breathe by himself and had to be put on a ventilator, quickly. They weren't surprised, and asked all the right questions, which she answered.

Looking back, she recalled the last words he and his wife heard from her. "Bill, we're going to take the best care of you we can."

Gasping, drowning—which is said to be the most terrifying feeling in the world—he managed, only, "Okay. . . . Thanks."

His wife, wearing her mask, moved to hug him.

"No, no, Winnie!"

She stopped, still. And then she said, "I love you, Bill."

Unable to get words out, he nodded.

Now, Amy hesitated before opening her "I"-pad to his family for the final good-byes. Had she done everything possible? Covid was a quick killer. Presenting in every organ system from liver to lungs to heart to brain, it's a pandemic inside the body. No one knew why one person lived and another one died. And often Covid patients didn't feel *well* but they didn't feel that they were *dying*, and then—*boom*—gone.

"We're going to take the best care of you we can." At the time, she had said to herself, "Time will tell." Now time had told.

Bill was about to die, peacefully.

Amy shivered. *Allegedly* peacefully.

She was the only one in the room with him. Their final good-byes would be on her "I"-pad. Saying to herself, *Okay, Doc, try to be there with them.*

She was fairly confident that the PPE obscured her face well enough so that his family couldn't tell that she was crying as she spoke to them. She didn't know if they could tell how badly her hands were shaking as she turned the camera on Bill and they began wailing—keening, led by his born-in-Ireland grandmother—wailing at the sight of his final breaths.

"We're going to take the best care of you we can." *Had I? Should I have waited? Others had died by my waiting. Would it have made any difference? I don't know. What I do know is for him and his family my best wasn't good enough.*

Someday I'll have to process everything I've been through. The lives lost, the suffering witnessed and experienced, and—a big one—the goddamn indifference by those who refuse to take even the smallest steps to lessen this explosive spread of suffering. A little handwashing, a bit of distance . . . a little cloth mask, for Chrissakes? Think the Lone Ranger if you want, a gunslinging American hero, or pretend you're robbing a bank—just do it! Have to process someday. But today I don't have that luxury. Tomorrow, the next set of patients will be waiting for me, and even when I can't go on, I go on.

Bill the mailman ended his rounds. Everybody cried.

Amy thought of Orvy and the party and what came to mind was him saying, more than once, "We doctors are always making a hundred percent of the decision on fifty percent of the data."

She looked at her phone: 4:35. Time to go home and party. She texted Binni to meet her in the parking lot.

But halfway down the stairs she got pinged for an urgent matter. She looked at her phone and grimaced. It was about Roy Basch. *Again.*

Roy had finally recovered and joined the team several weeks ago, but his behavior had gotten more and more problematic. He was irritable and quarrelsome, with occasional explosions of anger at his colleagues, and seemed detached from his patients.

He confided to Amy that he didn't feel quite as sharp as before Covid, and still felt fatigued.

On his first day of work at Kush Kare, Amy and his buddies from the House of God and Man's 4th Best Hospital—Hyper Hooper, Sev, and Eat My Dust Eddie—gave Roy a loud, raucous welcome. A crowd of maybe 20 workers gathered around him, brimming with satisfaction at seeing the three outstanding generations of doctors of their town: Orvy, then Roy, then Amy. Some were in tears.

Roy had been a star in the small town, a great Bluehawk basketball player and valedictorian, first ever from the city to go to Harvard, not to mention to become a Rhodes Scholar and doctor. The son of the town dentist, he was *known*. And he knew the families of almost everyone who was welcoming him. They reminisced about his basketball prowess, going to his father to have their cavities filled, his mother founding the Columbia Library, starting the candy stripers program, and chairing the hospital volunteers. Roy knew almost everyone in the hospital, doctor or patient. Until his parents retired to Florida, he'd come home several times a year, but he had not been back since they died.

All in all, it was a homecoming. He looked startled, probably from coming out of the dark closet of Covid, suddenly in the center of real live noise and laughter.

When Hooper and Eat My Dust had first seen him in the hospital, they were shocked. He had gotten obese. Not heavy, or overweight, but really fat. Double-chinned, belt-buckle-facing-down-from-protuberant-belly kind of fat. Roy, who had always been a trim athlete, was manifesting Couch Potato. Of course Hyper and Eddie kept their comments to themselves as they'd taken this in.

Now his face, even though fatter, was drawn, probably from the illness, and etched by the stress. The other noticeable change was that he seemed scared. In their year in the House of God, and then later in Man's 4th Best Hospital, they had never seen that look. Roy, scared? Never! Not once. And now he was hesitant, speaking a little haltingly, not looking into their eyes—in fact his eyes were drifting around to other people, to the details of the Emergency Ward as if it were a strange place to be (even though he'd spent months in worse emergency rooms). The most troubling, even in that first meeting, was how his eyes would wander, up, down, sometimes as if looking out a window. He seemed hesitant. Roy G. Basch hesitant? Eddie and Hooper looked at each other. *Did not compute.*

At first he was on a light schedule, to acclimate him slowly; so he was on half time, three days a week. And even with the deluge of patients, Leatrice Shumpsky—in charge of triage in Emergency—gave him the less traumatizing patients. All of them helped him out, hoped he would get better, to no avail.

Amy talked to Orville about Roy, and he was as surprised and concerned as the rest of them. He spoke to Roy several times by phone—Roy didn't want to do Zoom for some reason (perhaps his obviously fatter face)—but never got a straight answer to any questions. Finally, after a couple of weeks, Amy and Shump called a meeting to talk about Roy while he was off duty.

The team meeting was held in the doctor's fort in the emergency room. Amy was the leader, and they went around the room with their data. The most incisive were those who had been in the trenches with him, Eat My Dust and Hyper.

"I can't believe how heavy he's gotten!" Hooper said. "Not just weight—which to my eye now puts him in the high-risk category for just about every disease, especially cardiac and insulin-dependent metabolism—but worse is that he's not connecting with patients. I mean, hell, he used to be one of the best of us at that, the human connection. Forgive me, Eddie, I don't mean to imply—"

"No problem. I'm worse than you. My joking personality only works with about thirteen percent and with the others, I just focus on the disease. Not good, but that's their liability if they get stuck with me. I wouldn't recognize a compassionate glance if I got it in a Cracker Jack box."

"Think I don't know that?" said Leatrice, smiling. "Why do you think I triage all the creeps who hate doctors to you?"

"Hey, hey—designer doctoring? Perfect matches? I love it!"

"Great," said Hooper, having heard all this before. "When we got to Man's 4th, Roy was the best in connecting, which he learned from Berry, and patients loved him. Now, when I see him approach a patient, I say, 'Please please God, let him be human, or at least humane.' It's like he's gotten scared of getting even a little open to the patients."

"Have others of you seen that?" Shump asked.

Nods around the table.

"One of the things I've noticed," Amy said, "is that he might start off with a patient okay, but as it gets more complex—or, actually thinking of it now, more hopeless, with a risk of death or at least having to be intubated, he kind of, I don't know, shudders, and then, even though he keeps talking normally, he looks away. The connections break."

"Yes," said Sev. "I timed him and recorded an increased frequency of eyeblinks and look-aways."

Puzzled silence from all. *What is the little genius doing now?*

"I've got a metric that measures disconnections of docs from patients. He looks away more than any of you—it's in the pathological range."

Amy went on. "Does he look as if he's running away from deep feelings a patient had stirred up, or is it just because, well, something else is on his mind?"

Nobody knew.

"It used to be his forte," said Hyper. "How he could 'read' patients and connect—it was a talent. Breaks my heart."

"Let's just put this in a little perspective," Leatrice said. "I've known him for a long time too, and yes, this is an aberration, a sad thing to watch. But he's just come off of a horrific threat to his life, and he's trying to get back, step by step." She paused. "Has anyone reported his mistreating a patient, verbally or physically?"

No one had. And so they decided to continue giving Roy all their support—and a schedule that he felt he could handle—hoping it would get better.

"Tincture of time," Amy said. "Let's all hold the good, with him, in any ways we can. I'll have another talk with him, about our meeting, telling him we're sure he's on a path back to being the terrific doc he's always been."

That was a few weeks ago, and now Roy was pretty much the same, but it was clear that he had gotten the message, and he admitted to his old classmate Shump that it was hard for him, going from the hell of having Covid to treating it in the fierce Emergency and ICU Wards.

Now Amy was rushing to get Binni and leave the hospital for Orvy's birthday Zoom, when she was beeped to get back down to the ER, *stat*. It was another incident with Roy.

He was in a cubicle, red-faced and shouting at a patient. The commotion brought other doctors around.

"Hey, Roy, take it easy!" said Hyper Hooper, trying to make eye contact.

"Chill, dude, chill," echoed Eat My Dust, standing behind Roy, his strong biker arms wrapped tight around his chest to keep him from maybe killing a patient.

"Lemme go!" Roy shouted. "I won't take this kind of abuse!"

"Poor you, Mr. Bigshot Doctor," said a burly man with a shaved head and, under his mask, a bushy red beard—so his face looked upside down. He was wearing a flashy jacket with the name of a local cement company, Lone Star, and a homemade mask reading, "Donald J. Trump. The J is for Jenius!"

Amy stepped between them. "Okay okay, I'm the boss here. Cool it. *Both* of you."

"I can't deal with Mr. Niles Mork and—" Roy began.

"*Quiet! Now!*" They hesitated. Fell silent. "What's the problem?"

"He called me a kike," said Roy.

"'Cuz you called me an idiot sayin' the 'J is for Jeni—'"

"Calmly!" Roy said. "I merely pointed out your spelling error calmly, with a smile—"

"Hell you did! You was laughing and—"

"Cut the shit!" Amy shouted at the trucker. "Or we throw you out of here." She nodded to the new security guards, Butchy Lee Ervin and Chick Chick Hughes. They'd moved up from Transport.

"Hey, man, I'm the patient, and he's the doc, and I feel like I'm dying and you gotta take care of me—like in that there Hypochronic Oath—"

"Oh Jesus," said Roy, rolling his eyes.

"Enough!" Amy said. "Eddie, you take care of him."

"March!" said Eddie, rotating Mork like a trash can for pickup, and walked out.

Hyper Hooper, who'd been dead still, was looking Roy up and down, shaking his head as if he'd diagnosed something really bad that had caused this rage in his old friend.

"What?" Roy said to him. *"What the hell are you lookin' at?"*

"Nuthin', man," he said. "Gotta go—"

"C'mon, c'mon, let's have it—what?"

"Later," said Hooper. "Gotta go save people. Talk later." He turned and walked out.

Roy stood, shaking his head, looking out the window, thinking, *What the hell am I doing? You don't yell at patients, ever.*

"Damn right you don't! Didn't you learn *anything* from me, from the House and Man's 4th?"

"Fats?"

"Roy!"

"Roy?"

"Fats!" *In his enormous white coat, floating in the air up and down gently in the breeze, next to the tall Kush Kare flagpole. All that weight, afloat? And then gone! Have I gone nuts!*

"Roy," Amy was saying, "didn't you hear me?"

"Sorry, I was just daydreaming."

"Are you all right?"

"Yeah."

"I've got to leave," Amy said. "I suggest you call it a day. You're exhausted. I don't want you to wear yourself out. Walk with me, okay?" Her phone said 4:40. She texted Binni again, said she'd meet him in the parking lot. He texted back that he'd be right there.

Outside, she and Roy leaned on their adjoining cars, oven-broiled all day. Her Subaru, his BMW. The sun, desperately looking to get out of the August heat, stared across the Hudson to the cool Catskills, and relief.

Side by side, needing to talk but not talking. They were staring at the concave façade of the hospital emblazoned with **KK WHALE CITY** and the logo, a spouting whale, and then they lifted their eyes up into the distance, to the broken lines of tombstones wandering here and there in the Columbia Memorial Cemetery.

"Okay, Roy, what's wrong?"

"Gimme a minute." He closed his eyes and put his hands together, palms up, in a meditative pose, as if asking for alms. He stood there breathing, breathing. He opened his eyes, scanned the flagpole, the pines. No Fats. Not facing her, he said, "All the deaths."

"Yes?"

"Today was the worst. That child. How old was she, not even ten? She seemed okay, we did everything right, and then . . . gone?"

"I know. It's hell."

"She was Chinese, and I could see *our* daughter, Spring, in her. I mean, she's safe in Brooklyn. Really Covid-careful, but . . ." He paused, breathed. "It tore me up inside."

"I know how it is. I'm so sorry."

He turned to her, his faced twisted in torment. "So much death."

There were no tears in his eyes, Amy was surprised to see.

He turned to go.

"Roy," she said, "you and Berry are still going to Zoom with Orville and us tonight, aren't you?"

"Yeah. Wouldn't miss it." He managed a thin smile. "He's my God." He clicked his car open and drove off.

No Binni. Too bad.

She got in the car and waited. And waited more. As he'd gotten more and more into his research on Covid—monoclonal and stem cell antibodies—he was always late. *He won't have time to go to his house, change, and then make it back for Orville's party,* she fumed.

In frustration Amy banged on the dashboard with her fists, then backed the car out and started forward toward the gate when she saw him running awkwardly in his PPE to intercept her.

He jumped in the car, slammed the door, and sat there sweating and panting like a new Covid admission fleeing Kush Kare.

She shook her head slowly and, looking straight ahead, focused her anger on driving.

10

"Breakage!" Orville cried out in frustration. "Maximum breakage!"

It was Orville's real birthday, August 6, 1945. His false birthday, which he'd celebrated for the first 40 years of his life, was August 23, but his mother, a superstitious, fiercely cabalistic woman, had freaked out at the bombing of Hiroshima and bribed the military notary to change the birth date. Orville had not found out the truth until his 40th birthday, when she died and he returned from Italy to Columbia. Her will specified that to get his part of the estate he had to live in her house in the center of town for a year and 13 days continuously. Despite being in love with Celestina Polo, a spiritual fireball Italian yoga teacher, Orville had been dead broke at the time, so he joined aging Bill Starbuck as town doctor, planning to go back to Italy and Celestina at the end of the yearlong sentence. But he stayed, stayed diligently amid the breakages of Columbia, for these 35 years.

Stayed constant beyond reason, and never surprised by the town's spirit, either in reality or in Editor Lisa Cohen's recent celebratory trifecta in the *Columbia Crier*:

Police Seize 59 Firearms, 1 Monkey
Hooker Embraces Columbia Valley Agriculture
Officials Halt Lovers Lane Deal with Corkscrew

Now Orville was staring down his main enemy on earth, the computer. He shook his head in dismay. He had carefully set up a brand-new large monitor for his computer in the living room, a grand space for centuries of events like an international Zoom birthday.

I should have predicted it, the one time I really want the damn thing to work. Big plans for my 75th meticulously checked for days and bang!—a bad breakage, even for Columbia. Shit, do I hate computers! Maybe it's because Eleanor and Miranda bought me this gigantic and yes gorgeous computer monitor. The first law of dealing with computers in Columbia: if it works, do not try to make it work better, because it has secretly programmed the "Columbia app" to pounce, crushing the whole damn system. And here it is.

He checked his watch. The Zoom to Italy was supposed to start in 15 minutes. He had tested it out three different times, all good. But when he had tried to start the real Zoom meeting, he couldn't get out onto the internet. The only clue was "not connected to the server." He tried everything to connect to the server—but the pop-ups said that in order to make connection with the server, he had to be connected to the server!

Orville became enraged and had images of taking a log from the fireplace and bashing the machine to death and just doing what had worked for his first 75 years—telephone.

Miranda came in, dressed in a lavender silk blouse he hadn't seen in a while, one that always enticed him, the soft curves cradling her marvelous neck and framing her face, that red hair laced with silver now, and the eyes, those bright green eyes that he adored. When he was struggling to decide who to love, her or Celestina, and whether to stay in Columbia or take flight again for Italy. How precious every moment with her had been that year and 13 days in Columbia. He'd been so in love with Miranda! How he'd paid such acute attention to the slightest movement of her eyes, her lips, her head tilt, even her aura—shadowed by her post-polio body. And in the face of a disastrous mistake, the beginning of a shared good life. Life with suffering, to be sure, but the suffering enriched the shared love, as they walked through all of it, over and over, together.

"You look gorgeous!" he burst out, startled by a quaver in his voice, the clutch of deep feeling for her saving his life. "I'm so grateful for you!"

Seeing him so opened up, she got teary, smiled, nodded, took his hand. "Thanks . . . all these years now, thanks."

He nodded, and squeezed her hand.

"So are we ready?"

"Nope. Breakage of the whole system. I'll call Eleanor."

"She's just getting into the shower and, as you know, once in, she stays. Yesterday she reminded me again, 'You interrupt my shower, you die.'"

"What about Amy—is she back yet?"

"I heard her come in, but I'd guess she'll be a while changing and disinfecting."

"I hate this! Hate hate hate this town!"

"Really? Wanna move to Boca Raton? To *golf*?"

He screamed.

Boca Raton was where his parents had spent the winters in retirement. After his father dropped dead on the 13th hole at their beloved Conquistador Country Club—a rare uphill par 3—Selma never strayed from Columbia again. The one true thing that Selma and Orvy ever agreed upon? *Florida is hell.*

He sighed, defeated. Crumpled down into his chair, shaking his head.

"Why don't you call Clive?"

He blinked. Clive Lincoln was the owner of the famous 100-year-old Geiger and Lincoln Junkyard and Private Eye. Thanks to Representative Henry Schooner and the New York City art crowd, the junkyard had been designated a historical site and marked with one of those blue plaques by New York State. Clive was an auto-didact, a self-taught genius in "security" and computers and all else digital. Like Orville, he was born and grew up poor in Columbia; he had survived vicious anti-Black racism, as Orville had survived vicious anti-Semitism. They gravitated to each other, and lifted each other up, and out. Clive's life read like an adventure novel: cooking for the CIA in Guatemala during that 1954 war, escaping in disguise through Mexico, and then, alone, wild adventures in Chile and as far south as Tierra del Fuego.

"Why didn't I think of that? This damn Covid has gotten me so isolated, so into myself, way too much. I've caught brain mush. Yeah, I'm sure for Clive this is child's play. He can get it all set up, and then run the whole Zoom!"

He picked up the phone.

––––

Amy and Binni drove down the hill to Orville's house in silence. It would be tight to get to the Zoom on time.

Despite their trials at the hospital, with the insane schedules and pressure and Amy being the boss, they had slowly grown their love. They had fallen in love during the first hellish wave, and being to-gether helped them survive. They now were residents in that harsh little city of care that was the hospital that tore their hearts out. The love they were growing put their hearts back in, daily.

Amy's free time was mostly spent with Orville's family. Binni's was in keeping up his Zoom relationship with his first ex-wife and their soon-to-be-teenage daughter, who lived in New York City.

Binni and Amy had told each other their life stories, the censored versions that you tell to non-first loves. They would love to do outdoor things, but rarely could do them together. Amy was an athlete, braving whatever time she had to run in the cold, but Binni was doing nothing. One day she had surprised him with a high-end stationary bike that she'd custom fixed with a stand for his computer to keep all his data-grinding going. In turn, Binni, realizing that she loved cut-flower arrangements—exotic ones—found a local exotic Dutch gardener with a year-round hothouse who could keep sending arrangements at random times, with cards he dictated, some consisting of short poems by his favorite writer, Rumi. Even in the terrible stresses, as with all caring relationships they were finding the emotional distance that allowed them to be kind. They knew how sustaining this friendship was, and protected it at work, and outside. Because of Orville and Miranda's age, Amy had never brought Binni back to the house. This birthday Zoom in the Rose house would be their first meeting.

But Binni had been so late that he hadn't had time to go home and decontaminate. And she was stressed. Very stressed.

She unlocked her back door and went in. Distracted by thoughts of Roy's meltdown, she started to strip naked to make the post-Covid shift to protect her family.

With some irritation, she glanced at Binni. Still in the hospital clothes he'd worn under his PPE.

"You've got to strip too."

"But I have nothing clean to wear."

"Deal with it. Put your clothes in this bag. Leave your shoes and socks down here."

"And what if I—"

"No more talk; just *do* it. Hurry!"

Finished stripping, hands on hips, she glanced at him. He too was naked, and was staring at her, blinking, and smiling sheepishly, his hands covering his groin.

"Hands up!"

"I believe this other extremity is up as well?"

She looked at his erection. Then into his eyes. She glanced at her watch. "Good. C'mon."

The vintage 1875 stairway to the third floor was a work of art, a serpentine banister of gleaming hand-carved walnut. It spiraled up, stopping at two landings and ending at the top floor.

By the first double-back Amy wanted to make love to him right on the steps but was leery of splinters and there was no time to shower and make love and get to the Zoom. By the second double-back she'd forgotten all about decontaminating and thought only: Is there time for fast sex? They reached the top landing and went into the high-ceilinged loft with the giant plexiglass dome and the last sun slanting in. It was warm and they were sweating and panting. She turned to him—and was startled.

"You climbed all those stairs with an erection and you *still* have an erection?"

"And what was I to do with it, dear one?"

"This! Hurry!"

She threw her arms around him, and he around her, feeling the just plain stiffness of his interest, and laughing, out on that tricky edge of sex.

"And the bed is where—?"

"Onto the floor, right now!"

"Can't you wait a sec—"

"No!"

The floor was shining new oak, and August-warm, and the hard-wood against her back and skull and hands as she stretched them out to the sides, stretching this body that was hot and healthy maybe as a repudiation of all the shit and virus and insanity and death, and as if in penance for the death of Bill the postman she welcomed the pain of the wood against her backbone and hips and she opened up and let go, thinking *There is no promise to live anytime and that sucks*—but suddenly she stopped and cried out, "No! Wait!"

"What's wrong?"

"*You* get on the floor. Okay?"

"Okay!"

He did, his erection still hard and pointing up to his belly button, and she nestled it in and started rocking on it shouting and laughing and then she started to cry.

———

Given the strong Columbian history of breakage—and despite Clive's expertise in cracking codes of Bad Guys during our wars on four continents—it took him almost an hour. But Clive, sitting in his hi-tech "scrubbed" house in the middle of the junkyard, had finally prevailed against the crash, and the Zoom started.

Almost everyone was late joining—Eleanor from the shower, Miranda's son, Cray, in Milan, his wife Antonella and Fabio, their four-year-old. Still missing were Amy and Binni and Celestina Polo, the dear aunt of Antonella and the great love of Orville's Italian life.

"Time has no meaning for Celestina," Orville said. "She could appear anytime, or none. I'll give Amy one more call." It rang and rang. No answer. "Okay, let's start without them and—"

But suddenly there they were. Making an entrance.

"What the hell?" Orvy cried, looking at Binni. The others too were startled.

Binni was dressed in Amy's clothes. In the flush of lovemaking, Amy had celebrated by insisting that Binni—not a great drinker—down two stiff tumblers of Tito's Handmade Vodka, her favorite. Then, in their happy/silly state, they remembered he had no clothes with him and she had to find something for him to wear. He and she were about the same height and weight, and her first thought was jeans and a T-shirt, but that didn't radiate enough joy and flash for the celebration, so she ended up persuading him to wear one of her dressier outfits: purple slacks and a black silk blouse, unbuttoned a bit. She swept his black hair back and finished with a spritz of Chanel.

Seeing himself in a mirror, a tipsy Binni said, "Wow! This is classy! But am I still looking my gender, and not yours? In India, to dress up, you put on layers and layers, and this is freedom." He shouted, "Freeedom!" then blinked at the loud sound coming out of his mouth and said, "Am I not freedom guy now!?"

"You look great—really sexy."

"This whole escapade, dear Amy, is novel for me," he said, wobbling his head in puzzled but happy affirmation of this new free life breaking out, wave after wave. A broad grin upon his face, he was rocking on his feet, as if on a ship in a storm.

"Are you okay with wearing this to the party?"

"This is the most risk I ever take in my life but what could be better than to be in your clothes? It is a unqualififer . . . I mean quala . . . quala . . ." He couldn't get the word out.

"Binni baby, you are cool."

"Oh jeez, 'cool'? Me? Cool? This does not compute!"

"You are cool *and* hot. You are getting *down*, fella, down!"

"I love it! I have never been getting down. For the first time in my life I'm so up to be getting down!" He laughed, so hard that he bent over and lost his balance so that she had to catch him. "This is as farfar from our Covid-horror today, no more horror, just love."

"Let's put on our masks and go down there and make a grand entrance."

Which they did. All eyes were on Binni.

"Don't worry, everybody," Amy said. "We had to decontaminate. And he needed clothes."

But when Ben saw—and more clearly caught the scents of Binni and Chanel all drowning in Tito's vodka—he stopped, stared. He looked up at Binni, then Amy, in puzzlement.

The hair on his neck rose and he took a step toward Binni, and another.

"Rowwwfff!" A thunderous judgment.

Miranda, Orvy, and Eleanor froze.

"Hi, puppy!" said Binni, smiling, moving toward him. Unaware that with one slap of that giant paw, one snap of those teeth, no more Binni, cool or not.

"Ben!" shouted Orvy. "Come!"

Ben looked back at Orvy, but still didn't budge.

"He's okay! Come!"

Dogs love routine. Ben was relieved to be told what to do by Orvy, the familiar message, *You're so big you need to use your strength kindly and not roar or bark or bite and eat people except for intruders, and this Binni dressed in Amy's clothes is not one.*

But Ben was still riveted, not convinced. Staring at Binni he took another step toward him, then he stopped for a couple of fulsome sniffs, considering the assay patiently. Pause. And then, exhaling, thinking: *Maybe okay.* "It's *okay*, Ben!" said Orvy. "Be cool."

Ben pivoted to Orvy and plodded back to him, lay down, head resting on those two big bushy pillows of paws, keeping his eyes alert to this Binni thingee.

Binni, usually terrified of dogs, now smiled and waved happily. "Good doggie."

The Zoom was dazzling. Bonds of blood, and blood-in-spirit, lit up the soft night.

Only a few cherished nonfamily Zoomed in. Mrs. Tarr, a patient of great age who lived trailing an oxygen tank in a custom-made carrier and whose blood numbers and other tests were consistently incompatible with human life, and Robert Van Ness, Orvy's steady rebounder on the championship Bluehawk basketball team whose wife got Covid and was being cared for by Amy and—by some miracle—after weeks intubated, had survived, almost as good as new—mirabile dictu!

And, of course, Congressman Henry Schooner. His exorbitant "Rose Arrangement" had been delivered earlier in the day. When he came on Zoom—dressed casually immaculate in what looked like a safari jacket or a Soho version of the uniform he'd worn in Vietnam, he said, "Happy seventy-fifth, my dear best friend, joining me at seventy-five! As a great doc and person who has stayed to heal our town and health, I would ask your permission to start the process of officially recognizing your house for historical excellence as a doctor and a person of compassion and love. The only question is whether we should put the blue plaque on your historical little office building or on your historical home. All love from Nelda Jo and me. Your great mom—a mother to me as well—when I was down, she'd always say, 'Henry, so *what*? Henry, what *next*?!' What next, Orvy? All my love."

Cray was a lawyer in Europe for nonprofits trying to save the world, including the European Union and the United Nations climate initiatives. Orvy pointed out how great it was and what a coincidence that both Cray and Eleanor, with her whale PhD work in the Galápagos, were trying to save the world, on land, sea, and air.

"Go Cray!" yelled Eleanor. "Go big bro!"

"And you, little one. The smallest one in our family, and you're tackling whales? I love it! Come to Italy and do whales, okay?"

"Whales in Italy?"

"Well, no, but I can probably get you a grant to try to find some!"

Amy, who had always been something of a big sister to Cray, couldn't believe how he had grown in substance, in *being*, even, yes, in *gravitas*. A man, not a kid. The force of memory saw both at once, familiar and amazing, and happy! And having a second baby!

Miranda and Cray had Zoomed often in the pandemic lockdown, and before that, they'd seen each other every six months or so, either in Italy or some other sweet part of the world.

For Orville, with Cray safe in Italy and happily married and making him again a grandfather, and with Amy right here with him now, and having immersed himself in Zoom contact with his worldwide doctor-friends in the hellish pandemic? *Right now I've died and gone to heaven.* It brought him back to the first healing moment after the sadness and struggle of his first marriage and "amicable" divorce, when he quit New Jersey medicine and gave her all the money and the house. Then he'd joined Médecins Sans Frontières, and fell in love with Celestina. He'd said to himself: *Even a shy American can be happy in Italy, and I, Orville Rose, am just about as happy as a childless man can be.*

Now, looking at Miranda, he amended this: *Right here, right now, from all the decades since 1983, I have been and am as happy as ever— yes, ever. Unlike with Celestina, this one will last, at least until death.*

For most of the party, Clive was just hanging out in his box, silent, making sure there were no breakages. But in one of those moments when all goes quiet, he did something that he'd never done before, through a whole lifetime of knowing Orville, through harrowing danger and wild fun. In the silence, Clive cleared his throat once—twice—and said:

"Hey, Orvy?"

"Yeah?"

"I love you, man."

Orville, startled, fell silent. And then said, "And I love . . ." He choked up. Big silence. Everybody waited. "I love you too."

"Yes!" Miranda said. "Beautiful! And it's only taken three-quarters of a century to say so! Ah, you men!"

"As Shakespeare put it," Amy said, having been an actor as a teenager, now with mock-passionate drama, "'Oh these men! Oh these men, these men!'"

Orvy realized how rare it was spoken, yes, Clive's love, and his in return. They'd Zoomed rarely, and never yet taken a walk around town, or in the junkyard. Clive kept his place meticulously—his private eye office surrounded by all kinds of security devices, and the piles of metal junk wouldn't counsel any viruses, safe to be in, to talk in, to walk around the junkyard—which too was closed by Covid.

Got to make a date to go over there and talk—for about a week or so.

Several other dear friends joined the Zoom. But not Roy and Berry. A puzzle, and a disappointment—and then a worry. He couldn't believe that they wouldn't call—was something wrong? Well, if so, Berry would call.

Soon it was long after midnight in Italy. Cray and his family left to get Fabio and themselves to bed. Eleanor, shyly, gave Orvy her perfect gift. Since she'd been home she'd gotten out a professional set of colored pencils, and she would ask her friends to send a photo of their pet or favorite animal and would create dazzling portraits, full of feeling. She presented her father with a portrait of Ben in front of two of Orville's favorite worn old shoes—the ones he was wearing right now. The likeness, the capture of the love between them, was clearly full of Eleanor's love for man and dog herself.

Orvy was overwhelmed. Unable to speak he opened his arms to her, and she fell into them, and he hugged her, and she him, and then, calling to Ben, both hugged his massive head—taking care, of course, of the status of the drool.

After a rare full-body hug that lasted a while, and a kiss, Eleanor went to work cleaning up the living room and then cleaning up in the kitchen with crashing plates and silverware all in OCD joy, and then upstairs to her bedroom to keep on keeping on with her friends, all the while as she was working on her thesis and starting another pencil portrait.

Binni started to crash from his high of the Tito's, holding his head and yawning over and over. Amy drove him down to his condo on the edge of the bad part of town, helped him to find his key, helped him put it into the lock—"Why is this lock moving back and forth does it no wanna woannna the key?"—and she got him in and kissed him and hugged him a long, passionate, boozy good-bye.

Orville, Miranda, Clive, and Amy were too happy to go to bed, and sat with the Zoom still open, Clive in his Zoom box with Mississippi John Hurt now playing softly "Let the Mermaids Flirt with Me" on his 12-string Delta guitar. There was a relief, now, in the few remaining boxes of the screen, a welcome silence that was broken by the grateful talk about everything and anything. All were easing off, not wanting the magic of requited love to end.

"Roy and Berry didn't join," Orville said to Miranda. "Something's got to be wrong."

"Yeah," said Miranda. "Very strange."

"Clive," Orvy said, "can you keep the Zoom up just in case?"

"Sure."

After a few minutes, a new box lit up.

"Celestina?" Orville shouted.

"Orvy!" she cried out.

She was sitting on a meditation cushion in front of a golden Buddha as big as an old Fiat.

"Where are you?"

"In Villa Era, a meditation and Ayurvedic health center near our very lake, *Lago d'Orta*!"

"No!"

"Yes! The sacred place where we fell into the great love! A love that will never die!"

Orville checked out Miranda, who was rolling her eyes.

"Yes, yes," Orville said.

"Yes," she went on, "I was made the essential teacher here. Villa Era, in the town Biella."

"I thought you were living in Milan, near Cray and Antonella."

"Yes, I was. But with the second baby coming, and the virus in Milan, I picked up the—how do you say it—the gig here. I am now a *famoso* teacher."

"You look the same," Orville said.

"I am not and I am."

"What a wonderful surprise. Thank you!"

"Orville, I always am with you in my Buddha-mind, and right now it is for real, on the very Zoomer!" She peered into the screen closely. "I am so happy to see you all, especially Miranda the Saint and Amy—oh, and is that my dear Clive in the corner?"

"Nobody else, gurl! How ya doin'?"

"I love even more how you call me 'gurl.' Oh! OH!" She paused, choked up. "I am remembering with you and Orvy sending me on the secret mission to Guantanamo Bay to find out if the Pakistani pizza delivery man in Columbia was there—what was his name?"

"Aziz."

"Yes! He won his USA visa in the lottery, and wound up dead, framed after 9/11."

"That was a great thing you did," Roy said.

"Amen," said Clive.

"*Sì, sì*, it is not easy being a bodhisattva—a mere person following and helping others on the Buddha's way, but not going over into enlightenment for herself." She sighed as if exhausted from all her good works. "And now, even though there is no such thing as time, it is so late and I must sleep to get ready to the first meditation and dharma talk teaching at dawn. But remember, Orvillo! We will always have *Lago d'Orta*!"

Clive and Miranda grinned at each other.

Finally she said, "In our brokenness is our wealth, and I feel that each of you, gathered together in our Columbia sangha, is a *tesoro*— a treasure. Even for a bodhisattva." She wiped away a tear. "Many blessings to the birthday boy and to all and even though we are apart, we are loving each other in the very spirit. And you must visit here all of you and *ciao! Ciao!*"

Gone.

"How *old* is that woman?" Amy asked.

Orvy looked at Miranda. "You okay?"

"Very," Miranda said, shaking her head slowly. "You were the one real love of her life, and you left her for me. For her, it's in the present, all the time. How'd she sound to you?"

"Wild, still. And perhaps happy? Goofy, enlightened? When I let her down, I felt incredibly guilty." He went on, sheepishly, "As you know all too well, dear one, I don't run on fear, I run on guilt."

"Yes, yes. And my job all these years, Orville Rose, has been and will be to keep you safe and sound. I love you more than ever. *Ever* ever. Happy birthday."

"Right now," he said, "I'm so full of gratitude! The luckiest guy in the world!"

Clustering around Ben, they had a family hug, lasting.

"Clive," Orville said, "time to close the Zoom. You're a genius."

"Yeah, I know. Night."

They sat together, in silence, and then, stiff, got up to go to bed. Orville's phone rang.

"Orvy, it's Berry. Sorry to call so late."

She sounded scared. "Are you okay?"

"More or less. Is Amy there?"

"Yes, I'm putting you on speaker. Okay, go ahead."

"I'm really worried about Roy. He's been getting more and more agitated and down. He said today he got into a shouting argument with a patient—unheard of. *Never* before! He hasn't been sleeping—always taking some drug to sleep. He's in bed now. He can't really tell me what's the matter, just says it's horrific work. Says, 'I can't take all the deaths.' He wants to quit but he feels he owes it to you and Amy and the guys he rounded up. I don't know what's going on, or what to do."

"I've been worried too. Has he ever been this way before?"

"Never! Even at the worst, in the House of God and in Man's 4th—never treated patients badly. And he'd been really happy in Costa Rica, writing, Spring's doing well, got a steady guy . . ."

"When did it start, dear?"

"The first day in the hospital. Right away something got to him. It got worse, week by week, deaths and deaths. What can we do? I'm at my limit!"

"Do you think he's suicidal?" Orvy went on.

"I asked him, he said no. I believe him. But he feels trapped. Quitting would be even more depressing—he *never* lets anybody down."

"And when *I* asked him," Amy said, "he said the same: 'all the deaths.'"

"But that's so *strange*. He's had plenty of patients die over the years. Some horribly. Even, rarely, deaths because he missed something. But he was always able to let it go. This is different."

"I'd better have a talk with him," Orville said.

"I suggested that. He won't talk to you. He said, 'I'm not worth involving Orvy.'"

"But why now?" Orville asked. "I mean, he's so steady."

"I pressed him, and he said he has no idea what's going on. Amy, could it be from the Covid?"

"Could be," Amy said. "We've seen just about everything with Covid."

"But what I keep asking myself," Berry went on, "why is this happening when he has what he wanted—to be helpful during the pandemic, especially working again with guys he loves?"

"Sounds like depression," said Orville.

"He admits to some symptoms—fatigue, dullness, sleeplessness—but he says that's not it. One thing's clear: it began on his first day. He came home saying, 'the deaths.'"

"What I suggest," Orville said, "is to bring him and his friends together, Hyper, Eat My Dust, Sev—and get Shump, she's astonishing at this. Bring them all out to your house tomorrow evening, and set a long, uninterrupted time to talk. Open-ended. I'll be on Zoom. He's asking for help. Poor guy. I see him as a prophet—I mean *what he's been through as a doc?* My hunch is this is more a spiritual crisis than a psychological one."

"For sure," Berry said. "How 'bout at seven?"

"Done," said Amy.

11

"Damn it I'm telling you I don't know what's wrong!" Roy G. Basch was saying.

He was shaking his head and reaching for another hot pastrami on rye. Not only a hot pastrami, but the *signature* hot pastrami from the signature Katz's Delicatessen, on Houston Street below the Bowery, in New York City.

The Fat Man's choice.

The restaurant of course was closed by Covid, but their eat-by-mail catering was going gangbusters. This was the same Katz's whose World War II slogan was "Send a salami to your boy in the Army."

Roy had also accumulated a stash of Dr Pepper cream soda.

Now, mouth full, he went on, angrily, "I don't know what the hell's going on, but I really don't appreciate this 'intervention' or whatever the hell you call it. I told you, *twice*, I don't like surprises. Just leave me alone."

He bit and chewed the buttery spiced meat. Eyes closed, he sighed—an addict's hit of ambrosia.

It was sunset. The end of a dazzling summer day. Berry, Amy, Eat

My Dust Eddie, Hyper Hooper, Sev, and Shump were sitting with him in a circle on the grand porch of one of the oldest mansions in our county, 1834. Orville was on Zoom.

The sun was rolling down behind the Catskills, a wash of dark mountain reflected in the fierce ebb tide of the Hudson River. The lights winked on in the town of Athens, across the water. The Columbian weatherman had called for yet another in a summer full of hot, humid, mosquitoed nights. But there was the usual breakage in his weather-dyslexic brain and it was cool and comfy, even bracing. The pestilential mosquitoes were freezing.

Berry had not told Roy about the meeting in advance. As each of them walked in he became more and more pissed. Now they were at an impasse, Roy sulking. His coolness to the people he loved and who loved him was ugly. Worse, his stonewalling had only increased since they'd arrived.

Roy felt his mind narrow to a sharp point. A silent scowl was on his face.

What a contrast, his scowl, thought Amy, as she looked out over this opening vista. *How sad, not to be able to take in this glory!*

The elegant house faced west over the Hudson River, sheltered from the east winds, and nestled just below the peak of Mount Merino. Miranda, the official historian of town and county, had told her that the name "Merino" came from the early English settlers who had brought Merino sheep to forage on the mountain, breaking up nature by denuding the forest for grazing. To the south was the Rip Van Winkle Bridge, leading to the Catskills—every time Amy saw them fresh, she was startled by how tall, muscular, and wild the mountains were. In the strange late-summer cool air, the peaks seemed enormous, flowing like waves of water-made rock. The Hudson River was wide and tidal, up to five feet because of the onslaught of a glacier and then its melting, leaving a straight wide trough due north. In front of her now the river was split in two by an island,

Middle Ground Flats, guarded by an ancient lighthouse to warn vessels to take the passable left fork, because of the rock escarpment at the foot of Columbia.

Growing up with Miranda the town historian, Amy could not help seeing the land as the story. During the Revolutionary War, the Quaker whalers from Nantucket, their fleets decimated in the open sea by the British Navy, decided to find an inland port. The step-off to depth at Columbia was perfect for their whaling fleet. There they built a religious utopia. It didn't last. Fortunes were made in whale oil. The easy cash attracted gangsters, Legs Diamond among others, and whores. Columbia was known all over America for "the Block," its red-light district. If a certain conductor at Grand Central Terminal in New York City saw you were going to Columbia, he would punch your ticket with a heart-shaped hole.

In 1840 oil was discovered in Pennsylvania. The price of whale oil sank. Quakers left. The town was taken over by the whores and gamblers and crooks and just plain dumb thugs. Columbia had reached its peak population just before the American Revolution. Except for the brief religious and stolid Quaker period, it grew in avarice, prejudice, gamblers, prostitutes, and a penchant for money and violence.

"So, Roy," Amy said, "you don't have any idea why you're so angry at work? Why you took it out on the patient yesterday? And others before that?"

"Not a clue."

"Have you ever done that before?"

He looked at Eat My Dust and Hyper Hooper. "None of us *ever* did *that* before. Eddie, did you ever see me do that?"

"No," said Eddie. "I mean in the House, all of us got weird— each in our own ways. I myself was not sweet—imagine that? We give them all we got, *still*, to keep 'em alive, and they make us want 'em to die."

"With all the deaths now in the air, all the time?" Hooper said. "Brings it all back—I mean when Potts couldn't stand it and jumped from the top floor of the House. Y'*never* get over that."

Suddenly again, Wayne Potts was in the air, about to smash on the asphalt. *Never.*

"Yeah. And then we just went along abusing *ourselves*," Eddie said, "and *we* almost died. Something's eatin' you, Roy, and we want to help. I mean, you are *out* there, primed to explode. Man, I never saw you like that before, and—"

"Aw, gee, Eddie the cynic has gotten humane," Roy said sarcastically.

"Hey, me and Naidoo have *cats*, okay? I *love* our cats! Egyptian cats!" He brightened up. "You should see how they play together, it's amazing! I'm *good* with cats!"

"Cats?" Roy cried. "You?"

"Not soft for humans, baby, rarely soft for the humans. 'Cept for the basket-weaver guys. They're awesome."

"Good. For a second you got me worried—you and kitty-cats? You've been my hero and—"

"Me, hero? You must be in *real* bad shape."

"I *am*!" Roy said. "That's why I'm asking you about *you*! I mean, you're the only thing that keeps me going, Eddie, and now you've gone soft on cats? Jesus!"

Laughter all around, and then, sudden silence, one of *Does he mean it?*

Picking it up, looking sheepish, Eddie went on. "Nah, I don't really mean that, about the cats." Slapping himself twice in the face, once each way, he cried out, "*Bad* Eddie! *Bad* Dust! You're *regressing*!" He sighed. "But somethin's got its claws into you, and we gotta help." He squinched up his face into serious—a difficult contortion for him— and said, "I'm . . . I'm worried about you. All of us are, right?"

Everyone affirmed this, with nods and "you bets."

"So what's going on with you, kid?" Eddie asked.

Seeing Eddie open up, Roy shrugged his shoulders. "Dunno. Gonna get another sandwich."

He got up from his chair—or tried to. At about the halfway mark he started to wobble a little, and then there was a tug-of-war between muscle mass lifting versus heft of body falling. The tension was scary, and the wobble turned into his falling back down into the chair again, *hard*, so the chair let out a wood-shriek as if fractured. Jolted, shaking his head, Roy started gathering himself for another try—Berry was at his side, ready to lift and—

"Fat!" Hyper Hooper cried out, red-faced in fury, his thin, tight body leaping athletically up out of his chair to his feet. He stood in front of Roy. "Fat fat fat! There's an elephant in the room, Roy, and it is *you*! I don't know what the hell's wrong between you and your patient, but I do know that when you walked into the clinic the first time I said to myself, 'What the hell has happened to Roy, former Rhodes Scholar–athlete?'"

Silence from Roy, who looked shocked.

"When I saw you walk into Kush Kare, I couldn't believe my eyes, I mean that *this was you*? I went online and checked out your photos from when we first met in Man's Best med school, and you were an Adonis! Trim, muscular—six-four and one-seventy *at most*, right?"

"One-sixty."

"What are you now? *Two*-sixty?"

Roy didn't answer.

"When's the last time you weighed yourself?"

"I'm not taking this abuse! So long." But he faced the fight against getting up again without help, and it was not clear that anyone would volunteer.

"No exercise, right?"

No answer. Roy was gazing out, attention floating anywhere but at Hyper.

"Hey," Hyper said, "I'm trying to save your *life*, okay? Listen up!" Roy looked down. "You are morbidly obese. *Mortally* obese. Like Fats. You're at risk for everything. Isn't that correct? Eat My Dust, Berry, Amy, Sev, Shump?"

All yeses.

"Fats was our hero, yeah," Hooper went on, "and only once I tried to intervene. It was during our time at Man's 4th Best. When we had the picnic at your house? The only time any of us had seen him eat a meal outside the hospital. I confronted him, remember? He didn't listen. He's dead."

"Not because of food!" Roy protested. "You know that—"

"Of course I know, but he had *morbid* obesity. One day at Man's 4th I got his lab numbers—lipids, cardiac ejection fraction, and everything else measured were off the charts. Life-threatening. High stress, no exercise. You're a doctor, you saw it, we all did: *his days were numbered.*" He sighed, shook his head. "Now you're following in his shoes."

"Roy?" It was Berry. "Honey, we've been through a lot of hell together, and I've tried to talk to you about this, and I've given up. But I've got to say it again in public. There are a lot of stresses on you now. All kinds of triggers at work, Covid, being back on the front lines of medicine—and, maybe, even coming back home? But somewhere along the way, gradually, you've been identifying with the Fat Man. I've told you that." She shook her head in despair. "I don't know what to do anymore."

Roy shook his head. Said nothing.

"Fats was our hero, you bet!" Hyper said. "We all tried to be like him, but for his obesity. And we never said anything about his killer fat—except that once. Right?"

Nods all around.

"But I'll be good goddamned if I let you die too. Listen up. You had Covid, and I'm glad you made it through. But . . ." Again he paused. "Do you know how lucky you are you're not dead? Do you know why we prone fat people? People like you?"

"I haven't been paying attention to that kind of—"

"Because the single most important factor in death by Covid is *obesity—that ring of abdominal fat, that big gut*! And why is that? Cytokine storm! If you're not fat, when you catch the virus, your normal immune system sends out normal proteins to attack and kill the virus—producing at least some immunity. But in obese people, the fat can't recognize the good proteins and instead *attacks*! Spews out huge amounts of inflammatory toxic proteins called cytokines! The cytos destroy organs, especially the small blood vessels all through your body, and especially the lungs. And then you die a horrible death, drowning in your own phlegm!"

All through this Roy had been staring out over the balustrade west. He was looking at the Fat Man again, floating at the level of a young pine tree maybe 20 feet high—one hand on a fragile-seeming limb. He was as fat as ever and wearing a retrograde long white doctor coat, nicely cut and clean. *Amazing, to see him look so good, and so buoyant. Gentle up, gentle down, in the cool breeze.* Roy smiled at him. He smiled back.

But then suddenly the Fat Man's face changed, clouded, and he spoke: "Hey! Listen to them. They care. Tell them you see me! And tell them I'm all right."

"They'll think I'm crazy."

"You'd be surprised."

"Am I crazy?"

"How do *I* know? Sheesh! Gotta run, doing some work on the vaccine for Covid. *Ciao!*"

He let go and rose away.

"—and so the bottom line?" Hooper was saying. "Fat people die from their fat. Abdominal fat. You know how close you came to dying in your first infection with Covid?" This seemed to hit Hooper hard. He got choked up, took out a neat hankie embroidered "HH." Wiped his eyes, blew his nose. "The thing is, Roy, is that I love you and I don't want to lose you, especially by your inner fat fire! Your conflagration of fats! The good news? I can help you eat the right stuff—I puree veggies and fruit—they're the best-tasting shakes ever! Just gimme a chance, okay?" He paused, struggling. "I mean I love you, man," Hooper said softly, "but I don't love where you're at, at fat. It's like you're mimicking Fats, wanting to follow in his shoes, those big fat shoes, to his grave."

Roy seemed shaken. "Thanks. I hear you."

Amy glanced at Berry, then at Shump. In the glance was a first spark, of "maybe." A real connect, *maybe.*

In the women's glances to each other? *Do not talk. Let the silence work. And hope that none of the men talk, and derail it.*

Dead silence.

"I'm sorry," Hooper went on. "Fats is dead. And he made all of us kinda dead too, each in our different ways. That's when I really dedicated my research to fighting fat."

"Roy?" Amy said. He turned to look at her. "Have you been thinking of Fats much lately?"

Roy paused for what seemed a long time.

The birdsongs for "good night" went hopping branch to branch, away.

"Think of him? Yeah. I thought I was over him, but now he's come back, worse. I mean murdered in cold blood, you know the story."

"I don't," said Shump. "Would you mind filling me in?"

"I'd like to hear too, Roy," Amy said. "I never heard the details."

Roy glanced into the trees.

"Me neither!" said Fats. He was out on a bare maple limb, in his doctor's long white coat and for some reason a Great White Hunter safari hat. He was grinning. "Shoot."

As if talking to Shump, Roy said to Fats, "You never heard what happened?"

"Nope," said Fats, and Shump. "I got traumatic retrograde amnesia. My last memory is with you and Chuck, trying to get into my pants for the big meeting." He crossed his legs. "Shoot."

"Okay." Roy took a deep breath and spoke softly. "Fats was murdered in the office of the President of Man's 4th Best Hospital." He paused, getting a grip. "He was shot by Dr. Jared T. Krashinsky, who had just been fired as President. Krash and Fats had been childhood rivals in Brooklyn, with Fats almost always the winner. That day, Chuck and I were the last two guys to see Fats alive. We sat with him in the conference room of our clinic, just before noon. He was going up to the penthouse of the hospital, to lunch with the CEO. He said he was going to be offered the job of President."

Roy paused, eyes looking inside as if he were seeing it all again. He glanced at Fats, who nodded and lifted a salami in a thumbs-up.

"Fats was in a hurry, trying to stuff his big upper body into the jacket of a dark pin-striped suit. Awkwardly. The pants were only halfway on, thighs billowing out, big, tight, stuck. Chuck asked, 'Hey man, need some help?' 'Nah, I'm good,' Fats said. 'Trying to fit a fat guy into this suit is like unregulated health care: you get one part in, and another part pops back out—you can't cover them all.'"

Roy smiled, shaking his head in admiration at Fats—who smiled back.

"Unregulated health care—that was Fats. Even then, always thinking about better health care. I remember Chuck held one sleeve of the jacket in, while Fats and I struggled with the other. We asked where he was going. With pride and rare amazement he said, 'Lunch alone with Flambeau the CEO in his suite on the top floor—I can't believe I'm so nervous.' Never, ever, had Chuck or I or anyone else seen him really nervous, okay? That should've tipped us off."

He shook his head. Fats was nodding along.

"Y'have to understand: he never wore a suit, *ever*. And so I asked him, 'Why are you wearing a suit?'" Roy closed his eyes, envisioning it. "He said, 'My *mother* wore suits.'

"I don't think he'd mentioned a mother ever. Weird—another tip-off. And then he asked us, shyly—which he never was before—'Y'sure you can't persuade Berry to keep going with what she was teaching all of us yesterday, getting to we, in the mutual? It was terrific—out of this world! Maybe we can keep going, have another meeting *tonight*. I mean, didja see how good it went? How *deep* we got? In the *first meeting*? I'm on fire with this 'relational' model of hers—not I/you, but the shift to we. And tonight I'm free. Can we?' I gave him a look. He looked back in a weird way, an *unsure* way, as if chastened, or revealed? He says, 'Okay okay, so I'm just a hungry guy. I see something good, I want *more*. I try to control it, control myself, but . . . *but I can't.*'" Roy paused. "Fats, admitting a *flaw*? And clearly *asking* me for help? Never happen. I got a chill."

Roy turned to Berry and said, "You made a huge impression in that workshop when you joined us in the clinic, the shift to the 'we' and showing how it would help us all to use it; in medicine and, yes, life. In that last moment, Fats seemed more vulnerable than I had ever seen him except when Potts committed suicide. So I said to myself, *Answer him from your heart.* Thank God! My last words to him were what I think he needed just then, in all of that big wavering balance, now tipping to doubt. He seemed like he might be wondering what he hadn't understood, what vital sense he'd missed all these years."

Roy sat still. Staring past all of them, out into the trees, seeing that Fats was still there—yes. But now he was way out on the edge of the limb, not holding on, all of that enormous body and mind focus was lava moving toward him, his eyes lit up in grappling with a truth that he hadn't yet quite gotten—an exit from the false. On fire? Yes. *Tell him again. Talk to him.*

"If he were here right now, dear," said Berry, "what would you want to tell him?"

Startled, Roy looked at Fats. He seemed to be shifting all that weight around, fidgeting, trying to find a balance in the thin air. A shade, as if of sorrow, came over his face.

"Fats, my dear friend . . ." He faltered, wiping his eyes. Clearing his throat, looking up at him, Roy continued. "Fats, always wanting more of everything good—that's your great gift."

Fats stopped still, stunned. Chewed on this. Swallowed. And said, excitedly, 'Yeah! Maybe it is!'"

"And then," Roy went on, "Fats looked at himself in the call-room mirror and said, 'Wish me luck!' and he was gone. That was the last time I ever saw him."

Roy fell still. Staring out at nowhere. The words had gone, leaving the music of the cicadas. There was no breeze.

"It's carved into my heart. It's right here, right now. He took the elevator up and never came back. Krashinsky, who'd just been fired, killed him in the executive suite, then got into the elevator going down and shot himself. Sirens wailed. Chuck and I caught a slow freight elevator all the way up, raced into the CEO suite. Blood all over, people screaming. He was dead."

Silence enveloped them, a silence of horror and sorrow.

"Is *that* how it happened?" Fats cried out from above, so that it seemed to Roy that everyone would hear it. "Why the hell didn't you two stop me!?"

Amy asked, "What's your worst pain, Roy?"

"Chuck and I should have stopped you!" Roy cried out, shouting into the trees. Sighing, he said, "We told him the job wasn't right for him—but we never suspected the danger!" He took a tormented breath. He glanced up. "Sorry, my dear friend. Really."

Fats was taking out a big white handkerchief, then gave several blows of the nose. "Hey, it's okay, Roy. Jesus! What a story. No wonder I still need two cyclobenzaprines to sleep."

"Have you and the others ever gotten together and mourned him?" Amy asked. "Had a memorial? Anything?"

"No. All we had, two days after the death, was a funeral and burial in Queens. I know we should have, we'd been so close, in the House and Man's 4th. It was closed coffin, of course. But the end was so, so damn brutal and shitty, we all just scattered. Blown apart."

A quiet seemed to settle over him, and then over the others.

"A few years ago now, all of it came back," Berry said. "After you had a close call with death at our place in Costa Rica."

"Yeah. After falling down the mountain, my head stopped about three inches in front of a boulder that would have killed me." He took Berry's hand. "It brought back all of the pain of the Fat Man's murder—more and more pain. I couldn't get rid of it, seeing it. We spent a lot of time, Berry and me, talking, trying to find peace. And it worked. I *thought* I was done with it, anyway." He looked to Hooper. "But that's also when I started eating, getting fat. And kept going. Berry tried to help—her low-carb diet worked great for a while—but I stopped, got fatter than ever. Nothing else worked. Now, coming back here, being with Hyper and Eddie and back in a hospital again—in a pandemic in a hospital with owners who only care about money, not people? Depressing. Is *this* what medicine has come to?" He looked around the circle.

All nodded, and some cursed.

"How could I *not* think about death?" Roy said. "The death of Fats? Yesterday the death of that little girl in the ICU?" He shook his head. "I lost it! I dunno what to do. Maybe just quit?"

"You do that, man," said Eddie, "and I kill you."

"Good."

"Roy, this is Orvy." And there he was, on Zoom, looking older, like everyone now.

"Glad you're here," Roy said.

"Thanks for telling us all this. I think I might be able to help you through—from my experience, and all the Columbians I've seen. Okay?"

"Go for it."

"You've been thinking of the Fat Man?"

"Yeah, a *lot*. I mean I *get* it—coming back onto the front lines of medicine for the first time since Fats died? All the carnage. And now I'm as fat as him? *I get it*, okay? But lately, it's as if I'm . . . well, *aware* of him, all the time. Both his best and his worst and . . . never mind."

"Go on."

"He's gotten incredibly . . . *present* in my mind, and just . . . past the edges of my sight. As if he's *here*. I mistake other people for him—how could I not, with the legions of fat people here? Once . . . I even thought I saw him . . . flying through the air, all that bulk flying? Like he was trying to talk to me?" He paused. "*More* than once . . . Okay, a *lot*. I see him a lot, talking with me, just like always. Conversing. He couldn't be—or seem—more real. That's one reason I'm so tense—am I going crazy? I haven't dreamed about him for a long time. But this is new, ever since I've been doctoring again. I . . . I saw . . . saw him here, tonight, for a while. Am I nuts?"

"Nuts, hell! You're *lucky*," Orvy said. "Enjoy it. It's not going to last." He chuckled. "I've learned that the dead who talk to you are mostly helpful, if you listen. If they don't, or if you get scared and don't listen, it can be hell." He paused. "Can I tell you *my* story?" Roy nodded.

"My mother, Selma, and I had a horrific relationship. My first night back in town after her death, I saw her flying—dressed as Amelia

Earhart, goggles and all—hovering in front of me and talking to me and I answering—a real *conversation*. At first I thought I'd gone nuts, and I only disclosed it to one person around here, now my dear wife. My mother said the worst things to me, for months, blaming me for leaving Columbia, running away from her to have my life, out in the world. But looking back, the talks were absolutely crucial to our healing, both of us. The last time she talked to me—floating in the Courthouse Square at eye level with me, well, it was a moment of grace. She said, 'I see now that you weren't running *from* me, you were running *for* me.'" He paused, choked up. "I felt transformed with, well, gratitude. *And she never flew again.*"

"Wow. I'm stunned."

"I came to an ineluctable truth: the dead don't fly when there's love in the air." He smiled. "If there's no love in the air, y'get lots of unscheduled flights."

Berry said, "I know from my patients, when you make peace with your dead, they go away."

"Really? I thought I was going insane."

"I had that experience too," said Shump. "A lot of Columbians seem to. For a long time before I went to nursing school, I was a dental hygienist for Roy's dad. Nice guy, so-so dentist. He and I got to be good friends. He paid for my nursing school. And I *still* catch glances of him as I'm walking around Columbia, especially on Seventh and Warren where his office was. I see him drilling, smiling, and playing 'Yankee Doodle Went to Town' on the high-pressure-air instrument that he used to dry off cavities before putting in the amalgam." She paused. "You'd be surprised how many people see their dead flying around—and of course in dreams. It's like, if you still see them, it means you haven't mourned through the grief. Nobody admits it, of course. They think it's crazy."

"My favorite uncle," Sev said, shyly, "Moses Firmisht, the funeral director? The guy who got me interested in death and digits and pixels, which I resented, and I still see him sometimes in the corner of my eye, like in a chat room in Zoom?"

Amy said, "You told me, Roy, that what made you blow up at the guy was 'all these deaths.' Maybe, because it's the first time you've been back in a hospital since Fats died, and since you loved him and identified so tightly with him, well, it's brought out all the hell, all the loss. You've never really let him go. I know you thought you were done, and I'd guess this is just a flare-up." She put her hand on his. "This is how you're grieving Fats. We'll help."

"Thanks, thanks . . . It's amazing, really," Roy said. He paused, smiling. "And the miracle of all that weight being able to float up there like that? I've still got a lot to learn from Fats."

"You sure do," said Fats.

"We all do," said Hyper.

"*Amen,*" said Eat My Dust.

All were braced for how Eddie, giving in to a shred of hidden faith of some sort, would undo this rare show of normal.

Sensitive to a fault, he said, "Stop looking at me like that, or I'll start talking about my cats again." He smiled. "You *really believe* that I, Eat My Dust, would have *cats*?!"

Everyone stared. Then laughed. What was true? Who cared?

Silence, when all present could almost feel the night sigh.

Berry smiled, nodding. "I wish you'd told me, Roy. But I understand. There's still one question I keep asking myself. What do you guys think would have happened if Fats had taken up the job as President of Man's 4th Best?"

"First," said Hooper, "he'd have had a heart attack. And if he'd had a few more years? *Disaster!* The system would have gobbled him up in small bites! He wouldn't have lasted a year, if that! Right, guys?"

"No foolin'," said Eat My Dust. "Everything he believed in—and not just in medicine, but in life—was totally at odds with the . . . Let me use a *technical* term for 'administrators,' okay?"

No one said okay.

"Hey, I'm *dyin'* out here. Gimme an 'okay,' okay?"

"Okays" rattled around the porch, and then it was so much fun there was a second wave of "Okay!" shouted and sung, and then pounded on glasses with forks. And everyone laughed.

And it went on, one of those contagious laughs where someone stops and pulls herself together and looks at another trying to hold back and . . . bang!—laughter busts out again even louder.

Finally it was quiet, more quiet for the loud.

"What was the technical term?" asked Sev.

Eat My Dust composed himself, cleared his throat. "*Shitheads.* Fats was totally at odds with the money-grubbing shitheads at Man's 4th who only want to make money even though the one thing they don't need is more money. The rich and shameless."

"Roy," Shump said, "you told me that Fats was going to try to demonstrate how to put the human back from the top?" Roy nodded. "That could never happen. Before Covid, I did a master's degree in health care—Natasha and me both—an 'out-of-body' experience! The health-care profs wouldn't know good health care if they found it in a fortune cookie. They teach capital, not care. People like us, in the trenches and still caring, are crucial."

"Exactly," Amy said. "Fats probably would have tried to fight everything the board wanted—like building those swank satellites in the suburbs all over, right? What was it called? Friends? Pals?"

"*Buddies!*" said Hyper. "A fifty-billion-dollar holding company that bought up Man's 4th and all the surrounding hospitals with one goal—to squeeze out small practices and hike up insurance payments. The real business of Buddies was nothing much to do with health care. The business of money is money."

Around the circle, heads were shaking.

Sadness set in.

"I loved Fats too," Berry said, "all of us did. And a few times that year in Man's 4th, he and I talked, and he did try to take in what I was saying about how the health of a person—or an institution—is not in the 'self' alone, but in the quality of the connections. What's a good connection? A mutual connection. If it ain't mutual, it ain't that good." She paused. "When Fats heard that from me, he lit up, and said, 'Yes! But how do you learn this, and teach this, this mutuality?' I didn't want to interrupt the party so I kind of deflected it. 'C'mon, c'mon, Berry,' he said, 'hit me while I'm hot! I try my best to include everybody in my decisions.' So I said, 'Getting to mutual is the hardest thing to change in a big power-over system, and the way you get to mutual, all up and down your teams, is *real listening*, even to the disempowered below you.'"

"And what did he say?" Shump said.

"I think his words were," she imitated him, "'Sheesh! I got a lot to learn. Let's take a meeting, you and me, plan a workshop, *tomorrow*!'" Berry shook her head sadly. "Which never happened. He gave you all his best, and it was marvelous. But it was, sadly, in him alone. A lonely, brilliant guy. As in our poor nation—a long history of male heroes riding solo atop their faithful horse below."

"I never knew him," Amy said, "but he must have really believed he could multiply his clinic, to show the world how to 'put the human back into medicine.' Not likely. The goal of giant institutions is to generate giant money. They would have eaten him up."

"Well," Roy said, "growing up in the sixties, my friends and I learned that if we stuck together and marched together, we could bring more justice and peace into the world. We stopped the Vietnam War and we put the voting rights laws on the books." He paused. "And so when Fats went up there *alone*, he was doomed." Roy looked around at each in turn, then went on. "The only threat to the dominant group—be it racial, ethnic, sexual preference, whatever—*is the quality of the connections among the subordinate group.* Fats was great, *truly* great, but if you think about it, *that's* why he wouldn't have had a chance up there, why he died." He gazed down. "And it hurts . . . *badly*. But tonight helps." He smiled. "Maybe he knew, right then, that we—each of us in our own way . . . didn't need him anymore."

No one said anything for a long time.

"We all have to learn what Fats couldn't," Berry said. "Start where he stopped. Each of us has a time to flower, and then pass it on. Roy, and all of us, we have to try to learn what Fats didn't know, couldn't know. Young doctors like Amy are knowing it *new*, and the next generation will be a *new* new. Fats tried to show how the new clinic could 'Put the human back into medicine'—a brilliant quest— and, for that magic year, it was wonderful. He couldn't work in that system. But he left a way for this generation to work to do it new, and never to forget the human. How to do it? In this mess of health care? Amy and Binni, and those already coming up behind you, will have to do it. But we're not alone, we're joining in the here and now, with the pandemic, and our national grieving, finding a way."

"It reminds me," Roy said, "what Chuck said at times like this, a gospel lyric: 'Them that know, they know that they know. Them that don't know, they don't know they don't know.'"

"There it is," Eddie said. "Basketmakers unite!"

The silence deepened. No one knew what to say, but no one wanted to go.

Roy turned to Berry and took her hand. "Dear one, thanks."

They hugged, for a long time. Hyper starting counting, "A-one, a-two." Everybody laughed.

Berry spoke up. "Can we take a moment before we go, to end with the Buddha's blessing?" Nods all around. "I've got some candles.

Here, each of you take one. Each has a holder below it. Roy, turn out the light?"

He did so. There was no moon. Things went black. Berry lit her candle, and lit Roy's, and he lit the next, around the circle. When all were burning, softly framing each face, Berry spoke.

"So much is going on right now—Covid surrounds us, the whole world, surrounded by death. It calls up our grief, fear—rage at our helplessness. At our hearts, in our hearts, are the three hindrances of the Buddha: hatred, craving, and delusion. We are, every day, at our limit, thinking that we can't go on helping others, yet we go on. And we *do* help others, we really do." Then, closing her eyes and putting her hands palm to palm at heart level, she said, "May all beings be happy. May all beings be free from suffering and the roots of suffering. May all beings see and be seen with the eyes of loving-kindness." She paused. "Let there be peace."

A moment, and then she looked around, nodding at each of them, one by one, at the only part visible: their face, softly aglow and flickering, yes, but staying lit. Another moment, still.

"Now, on three, we all blow out our candles together. One . . . two . . . three!"

12

The day after Labor Day.

The virus in this second wave had been more hellish than ever. The number of American Covid deaths had been going up in remarkable parallel with the Dow Jones: 294,000 Americans dead, and the Dow Jones closing at its highest *ever*, blasting through 29,000.

The surgeons were still not performing "elective" surgeries. Without them, a huge quantity of insurance payments were lost to Kush. But of course the insurance companies were still receiving monthly premiums. United Health Care alone made billions.

Not that they weren't altruistic. The profits at United were being distributed to executives by way of bonuses. What luck! Go, Covid!

And what bad luck for Kush Kare. They and other private equity hospital chains were bleeding out.

In response, Jason Kush of "the Unseen Voice" Kushes had a great idea: start admitting jackpot patients again, for nonemergent surgeries.

It was such a bad idea that the surgeons wouldn't touch it. Catch Covid? No way.

Corners were being cut, equipment was slow to getting restocked—especially the protective covid N95 face masks and other gear that kept everyone safe—and here and there, workers disappeared. Quality was shredding. The contract with Scomparza Ambulance and Taxidermy was canceled because they didn't own the big refrigerator trucks to warehouse the overflow of bodies. Somehow KK got a bargain lease on trucks emblazoned CHICKEN OF THE SEA TUNA. Macabre, yes. As is so often the case in our great country, you can't invent this stuff.

There were new firings of "non-necessary groups"—such as security guards, recently hired lab techs, and, most painfully to KK, clerks in the billing department. And by choice, there was again a departure of more nurses and nurse assistants. Kush Kare would not raise their pay, nor hire more nurses.

Amy's intensivist team, dependent on a full cadre of nurses to staff the overflowing ICU, suddenly had a big problem. One day when the usual morning patient conference meeting was about to start, a text came from the best and most hardworking intensivist nurse, Debbi Silk: "I need a brief Zoom with you all this morning." When she got on, she looked worn, eyes red and lips set in a tight line. "Sorry to take your time," she said, "but I can't go on. I've quit."

All were stunned. She, the best, calmest, most honorable and most judicious person, quit?

"Last night was a nonstop nightmare. Jan, the other nurse on shift, didn't come in at the last minute—might be Covid. I was alone, to take care of eight really sick patients, five on respirators. I tried to call for help, there was no one. Respirators, infusions, medications. And fighting to complete the protocol-administrative crap! It seemed everyone had a full bedpan! Then with only two more hours to go, I had been trying to wean one of the Covids off the vent—a sweet guy named Roland—and as I tried to get his bedpan out he suddenly swung his arm and hit my visor, hard! And suddenly I was breathing all this hellish air, and I shouted, 'Shit!' and holding my breath I settled him back down and the bedpan clattered on the floor and I got out of there with the bedpan and . . ." Her voice sped up and she said, "I thought, 'Good for you, Debbi, you actually do help most of the people and hold the hands of dying patients and risk bringing Covid home to your family, and you try hard with Roland who's probably going to die anyway no matter what I do and sometimes I get fierce abuse and now I'm going to get Covid and one of you will be intubating me and I'm going to die but . . . IT'S OKAY, ROLAND, IT'S REALLY OKAY!" She shook her head, and then was gone.

The team was silent.

———————

Given the deterioration of KK safety and quality, more of the nurses with families just gave up and stayed home to be safe with their beloveds. Others, the younger, single women and men, went traveling to better and safer hospitals, and higher pay.

It was a remarkable fiscal moment: the squeeze on KK and other hospitals by the new traveler nurse companies, TNCs. They would charge a hospital like KK a fortune, and impose onerous contracts. KK of course said no. But if the nurses joined a TNC, their pay was huge and they would be placed at better-run, lower-cost hospitals in the Midwest and South. Another company had outfoxed KK on making big money.

There was a catch. They were mostly red-state hospitals, sometimes regional hospitals. The traveling nurses thought that the work would be safer in the Midwest and South. But they soon encountered a similar bottom-line squeeze as they'd had at Kush. And even more dangerous, in these remnants of the heartland (and almost a neat map of the old Confederacy), wearing masks was a sin against freedom. To males, masks were not cool: "It makes me look like a nurse" or "It makes me look as if I'm wearing my underwear" or "It looks like my daughter's training bra." Super-spreader unmasked events in this, the spare-tire belly of America, were rife and deadly.

The bright red states, the gun fire states, compared to the Kush Kare blue, were now an even scarier place to work and live.

———

But by some miracle, the Labor Day weekend had been surprisingly calm, in the number of Covids. There had been the usual horrors, but not as many as predicted. The reason? The *incubation period*. The way that the virus took its own sweet time incubating before saying, in horrific ways: "Hey, I'm loaded, locked, and ready. I'll be *ba-ack*!"

And so the long Labor Day weekend brought mostly the normal holiday hell. There was a dire shortage of Covid tests, which made things easier for the team, as in the House of God Law Number 10: "If you don't take a temperature, you can't find a fever." And then you don't have to work up that fever. And even if you could find a reliable test and sent it off for analysis, you couldn't count on getting the results in time to matter for starting treatment. Amy and her team had to rely on the old standards to make diagnoses: patient history, physical exam, and lab values.

Luckily most patients over the long weekend did not seem to have Covid but had all manner of injuries and syndromes of the usual holiday fun. Fueled by alcohol and drugs, signature Columbian car crashes came to the fore. On the twisty, hilly, broken-down roads in Kinderhook County, 18-year-olds driving 90 crashed into 90-year-olds driving 18. Most were drunk or high.

The national holiday celebrated solidarity in "labor." But it seemed more a celebration of violence. In Kinderhook County the violence was mostly human-to-human but spilled over into human-to-animals: from friendly dogs through fierce cats to docile livestock—all dead.

And this particular Labor Day featured gunshots.

The *Crier* headlines over the holiday weekend had been, for the past three days:

Man Critical after 2nd Columbian Shooting
Shots Fired Again in Broad Daylight in City
Shootings Draw Ire of City Business Men: Teens Charged

The last headline elaborated: "Police seized a defaced Ruger 380 handgun with six rounds of ammunition in the magazine, an AR-15 (ArmaLite) semiautomatic rifle with ammunition, an AK-47 semi-automatic rifle with ammunition, and a 12-gauge shotgun with ammunition. One of the teens was in possession of more than $1,400 in cash. Both juveniles were released on their own recognizance to their mothers."

The "Man Critical" had been shot in the crotch—ouch!—and knew it. He was helicoptered from KK's rooftop up to Albany and died. The second and third *Crier* articles detailed a heartwarming spray of live ammunition all around Fifth Street and Rope Alley, shattering the windshield of a passing car, another bullet entering a second-floor apartment just above the bed of a napping three-year-old, and other close calls all over the neighborhood.

Amy had been surprised at the violence, drugs, and poverty she found on her return home. She asked Orville and Miranda what was going on.

"Starting in the eighties," Orville said, "New Yorkers began to migrate from the city to Columbia to escape the epidemic of drugs and guns. But after a while, imagine their surprise to find themselves in the middle of an epidemic of drugs and guns here. How had this happened? Well, the drugs used to come from New York on express trains straight up to Albany for distribution. Eventually the police clamped down on that route at the Albany end. Columbia was the last stop before Albany, and even back then, our town was a good place to deal the drugs, not to mention it was a short drive to Albany."

Miranda, the town historian, had a deeper view. "From the time the Quaker utopia was founded just after the American Revolution, whenever Columbians had a choice of spending money and effort 'for the common good' or doing something for themselves, they chose themselves. Read my book, *The Columbian Spirit.*"

————

At noon on the Tuesday after Labor Day, Amy had just finished dealing with a farmer with the chief complaint of "My wife tried to slice off my ear."

"Why did she do that?"

"She said, 'Y'never listen t'me so you won't miss it.'"

As Amy left for the team meeting, she thought of the First Law of the Columbians: "Everything happens with maximum irony."

On the way to the team meeting she got a call. It was Erin Burke, a 25-year-old legal secretary in town whose mother, Juliet, had collapsed at work and was admitted in bad shape—a sudden onset of soaring fever and wheezing.

Tests clearly showed she needed to be intubated. Juliet, gasping and crying, had begged to have her daughter come in before she went under. Amy located her, told her to come right away. But because of the new shortages of nurses and other clinical staff—especially in the ICU, where the respirators were—KK had instituted a rule that there could be no visitors once the patient had been transferred to critical care to be put on a ventilator—except for one or two relatives for the final good-bye across the glass. When Amy gave Erin the bad news and prognosis on the phone, Erin said she'd be right in to see her mom, but she arrived too late—Juliet had already been transferred, and the rules stated she could not have a visitor.

"Please, please," Erin said now. "We're the closest mom and daughter in the world! She must be crazed not being able to see me—and if this is the last time . . ."

Amy listened to the wrenching tears.

"Okay," she said. "I'll tell them to hold off—and I'll sneak you in. Come around to the hospital's back door—you'll see trucks that say 'Chicken of the Sea'—go to the door that says, 'NO ENTRANCE HI VOLTAGE.'"

In four minutes the phone rang again. Amy opened the door, and they raced up the one flight to the glass-walled room where the intubation was just about to take place. Nurse Surrey was on duty, and Amy knew and liked the doctor as well, and she whispered what they were doing.

In rushed the daughter to her mother. Waves of heartbreak, and a sliver of joy.

Tearful, Amy went back down the stairwell, thinking of how she never got to say good-bye to her mother—and father—before they died in a plane crash while on her mom's dream trip, "doing Alaska."

———

Earlier that day she had gone into the office at Fifth Street. Even with the mask dictum and the footsteps painted on the street for social distancing, for the first time in over a month it had gotten too dangerous to see patients in that confined space. A lot of them simply would not wear masks. And after a few incidents when Amy came into the tiny waiting room to see one—or two or three—unmasked patients, and had a hard time getting them to leave, she gave up, shut down, and put a sign in the window: **CONTACT KUSH KARE**. Almost all her patients were now being seen through the emergency room.

Orville had stepped in gladly, increasing his Zoom doctoring. He was more and more adept at Zoom and liked the challenge of doctoring from home. The patients soon liked it as well. But there was a big problem: there was still not much of a Wi-Fi network in town, and out in the county it was terrible, worse than Wyoming. Battling breakage, Orville tried to diagnose and treat patients over the phone. He'd known most of them for decades, known their parents and children too, and it worked fairly well. For many patients it got to be like a call in to "a doctor TV show." Luckily, studies showed that 80 percent of people who come to see a family doctor have no identifiable physical disease. The issue for Orvy was catching the other 20 percent. It was a lot harder through pixels than in person. But he had "seen everything" by now, and rarely made a mistake. And he was such a nice, attentive doc that his patients hung up feeling better, sensing good doctoring: *Someone is with me in my suffering.*

But this morning Amy had to meet a patient in the office. She'd gotten a call from Alice, the young woman she'd seen out in the county on Memorial Day, when she'd had to break the clavicles of the baby to save both mother and child. What was the husband's name? Royal. And the baby? Forgot. Alice had sent photos of the baby a few times, all doing well, with her husband "totally in love with her—and with me too."

"Everything's fine with us," she'd said that morning on the phone, "but my new best friend is in bad trouble and kinda might die?"

"From what?"

"She's going to have twins, and she's having problems."

"What problems?"

"Kinda like mine. But she's, like, even more enormous. She's a wonderful person and been stayin' with us since two days and last night her water broke and she's, like, having contractions and she's groaning and pushing but nothing's happening. I told her you're an expert. We don't know anyone else to call."

"Has she been seeing a doctor or nurse?"

"Nope. She's illegal. Guatemala. A picker, working on Bothways

Farm nearby us. Doesn't have a car even. Or a guy. Or money or much English. Royal says he can pay you cash, some at least. He likes her too and she's got nobody else in the whole world so we want to help and he's got the pickup ready to rock and roll to your office— oh, hang on, Royal's sayin' somethin'." A pause, then: "He's tellin' me to tell you he's wearin' masks *everywhere* since you came—and that he can get us there in twenty minutes max. Please?"

Bad news. Kush forbids any obstetrics—and this is why. I could try to get her to another hospital—but not for an hour. Maybe I can deliver her in the office? Twins, with no prenatal care? Questionable. But I can assess, and go from there.

"Okay, come to my office."

Fifteen minutes later Alice came into the room, cute baby in her arms. Royal was straining to get the large patient, Cristina Galeano, up onto the examining table. She was breathing heavily and terrified, sweating, eyes popping out, wringing her hands—scarred, blistered hands. Amy sensed her panic, and danger. Her blood pressure was falling, her breathing was labored, and a quick exam showed that the two babies were in a lot of distress.

"She needs a C-section, right away," she said to Alice, and repeated it in Spanish to Cristina, who nodded. "Royal, get her back in the truck and go to Emergency. I'll meet you there."

They left. She called Leatrice Shumpsky.

"I've just sent a pregnant patient to you, and I'm on my way in. I need to do a *stat* C-section, twins, eighteen-year-old mom, no prenatal care. Obese. Illegal immigrant, no insurance. Spanish-speaking, little English."

"Hmm. Any *other* KK rules you'll be breaking?"

"I'll try to find a few more by the time I get there—less than five minutes."

"Done."

"Oh, hey, what about the anesthetist?"

"There is no anesthetist."

"What? There *has* to be an—"

"She quit last night. I'll try to find somebody."

On the way, Amy felt a sharp hit of risk, a good sign, saying to herself: *If there's one thing I know how to do, it's this. Emergencies bring out the best in us, it's what we docs do—and even crave. We're the ones who run toward the danger.*

When she got there, she met the anesthetist: Natasha the Tolstoy reader from the executive floor up under the helicopter bull's-eye.

"You?" Amy said, startled. She'd never seen her outside her domain.

"I used to be in anesthesia. And I'm glad to help. Let's do this."

It was a boy and a girl, both okay, and the mother too. From open to close, 20 minutes.

And the clavicles of Alice's baby had healed just fine.

———

After the Berry "intervention" with Roy and the group at his house, the team decided to have a recurring meeting to stay connected. The only way to keep it going was to do it at work in the emergency conference room—much like the Fat Man had done in Man's 4th Best Hospital, calling it "the Check-in." Fats described the agenda as going around the table to share what's up in your life, and then, briefly, problems with patients, staff, or screens. Roy had put "The Fat Man's Guidelines" on the chalkboard:

1) Your life outside medicine.
2) Your life inside medicine.
3) Your part in medicine in the world.

Amy scheduled the meeting for 20 to 30 minutes first thing in the morning. They went around the table to hear about anything pressing—both bad and good. Anything *except* patient care, which was done at change-of-shift. Hyper, Roy, Eat My Dust, and Sev knew from Man's 4th how valuable even a short meeting could be in dealing with work and life, and spread their enthusiasm to Amy, Shump, and Binni. Even the growling Eat My Dust seemed to be okay with it—letting the others know by looking like it was not okay. Since it had started, shortly after the meeting about Roy four weeks earlier, all of them had been surprised at how much they had come to value it.

At Roy's house Berry had told them, "Connection comes first. Think about the first meeting you have with a patient. If you're connected, you'll hear everything, the whole story; and if not, not. Good connection is good medicine."

It had been a treacherous, up-and-down month with Roy—and for them trying to help him. In the hardest times—like when he had to be physically escorted out of the emergency room because he was getting triggered back into the despair and anger—each of the team helped. He was so beloved by most of them that walking him out from hell toward sanity had become the second purpose to their lives. And the first purpose? Staying alive themselves.

As Berry had said, "Roy, without knowing it, has been grieving all the Covid deaths, all the suffering. We have to do our part to bring him back to where he can feel the deaths without rage, and the sadness without wanting to kill himself. To hold rage and sadness *without trying to run from it*, until we all find the softening touch of sorrow. Healing."

Amy worked with Berry to keep in view the crucial action for the team: "We have to make an effort to be with him, each in our turn, all the time, to start with. He's grieving for us all."

Sev had created and monitored a schedule on their individual phones, except Roy's. At first someone had to be with him at all times. At home, Berry and Hooper were on watch.

After that first meeting, Hooper had moved into the fully

furnished carriage house behind Roy's big house. His goals? Weight loss and fitness.

He offered to be Roy's "food and exercise trainer," to get him back in shape in body and mind, "the Hyper Way."

The key, in Hyper's mind, was a system he had perfected as professor in whole health at UCLA. At its core was exercise on various brand-new machines, and a diet high in pomegranate shakes, low in carbohydrates—which led Roy to a grand diuresis, up at night for a week peeing, and losing weight fast.

Hyper's mantra: "No carbs, no craving. No craving, a life."

Gradually, Roy felt better. Not only because of fitness and a sense of lightness, but also because of the incredible "coach" that Hyper was. Any and all resistance from Roy was neutralized by Hyper's unstinting belief that Roy would "win."

And when Roy tried to escape the regimen, Hyper would say, "Listen up. Carbos cause craving. No carbos, no craving. No craving, y'got a life."

And he did.

————

He started to come back to work, first on half days and easy cases, gradually working toward the hellish. The red line would be if he got into fights again with patients. A few times he came close, but he never stepped over.

Now he was back to a normal workload. After he'd checked in, Amy asked him, "How have you survived the reentry?"

"First, Hyper's shakes and, well, his love."

Hyper beamed.

"And I used my, well, call them *encounters* with the Fat Man, as if he were still really here, with me, and with all of us. The weirdest thing was that it was mutual—last night, when I saw him floating up near the carriage house cupola, he said, 'Even a Fat Man can fast on Yom Kippur. Basch, I'm *fine. You're* fine. Berry's got it right, we made it to mutual. So you go for it, okay?'" Sheepishly, Roy said, "I said I would."

"What you did in the last few days was great," Amy said, "to figure out what was going on with that woman? Saved her life. Tell the team."

"Thirty-four-year-old woman with a house out in Red Rock. Came in on the weekend with a fever of a hundred and five, oxygen eighty and dropping, bad chest X-ray. Looked like Covid, intubation. But I knew Red Rock well, and even when I was in high school I knew it was 'tick heaven.' I got all the tick assays *stat*, and luckily the next day she came back positive for babesia—she had babesiosis! Started her on antibiotics, and they worked."

"Babesiosis?" Hyper said. "Never heard of it."

"Nobody has, except this nerd in the lab. Luckily we here in Kinderhook County have the most tick disease in the USA—they went wild to diagnose this one, their first. It's really rare."

"It's the hardest thing we do right now," Amy said. "In the pandemic it's been Covid Covid Covid, and then someone throws in a tick and unless we keep alert, people die. Great save, Roy!" She smiled broadly. "Glad you're back." She looked around the table. "How 'bout it?"

Applause and whoops.

"Next," said Amy.

"I shall go next," said Binni. "In this lull we have made strong progress in our research. I just got the okay from the Food and Drug Administration to go into 'compassion' usage to infuse our biologic— isolated from human bone marrow mesenchymal stem cell or stromal cell—which we grow in culture. It provides bioactive signals that have been shown to modulate inflammation and direct cellular communications." He smiled, rolling his head. "And so as of this morning we can *use it on anyone in APD*"—acute pulmonary distress—"mainly Covid, and—"

"What?!" Hooper said. "FDA approval?! Holy shit!"

Everyone cheered. He'd rarely talked about his research, and now he'd solved Covid? Who knew?

"Yes, yes, I and the team are quite excited. It will help people, especially in rather hopeless cases. And it is ready, *now*! Our company is called ExoFlo, and we can now legally try it right here on Covid-19 patients who are not responding favorably to standard care."

"Dying patients?" Amy asked.

"Yes. Especially APD syndrome. Each of you, please use your judgment. There are no side effects, so we're way ahead of all the other drugs. Try our parenchymal stem cell infusion as a first treatment. And so please contact me for—"

Crackling in the intercom. And then, there it was: the Voice. All over America, through KK intercoms came the Voice. In calm, strong, even *caring* tones he talked, seeming to talk to each of us individually, and also sent in text to all our phones and e-mails:

"Well, stakeholders, Jason Kush your CEO here! We got through the Labor Day weekend, with banner doctoring, nursing, and Kush Kare care. In appreciation for your good and hard work, we are offering new ancient ways to get that darn tightness out of our bodies and minds. Studies from The World's Second-Best Business School show that wellness brings fiscal returns. Starting today, as part of our Wellness Program, we are offering *free* daily video yoga sessions—a surefire relaxer at all Kush Kare sites. Once per day on all your screens you can participate. Each day has a unique 'taste' of yoga: Monday through Friday, the titles are Yoga for Humor, Yoga for Finance, Yoga for Rage, Yoga for Yoga, Yoga for Pets. Be well, and keep caring." Gone.

Everybody looked at everybody. Giggles broke out. A few curses.

Shaking his head, Binni said, "Okay, just remember to try stem cells from ExoFlo. Deal?"

More whoops of congratulations.

Amy looked at her watch. "Okay, anybody else?" She looked pointedly at Eat My Dust Eddie, who was sitting with his jaw clenched. Finally he said, "You don't want to hear this. Let's go." He started to get up, but the others shouted him down.

"We want to hear, Eddie," said Amy. "Honest."

"Okay. I've had it. I mean I really have *had* it. You all know I got kind of, well, *entranced* by the basket weavers out past Copake Falls, around a lake called Little Bash Bish, in the Taconic Mountains. Native Americans. Their patriarch, Mike Fiddler, has been my patient?"

Nods.

"You might remember a while ago when I was talking to him on the phone—trying to keep him away from treatment in hospital, because of Covid? He had mixed up his heart meds for his asthma meds and thought he was dying. After I straightened him out, he invited me to come meet their tribe. So I've been going out there spending time with him and the tribe whenever I can. They've got houses, appliances, all the modern stuff. But they've been there forever, have their own language. In this world, something pure— imagine? Make their money selling incredible reed baskets—they have an art dealer in Soho. These people, well, they're real, no bullshitology. *Good* people. The last thing they need is a case of Covid! I'm helping 'em be real careful."

He paused, looked around.

"Y'think I've gone crazy, right?" He smiled. "A basket case?"

Laughter all around, and relief.

"But it's really getting to me lately, being with them, and then coming in here and being with some of the people we have to deal with. Talk about culture shock—to all *this*?" He shook his head in wonder, and sadness. "I've been really careful with them, decontaminating before showing up there, wearing a mask always, social distancing. "And guess what? If you can believe it, I got *them* all to wear masks, imagine that? That's the trust, and openness we have." He nodded. "So I've had it. I really have had it!"

"You can't quit, Eddie," said Amy. "Please don't—"

"Quit?" he snapped. "What are you talking about? The Eddie does not quit. And at my age, I've finally got my first case of good luck." He paused. "All of us are flat out. Ripped apart. When we leave here each day we leave all the energy we have, taking care of patients, and each other. Drained, right?" Nods all around. "And now in this second wave, getting less and less support in here, we're really getting killed by one thing: *the goddamn idiots among the Columbians who are not doing the one true thing they can do to help—masks. They will not wear masks*—am I right? Am I?" He shook his head in dismay. "So right now we're way over three hundred thousand deaths in the US. Americans have stopped pretending to follow the guidelines—no masks, no distance. With the blessing of the President. The basketmakers have opened my eyes. It's time for me as a doc who's on the front line of this war against Covid—and getting abused—to get on the 'net and tell them in detail what I and we are seeing here every single day, and how a million more will die because of them not doing the simplest thing in the world: *wearing a mask*." He nodded. "So I'm thinking of going public. On Facebook. A nice note, on Facebook."

Amy sat there stunned, grateful for his just plain humanity—and bravery. She looked around. All were asking themselves, *Should I offer to join him? Should we do it as a group? Eddie, of course, would never ask anyone to join him. It wasn't Eddie's way.*

"You'll get killed," said Shump, finally. "You'll get it in the neck! People on the internet are crazy, violent. You're a public figure—they can walk in here and shoot you. It's not uncommon, now, doctors getting shot in hospitals, right?"

"But it's not just about you, Eddie," Hyper said, "we'll *all* get it in the neck. It's the Nazis all over again: 'You kill one of us, and we'll kill *all* of you,' okay?"

"Eddie, you're amazing," said Roy. "We stuck together in the House—I, you, Hooper, and Sev—and Berry. And it worked! We helped get the laws on the books for limiting on-call hours to eighty a week! We'll stick with you—behind the scenes. Right?" He glanced up, and around, as if hoping that the Fat Man had heard it.

Roy went on. "We made it easier for the ones who came after us. Now they have a life."

"We nurses know a lot about trying to keep this all human," said Shump. "For us, for patients, docs, and others. When we take action, we almost never lose. We're with you."

"But, Eddie," Amy said, "it's getting dangerous now with the crazies online. Do you have any idea how you'll get smashed?"

"No."

"I hate to think," Amy said. "It's too risky for me, as leader. But I'll stand with you."

"Eddie, please listen," said Hyper. "They'll kill you. They're crazy and have guns and could *really* kill you. Think of us, and your family. And what we're trying to do here. Don't do it."

Eddie nodded slowly. Finally he blushed red. "I love you all."

———

At the end of the day—early for once, only six o'clock—Amy was with Shump in the on-call room checking on everything before she left.

Earlier, her post-Cesarean visit on the ward to examine Cristina and the twins was happy; as she said, "The happiest moment of my life." The fact that she was an undocumented Black single mother meant a life of scrabbling to stay alive. But she already had a great, experienced friend, Clavicle Mom.

That night Amy and Binni had planned a twosome celebration dinner at his condo. They would be ordering in—*again!*—from Big India Restaurant, a hole-in-the-wall that had taken the site of Whale City Pizza. Big India did basic Indian cuisine they loved. Amid the crazed and tentative and fractured Covid time, it was *reliable.* Day in, day out, seven days a week, good hot fresh food, specializing in dynamite tandoori in a real clay tandoor. Baingan bharta and palak paneer, and popadams were so just plain spiced-up and *there*, they blunted the taste of death and disease and heartache they'd just come from. She couldn't wait.

The day's meeting had been a rare high. Roy was finally back. Now before heading home Shump and Amy were in a rare loose, happy mood, about to celebrate with a bottle of good wine from a grateful family.

"Don't get mad at this," Amy said to Shump, "but right now I feel happy."

"Me too. Catch it while you can."

"I mean to see Roy back—our somehow getting him back here in one piece—the closeness today between all of us, seeing Eddie open up with—what?"

"Kindness!" said Shump.

"Yes! To feel this closeness? After what? *Eight months?* Think about it—harsh, stupid, KK shit," Amy said, "but we're all still here!"

"Unless this is heaven," said Shump.

Knocks at the door.

"Enter to grow in wisdom!" Amy called out.

Two men entered. They both wore oversized phony gold badges shouting KK MEDICAL SAFETY AND SECURITY. One they loathed. In a dark suit and regimental red tie, he was the tall, thin, baby-faced man with a face so narrow it was as if he'd got someone so enraged that they'd crushed it from both sides so that looking at him straight on, he seemed giraffish. His slicked-down black hair was a tar field, his part a white pipe. His badge reminded Amy and Shump that here was Kenneth S. Miller Jr.—but with a promotion. He looked like he'd been starved half to death.

The other man, Butchy Lee Ervin, was Black, tall, and wide, in a KK police-knockoff uniform. His white-speckled hair showed he was at least two generations older than Kenneth. He had a solid, commanding, and calm presence, a round face with a slight sense in the lips of a smile, and kind brown eyes. Everybody at KK knew him and liked him. He had helped them out on just about everything they had asked for, all through the long Covid months.

Kenneth read from his notes. "Dr. Rose, as you know I am Safety and Security. This is Butchy Lee Ervin, also Security. You have—"

"Hey, Butchie!" cried Amy. "OMG—welcome again to our turf."

"Thanks, Amy. 'Lo, Shump. Is that basketball star of yours still working out during Covid, even with no games around?"

"It's the only thing keeping him going! Six-one, and the other day he dunked!"

"Jesus!"

"Excuse me," Kenneth said, "I have serious business here."

"And how *you* doin', Butchie?" Amy asked.

"Oh, y'know, a day late and a dollar short. But whenever I see you two, I'm lifted up—"

"Let's get down to business," said Kenneth. He took out his cell. "You, Dr. Rose, have *two* serious breaches *in the same day*! Number One Violation, 374.9P: the KK total ban on obstetrics, including deliveries. Number Two Violation, 2007.7D: allowed daughter to see mother in Intensive Care before she was placed on a ventilator, knowing that the only permitted visits, including of kin, are at death. Arranged in advance. Insecure and dangerous. Very punishable. What do you say?"

"You said *two* protocol breaches, but that's wrong. How did you count them?"

"Obvious. One woman birthing, one woman visiting not before death. Two. Women."

"But from my recent reading of the manual," Amy said, "*each person* is counted as one breach."

"Correct. The mother birthing is one. The non-deathbed visit of the daughter is two."

"I think you're going easy on me, Ken-*neth*. Listen carefully. If there's a mother birthing, then there is a *baby*. Total of two human beings, right? Two breaches *right there!*"

"Okay then, the total is three."

"Nope. You missed something, Kenneth."

"No, I did not."

"Did you know that there were *twins?*"

Kenneth's jaw dropped. He popped it back up. He did not answer.

"Hey hey hey!" said Shump. "You're making it all the way up to *four*! Nice goin'!"

"And," Amy said, "two crucial matters to make sure I'm not at odds with Security—and I *want* to be secure, okay?"

Kenneth didn't say okay.

"So!" Amy went on. "I read in the large KK Security Manual, not your little condensed version, that if there are four breaches by the same doctor in one day it's a federal offense, correct?" No response. "I mean, Kenneth, how do I know my offenses, if I don't know *how* I was insecure?"

Everyone but Kenneth was having a hard time not bursting out laughing. They waited.

Kenneth's eyes in that narrow face narrowed. "I know what you're doing and it won't—"

"Hey hey," said Roy in the doorway, "is that my great old pal Butchy Lee?!"

"Roy! Hot damn! How y'been, buddy?"

Kenneth looked like a hot geyser was about to lift the top of his head off. He turned red.

Amy worried that he might burst, and hoped so. "Hey, I got an idea, a proposal that can straighten this thing right out. How we can reach a consensus?" He nodded. "If you can *put the two babies back into her uterus*, we'll call it even. Okay?"

Everyone looked at Kenneth. He snapped shut his laptop and rushed out of the room.

"Well," said Butchy Lee, "gotta go. Man, I miss you, Roy. How 'bout we have a coffee sometime, outside this"—he looked around, whispered—"bullshit hospital?" And left.

Feeling pretty good as they walked through the emergency rooms, Amy and Shump caught up with Sev, also leaving for the day. He was scuffling his feet, as if he had no more lift in him. The little mathematician looked like he had been shot out of a cannon and was now totally wiped out. He said to Leatrice, "How long have you been working here in Emergency?"

"Ages," she said. "Many many years."

"You like it?"

"Love it. Wouldn't work anywhere else."

"But . . . but . . ." He tugged his beard. "But it's a kind of hell, isn't it? Seeing the worst? Facing the anger?"

"You bet."

"*Nu?*" he asked, and was met by her look of bafflement. "In Yiddish it means, 'so, explain.'"

"It's simple, really. By the time they've been waiting to see me—maybe an hour or two or more—they're angry, and when I finally call their name they scream at me, 'Fuck you!'"

She looked at Amy and smiled. "And then, if I help them, on the way out they give me a hug."

13

"You're the whale, Dad, okay?"

"Okay."

"And, Mom, you're in the whale-watching boat with me."

"Got it."

On a calm, clear afternoon, Eleanor stood on the edge of the back lawn, holding what looked like a large silvery insect with four feet and four propellers for wings.

"I'm with Hector in our little boat off the Pacific coast of Ecuador, in the Galápagos. I have to keep the drone steady above the whale and her newborn babies. I'm going to fly it out over one of the whales, get my video, and then my assistant is going to fire the crossbow probe into the whale from the boat to get our specimen. Got it?"

Two "got its."

"But doesn't it hurt the whale?" Miranda said.

"Nope. It's like a little pinprick in all that blubber. And then, the hardest thing, and there's no room for error, I have to land the drone safely back onto our boat in a thirty-by-twenty-five-inch landing spot—I'm using that cardboard box over there to practice. The Pacific is rough down there, rising and falling with a significant swell, okay? It is *very* delicate work."

"I thought you were an expert already," Orville said.

"I'm going on to these advanced moves, pretending there are different winds."

"And you're sure that the probe doesn't hurt the whale?" Miranda said.

"Nope. It's just a tiny prick, to get a sample of tissue. It's the only way we can measure the corticosteroids, to find out what stresses the whales are under. We do *not* want to land an expensive drone in the ocean. So first I'll do some runs just to put it down on the stationary box, and then, when I think I've got it, I'll want you, Dad, to leave the whale and carry the box around, and up and down like you're on a boat, okay?"

"Okay!"

With a sudden *whirrr,* up went the drone—its four propellers and several gyroscopes attuning it to the slightest nudge of Ellie's command, rising fast over the towering oaks, and then moving this way and that to mimic chasing the whales. It was a series of quick turns and static hoverings—during which Ellie cried out, "Okay, here comes the harpoon!" And then, as smooth as a small wave it came back down and, with remarkable delicacy and precision, landed in the center of the cardboard box.

Three cheers. To Miranda and Orvy it was astonishing.

It's a perfect fit, Orvy said to himself, *Ellie working with animals in a way that puts her in control, for the unquestionable good, of protecting the whales and their babies at the yearly breeding—with the hope that Ellie had often talked about, of making humans appreciate and protect animals. How fitting,* he thought, *that this little drone which had ruthlessly killed so many of our "enemies"—whole families in Afghanistan gone in a sudden puff!—can do something good in the world.*

The threesome did several more flights, with remarkably increasing difficulty, up and down, zipping fast in and out of the trees, down and up, as far away as she could get—a perfect learning curve—ending with Orville picking up the empty cardboard box and walking along with it as if it were in the small boat riding the waves, so that Ellie had to gauge the movement and make a safe landing.

"The one thing I don't want to do," Ellie said, "is land it in the water."

"What happens then?" Miranda asked.

"A thousand dollars charged to your credit card, and no PhD for me."

This was the final hurdle. Since she'd been home, she'd finished two hurdles: first her comp exams, and a few weeks ago a presentation of her final fieldwork. All three of her professors were high on the project to find out how to make the whales and the humans able to coexist, to the benefit of both. She hoped that her publications would move other countries to regulate the whale-watching boats and pay the fishermen who run them.

In the practice with the drone, there were no screwups. With high hopes and a sense that they had all contributed as a family to make this work, they went in to start dinner, feeling high.

———————

But dinners had become, over all these months, a trial. Each of the three had a particular food regimen. They were now six months trapped inside the house, with pandemic danger all around. Six whole months of repetitive life. Trying to feel alive, and even "new," in the boredom. Each of the three prepared their (mostly) separate dinners. The kitchen had been remodeled years before. But to Ellie it seemed badly organized, especially in terms of utensils and labor-saving items. And so ever since she'd been home her mission had been to "bring it up to speed" by ordering the hell out of every new pot or pan or utensil or special easy-open glass (not plastic) tub for leftovers. This was a tough standard for older parents. Worse, with each new arrival, Orvy, Miranda, and even Amy had trouble finding things, because of Ellie's reorganization of the cabinets. Not to mention composting—easy for food, but the two other bin categories, which were not easily decipherable, recyclables versus trash.

Eleanor was the Climate Police. The rest of the family's goodwill was no match for Ellie's saving the planet. And there was no arguing with her—who, aside from lunatics, could possibly *want* global warming?

Thus, dinner preparation was always tense, filled with land mines, and with shotgun crashes of pots and pans and drawer slams and, often, shouts. Each of the four of them—Ellie, Roy, Miranda, and Ben—had special food management. Amy, from all her travels throughout the world, and the fact that she rarely made dinner with them, was easy. Orville and Miranda, during the first few months of Ellie's kitchen "upgrade," had been hit hard.

All of them had been trained, and often traumatized, by their family-of-origin meals. Orville was especially vulnerable. His mother had been an expert at banging pots and pans, screaming, burning meat, and—having grown up in the Depression—keeping an Amana refrigerator so full of food that you could not shove a toothpick into it. Ellie also liked a stuffed fridge. And so now, again, Orvy was phobic to open the refrigerator door.

His solution? Grilling. He got a top-of-the-line Weber gas grill set out under the high Victorian roof and higher sky, for all-weather grilling. Now, at every dinnertime, he could hear from the kitchen, much muted, the bashing and clashing from Eleanor and Miranda.

Ellie followed a strict vegan menu—no meat or fish or other vaguely live creatures, no egg or dairy, but plenty of sugar, while Miranda full-throatedly embraced meat and fish and egg and dairy and all vegetables, avoiding only carbs. Orvy was on a no-red-meat and low-salt, low-carb diet, with a mordant fear of fresh vegetables. Ben was food cool.

The issue was not getting the food. Ellie had been a genius in organizing regular deliveries not just for each of their disparate food preferences, but—God bless her—for Peet's coffee: French decaf for Orvy, and Italian for Miranda, in sufficient quantity to finish her tome on Columbia's one local hero, General Worth. He was famous for breakages in his character that ended a dazzling career in the holocaust of the Indian Wars. His name remains to this day in Fort Worth and Lake Worth.

The only other major difference was in what shows they could watch "as a family." There was really only one that they all enjoyed: Stephen Colbert, broadcasting from a closet-like room, maybe in his apartment.

Lately Ellie had been secluding herself more—working on her thesis, trying to get back to the Galápagos to finish her research, and teaching at Duke: virtual classes in biology and ethics and animal behavior. When she did come out of her room she was often tight as a drum, her targets being Orvy and Miranda, and the rest of the world. As the months of Covid isolation went on, her flights of raw anger had become more fraught. The last few days were all eruptions. And so they did what they'd always done with much success—a family meeting after dinner, phones put away.

One of her best traits—in addition to making sure "that you two don't die"—was her compulsion to keep the house neat. She always washed and dried the dishes fast and furious, so that you never found a speck of food or dirt. But she criticized them a lot and severely, as if she herself was both the Earth and its climate. For instance, of using plastic sponges instead of silicone sponges: "Silicone doesn't add to the nondegradable plastic." In all the months so far, she'd held to her convictions, and almost on a weekly Amazon basis, yet another "clean" climate changer would arrive. But she was judicious. When she found out that cleaning the dishes by hand in the sink used more water than a dishwasher, she switched. But then she found out that "this old dishwasher is not working at its max. Plates and utensils come out dirty. I'll see if I can fix it."

The next morning they came down for breakfast and saw her on the floor with the dishwasher in pieces. By noon it had been reassembled and passed its test. Another bright shining moment for Ellie? She had found Orvy's Cuisinart blender, a French relic from the late '70s that was the first real restaurant machine sold to non-chefs— and it still worked! Ellie and Cuisinart had an ongoing love affair, which benefited all: every day she made a special shake of fruit, protein, and who knows what other healthy ingredients and shared it with Miranda and Orvy. And it was dynamite. A little gritty with the mulched seeds, but explosive, nonetheless.

So before the meeting began, she first washed the dishes, declining their offers to help. While each of the three had grown more isolated, connecting to the outside world only through Zooms and phones, Ellie was suffering the most. In her little trapped family, she was more so.

And so after the crashing and bashing sounds of dinner cleanup had echoed off, Ellie had filled the dishwasher and cleaned the long cherrywood table that could be extended to seat 12 but hadn't done so for six months. Cleaning it was a bright spot in yet another dull and scary day living with Covid. The mere three of them heightened a sense of loneliness, the table orphaned. Now, all three "I"-phones had been deposited in the inlaid wooden box Orvy had gotten in the Grand Souk of Marrakech half a century ago. The meeting was going to start. Their food, tailored tightly for each, was making its way down the long and twisting journey of absorption. All of them held a glimmer of this being something new. And even if bad, a *new* bad.

"I try not to say anything," Ellie said to Miranda, "but, well, one problem I have is about how you never close things, okay?"

"What things?"

"The refrigerator door, the stove door—any door, in fact, like the front door—and the tops on every kind of bottle and package, not to mention lights—I don't think I've *ever* seen you click off a light, except maybe when you go to sleep. I keep on having to walk around the house and turn off things, close things."

"Why does it bother you?"

"I don't know, just my neat-freak streak, I guess? But also it's wasteful, electricity and all."

Miranda nodded, took a deep breath. "I never really noticed it," she said. "Thanks, dear. I'll try harder to turn things off, okay? I guess I'm a person who likes to open things up, not close them down. Maybe it comes from being a historian. You have to be open to whatever comes up. You know, when I used to teach history, I'd ask the class to write down what the weather was outside today. I'd collect their answers—they'd all say the same thing, versions of, say, 'It was a beautiful sunny day.' And then I'd read mine: 'It poured cats and dogs all day.' And then I'd say, '*This* is the one that will survive. The false weave of "true" history.'"

"Cool! I mean it's not a really real big deal, but everything in energy and climate helps."

"Agree completely," she said. "The only way we're going to make any progress is to stick together, on everything."

"We'll all try to do better," Orvy said. "You know, El, we're really trying to get with the program on climate change. We really are."

"I know."

"And the only way to get there," Miranda said, "is we all have to do it *together*."

"I don't know about that," Ellie said. "We can't rely on other people, we've each got to just do it ourselves."

"What about all the millions of people who are like you, dedicated to working together?"

"People are selfish."

"In the long run," Miranda quoted, "the arc of the moral universe is long, but it bends toward justice. Violence only gets violence, hatred only hatred, okay?"

"Yeah, *ideally*," Ellie said, "I give it a reluctant 'maybe.' But you'd be surprised how many of my friends agree. I hate to tell you guys, but my generation's full of a lot of selfish people."

"You can't do it alone," said Miranda.

"That's my point! Welcome to my generation! You don't know my generation! Yesterday someone posted a review on Yelp of Old Faithful, trashing it and Yellowstone—trashing the national *park*! And these are the people who will work *together*?"

"Which means," Orvy said, "to get the ones that aren't like that to join—"

"Why d'you think I'm killing myself for animals, for whales? I mean these poor animals! Today's headline in the *Crier*? A woman tried to saw off her dog's head with a sword! Why do you think I'm with the animals?"

Roy and Miranda looked at each other.

"You *do* know," Miranda said, "that we're really glad, and proud, that you're working so closely with animals. It's a real gift. I'm reading a book by a Black woman ethicist focusing on animals. She says Black people look at this from a different angle, to share with them the oppression by 'the great white hunters,' and to stand with them, and in that way honor them."

Ellie looked up, eyes wide, shaking her head in dismay. "My opinion, having worked with animals all over the world now—let's not forget a month on a tiny deserted Australian island studying miniature penguins—is that's a really sentimental way to view animals, hunted or not. They're *animals*, okay? What she's saying is her opinion, and so be it. Just an opinion. I've got my own opinion—based on years, now, of working with animals all over creation." She looked down at the table.

Silence. Orville and Miranda looked at each other. She nodded to him to say something.

"And so, Ellie, I guess you don't want to listen? You'd rather just have your own opinion?"

"Sort of."

"And on this, you'll stick with your *opinion* of your opinion, right?"

A slight smile. A glance up at Orvy. "Yeah."

"Hon," he went on, "it's really hard now, for all of us. This isolation, not being with friends in person."

"Yeah. Real hard. I love my friends, but Zoom's not the same."

"Yes, honey," Miranda said. "I agree. It's harder to make real contact."

"I wish I lived in a time without social media. I really mean it! Online everybody's trying to make a mark. I mean when we were kids in soccer everybody got a trophy. I'm talking about the ivory tower kids—I can't talk about the poor and all that. But for my generation, now grown up, we have no easy way to get praised. The competition is fierce. What's success now? Online and TV. All the time having to be better and better, fighting against others to *get* that trophy. Everyone trying to be famous. And we're setting the stage for the next generation! They're even worse."

She looked at Orvy, then Miranda.

"Now we are trying to identify ourselves against all the noise of the others, trying to make our mark. And of course some of us are great. Greta, Malala, the Parkland massacre kids—finally a time for women! Thank God! All of us others have five minutes of fame and attention. Doing it all in pixels online—you kind of have to be a sociopath. And the new generation is worse! All this spam that clogs everything important is that next generation trying to get out there and be noticed in the chaos. I try to date, right? One guy's profile said 'animal lover.' Turned out he didn't love animals at all, but was focused from when he was fourteen on quote 'curating my brand.'"

"No!" Orvy said.

"Yeah. Y'think I've got it easy right now? You want me happy and cheery, instead of monstrous?"

"You know we don't see you that way," Miranda and Orvy said, almost together.

"Yeah." She seemed to blush, turn away. "But you're right, I'm not doing all that well with people . . ."

"Of course not, honey," Miranda said. "How could you, stuck in here and—"

"Don't be *nice. The reality isn't nice.* It's more or less how my life's been going in North Carolina. Except for my friends and going hiking, camping. But I haven't met any possible guys for ages."

"What about that PhD candidate in your program?"

"He was okay. At least he earned himself two clicks—but he's basically gone."

"Two clicks?" Orvy asked.

"Like on your computer, you have to click twice to open an icon up, right? In this case, with the guy, it was difficult to connect. He was at the University of Exeter, in England, for postdoc. On monkeys."

"But you really have worked on trying to maintain friendships?" Orvy asked.

"Sort of, yeah. You both are pretty good at it, so I did learn something from you the first eighteen years. And to tell the truth, I know kind of how to fake empathy for someone else, but I don't really *like* to go after people, ask them about their inner world, and then, usually getting their story of woe, and even of, well, triumph. Both of those make me feel even more inept. I can give practical advice—I'm good at practical advice—but I don't really like doing it. Most of my friends think I'm a big help to them. And, in a way, I am. But it's not, well, fun. I *hate* the idea of going"—she snapped her fingers in rapid succession in a way that was, in Orville's hearing aid, incredibly loud and jagged, like an old power switch, *snap snap snap!*—"'Oh, tell me more'" *snap!* "or 'Maybe you're depressed?'" *snap!* "I'm good at faking it, and I keep a kind of fence around my own emotions. I don't risk things. I'm sure you noticed. I don't want to go into another person's swamp! Not that I *like* being that way, but that's me. I don't like to explore *their* crap! It burdens me even more. I hate to say it, guys, but I'm dying to get back to the Galápagos. Ecuador can't open up soon enough!"

She fell silent. Ben got up and walked around the table to each, clearly having picked up the tension, and the hurt, determined to help them out of it. He sat next to Ellie, eyes on her.

"Do you ever ask questions?" Orvy asked.

"What?" she seemed startled.

"Questions? Forgive me, hon, but I just wonder if you're missing something?"

Ellie stopped, eyes widened, then blinked. "What do you mean?"

"Maybe that you're missing something by not asking?"

She seemed stunned, and turned red in the face—had they ever seen her red-faced?

"You don't understand," she said, although not with real conviction. "My life is going nowhere. *I'm* going nowhere. I've got no one. I can't even get a boyfriend, and I'm going to *solve the climate*? My life is nowhere, I'm nowhere and . . . *and no one can help.*" She got up. "*Especially not you!*" And stormed out.

Orville and Miranda stared at each other. Ben got up on all fours and stood there, nose at table level, big bloodshot eyes looking back and forth between them, and then looking at the doorway where Ellie had just disappeared.

"Poor kid!" Miranda said.

"Breaks my heart."

Ben was still listening carefully, awaiting, if not an explanation, his orders.

"Ben, go to Ellie."

Solemnly, he padded out.

———

Exhausted and happy, Amy climbed slowly up the three flights and opened the door to her haven above her small family.

She and Binni had been so wiped out by their workday—and even by the excitement of FDA approval, which would require even more work to roll out—that after arriving at his condo and decontaminating, they only had the strength to order from Big India. The FDA approval was opening, for the first time in his life, a path that might well end the scrabbling for money to cover his huge med school debt and also for his two alimonies.

Opening her door, Amy paused, and smiled. To celebrate, Binni had surprised her by taking out of the refrigerator a chilled bottle nestling inside a hand-painted box. "A top champagne. Louis Roederer / Philippe Starck. The best that Columbia carries!" With great panache he uncorked it and hurriedly poured it into two crystal glasses. But instead of a healthy "pop" and a gush into the glasses, there were no bubbles. They stared at it. He was crestfallen. Breakage! Amy suggested they drink it without the bubbles. They did. It was good.

Soon the booze was diffused through both their blood volumes, and they got giggly as youngsters who didn't face each day sure of death and sorrow. Just in time, the pizza arrived—a kind of giant naan carrying sharp spices: turmeric, cumin, palak paneer cheese, and a tandoor tang. They sat out on the small balcony overlooking the Hudson and the shadowy Catskills—always seeming at first sight grander in height than they truly were. Binni was as happy as Amy'd ever seen him, and it was infectious, at first joking and then sobering, opening up, risking.

"Dear one," Binni said, "you make me so happy. When at work, and at my last wits, and I see you coming along a corridor toward me, I feel a bounce in my heart. A real bounce!" He laughed. "Sometimes it is so bouncy I take a beta blocker, if I have to get back to work!"

"You're joking?!"

"No. Seeing you—especially when you just drop by and say 'Hello, Binni'—I love your voice!"

She smiled. "Yes, yes, that 'zing' goes all over me too. In all this . . . the work . . . you keep me going, every time I see you." She paused, and then said, "I love you."

He blinked, and then smiled. "I love you too."

Their parting had been a kind of watershed. Their hug good-bye was less erotic than just plain happy.

Driving home, she felt something new, something else. *What was it? A future together.*

Now, all Amy wanted to do was take off her clothes, set her alarm, and tumble into bed.

But before she could undress there was a knock on the door, and a deep-voiced "Ruff!"

There stood Ellie and Ben. Both seemed upset. Before Amy could say anything, Ellie ran into her and hugged her, crying. Startled, Amy held her as her body shook. After a few long moments, Ellie pulled back.

"I'm sorry, I know you need your sleep, but—"

"C'mon in. What's up?"

"A terrible meeting with Mom and Dad."

Ellie took a few steps, but then turned to Ben. He had twisted his huge head a little on its side, as if wondering if he had now done his love-duty to help—delivering Ellie to another good human—and so could go now.

"It's okay, Ben," said Ellie. "You can go. Thanks."

It almost seemed to both of them, standing there, that Ben

nodded, but maybe not. He clomped carefully down the old winding stairs.

"I wish I were Ben," said Ellie.

"Me too. But it's a hard wish to have granted, right?"

"Yeah, especially if you don't know who to ask."

"Want something to eat?" Amy asked. "Drink?"

"Something alcoholic?"

Amy glanced at her. Ellie rarely touched alcohol. She didn't like her mind getting fuzzy. "Let's not go down that route yet," she said. "What's up?"

"Family meeting. Mom, mostly, and Dad. It was terrible. I lost it. Got furious. Stormed out."

"Sorry to hear that. I know what those things are like. There are better ways to deal with your mom."

"You're right," Ellie said. "That's why I'm here. Pellegrino?"

"Good. It's so hot up here, how 'bout we go up on the roof to talk?"

"Deal."

The Columbia County weatherman had forecasted cold pouring rain all night, ending in the morning.

When Amy opened the trapdoor in the roof and looked around, the sky was diamond-clear and the stars were sparkling and Venus seemed to have grown up—the dark was studded with constellations. The air still held the warmth of the sunny day, and the tin of the roof was warm under their butts.

"What's up?" Amy asked.

"What isn't. It's Mom, but it's really me. I'm a horrible daughter."

"Anything in particular?"

"I was nasty. All I wanted to really do was be okay with them, and not get angry. But I blew up and ran out. They're old, and anything can happen, and it's a real small family, just me and them and you and Cray on Zoom." She squinched her face up tight, shaking her head. "I feel horrible."

"I know what it's like. I treated my parents terribly. Orvy was my savior for a long time, and then, when I could, I headed west, all the way to Stanford. Then I ran all over the world. But here I am. Go figure."

"I can't seem to be just, I don't know, *kind*? Not even like *kind of* kind? And the blowup was so stupid!"

"What was it about?"

"Well, um, yeah. The way she never *closes* anything. Y'know what I mean?"

Amy burst out laughing. So hard that she couldn't stop.

Smiling, Ellie went on, ending with what a terrible daughter she had been, and still was.

Amy listened to the long litany of failures.

"Y'know, El," she said finally, "Orvy always told me how, when he was feeling like shit, he would come up here. He called these two trees—the oak and the copper beech—'my dear companions.' Orvy had about the worst relationship with his mother of anyone I've ever met. And I had a bad time with both my parents. When it came to college, I ran as far as I could, and didn't come back, really, until Orvy needed me, for this—"

"Is this relevant?"

"Hmm," Amy said thoughtfully. "No, not really, as long as you think you can trust me to help you maybe walk through all this, in this terrible isolation at home that's driving everyone nuts, and your stalled whales and all. I mean give yourself a *break*. You're a great kid, and you're doing far-out work, and it *will* work, do you understand?"

"You're psychic?"

"Oh yeah."

Ellie was taken aback. "How can you be sure?"

"I just *know*."

"You don't know about the whales."

"I know about you. I *believe* in you, kid, okay?"

Ellie stopped fingering her neck charm. "Go ahead. I'm listening."

"Good," Amy said. "I hope I can keep your attention."

"It's harder than *me* keeping it—but give it a shot."

She smiled. "It'll be worth it, I promise. It's something that Orvy told me that saved him when he was young, and when he told me, it kind of saved me too. When he was six, and he was lying on his back in a field down the road near their house, looking up and watching the clouds passing across, suddenly he had a vision—that there was 'something else,' that the world wasn't just about what you see and feel, but that there was something else—some whole of which he was just a part. And he ran home and told his mother, saying 'There's something else, there's something else!' And she said, 'I'm sorry, Orvy, there's nothing else but this.'"

"Bummer!"

"Exactly. And then all those years later, he told me this and then said, 'Ame, I've been trying to hold this vision my whole life, like when I was far away with Doctors Without Borders and running around the world, I felt that I was *worth* something, you know? Because of being part of that something else. And I've held that vision my whole life.'"

"Wow!" said Ellie.

"Have you ever felt anything like that?"

She was silent for a moment. "Sort of. And I can see how he tries to do that, keep being a part of that . . . that something. And yeah, me too, in my own way. Makes me feel better. Affirmed."

"For me," Amy went on, "that moment changed my life. Now I'm passing it on to you."

"And could it for me? I mean change my life?"

"You'll find out. Just keep *trying* to be in good connection with your mom and your dad and me, like I try to do even with my poor dead parents. The trying is all."

Ellie fell silent. "Y'know, tonight one thing that happened, right at the end, Dad asked me if I ever asked my friends questions. I said, no, not really. It's real hard for me to do."

"It *is* hard—I know what it's like—but not as hard as you think. Being with others, *open*ing up, others might just open you up more too, right?"

"Like Mom."

"Yes."

"Instead of trying to close things down, staying in my own little trap?"

"Yes. Y'know, El, I think you're great. You're right where you need to be right now. Open up a littlelittle, then a more little. Downstairs with them you opened up a possible new chapter. And one thing I've learned in this—I don't know—yeah, rough-edged world, is that at the end of the day, it's just all about walking each other home."

"What does that mean?"

"It means we're all here for each other."

She opened her arms to Ellie.

Ellie hesitated. Then she opened her arms and they hugged so hard it was almost painful, and then they let go.

When Amy, Orvy, Miranda, and Ben came down for breakfast, there was a note on the kitchen table from Ellie, accompanied by a colored-pencil drawing of the five of them, close together:

"You're the only ones I trust enough to take advantage of, and love."

14

They told him not to do it.

He said he was going to do it.

They told him again, "Don't do it."

He said again, "I'm going to do it."

They said that if he did it, he would get it in the neck.

"I can handle it," he said.

"But all of us will get it in the neck too!"

He did it.

He got it in the neck. All of us would get it in the neck too.

It was a few weeks later, beginning of October. The infection rate was the highest since the pandemic began. All 187 beds were filled up, and new cases were piling up in cots in Emergency and up and down the hallways. Ventilators were scarce. Non-Covid patients were not welcome. Those with mild symptoms were advised to stay home—and even broken legs or other diagnoses were told to get someone to drive them up to Albany Medical, an hour away.

The second wave seemed to have dug in its claws for a long, *long* stay. Everything was worse, including morale. But to the owners the worst of the worst was not "patient care," but "fiscal care." Kush Kare was cutting corners Karelessly. People were getting fired—even some of medicine's heart's blood, the nurses—the ones who were exhausted and because of Kush could not live up to their oath of care. Some of the most meticulous, in fact. And if nurses got sick with Covid or anything else and had to take time off, often as not they did not come back.

It had gotten so bad that sometimes when one of the doctors said, "Get the nurse!" the response was, "What nurse? There is no nurse!"

Just as bad was KK's "Up Your Kare" campaign. Its main "action item" was a shortage of PPE, including that contagion-fighting miracle, the hard-plastic face helmet. The shield enclosed your head in plastic, muffled sounds, and at first it was hard to get used to—like a real space walk. But after that it provided a great sense of safety. In fact, when doctors and nurses took them off to leave, they had a shot of anxiety, feeling that they were missing something, even at home. Like losing your wallet. The ritual donning and doffing of the safety protection coming to work and going was no more. In a strange way, its protection was missed.

And so now fresh clean safety coverings—from helmets to shoe booties—were scarce. It was suggested that the team do better recycling.

Again Amy tried to bring this to the attention of the administration. First, on secure e-mail to the several listed hospital administrators, she got bounced around a few times until she got nowhere. Next she tried calling them, including what looked like the phone number of the top administrator, and received no return calls. She was then shunted to an e-mail address for the Help Portal. Rather than go into *that* cesspool, finally she found an allegedly direct line to the President, Jason Kush, and left a message saying it was an urgent matter. Finally she got a call back from a second vice president, a woman named

Reggie. Amy explained to Reggie in detail the dangerous shortage of PPE and N95 masks. Even disinfectant for staff.

"In fact," Amy said, "some of the doctors and nurses—none from my team, but it *affects* my team—are hoarding them in their lockers."

"Hoarding? Hmmmm," Reggie mused. "Don't you have a master key?"

"They're using private, sophisticated locks. It's a matter of life or death."

"Matter of life or death. Hmmmm. Let me make sure I've got this perfectly *straight*, for the President, Mr. Jason Kush. He wants things *perfectly* straight. You said 'Private, sophisticated locks'?"

"Correct," said Amy.

A pause.

"Sure sounds like hoarding to me, Amy. Good job. Go on."

"Yes, they're hoarding, and so we don't have enough."

"Of what? Can you send me a list of—"

"Of what they're *hoarding*? Everything we need!"

"Everything we need. Hmmm." A pause. "Stay with me here, girl-buddy. If they don't have *enough* of what they *need*, it's because they're *hoarding*! Use an established business model—optimize it. Meld the thing out onto the back end and . . . case closed! It's in your bailiwick now, right? In *your* sweet spot. Tell them to stop. So glad that we got that one straightened out. I'll brief Mr. K when he gets back and he's, like, unbusy?"

"What about the government?" Amy said. "I heard that both the federal and New York governance was offering to help with protective garb. For free. Has Mr. Kush contacted them?"

"Federal and New York, contacted them? Hmmm. I'll ask. I mean if they're free, why not?"

"Hmmm, Reggie. Good thinking."

"But to be truth-ish, Amy, Mr. Kush has a kind of, um, in your lingo, *antibody* to the government? He hates 'em. This is why I get paid the big bucks and, like, have a nice—?"

"So Kush could care less? Well, if you ever find him, *tell him to call*!"

But the receiver had gone dead.

No one thought they could try to work with even *tighter* control of gear, but what else could they do? Result? Buy them from Amazon, and more padlocks on lockers.

The daily question for Amy's team? How can we make it through just one day? Amy and now Roy were trying to get Jason Kush to stop doing what he was doing, or else. He was always *out and would get back to you soon*. Finally with repeated calls by Amy and Shump and Maintenance and Cleanup, there was an e-mail from one Ken Baiter, third in command of "the Columbia and Albany NYS KK Region" that read:

> Great work. You guys are stars in the crown of
> Kush Kare! Keep up the good work.
>
> CC: Jason Kush

Finally Amy took this dilemma to Orville.

First he said that it was "appalling and expected." He considered. "How much equipment do you need?"

"Are you kidding? We need truckloads!"

For a few moments he stared at nothing, and then he nodded and said, "Okay. I might be able to help."

———

That morning the team was gathered in an emergency "connection" meeting in the call room.

"Okay, Eddie," Amy was saying, "so despite all of our warnings, you did it. How in God's name are we going to deal with this mess? Note that, despite your doing what we warned you *not* to do, last night you did it and you've been getting it in the neck and posting more at five this morning. First, Eddie, you've gotta stop!"

Silence. All of the team stared at Eddie, their attention on a new sartorial touch: instead of the motorcycle cap, he was wearing what looked like a real bald eagle feather fastened into his hair at the temple and extending back over his ear onto his neck.

Eddie said nothing. He crossed his arms over his chest.

"I mean, *Facebook*?" Amy went on. "You told me you don't *do* social media, right?" He nodded. "And you joined it, fell into that sewer? Created a page?"

"Not exactly. I don't know how to do it. The chief of the tribe did it for me. I just talked."

"Chief of the tribe?!"

Eddie shook his head. "I can't talk about it."

"But we have to—"

"It's personal."

The room fell still. Had Eat My Dust again, like in the House of God, gone nuts?

"Eddie," Roy said, "we've been through hell together. I know how you feel, guy, and if we could channel the Fat Man right now, I can almost see and hear what he'd be saying."

"What would that be?"

"First, he'd say, 'When you're resisting an unjust system, don't stand up alone—*stick together*!' Right?" Eddie nodded. "Second, he'd say, 'Y'gotta be *deft*. When you're going up against the whole big system, you don't just bash away,' remember?"

Eddie shook his head, battling with himself. Finally he said, "Cool."

"And," Amy said, "you've been isolating—out of touch with us— not talking much for a week, maybe more, just putting in the hours. It's like you disappeared. What's going on with you?"

He closed his eyes, took a slow breath in, held it, pursed his lips in a little "o," and let it out slowly, whistling. He opened his eyes. Looked surprised at being back with the team. He looked around, face by face. Finally he said, "I've moved. I'm renting a house out near the basketmakers."

"Jesus!" cried Hyper. "I thought you were living in town, over Lebowski Bar and Beef."

"My main goals are to keep the tribe healthy—Covid-free—and keep them as secret as I can. My main challenge now is keeping Chief Ralphie alive. They know I can help them. They trust me."

"Amazing," Amy said. "Good for you—really! I'd love to see the baskets. But exactly *how*, Eddie, did you get from basket weaving . . ." She paused, tried to stay calm. "To us being a target in a Facebook war? We're already getting it in the neck. All of us!"

"You don't see the *connection*?!"

"No. I'm an earthling."

"You sayin' I'm *not*?!"

"Eddie, listen. I and the team know *for sure* that deep down you are an earthling, okay?"

"*Deep down?* Not in my appearance?"

"All good. Tough and handsome."

"Okay. Got it." He adjusted his feather. "As you can imagine, I'm going through a few new paradigms, y'understand? It used to happen a lot, after we lost the Fat Man, and me and Naidoo went back to Naples Beach, CA. It's New Paradigm City."

"Good," Amy said, "all good. Now. I just want to go from A to B, 'B' being your start of a national war on Facebook that we doctors and nurses can't win."

"Nothing personal, then, right?" he asked, doubt on his face.

"I'm always *with you*—we *all* are. Never forget that. The A-team 'we,' right, guys?"

All around the table there rang out variations on "Right."

"Cool," he said. "The 'we' together, always. Us against the motherfuckers. All of whom are dumb as flagpoles." He paused, closed his eyes, took a deep breath in, smiled it out.

"Okay," he said, "this is how it all came down. As the deaths rose, all of us kept on publicly advocating for masking and distancing—me the loudest about it, I know, I know. I became the face of oppression in the minds of others; the worst, friends and neighbors. You all know this—it's been going on for months. All of us getting threats against us and our families—they assumed I had kids—for trying to get people to wear masks. They found out my cell number. I changed the number. They showed up at Lebowski's bar, hassling him for my new address. Wrong guy to hassle. He practically killed a few. All because of a mask? A piece of . . . of *nothin'*? A disposable item?"

He took a deep breath.

"They were shrieking like banshees come to take a damned soul to hell. Telling me I was an asshole with a God complex. That I'd *chosen* my job and I needed to just shut up and do it. 'You get paid,' they said, 'you're not a volunteer, you make good money!' I got calls that tried to strip away any shred of humanity I had managed to retain, and to ensure I understood that I had no value as a human being in the minds of the very people I was fighting so damned hard to save. The whole thing, I mean, I got to feeling like I was fighting a war in which both the enemy and the homeland are attacking me!"

He shook his head.

"So . . . There was one night recently that I almost didn't survive. I'd had five Covid patients die that day, none of their families allowed to be with them. I cried with them over the phone and, in some cases, outside of the loved ones' rooms. I tried to provide what comfort I could, but it was never enough."

He paused, wringing his fingers, battling with himself.

"Yesterday I finally got up the guts, or maybe couldn't take it anymore. Knowing it might not help, I got Chief Ralphie to get me a Facebook profile with a nice photo, suit and tie—and I posted. Pleading with people to take this situation seriously. I couldn't be with my dear wife or any other living person and I was facing down this abyss alone. I almost lost it that night five patients died. I knew, like we all do, how to exit painlessly, and I had the drugs."

He stopped, shaking his head slowly. Then he sighed, and adjusted the feather.

"I was saved by a . . ." He choked up. "By a random call from . . . one of you. Who said to me, quote, 'All day long you seemed off—I mean *more* off.' Which made me laugh. On the edge of killing myself and I'm *laughing*? Snapped me out of it."

The group was silent. Who knew? And which one of us was it?

"Facebook *exploded*. The doors swung open to all the bigots and crazies. As you said, Amy, all of us have been getting it in the neck for a while and so will we all . . ." He gulped, near tears. "I'm deeply sorry for starting this. Never again."

"Good," Amy said.

"Hey, big fella," said Hyper, "none of us can count on the luck of someone being there at the right place at the right time. Chancy, right? If you want to kill yourself or do any other shit, do not isolate! Move in the exact opposite direction—to connect—and pick up the phone and make the call. Call me anytime—I never really sleep. We love you. Period. Like Berry said, 'Isolation is deadly, connection heals,' got it?"

"Got it," Eddie said. "I'm sorry, so sorry. Gratitude. For all of you." He sighed. "Let's go."

"It's so sad!" Roy said, not moving, "and whoever saved you, thanks. None of us House of Godders could keep going here without you." He found himself looking up and away as if Fats would sail into view—all that weight sailing so weightlessly and so often, a real comfort now. A buddy. *Nope. Nothing. Keep going. As if the Fat Man is saying to me by his absence: "Bring me in yourself."*

"I'm remembering the day," Roy went on, "after Potts jumped out the eighth-floor window, and Fats and I were totally down, sitting there in our own worlds and not knowing what to say—sitting in the on-call room in that hellhole of 4-North?"

Groans from Eddie and Hyper.

"So Fats and I are not saying anything, each of us just in our own hell, going over and over it in silence. Finally I say, 'What the hell do we do now?' and Fats says, 'Linking pinkies.' I ask what's that? He says, 'In Brooklyn, when we were really down and didn't know what to do, we linked pinkies, and squeezed. It's a way of saying to the people we love, "Hey, *he's* dead, but *we're alive!*"'"

Roy held out his hands and offered one on each side. All of the team did likewise. "Now on three, look around and *squeeze*, and show 'em to us all," said Roy. All squeezed. And then all raised their linked pinkies high, dancing up above the tabletop—to where Fats might be—and then let go.

And somebody cheered, and then all cheered, louder louder, and then everybody laughed.

"But, Sev," Eddie said, "anything I can do to get my post off Facebook? Press delete maybe?"

All burst out laughing. Sev shook his head.

"Eddie, my friend," said Roy, "you're a guy with a glorious disregard for all restraint. All you need right now, big guy, is a little fine-tuning." He stared at him, hard. "Do not post anything else, and don't look at who's commenting on your post. Got it?"

"Got it."

And then, because Eddie didn't die, they all went back, energized, to do the impossible work.

———

The first test of Eddie's restraint would come that afternoon on a Zoom with the KK Covid chief infection prevention officer, who was speaking from an undisclosed location. Roy volunteered to be on the Zoom with Eddie, and instructed him not to talk except to apologize. He agreed.

Chief Prevention was joined by the on-site prevention pod officer, a young man named Rolf. He had okayed taking a Covid patient out of isolation and off of precautions by simply looking at a list and determining that enough boxes had been checked. The patient had continued his clinical decline: but there were signs of hope.

Roy made the exact same case as the now-silent Eddie: case studies had shown *active Covid viral shedding* in immunocompromised patients for up to 180 days! But the patient had only been there for 11 days. Young Rolf made it clear that by overriding him, Eddie had "upset the higher-ups" because he was making the Covid KK care numbers look worse, and he was also forcing nurses and others to continue to wear full, *costly* PPE. In his previous talk with Rolf, Eddie had shouted down the junior infection boss, saying, "I'm not willing to bet our nurses' *lives* that this patient is no longer shedding infectious viral material all over the place, you child, you . . . *kumquat*! You think the administrative status quo is more important than my clinical judgment?"

Now Eddie was twisting himself in torment to say nothing. Roy held up his index finger to say, wagging, "Zip your mouth." Eddie did. And then he took a deep breath in, and out. Told to be silent, for once he did so, and turned it all over to Roy. In fact he sat quietly, eyes half-closed, once in a while nodding—as if following the reeds making their path through a basket.

After a few more minutes, Roy got exactly what he wanted: saving the lives of the caregivers. Chief Prevention had given up.

Roy hung up and, when he turned to speak to Eddie, found he was sound asleep.

He and the rest of the team, for at least one patient, had prevailed.

Later that night, in what seemed a moonless clarity of stars, the helicopter began to slow down.

Looking out the passenger windows were Roy, Amy, and Natasha, the nurse and director of the private KK ward for the rich. Roy and Amy had gotten an urgent call from Natasha to appear at her hospital unit on the top floor beneath the helicopter bull's-eye just after dark. She was not able to say why, other than that it was not anything to do with Kush Kare directly, but "Congressman Henry Schooner, via Orvy. We need two squeaky-clean witnesses with us."

Now, after about an hour's flight, up ahead was a circular tattoo of powerful spotlights reaching up to them, clearly indicating the bull's-eye for landing. At the far edge of the circle were three small figures standing in the shadow of a large tractor trailer.

The pilot, Henry Schooner, was dressed to the nines in a crisp "war-pilot-flyboy jumpsuit" festooned with colorful bars, silver and gold medals, and a Purple Heart. Schooner hovered delicately as a hummingbird over the center of the circle, all the while chatting a kind of military shorthand for setting them down. Henry, flying a chopper? Orville had never really believed that Schooner played an active part in the Vietnam War, but here, finally, was proof. Unless he'd just taken chopper training. And if the medals were ersatz? Who knew? As Orville always said, "Y'know, even to this day, with Schooner, y'*never* know, y'know?"

Schooner set 'er down with a gentle bump.

The helicopter ride had been so noisy inside that only through the intercom could anyone be heard, and only Schooner and Natasha had headsets. Clearly, the two of them were in cahoots and didn't want their secrets revealed. Henry had not told them anything about this mission.

"Because I want it to be a surprise," he had said. "Trust me."

Which was the opposite of what Orville had often said: "Don't trust him."

Amy and Roy didn't know Henry well—Orville said nobody did, really.

"Over the decades, he's mellowed," Orvy had said, "as terrible tragedy in any family will do. Suffering always softens, right? We have actually become real friends. But he's still more truly transactional than true."

Before they had gotten blanked out of the conversation in the chopper, Roy asked Henry, "What's this all about?"

"It's about helping you great docs out," Henry had said. "I've been in Congress for so long—first elected in 1980!—the year Orville came back home? I've finally, only recently, gotten my dream. I'm the chairman of the Ways and Means Committee. Know what that's for?"

Neither Amy nor Roy knew what.

"It's money, pure and simple. Your taxpayer money. *For getting money by whatever 'ways and means' you can.* I'm the last signature on how to spend it. And this—this! This is the best 'what is it for' I've heard in about twenty years. Usually the members are doing nice civic things like the 'ways and means' of buying more pigs, or stealing more cash, but now, with this crook of a President, people are at the trough. Doing a lot of really illegal shit. The money often goes to 'MFDDs.'" He paused. "All things are for money."

"To what?" This from Amy.

"'Money For Donors Direct.' MAGA shit. No intelligence required."

"How'd you know that?"

"Ways and means, honey, ways and means. You have *no idea*. Now I'm going to click off so I can concentrate on getting this thing up in the air. And also so that you'll always be able to plead *plausible deniability*, a concept perfected by Reagan and our native Philmont psychopath Lieutenant Oliver North, Reagan's guy in stealing the reelection from Jimmy Carter via Iran-Contra."

"What's that?" Amy asked.

"Oh boy I'm feeling old. I better sign off." He pulled a lever and the copter jolted harshly.

"Wait!" cried Roy. "How long since you flew a helicopter?"

"Let's see . . . eleven years. But it's like riding a bike, in three dimensions. Now, where the hell is the Up switch?"

"*What?*"

"Joking. Like riding a bike. Well, not really, a lot more difficult, actually; it's learning to ride a bike while patting your head and circle-rubbing your belly. Look, what will help is if you pray for me. We'll talk when we're on the ground, in forty-five to an hour. If we make it."

Click.

Forty-five minutes later, when they landed, Natasha went first, Roy and Amy followed. They looked back. Schooner, clearly by plan, was not coming out. They walked to the back of the enormous truck, emblazoned with the Amazon trademark smile-swoop. Clearly it was a brilliant dupe because of its prevalence in everyday life, everywhere. The most recognizable logo being the least suspicious.

Clever. Clearly not amateur hour.

Natasha handled some kind of transaction, speaking in a Slavic tongue, maybe Russian, or Ukrainian, or one of the "-stans," say, Uzbek. She inspected the load in the truck.

Then "What?!" she cried out, sounding alarmed. More Slavic talk, finishing with *Da, da*—Yes, yes. "Okay," she said to Roy and Amy, "we gotta get this monster on the road. Gotta leave *now*. Have a safe trip back."

"You're not coming?"

"I'm driving shotgun with the guy in the truck. See you tomorrow if . . ."

A shout from one of the Slavs, then gestures and broken English conveying that someone was heading toward them, and that they had to get going or else!

"Or else what?" Roy asked Natasha, as she turned toward the cab of the truck.

"Or else we lose it."

"What is it?" Roy asked.

"Ask Henry. Go!"

"And if we don't get it and we lose it," Amy said, "*who* gets it?"

"Ask Henry."

The driver got in. The other guy jumped into a BMW and floored it, spitting dust and pebbles, and disappeared into the woods.

"Go!" shouted Natasha. "Into the chopper *now*!"

She hustled around to the front of the truck. The door slammed and the diesel engine as loud as a train kicked in, and remarkably quickly the truck was moving.

Roy and Amy ran to the copter. Even before the door slammed Henry had kicked the dallying blades into a whir.

Before they took off, Roy shouted, "What's in the truck?"

"PPE and N50 shields and every other Covid-protective garb and matériel, down to booties. Natasha and I calculated it would get you through three months, maybe 'til the third wave hits. Buckle up."

"*Third* wave?!" Amy shouted. "Are you sure?"

"Guaranteed. At *least* third."

"Does anybody else know this yet?" asked Amy.

"Officially, nobody."

"Unreal."

"And who would have gotten it if we didn't get it first?" Roy asked.

"Can't hear ya. Shout!"

"*WHO* WOULD HAVE GOTTEN IT IF WE DIDN'T GET IT FIRST?"

"JARED AND IVANKA."

"You're joking," said Roy.

"Not. Their hired thugs are"—he glanced at his watch, a bejeweled one that timed everything on earth as it is in heaven—"eleven minutes away. Okay, I'm muting myself again, so I can concentrate, 'Nam-like."

He paused.

"Hmm. I forgot where the Up button is on this damn thing. Either of you remember?"

Roy and Amy screamed.

"Joking! Relax. I'll pipe in some of my favorites. God bless you and God bless Columbia."

Click.

To the music of Bob Dylan, starting with a little-known *Biograph* song called "Up to Me," they all rose like magicians and flew like angels, for home.

Dylan? Schooner?

Roy looked out the window to see if the Fat Man was flying tonight—but no. He sang along to the chorus of the Dylan song: *No one else could play that tune, you know it was up to me.*

15

With Binni on the front lines of the pandemic, his ex-wife Chris—her Indian name was Krishna—had not let their 12-year-old daughter, Razina, visit him in Columbia. Before Covid, she'd made regular trips, and both father and daughter always looked forward to them. He had explained all the risks and benefits to Chris. He went through his total antiseptic routine, one that had never had a breach. Razina would have the guest room, where no one had slept since the pandemic began. But no luck. Of course they had Zoomed frequently, but as time had dragged on, much of the fun had gone out of it.

Recently Chris had hit a seam of gold: she was a new partner in a Wall Street investment firm in private equities. Living on the Upper East Side.

Chris viewed life more and more as a spreadsheet of an investment, all about risks and benefits. Risk, of course, was prime to her life now. Years handling astronomical amounts of money had seeped into all parts of her life.

And now as his stem cell infusion had been given FDA approval for "emergency use" when sure death beckoned, she'd raised the possibility of making an "equity-platform" investment. She was even more interested when Binni joined the biotech firm Moderna, which was the front-runner for making a vaccine—as soon as January.

Still, the risk of Raz traveling and staying with him for two nights made her hesitate.

He was heartfelt with her, talking about how much he missed Raz, his dad-longing. Binni presented his proposal: taking time off from five on Friday through five on Sunday. An evening alone with Raz's favorite Mexican takeout. Saturday outdoors doing something with Amy and Eleanor. Another sleepover and an afternoon return to Chris. The risks were low. To her they were high. But before Covid, she had allowed Raz to take Amtrak two hours up and back for a weekend or even a day. Chris, after the divorce, threw herself into Razina and a killer, Midas-level job. Like Binni, she had not had a serious love partner since the divorce. Binni now told her that his relationship with Amy was serious. She was glad for him.

And so Chris had "gotten on board" with Binni's plan for the visit. He was surprised at her change of heart. The answer?

"I'm so glad she has you as a dad," Chris said. "I've realized that I am a great mom and you are a great dad but the two of us together are not so good. Okay, Binni, your schedule of activities passes muster! Have good fun!" She paused. "Oh, and I hope you'll come to me at Mnuchin Equity for the 'lock-down' first investment in your cute little stem cells."

———

Now it was mid-October. The second presidential debate, when Big Mac, challenged by Biden to deny his links to white supremacy groups, turned to the camera and said: "To the Proud Boys, my message: 'Stand back, and stand by.'" Half of America gasped.

By some miracle of the gods—despite the high titer of Columbians who didn't mask or socially distance—there was a glimmer of an easing of Covid. Was the second wave receding? Too early to tell. But in the crisp, deep autumn there was a sure indication of the fiscal weather for some doctors: Kush Kare surgeons had again started cutting and sewing and humming as they walked into the operating rooms to do their nice, civic duty for Columbians, like sewing back on a pinkie or a thumb or a leg or the good part of a head (yes, a head!)—not to mention hernias, hemorrhoids, livers, flanken, and kishkes and other tasty morsels that were their bread and butter. They were doing good "lucrative" work, optional and elective surgeries, cheerily whistling to and from the operating suites. They and Kush Kare were making some money.

But the biggest change at the hospital was not the weather, or the surgeries, but the miracle.

A whole truckload of PPE and other items to help all frontline workers to actually work in safety. The gowns and helmets and everything else were not the schlock that KK had handed out before, and stingily; these were top-of-the-line brand-new masks and equipment. No one knew how it had happened.

KK tried to take credit, per Marx—Groucho, not Karl: "Who y'gonna believe? Me or your own eyes?" The nurses—from Natasha on the top floor down to Shump in Emergency—said they knew the truth, and that it was *definitely* not *in any way* the administration. All kinds of romantic tales were told, but whoever did it was never identified. Yes, an Amazon truck had pulled up in the dark of night and was emptied into a prepared labyrinth of lockups. The *only two people* who had access to this hoard—to prevent hoarding—were the two head nurses. They kept control of every piece of the shipment, in off-site-but-nearby lockups, with clear rules as to who and how they would be distributed, with the unspoken understanding that NANA—no admins need apply. They were joyous about this find dropping into their laps—and would distribute it fairly. No one messed with either one of them. All knew that if they tried, they would be crucified—without anesthesia.

All over the US, hospital administrators had been trained in an MBA course that taught the BSM—the business school mindset, or managerialism—and now went on Amazon to try to buy the swag. But they could not. This confirmed what everyone knew, that graduates with MBA degrees are perfectly unprepared to manage any industry, a tattoo parlor, a government entity, and least of all, a hospital system. When they tried to click on Amazon for their hospital's orders, they got: "Out of stock." And they were not able to find another seller, at any price they wished to spend.

In a team meeting near the end of the *first* wave, Shump had said, "This thing that we've been through has been *beyond*." Now, as it *seemed* the second wave would lessen, she said, "This thing will be *beyond* beyond!"

But as the job got a bit easier, the rage against masks and social distance spread. Every Saturday at noon now there was an unofficial drive-through protest starting at the river, up to the hospital and around the circular **EMERGENCY** drop-off at the front door, shouting, honking, cursing, and threatening—and then going back down to the Hudson, and home. They were emboldened by Big Mac's new slogans: "The election is rigged—fake news!"

————

Razina was delivered to Binni's town house on Friday evening by a town car whose driver Chris always used. Betsy Q. Ross was "a long-time germaphobe" with a love of driving in town cars. After dropping Razina off, she would drive back to New York Friday night and then come back up again on Sunday afternoon to drive her back again.

"My limo is my home," said Betsy.

"I don't feel I've got much in common with Razina," Binni said that first night to Amy. "We didn't really talk, just watched some things on her computer. But just spending the night alone with her was wonderful and puzzling. It was like she is all new, and even though she is only twelve, she seems to be pushing sixteen."

"What do you expect after not seeing her in person for so long? Don't worry, I've come up with options, from eleven in the morning 'til late, that she can choose. And listen, even if she wants to do something else and we hate it, as long as it's safe, we do it. Between Ellie and me and Ben, we'll have fun."

"How do you know she likes dogs? In India they are not pets."

"Number one, he's not a dog, he's a spirit. Number two, three girls and one spirit and we're good." He groaned. "Okay, okay," she said. "Was there any—and I mean *any*—hint so far of the fact that you are her father?"

Silence. Then: "The only thing she said, as she was closing the bedroom door, was, 'I'm curious about your real life, Dad, g'night.'"

"And you don't think that's *gold*? Ohhh, you men, you men! Like us women's voices are too high for you to hear?"

———

"You're coming to pick her up in half an hour and she's still sleeping," Binni said the next morning. "Should I wake her up or not?"

"Wake her up."

"But she's nasty when she's sleepy and—"

"Listen carefully. Wake. Her. Up. We've got a lot to do today. It is carefully planned for things she will love and you will come out smiling. Oh—does she have any pins she wears, like on her jackets or whatever?"

"Black Lives Matter."

"Couldn't be better! Later today we're all going to a BLM rally, put on by the high school kids! You said she likes to read. What's the title of a favorite book?"

"Not a book. Plays. Not just plays, Shakespeare."

"Great! I was into Shakespeare and even performed as a teenager. What's her favorite play?"

"*Romeo and Juliet*. And it was funny, but after we took her to that, she could almost say a lot of the speeches! Amazing. In fact I asked her how she could remember those plays, I mean such old language, and she said she just *did*. We went to a lot of Shakes—"

"Jackpot! Wake her up!"

"But—"

"Now!"

———

When Amy met Razina at the front door of Binni's house, she found herself thrilled, a thrill rushing from her heart down to the gut and up to the brain. The 12-year-old seemed so reserved, almost fragile, with a quick look into Amy's eyes and then looking away. A long light-brown face, dark eyes that seemed . . . the word that came to her was *elegant*, and lips that were pursed a bit, as if really trying not just to see, but to understand this first woman her father had introduced her to. On their last Zoom call she had asked, "Are you in love, Dad?" and he had said, "Yes." He had told Amy afterward that he felt he'd made an error—Razina's face had suddenly tensed up, like water can tense up in a pond in a sharp gust of wind. He had not talked to her much since then. But when he asked if she wanted to come for a visit, she jumped at the chance. Binni had said to Amy that "she has our courage, both mother and father, for sure. And it seems that her brown face now is making her test that courage in America."

On her first meeting with Razina, all this came into Amy's focus. *I know how scared and hopeful and totally alert you are, Raz—even though you hide it well.*

"Hi, Razina," she said now, taking off her mask—Binni had agreed. "Glad t'meet you."

"Glad t'meet you too, Dr. Rose. And everybody calls me Raz."

"Hey, no 'doctor' today—call me Amy. We're all civilians now. If it's OK with you, we're going to walk up four blocks seeing some of the town, then over to visit my uncle Orville and aunt Miranda, and their daughter, Eleanor, and Ben. Let's go."

"Who's Ben?"

"Ooohh, Ben? The best. A surprise." And then, as if she'd just noticed it, Amy said, "Hey, girl, I love your BLM pin. I'm wearing mine too, see?"

"Saw. First thing."

"And we're in luck! Just by chance, the senior class of Columbia High are holding a BLM protest at city hall later. I mean, you probably don't want to waste your one full day here with your dad, and—"

"Not a waste."

"Oops, sorry. It's *key*, right?"

Startled at Amy's clarity, Raz said, "*One* key, yeah."

"Exactly! Let's walk." Putting on their masks, they left.

They walked a half block over to the main street, Washington, and turned up onto Promenade Hill for the bracing view opening up over the Hudson and the Catskills. Amy told her that this created a safe port for the Nantucket Quakers to launch their whaling ships all over the world. They turned and started up Washington, the spine of the town, uphill and arrow-straight up to the hospital, the cemetery, and the reservoir.

At first they had to tiptoe through the downtown sidewalks, the night's detritus of empty booze bottles and used needles and even, given the epidemic of guns, spent shell casings. They had to pick their way past the drunks on doorsteps, and worse.

When they crossed over to safety, at the old opera house, Amy stopped and asked them to look at it. A soaring brick building that had been a year into renovation and about to have its grand reopening—just in time for the pandemic to close it.

"Y'know, Razina," Amy said, "at about your age, I was in a play in the opera house, a real production with adults playing the main parts. I was wild about the theater, and it was, of all things, *A Midsummer Night's Dream*."

"Really?"

"Yes."

"Which character were you?"

"The Queen of the Fairies."

With eyes wide, Raz said, "Great part!"

"Great," Amy agreed. "And I've never forgotten the lines."

Sleep thou, and I will wind thee in my arms.
Fairies, begone, and be all ways away.
So doth the woodbine the sweet honeysuckle
Gently entwist; the female ivy so
Enrings the barky fingers of the elm.
O, how I love thee! How I dote on thee!

Razina stood stock-still, trying to grasp this. "How *old* did you say you were?"

"Twelve."

"I'll be thirteen next month!" Her eyes were wide. "Wow. I love Shakespeare. The first time my mom and dad took me to see *Romeo and Juliet*, some of the lines just stuck in my brain, even now. I mean I didn't have the, um, *experience* in love, and I don't yet, so I can't understand and act the parts yet. But I read and watch videos of the plays, and sometimes one or another speech will help me to understand, well . . . *life*? Even *my* little life!" She hesitated, clearly wondering if she should go on with this.

"Yeah?" Amy asked. "Can you give us an example?"

"Sure. Sometimes when I'm working too hard at school, and I'm really tired and not wanting to study any more bummer stuff, I think of Shakespeare. And when . . . um . . . *some* people make me want to work all the time to get in the next school so that I can work all that time to get in the next and the next and . . . Never mind. Let's go."

"Tell us, honey," Binni said. "Maybe your words can help us too, in our drudgery—right, Amy?"

"Absolutely! I am way way *way* too hardworking at doctoring. And your dad, not just doctoring, but also working to find a cure for Covid."

"Is *that* what you're doing here, Dad?"

"Trying."

"Why didn't you tell me? That's so cool."

"Sorry."

"Raz, your father is amazing, even if he is shy about his, well, incredible accomplishments."

She was looking at her father in a puzzled way. Clearly this was news. Binni hunched up his shoulders and smiled bashfully, his arm in an "I just don't talk about it" gesture.

"Well, maybe this will help you too, Dad." She paused, then in a firm, clear voice recited:

> *If all the year were playing holidays*
> *to sport would be as tedious as to work.*
> *But when they seldom come, they wished-for come,*
> *and nothing pleaseth but rare accidents.*

Silence. Amy and Binni were looking at each other, letting this sink in.

"Wow!" said Binni. "Bravo!"

"*Henry the Fourth*, part 1, act 1 scene 2."

"Now *that*," Amy said, "is *amazing*! And *how* you recited it was astonishing. That's some gift!"

"She has a great affinity for Shakespeare's plays," Binni said, in awe. "Almost a photographic memory. I don't know how she does it—sometimes now, I can't even recall what I had for lunch."

"Yeah, but it's because you can remember a gazillion sequences of stem cells and all."

"And your mom?" Amy asked.

"What do you mean?"

"I mean, what's her, well, what does *she* live by?"

"Hmm. Well, she's nice." Raz paused. "Except when moms *aren't* nice, y'know?"

"Do I ever!" Amy said. "I remember when I wanted to mop the floor with mine!"

Raz laughed hard, covering her mouth. "She works in finance. I think she wants me to wind up doing money too."

"I doubt that, Raz," said Binni.

"But she *did* want me to go to those real pre-pre-Harvard prep schools, right from the start." She turned to Binni. "Thanks for letting me go to Fieldston. Like I've got great girlfriends now, a really tight group of us that hang together—I'd've, like, gone crazy without our Zooms! We all would've. We all are having trouble with the boys—you wouldn't believe what jerks they are! It's like we're a lot *older*! But I have a lot of elective classes and right now that's the Bard, and stage design."

"Wow!" said Amy. "You are something *else*! You're going to love my uncle Orville and his wife, Miranda—together they're the best. They were like parents to me. He's the reason I got into medicine. And their daughter, Eleanor, is something else, studying whales—imagine?"

A smile from Raz. They started walking again.

But then she fell back a bit and fell silent, dawdling, so that she was several steps behind. Amy glanced back at her. She was pretending to look into the window of a refugee New Yorker's antiques store, Five Figures North—399 dollars for an old milk churner?

What made her fall back? Amy wondered. *Was it mentioning mothers? Simple shyness? Like with born actors, offstage they are terrified.*

At the Courthouse Square Amy led them up the driveway of the Victorian house, opened the gate of the high wooden fence, and walked into the large back garden bordered by soaring pines and holly, the massive copper beeches, a severely straight larch, and maples. Binni and Raz followed. Amy had told Miranda and Orvy what the story was—how delicate it was to help.

Orville and Miranda were on the wide, welcoming porch, he at the Weber gas grill, coaxing both meat and vegetables into good food as he had coaxed his patients into good health or at least living with disease. In addition to Zooming with his outpatients, he had grown intensely in touch with many of his doctor pals all over the world who'd been with him in his time in Médecins Sans Frontières. And now he was also in touch with some of their doctor children, and even grandchildren. All of them were sharing perspectives and clinical ideas about Covid, and also strategies to stay sane and be prepared for the moment of real change, once the dust of the pandemic had cleared. All over the globe! *And even, finally, for our poor fractured America.*

Miranda was busy tossing a spinach and feta salad and rushing out the knives and forks and fluted glasses for champagne toasts. Eleanor was in the backyard flying her new drone. Ben wasn't there—strange.

Everybody, of course, wore masks, and kept a sensible distance from each other.

"We're here!" Amy called out, coming in first, walking up on the porch. "Eleanor," she shouted and waved, "come meet Raz!"

"OMG!" Raz said. "Is that a drone?" Eleanor waved back, landed the drone, picked it up, and walked toward the porch.

"She studies whales with them," Orvy said, "in the Galápagos.

It's so she can study them from above, without stressing them out. But she can't get there, now, with the Covid. She's here on a 'reverse-parent' study—me and Miranda are the whales. She's taking care of us old gomers."

"May I present my daughter . . ." Binni started to say, but at the word "daughter" he got choked up. He cleared his throat and finished, ". . . my daughter, Razina."

"Hi," Razina said. "Thanks for having us."

All at once Orville was jolted by seeing just how much Binni loved her, how he had missed her. *We fathers can love our daughters insanely. All kinds of fierce dad-energies soar up, in jolts of clarity. I've gotten so goddamn dull and fuzzy during this damn Covid. How much I missed this, seeing new people—or even old friends and relatives—and Zoom doesn't give you that, that spark. And to actually see Amy in love, and with a helluva good guy and trying to manage this—what?—this daughter so fresh, there seemed to be sparks all over her! How rare, now, is that?* Seeing her spark brought tears to his eyes.

"It's great to meet you in person, Razina," Orvy said. "Or Raz?"

She nodded, shyly.

"Your dad talks about you all the time."

"Thanks. I, well, he's a noble dad."

"And with his discovery, a new treatment for early Covid, he's soon going to be a No*bel* one too—you just wait and see."

"He has a treatment for the pandemic?"

"No, no, Raz, just working on one small part of it."

"Too modest," Orvy went on. "A course in med school that I flunked. C'mon, let's eat."

They started in, happily, raucously to talk. Except for Ellie, sitting between her father and Amy. She had gotten more and more silent, quietly bit by bit, scooch by scooch, her chair farther out on the already wide circle, so that she would not have to talk. Occasionally a question would be addressed to her, and she'd answer, but shyly. With their glances around the table, the others shared a tacit agreement to let her find her own way to be there—they'd had a *lot* of practice since Ellie had come to live with them.

Binni had told Amy how shy Raz was. Amy had talked to Miranda, Ellie, and Orvy, about how to help her feel at home. Now as they noticed Raz squirming and not talking and inching her chair back from the circle, they glanced at each other to activate their rescue.

"Well," Ellie announced, "I guess I'd better go back on the lawn down there to finish tuning up my drone before we head off to the BLM rally, okay?"

"Okays" came flowing in.

"It's a two-woman job," she said. "Raz, wanna help?"

"Sure."

With bated breath, the others watched the two girls, separated by almost a generation, walk off and stop in a flat "landing" area away from the huge trees—killers of drones. Ellie, with Raz watching carefully, took the drone up high and brought it soaring down to maybe 20 feet above them several times. Then she gestured to Raz that she could try it. The back porch audience held their breath—most of all Binni. They watched her ponder this, shyly, assess it, but then shake her head no. The porch crowd groaned.

Miranda turned to the others. "Okay, Plan B. I'll activate the fail-safe." She turned back toward the house and whistled. Once. Twice. They all waited. Nothing. "Damn!"

"Just wait," Orville said. "He forgot his hearing aid today."

They waited. Glancing between the back door and the little girl standing there with arms crossed, watching the drone and looking really lonesome.

A soft brushing sound from the kitchen, then a skillful push at the door handle, and there was Ben, carrying his leash in his mouth.

Orville bent down and spoke to him, and gestured down the lawn to the two girls, fed him a treat, and showed him that there was another to be had—perhaps maybe a bag of treats—if he did his duty well. Rolling his head into a "got it," he lumbered slowly—even seeming more delicate for all that bulk—down the stairs and, in a majestic gait, made his way slowly to the girls.

Ellie was showing Razina how to store the drone for carrying it over to the BLM event.

Ben was slowly making his way grandly, a pasha of a pup—to them. He looked at Ellie, who looked at Raz. He, sensitive giant—he would *have* to be one, to survive—followed Ellie's gaze toward Raz. And then, for some reason, perhaps the fact that Ellie was, head down, busily collapsing the four legs and snuggling them into their places, he chose Raz. It may also have been the few treats that Orvy had slipped into her pocket before she left the porch.

Raz and Ben held each other's gaze, and then suddenly Ben rolled over on his back and put his four pie-tin plates of paws up and huge red tongue lolling to one side and waggling, and then he seemed to be waggling all of him, his black coat in waves of muscles.

"He wants his tummy rubbed," said Ellie loudly. "He likes you. Pat his tummy while I store the drone, and then we'll take him for his quick walk in the Courthouse Park."

Raz patted.

Ben seemed to smile.

"Here," said Ellie, throwing Ben's leash to Raz.

Ben, seeing the "walk now" cue, seemed almost to smile.

Raz hesitated.

"He wants it on! He loves it!"

Raz snapped the leash into the collar.

"Ready?" asked Ellie.

"A little scared."

"No need, he's only eaten two girls your size in the last month."

Raz broke out laughing. The porch crowd laughed too.

"Listen up," Ellie said, taking charge again, "he knows you're part of our pack now, and if you ever were in danger, he'd kill to get you out. But you've got to help too."

"How?"

"Pick up the gigantic poops, with that reversible green poop-grabber on the leash. Let's go." Soon the whole family and Ben—Orvy leashed to him—were walking back across Washington on Fourth Street, toward Underhill Lake and Columbia City Hall where the BLM rally would take place. It was strange, this, their first excursion since, well, March 2020—almost ten months.

Amy and Binni were walking in front of Razina, who was taking up the rear. Miranda was making a real effort to engage her, but Raz didn't seem very talkative. As soon as Miranda moved away to be with Orville, she came up to Binni.

"Dad?"

"Yes?"

"I want to live with you—with all of you!"

"You what? How can—"

"Listen! I need a break from New York, and seeing you again and . . . and this amazing family? Amazing! It's like—I don't know—a three-ring circus, or like a play where everybody's playing a part without even knowing it and loving and brash and, well . . . dramatic! Even Ben! I never saw anything like this in my whole life!"

Both Binni and Amy were stunned, and stopped walking to face her.

"But there are so many obstacles to—" Binni began.

"*Listen* first, then tell me no, then listen some more and tell me yes." He nodded. "I need a break from New York, and Mom needs a break from me—and me her. I can—"

"Did Mom say she needed a break?"

"Not explicitly. But it's obvious. We clash, without clashing. *So listen.* I can do everything I do on Zoom for school from here, see my friends, do my work. It'll be easier because of less tension. And my best friend Eliza moved to New Mexico with her parents and I don't think I can *stand* the boys in my class anymore without her." She caught her breath. "I want to be with *you* for a while, not Mom."

"How long?"

"Don't know. Like, open-ended."

"But I'm never home."

"Good. I work better alone, and I can get to know the Roses better—maybe work toward being, like, Rose-worthy, I mean, Amy, like an honorary Rose?"

Do not answer. Despite it seeming so "right" and feeling so excited, do not talk. "Binni?"

"If Dad says yes, I can have you as a friend, Amy, right? Bringing me out, like you're bringing my dad out?"

Binni was astonished at this, flinching as if he'd been punched.

Amy and Raz laughed.

"But I mean it," said Raz. "I haven't seen you so happy since I was a kid! I mean the Roses are fun! And they joke and tell the truth. We never did any of those things, right?" He thought for a moment, then nodded. "I'll fit right in," Raz went on. "And you're already fitting in."

"How can you know that?"

"Da-aad. Have you looked in a mirror lately?"

He seemed to be trying hard to answer, as if being quizzed on a sequence of messenger RNA.

Amy and Raz couldn't help laughing even more. The laughter was infectious. He joined in.

Catching his breath, he said, "Well, well. That's why I love Amy and her family. It reminds me, sometimes, of my big crazy fun family back in Varanasi."

"How cool is *that*?"

They were almost to the rally. Walking alongside them now were a few high school students holding BLM signs.

"Dad, I'm dying in New York."

They stopped walking.

"She'll never agree," he said.

"Here's what we do. First, I get on the phone, *alone*, and threaten not to come home ever again and I want to end your joint custody."

"She'll never agree to—"

"Daa-ad, of *course* not. And then I'll say, 'So let me live up here for now.' She knows, of course, that possession is nine-tenths of the law. She'll talk it over with her new boyfriend, a lawyer—and I overheard him say he's not ready to have a child around!" She shook her head in dismay. "He's forty-three, and not *ready*?"

They were walking into the circular drive around city hall, the limestone building that had been built as the first lunatic asylum in the country, founded on the radical Quaker model of "caring" for the insane.

"If we do this, Dad, maybe I can really start to feel I'm *worth* something again, or will be, sometime."

"You? *You don't feel . . . ?*" Binni was astonished. "You're that, um, *down*?"

She paused, trying to keep in control. "I'm trying hard to hold on to, well, my vision of my life, but now I need your help, and . . . something I never expected 'til today . . . *both* of your help—and the Roses too. All of you." She sighed. "I've been so down. I didn't know what to do with my life. Now, I'm so grateful, 'cause all of you are so, like, caring. Crazy caring."

Tears came to Binni's eyes. "Okay, we'll try it."

"Yes!" she said, punching the air with a fist.

"I've really missed you, Razina. A *lot*. The only thing that's kept me sane in this mess, well"—he choked up, went on—"has been my two girls!" He opened his arms to them.

They all came in. Amy started crying, and then all of them did.

"So," he said, "we'll talk to Mom. I'll tell her I want this arrangement until I can't stand you anymore, little lady!"

"That means I can stay with you forever!"

They were on the edge of the circular driveway, and the other Roses and Ben had turned back, watching their long, threeway hug.

And then they shouted back to them to come on. The demonstration was about to start.

16

Orville, walking with his little group toward the gathering, all wearing surgical masks, was talking with Amy.

"She took one long look at us," Amy went on, "and she told Binni that she wants in."

"How good is that!" Orvy said. "Amazing. For a lost sad girl, in a couple of hours to catch the spirit of this crazy family? To see her open up, get touched by a new shared spirit? To have just plain fun, and heal? Strange thing about the word 'heal'—it goes both ways. Heal others and you heal too. This is as good as life gets. Hey, look—Roy and Berry, and their daughter."

Roy caught Orville waving at him and started to lead Berry and Spring over. Roy and Berry had met on the date of the Martin Luther King "I Have a Dream" speech. While King was speaking at the Lincoln Memorial, they were at Tanglewood to hear the Boston Symphony. Their parents had arranged the meeting, a picnic on the great lawn, but they ran from them and illegally snuck into the shed and fell in love. Together and separately they had been at a ton of demonstrations—Roy during his Rhodes at Oxford, when the relationship with Berry crashed—had gone "full '60s," taking up just causes like Vietnam and what is now called Black Lives Matter. From then on, whenever he got discouraged about the chances of his poor USA awash in money instead of democracy, gun murder and neglect instead of kindness, he'd hear a simple phrase in his head: *Hey, wait a second—this is unjust. Someone has to resist it, and—in the novels— it seems to be up to me.*

Now Roy led Berry and Spring toward the grassy middle of the circle that the tarmac made at the front entrance of city hall. As he walked, he glimpsed something in the trees.

"Fats?" he said.

"Roy?"

"Roy!"

"Fats!"

And there he was, floating, hovering near the top of a young pine. One hand grasping a branch, he bobbed up and down calmly. Amazing that that little branch could tether and support such a big, fat man—fatter now than ever. In most of his previous spectral appearances he was in his doctor clothes, sometimes crisp and clean, other times as bloodied as a butcher. Now he was wearing, of all things, an old-fashioned flight suit, like Lindbergh on his transatlantic flight. Fats, with all that weight, on such a thin branch?

And then, as if hearing him, Fats let go and said, "Look, Ma, no hands!"

"How are you?" Roy asked.

"Who knows, kid. Above all, I'm still dead."

"What's it like up there?"

He paused, as if making sure of a tough diagnosis. "Yeah, it's like a tough diagnosis. Let's say, 'You'll find out.'" He was gathering himself up to go. "Have fun and always watch out where you stick your pinkie and—"

"Wait!"

"Yes?"

"Do they tell you when *other* people down here are going to die?"

"Oops, they're starting, and I want to make sure to have a good perch. But there's one thing you have to remember, when you're in a tight spot, like now."

"How is this a tight spot—"

"Stop with the questions, Basch, and listen up! For your safety and health." Roy stopped. Fats smiled and went on, "There's one thing I always said to you in the House of God, when you wanted to go up against the money-power shitheads, remember?"

Roy tried to recall, tried hard, but nothing. "No."

"Sheesh! Why do I waste my time? Well, rumor is, it's 'cause infinite time *may* be all I got? That, and *food*! Heavenly! As much as the Katz Deli can deliver down here and—"

"Down?"

"Up. Sometimes I mix 'em up. Listen." He paused, inflated even more, if that were possible, seeming to block out the high sun, but casting no shadow on the tree or ground. "I said," he went on, "I said be *deft*."

"What?" Roy said. "Be deaf? What does that mean—"

"No no no." Fats sighed in dismay. "Dee, ee, fff, tee. Deft. When you go up against the Man, don't go right at him, be deft. Like now. Believe me, you're gonna need to be deft, soon. Bye-bye." With a slick, tight bank, and more grace than he'd ever shown alive, he was gone.

"What'd he say?" Berry asked. She knew what the sudden blank look in Roy's eyes meant.

"All well. Be *deft*."

"Sounds good. C'mon."

The turnout was not all that large. The 40 or so members of the senior class were able to socially distance on the steps to the entrance to the building. They were finishing setting up the megaphones and organizing who did what when. Of the class members who'd shown up, there were only about 10 boys. Amy was surprised at how few families had come out to support their kids; maybe a dozen, mostly women.

Roy, Berry, and Spring caught up with the others on the grassy raised island, around which the cars drove to get in and out. Introductions and small talk briefly reigned.

Spring and Raz decided to join the students on the steps.

Ellie was excited to capture the event of her alma mater. She'd been in the Columbia school system all the way and was still a loyal Bluehawk—dead set against going away to private school in Massachusetts. Now she had unpacked the drone to film it, and later would synch it with the students' soundtrack and do interviews. A reporter from the *Crier* might want photos. As the event began, up the drone went, high enough not to be distracting.

Amy was still floating on air, thinking: *Binni was so happy on the walk over, and so nervous too. "This will be very challenging," he said. "I hope I am not intruding on your life with this, but I will need your help. I'm scared that I won't be enough." And without thinking I said, "I will be with you, Binni. Count me in, one hundred percent." Even thinking of it right now, I'm so happy. I feel so good. Do not start crying, okay? So, big shot: I hereby commit. I commit.*

The Columbia weatherman had predicted heavy rain continuing throughout the day, with storm warnings. As was understood by the Columbians, the forecast was a reliable breakage, and it was a crisp, sunny day.

The speeches began. But the bullhorn didn't really work that well—and a lot of the words were swallowed in echo, filtering down to the small crowd listening below. But the students seemed to hear just fine—on the steps, and the ones on the circular driveway below.

There were no breakages. Kids and parents relaxed. Speakers took turns talking about the police atrocities and the greater problem: the fact that the United States of America was now as bad as, if not worse than, ever. They shouted out simple slogans, variations of Black Lives Matter, and the crowd called back.

The kids were arranged on the steps around their leaders, rippling all the way down to the sidewalk, into the road. Their parents were standing in the grass circle with the broken fountain, upon which in Becraft limestone was the "Town Seal of Columbia, 18th century": Neptune, with trident, sitting astride a spouting whale, facing backward.

At the top of the stairs, behind the students addressing the crowd below, was the entrance to city hall. Suddenly the door opened and a man came out, taking off his mask.

He was sort of pear-shaped, with a small head and thin hair, and wearing a red golf shirt open at the neck. In his hand was a rolled-up document. He put a pen back into his shirt pocket, looking down at it. It seemed he had been inside getting something, perhaps a permit. When he looked up and saw the crowd he was startled—he jumped back, as if scared by the size of the crowd.

His reaction was comic, and everyone laughed.

Looking out over the crowd, he was embarrassed. He turned to the leaders with the megaphone, and asked, "What's this for?"

"It's a rally for Black Lives Matter," said the leader.

He looked up at her, and down at the crowd below.

"Yeah, well," he said, with contempt, "and do Black *babies* matter too?"

A gasp from just about everyone. A murmur swept through the crowd. The student leaders looked stunned, not knowing what to do.

The man pushed his way down the stairs and started across the street toward the grassy circle, pulling his car key from his pocket. He pointed it at a truck parked on the other side, and it unlocked with a *squileeep!* that, in the portending silence, seemed loud and scary.

It was one of those high-off-the-pavement, extra-long pickup trucks with a back seat. Orville and the others saw in each other's eyes the same worry: he might have a gun in that truck and this is how people get killed. They prayed that no one would shout anything at him.

"Asshole!" a boy yelled as loud as he could. "You asshole!"

The man stopped, turned, and started walking back across the grassy circle toward the kid.

Orville stepped in front of him, started to try to talk with him, looming over him.

"Get outta my way!"

"Cool down, don't lose control—"

"Outta my way, old man!"

Orvy didn't move and, as Amy and Roy rushed over to help, the man shouted, "Fuck you!" and pushed Orville, who fell to the ground. But when he turned to run, he tripped over someone and landed on top of Orville. Others tried to separate them, but the guy ripped the mask off Orvy's face and, coughing and cursing, spat at him, "Fucking cunt!"

Then, seeing others come running, he got up, ran to his truck, revved it up, and drove it back fast around the fountain circle, wheels screeching, and it looked like he was going to plow right into the kids and parents in the road who had gathered there to try to help.

Everybody was screaming, throwing BLM and other signs at the truck as it barreled down on them, and then it seemed to swerve and slow, and miraculously didn't hit anyone, and was gone.

Orville, wiping his face, was the only one who might have been hurt. But he got up on his feet and on brief exam all the doctors agreed that it was nothing serious. Putting on a fresh mask—Orvy always carried spares—he insisted on walking home.

———

When they got to Washington Street, Binni and Raz turned to go down to his house, said their good-byes.

"I'm so sorry this turned out bad," said Raz.

Ben, clearly worried by what had happened to Orvy, whined at Raz, wanting a pat, which she gave, a pat and a hug.

"We doctors are with you, Orvy," Binni said. "No matter *what*."

"What could be better?" Orvy said. "And *you* be well as well. See y'soon."

Orvy started walking briskly along Fourth Street toward home. "Who *was* that guy anyway?"

"I asked around," Miranda said. "No one had ever seen him before. You might have been exposed—we've got to trace him, get him tested."

"Yeah."

"The good news," said Ellie, "is that the drone got it all on tape—his attacking you, his license plate, too. I already called the police and sent the link to all of it. They said they'd meet you at the hospital."

"Hospital? In a pandemic? Packed to the gills with *sick and dying people*? I'm a doctor! Doctors don't *go to* hospitals. We go *home from* hospitals. Keep walking."

At the house, Roy, Berry, and Amy confronted him.

"Orvy," said Roy, "you've got to take this seriously. We've been through it, and even a minor case is hell. You've got to take this seriously—at least quarantine yourself, keep open to any symptom, get tested." He paused. "I'll be on the case. Remember—a doctor who treats *himself* has—"

"A fool for a patient. I know." Orville took a deep breath in. *How good, right now, a clear breath is. Very scary, this. You've got to find the best current treatment, from all the docs you're in touch with. And do it fast, while you can. Right now.*

Visibly shaken, he said, "Of course I'll quarantine. Miranda, can we make my office into a bedroom? I'll touch base with my doc friends, especially since this may turn out to be . . . 'personal,' right? I want to know what's working all over the world, if anything."

Miranda shook her head. "Don't say that."

"I know, I know. The odds are that Mr. Neanderthal wasn't infected, and anyway he gave me only one or two coughs. But I better not be face-to-face with you all until I'm clear—probably a week, to be sure. We can designate the guest bathroom right outside my office only for me, okay?"

"We'll get you tested every day," Amy said, "starting tomorrow. I can get test kits for all of us. Including Binni and Raz."

"The symptoms are key," Roy said, "not the furshlugginer tests—imagine, after a second wave has come and almost gone, and we *still* don't have accurate tests! Last I looked, the quality of American health care has fallen below Togo. So we've got unreliable tests *and* not enough of them. I can't recall if they err over-positive or over-negative?"

"No one knows," Amy said. "Probably both."

Roy said, "It's the symptoms that we need to watch for—any symptom. I tested negative the whole time I was tested in our apartment, but all the while, subtly, I was getting the symptoms. Write down anything weird, okay?" He paused, choked up. "Don't be no hero."

"Were you?"

Roy grimaced, then smiled. "Of course I was. I just gutted it out. *Bad* choice. I was lucky."

"Me too," said Berry. "I know what it feels like, and easy to miss. Especially with the typical aches and pains and forgetfulness of age."

"What age?" Orville said. "Right now, I can't even *recall* my age. Is that my first symptom? Covid dementia?"

———

After a few days in quarantine, the jokes from Orville, and anyone else who knew him, stopped. His vital signs and the Covid test were negative, and he had no symptoms. But he was sore all over—like the clenching up the day after a car crash. He had no temperature, shivers, or coughing. The second wave was almost to November—a lull before the hell of the holiday season—but because of masks and distancing, it might have been lessening in New York State. In the South and Midwest it was steadily, scarily rising, high and fast.

And so Orville and the others started to think he'd beaten it. They were all so worried and distracted. After four days, just as Orvy was thinking he'd be okay to lift the quarantine, he ordered a Pizza's Pizza, hot, with pepperoni and double garlic.

"There's no garlic on this pizza!" he said on his phone to Miranda in the kitchen. "And the pepperoni I can't even taste! The only good part of it is the crust and the cheese!"

When Amy came in that night and heard it from Miranda, she went cold.

"What?" Miranda asked, seeing the instant change in Amy's eyes.

"Loss of taste and smell is classic for Covid."

"Oh," said Orvy, on the phone. "Yeah, I forgot. Shit!"

Amy got her black bag and took out the automatic thermometer "gun" and pointed it at his forehead: 99.7. She put the tip of his index finger into the oxygen saturation clip: 92 percent.

"All normal," he said.

"Not quite. Here," she said. "Let me get a test." Then, "Head back."

"They're notoriously bad, and—"

"You are not the doctor now, I'm your doctor. Nostrils up!" She scoured both nostrils.

And then, even before the test result, it sank in. There was a good chance he'd caught it.

Amy sat him and Miranda down, to plan. "You're trending, Orvy. There's a fifty-fifty chance you have Covid."

"I'm not going to the hospital," he said. "As you and every other doc knows, hospitals are dangerous to your health."

"Thanks a lot, Unc. Jesus."

"You and your team are terrific. But an overextended hospital and an exhausted team? And since I know most everybody, and they me, I'll be the 'star' patient, which might kill me."

"True. So what do you suggest we do?"

"I'll start right here, right now, with Binni. He's on the right track with IV infusions of cloned fetal stem cells—it got FDA approval for special cases. Do you think he'll call me special?"

"Absolutely."

"And maybe monoclonal antibodies, right?"

"I can get us that, yes."

"And, just a hunch, but a lot of my European contacts are hot on high doses of steroids."

"Good. Real good. But as you know, they're all IV infusions, and over time, have side effects that have to be watched for carefully, all right?"

Orville groaned. "I know. But I'm skeptical of Kush Kare—especially with more and more nurses quitting. They're indispensable."

"No problem," Amy said. "We'll put you on the top floor, in the Diamond Suite."

"Isn't it filled up with the Diamond Rich?"

"Nope. It's almost never used—maybe once or twice in all these months. The rich want to go to the name places that nobody else can afford. They buy the idea that the greatest expense is a sign of the best care in the world. The Mayo Clinic allows them to land their private jet at a runway that rolls them right up to the entrance to the hospital and then get whisked up to the private suites. They're making millions.

"Okay, hang on." Amy called Shump, put her on speaker, told her the story, and the plan.

Silence.

Sounds of Shump clearing her throat a few times, then blowing her nose. "Sorry. I love that old guy—always have, since second grade and . . ."

They waited for her to stop crying.

"Okay," she said. "It's scary, but we will save him. Right?"

"Or die trying—did I just say that?"

All laughed, the sound somehow cleaning the air. *Yes, we will save Orvy no matter what.*

"Thanks, kid," said Orville. "But I've got one condition, to put my life in your hands, and the hands of that phenom Natasha, okay?"

All said okay.

"There are two beds on that top-floor luxury ward, right, with two ventilators?"

"Right," said Shump. The rich guys want two there, in case one breaks. Which is never.

"While I'm there, I want approval over who gets the second bed and ventilator, if needed."

"Anything you want," Shump said. "Natasha will be on board for anything you want, honey."

"I *don't* want one of those rich white *shmuckelzagers* to get that bed. I want a POC."

"A POC?" Shump asked.

"A person of color."

Amy looked at Orvy, puzzled.

"Black Lives Matter."

———

Luckily none of the others at the protest tested positive. In the days following Orville's admission to the hospital, as he developed most of the symptoms of Covid, he also got all the treatments that he and his world network had figured were the best. It's possible no 70-year-old man had ever received so many meds in such a short period of time—Orvy wanted to go all out and the team agreed.

When Binni did his fetal stem cell infusions, he could barely see through the nervous sweat. Using his rare procedure might—given the other rare treatments' side effects—harm Orvy instead of help him. Roy, who had knowledge and experience with monoclonal antibodies, administered those. The high-dose steroids were administered by Natasha. It was not rare for a patient to get these treatments, but it had rarely been tried in quick succession. Everyone was going all out—the risk taken because of the love given. Love does that.

Luckily Orville had stayed in good shape. His careful eating—Miranda's fierce vegetables, daily being walked by Ben, had kept him thin. The "best" predictor of death was gut fat: the spare tire around the abdomen.

In the first week, before all these treatments were finished, Orville had one "high" day, one clear day! It was the steroids. He was talking faster and thinking more clearly—but he got manic, sketching out how to fix world health care by an eight-part plan based on a specific kind of castor oil from his childhood. And it might not have been only the steroids, because his temperature and oxygen trended a bit better. A ray of hope, of not needing a ventilator.

That night, Miranda decided to sleep over at the hospital, as she often did.

"I want you to see something, dear," Orville said, not gasping as much that night because of the day's bolus of steroids. "I feel clearer. Something I just recalled that I never told you. Come with."

Natasha helped him into a wheelchair, and Miranda pushed him toward the wall that was all window, looking out over the little town.

"This used to be the top floor of the hospital," Orvy said. "You could get out onto a balcony back then, and see all the way across the river to the mountains. It was winter. The first time I was planning to stay over at your house—Cray was on a sleepover at Schooner's house? I was taking calls from your house up in Columbiaville. It was the first time we made love, remember?"

"As if I was there right now again, yes."

"And then way past midnight, the hospital paged me to come in. A delivery of twins. The couple was Black and poor, and something was terribly wrong. I raced down here—twins, fetal distress, I had to work quick, do a C-section."

He paused to take a better breath.

"Twin boys. One was normal, the other was microcephalic, his head the size of a small doll's. He soon died. The father wanted to see the dead baby. I said to him, 'Okay, but you'll never forget it.' And he said to me, '*Him*. I want to see *him*.' It startled me, being called out. Rightfully so. And when he saw his son, he reached out a hand and touched the perfect shoulder, and then the squashed head. He bowed his own head and crossed himself, prayed. He looked at me, his eyes wet, sorrowful. He said, 'Thank you.' And I said, 'Thank *you*.' Feeling, in him, the power of facing *into*, in a world that as a rule turns *away*."

"Beautiful, love. The spirit!"

"Yes. The divine in us." Tears came now, *good tears. She's teary too. Arm around my waist. She's strong, I'm fading. Fear raised its ugly face. Then left.*

"And so," Orvy went on, "that night during a break in the emergency room action I came up here for some quiet, out on the balcony. I searched my pockets for the half-smoked Parodi cigar I always had, and matches. The night was crisp. The little town was iced up and the air tasted like cold quarters and seemed stretched tight as an eardrum so it was like I could hear *everything*. You know that kind of night?"

"I do."

"And I thought of the dead twin who would always be almost there, floating there like all the dead, and the live twin. And then . . ." He felt tears coming, swallowed them down. "And then I thought of *you*, of our histories and of our lovemaking that night, and I whispered . . . '*This* is the one that will survive.'"

"Oh my!" she cried out. Tears came to her eyes, rolling down her cheeks. "My dear one."

They fell into each other's PPE.

———

At the same time, hearing that Orvy was having a good evening, Amy, Binni, Roy, Hyper, and Eat My Dust were walking out of the hospital to their cars. Their spirits had been lifted a little by the news that Orville had had a good day, and also by the slight but clear decline in admissions as if, by chance or fate, the second wave was finally waving good-bye.

They were getting out early, just six o'clock—the time during the first wave when Columbians, taking their cue from the New Yorkers, would come up to the hospital and applaud as we came out, singing all the time, inspiring American songs like "God Bless America," "The Star-Spangled Banner," or even "Take Me Out to the Ball Game." It was great!

But now the singing was gone, replaced by drive-by invective—even hatred—as if we'd stopped trying to give every person all we had? Somewhere the gratitude had turned to rage. Nothing had changed in the care of the patients—ever since the first wave it was often hard to treat the patients promptly or well, and lying on a stretcher in the hallway was often the case—but still they had sung.

Why all of a sudden had appreciation turned to rage?

A lot of it still focused on Eat My Dust's Facebook posts, about masks and distancing. And the Big Mac knew which words would mobilize his millions.

So the six-o'clock drive-by was a ride of rage.

Eat My Dust Eddie's main concern was to make sure they didn't find out about his connection with the basketmakers. He hadn't been able to see them for at least a month now. Eddie always had trouble making friendships, and he was missing this one dearly. He got more depressed.

Most evenings the security guards would escort the doctors to their cars, but that evening there was an emergency somewhere else. It was as if the drive-bys knew it, and lingered, some even stopping their pickups to curse them out. The doctors and nurses were stranded on the pavement, unable to get to their cars. Staring out into the face of hatred. They just stood there in the lee of the entrance, stuck. Fearful it would get violent, as it had elsewhere—say, with the appearance of some nice new guns.

All of a sudden there was a loud coughing KA-BOOOOM! and then a roar of a big tough diesel-throated engine—*ka-thumpp, ka-whampp*—and several backfires. And out of KK's ultraprivate service road emerged an armored Hummer kind of truck with a turret on top and riveted dust-colored armor plates all over behind which to shoot without being seen—like the ones we'd all seen on TV in the 20-year folly of a war in the sand and dust of Afghanistan. It stopped right in front of the docs, blocking the other traffic.

Wa da boom went the diesel engine, *wa-da-boom wa-da-boom*— a reassuring sound.

Two hatches opened in this monstrous armadillo-like, well, *thing*. One hatch on top, one hatch on a blast-repelling opening in the lower level, over a wheel bed. All in freshly painted tan, strong heightened tan, oiled up, testosterone bodied.

Out of each hatch popped half a policeman. In the turret on top he was fat and red-haired and red-faced. In the other, from the lower deck, was a matchstick with deathly white skin and dark black hair. Both wore bright red earmuffs, making them look like teddy bears on Christmas Day.

"Gilheeny and Quick?" shouted Roy. "You, here?"

"Would we be policemen if we were not?" said Sergeant Gilheeny, the red and heavy one.

"For what are friends for," said the black-haired matchstick, Officer Quick, "if not for this? We heard how badly this is going for you all. So we came to protect our dear docs again, from the House of God all the way to Man's 4th Best, and now this. Fifty years! And we would hope that you'd throw in our annual checkups in return?"

"Where'd you get the . . . the what the hell do you call it?"

"Standard-issue tank: Iraq War and then the twenty-year Afghanistan folly," said Gilheeny. "Towns like Columbia are getting them for free, via His Honor Henry Schooner. He's given us full use all the while we're here. And we've got an open-ended stay."

"He bought it?"

"Well," said Gilheeny, pursing his lips, "let us just say that he donated it to Columbia via his clout on the Ways and Means money, for as long as it is required. In fact the US Army is practically givin' 'em away to a lot of cities now, to quell the locked-and-loaded legal protests."

"To fight the race wars," said Quick, "and worse wars; vide fascism growing all over the dull underbelly of our divided once-great national nation. A task that the Fat Man would have welcomed—yes *welcomed!*—in its dark and ironic waste, may God rest his soul."

"Yes, yes!" said Gilheeny almost happily, as if at the conundrum of democracy failing. "We've become a kind of home-fried Afghanistan, have we not?"

"But . . ." Roy asked, "how the hell were you in touch with Henry Schooner?"

Gilheeny looked to Quick, Quick looked to Gilheeny.

There was a pause, and then Gilheeny said to Quick, "Your turn."

Quick smiled. "Would we be policemen if we were not?"

"And now to work," Gilheeny said. He and Quick popped down into the guts of the thing, and in unison pulled down the hatches with two great metallic WHOMPS!

A roar. A flashing of lights.

As they moved to get rid of the circular traffic of legions of Big Macs, out of the Hummer's main gun barrel came a strange noise, and when the turret aimed it at a car, the driver jumped as if he'd gotten a shock, stalled for a second, and then frantically drove away.

In a few minutes there was a blessed silence.

The bestial armored vehicle gave a couple of soothing *toot-toots* like a toy train and rumbled down the hill after the cars and then sat there, setting up a checkpoint.

In the parking lot, the little group of docs and nurses and techs and good citizens shook their heads at what had just happened. They looked at each other.

Suddenly Hyper Hooper pointed back at the hospital's façade, shouting, "Holy moley! Look!"

On the high concave wall of the main building was an even more enormous banner than before and upon it in artery red was a simple message:

KUSH KARE IS SHIT

Each of them looked at the others. Phones came out, photos and videos were taken and sent all over the world, in an indelible instant.

Eat My Dust Eddie said, "Finally, finally!"

"Okay, big guy," Roy asked, "what's this 'finally'?"

"This," Eddie said in a voice of awe, "this is finally proof that there is a loving God."

Smiling, with a lift in their steps that was, yes, a lifting up, they left.

THE END
OF SUFFERING

"We know now that Government by organized money is
as dangerous as Government by organized mob."

—FRANKLIN DELANO ROOSEVELT (1936)

17

Two weeks past Thanksgiving, two weeks to go to Christmas.

Before the start of these double-barrel holidays, almost all Kush Kare doctors had warned their patients to be even more careful to wear masks and maintain social distance from their loved ones and others, especially if their loved ones didn't love them enough to wear masks and maintain social distance. There were also stern warnings from the CDC against holiday travel, especially on buses, trains, and airplanes.

Roy reported to the team that one young patient had said, "But I want to make sure that I get to see my grandmother before she dies." To which Roy replied, "Great, great! Because if you *do* go see her, it might *be* the last time before she dies—because of you."

"And what did he say to that?" Hyper Hooper asked.

"I believe his words were, 'Hey, thanks, Doc, for letting me go. I'm with you, a hundred and ten percent.'"

If the first two Covid spikes could be referred to as waves, the third was a tsunami. A rushing tidal wave of human suffering that crashed through the hospital and flooded beds—first the ICU and then spilling out into every nook and cranny that could fit a bed (except for the one empty bed on the top floor). The corridors to and from Emergency were lined with patients on stretchers. Some heart attacks were treated by nurses in the corridors—how ludicrous was that! The team had never encountered as many patients as sick. If asked, any of Amy's team would say that they didn't really know what the hell they were doing, but they had gotten expert in doing it.

For instance, they still didn't know what the optimal timing was for intubation. Looking back at patient outcomes from the first wave, they'd concluded that they'd been intubating too soon. In the second wave they had shifted to waiting much too long to intubate. During the third, they were trying to find the ideal middle ground. The decision became easy at one point when they ran out of ventilators.

KK never admitted publicly that during the third wave they were running out of many necessary things—not just ventilators, but nurses, BiPAP machines, high-flow O_2 systems—all the things that keep patients alive. Keeping dead patients dead made KK care a lot easier— they could move on to billing them and their surviving relatives.

During the holidays there was a new level of indifference on the part of the bosses to the suffering of the workforce: nurses, doctors, respiratory techs, cleaners, and all the others who risked their lives 24/7. Instead of shutting down lucrative elective surgeries again—to redirect help and matériel to Amy's frontline intensivists—KK sent out a memo that they would "ramp up and risk our brave surgeons' lives" by doing *necessary elective* surgeries, which would be billed at "combat" pay for the whole surgical team, while flouting the detailed Covid safety guidelines. Long ago it had become clear to the intensivists that in the private equity system the doctors were only as good as their ability to bring in money. And surgery was the linchpin of hospital money.

Also, to stop the bleeding, like any sharp businessmen, KK hired a top-ranked publicity group to attract new customers. One

TV commercial showed a wonderful family frolicking in their back-yard swimming pool, three generations smiling. Except for a slightly overweight but gorgeous mom clutching her belly and grimacing, pushing back her plate piled high with rendered-fat stuff. Suddenly, a doctor appears in surgical garb and says, "Let Kush Kare take out your gall bladder, and we'll take out your second one free!" Was this a joke? A mistake? Who knew?

At one of the team meetings during this brutal holiday season, all members were mostly quiet, depressed and exhausted, body, mind, and spirit. Silent gloom.

"Luckily it takes energy to be depressed!" Hyper cried out. "So I'm good."

"Yeah, well," said Eddie, "I wish I were you, man, because I've got just about enough energy to spare, and I'm using it productively. To rethink suicide."

"Great, great!" Hyper replied happily, as if he hadn't heard what he'd heard, "all we have to do to stay alive is to pull the plug on all our emotions, and muddle through the day. I'm bad, I'm mad, and I'm glad of it."

Most days, a member or two of Amy's team would seem to disconnect emotionally, and muddle through the day. Often, the entire purpose of waking up in the morning was to try to survive until it was time to go to bed.

The patient load ballooned. Amy demanded help from the administration. They responded by offering to pay other specialties—nephrology, cardiology, dermatology—to help. At twice the pay of the team members who would be supervising them! The team was outraged but soon realized that it was just another in a long exercise of "good business" kicks to the groin. It turned out to be irrelevant, because the other docs wanted no part of hellish acute care with its high risk of getting the real bad shit or dead. Better to watch it from home on TV.

Among many Columbians, the disregard for the danger of the pandemic continued. The team stopped trying to educate patients about masking and distancing. It took too much emotional reserve to deal with the fiery, moronic backlash.

The team's single goal was to survive, so they could help others survive.

The nurses had it the worst. Now when each nurse had to cover seven beds per shift, often Covid at various stages, they felt they were at their max. When colleagues dropped out and could not be replaced easily, that number went to ten beds. An impossible situation. Errors ballooned. Many nurses were stretched so thin that the docs and others watching them work couldn't fathom how they didn't break. Some did.

One morning Shump came into the team meeting half an hour late, looking like all the life force had been squeezed out of her. Known for her energy, she just sat there and looked unplugged. Everyone waited for her to speak.

Finally: "There had been nurse cancellations up on the wards, and we were also down one in the ICU. I had to find a way—I got two clinical nurse assistants. Only me and them. And the house staff was great: cleaning, delivering things—plethora of bedpans. We managed pretty well to do the meds—not much else. All night long I'm mostly alone—feeling really alone, lonely! Mainly a lot of suctioning out of secretions—*secretions*! It's the worst—drowning—dying—in your own secretions! One old guy was so sweet, really fearing death—dying alone, you know? Lovable guy. One of the housekeepers is learning Reiki, and we all put our hands on different parts of his body, comforting him, at least for a while. But it all felt so . . . *lonely*! Lonely as death."

She shook her head.

"And at about four in the morning I had to go through the dying moments with a twenty-year-old girl, her family on one side of the glass and me on the other holding this . . . this saintly young girl . . . until she . . . stopped breathing. And I had to rush off! Someone dying somewhere else!"

She looked around the room. "I'm not sure I can do another night like that. And then just before I could leave, I was suctioning and got . . . got all the stuff on my PPE and that was it! It like exploded, seemed to aerosolize! Somehow I thought they'd broken through the protection and had gotten on my goggles, forehead, eyelids, neck, ears? I stripped and showered here, not wanting to bring it anywhere *near* the house. I wrapped myself in fresh scrubs and drove home. I stripped again outside the house, and stayed in the shower until I kind of felt like I-don't-know clean—*porcelain*-clean? Best shower ever."

She shook her head sadly, and then, angry, said, "Goddamn it, that's it! We've got to get more nurses in here, okay? I don't know how, but I know we have to! *Period.*"

———

And still there was no treatment for this disease.

Intravenous medications of three drugs, right away, might help: steroids, remdesivir—monoclonal antibodies—and for the first time Binni's approved, targeted stem cell infusions. Otherwise, after almost a year fighting Covid, doctors all over America and the world were *still improvising*, making it up as we went along, clutching any new hard sliver of data about the virus.

The best treatment would be a vaccine. In fact, Moderna and Pfizer were close. Binni's discovery had been noticed by Moderna in Boston. They offered him a position. He said he couldn't leave Columbia. That was fine—as long as he had good Zoom and safe access to high-powered Moderna computers, which he did. He talked it over with Amy and Razina. They were fine—and proud. This also solved a problem. His ex-wife would only let Razina stay with him if he was not in the hospital all day and night. When Binni *was* in the hospital, Raz could be with one or more Roses. And it was an astonishing moment for Binni: at home on a little screen, helping to tweak messenger RNA chains! To win the race to the cure.

And what a time to join Moderna! In a few days the first injections would be given, to health-care workers. A jab in the arm, and *So long, virus!* Like the yearly one to protect against the flu, like all the childhood viruses. Surely, *surely*, the scientists were saying, a broad vaccination rollout could come in January 2021! And of course it would be embraced by all! *So long, virus.*

On *Morning Joe*, the President had not conceded to Biden. "Fake news," he said. "Stop the steal." Asked if he took responsibility for Covid deaths reaching 350,000, he said, "No."

———

Orville was still in the hospital, up on the private floor. Amy and the others had agreed that she and Natasha would be his lead doctor and nurse. "Doc Orvy" had doctored Columbians forever, so many were paying attention to his transit along the difficult path to recovery. This awareness meant that there was a microscope on everyone involved in treating him. The community love for Orvy was so *there*, and gratifying.

The "BLM case" at city hall had gotten florid in the press—Ellie's drone tape had captured it all—both Orvy's life-and-death battle and also the arrest and charges against the guy in the truck who attacked him. Luckily, to the press, after a really long time of trying and failing to get interviews from the docs, it was old news. It stopped.

Amy went to see Orville two to ten times a day, depending. Her whole team—especially the science nerds Binni, Hyper, Sev, and the remarkable Nurse Shump—were totally on the case, with contacts all over the world. Eat My Dust Eddie was still hated and hassled for his Facebook pleas, but on a secure flip phone he was consulting with his basketmakers. None of them had caught Covid, using their natural medicines—which Orvy could try if needed. Orvy's symptoms were classic Covid—high fever, coughing, intermittent difficulty breathing. A persistent headache, which was unusual. The goal was never to go over the red line of intubation.

On one particularly bad day and night and day, with his oxygen saturation bouncing around as if the virus was trying to carom farther from his aching head into his lungs, Amy almost never left his side. Roy, as the senior doctor, took over leadership of the team, as the level of horrific suffering and dying went up even higher.

Orvy had fought it out, day after day. A few times, Amy had almost given the order to intubate him—all the numbers lined up to do it. But then, remembering Orvy's mantra "Tincture of time," she waited longer on the knife-edge. To some on the team her daring was down to being too close to him emotionally, and the time went on into the night, then over into the morning—watching him laboring to breathe, keeping the emergency meds ready, and the intubation option always in the offing. At one point Natasha and a few others— thinking that she was "too close" to him to be "objective"—tried to persuade her to "bite the bullet or else we'll lose him!"

At every downturn Amy did her inner-doctor scan of whether or not she was being "objective." And then she realized that it wasn't only a matter of objectivity, but it was also a matter of what good doctors do: being willing to *be with him, and in great care with him.* As if she had hyperacute observation and understanding of that observation, from all the years of all the patients who had been in this spot. *No, I'm in an exquisitely clear moment, almost seeing him from his whole life to his lungs. They think I'm too close to him, too involved? I know him, and know myself, and however strange it is for a doctor to say, "As long as I'm sitting here with him, I promise you and him—I won't lose him."*

———

Finally, step by step, taking an eternity and an instant, his breathing edged back.

There came a day when he was clearly on the mend. Still in the hospital and demanding to get out, still weak and headachy, but, yes, mending.

"Hospitals are dangerous," Orville repeated ad nauseum. "Get me outta here."

That fine day Amy and Roy were with him. Miranda and Ellie—and Henry Schooner from his office in Washington—were on Zoom. A fervent celebration.

Orvy was rolled out in a wheelchair through the deep crowd of hospital workers and Columbians, everybody cheering and crying, crying with joy. The wheelchair seemed gigantic and made him seem even more frail and collapsed, almost overpowering him. He was bundled up and blinking in the sharp low winter sun, and his waves in the bulky cloak he was dressed in seemed feeble. There were so many people that Gilheeny and Quick in the Humvee had to control the flow. Somebody started singing, "When you walk through a storm keep your head up high . . ." But it petered out quickly on the other verses, and someone else switched to "God Bless America." He smiled broadly and waved weakly—and demonstrated a series of deep, coughless breaths—to more cheers. A beloved of so many.

And all that cheering and shouting was nothing compared to one other person who for some reason hadn't *ever* come to visit him, in all that time?

"WROWLLLLLLLL! WWWWROLOFFF!"

———

They were sitting around the long kitchen table with coffee and Iggy's chocolate croissants with Amy, Miranda, Eleanor, Roy, Berry, Binni, and Raz.

"So, Dad," Eleanor said, "what do you think made you make it? Was there anything that brought you back?"

"Good question, hon." He thought about it for a long moment. *There was one day, one moment, something when, with all the pain and fear and death right there, and I finally had had it! I wanted to just let go*—was *letting go, and something else happened. What was it? Yes!* He said to her, "You're not going to believe this. Y'know, Roy, it was something you did, when you stayed the whole night with me, at one point reading out loud to me? I forget the book, a novel?"

"My favorite, *Of Love and Other Demons*. Gabriel García Márquez."

"Yes! About a doctor, treating a girl bitten by a rabid dog?"

"That's it, yes. His name was Dr. Abrenuncio, a Spanish Jew."

"His prescription was wonderful: flowers, and . . . what was it? Yes! He talked about how 'no medicine cures'?"

Roy nodded and smiled. "It's my favorite passage. In Dr. Abrenuncio's words?" Roy closed his eyes, recalling. "'Play music for her, fill the house with flowers, have the birds sing, take her to the ocean to see the sunsets, give her everything that can make her happy. . . . *No medicine cures what happiness cannot.*'"

"Yes!" Orvy cried out. "'No medicine cures what happiness cannot.'" He paused, shaking his head at the simple mystery, so devalued now in modern medicine. And then he went on, in a kind of awe. "And then I saw in my mind's eye the happiness that I have had, and do have, and will have if I live! There was a *click*. Like a shutter. *Click!* To remember it. That night I slept well and woke up knowing I wouldn't be dying this time around."

Weeks later, Orville was sitting on the couch. Seeing Amy looking so happy to see him alive brought tears to his eyes. *What a weepy old man I've become!*

Seeing him tearing up again brought tears to her own eyes! *Like a love ritual, affirming that all is precious and nobody's gonna die today.*

"Sad to see me, eh?" she said.

"You look wonderful right now. All good?"

"Because of you, yes." She handed him his coffee. "You're a miracle, Orvy. What you went through, the odds? Coming out of it scot-free, no residua, you look great, back to normal. You are so, so lucky!"

"I got great care. Strange, being out on the edge with death, I really did *feel* it, that damp chill and invading panic . . ." He trailed off. Looked concerned.

"So you're back to being your own healthy, intolerable self. Even, go back to work? Going firsthand through hell and coming out great can help others?"

"Agreed." *Should I tell her? Gotta tell someone, and she's now my doc.*

Amy was so acutely attuned to him now that sometimes she felt she could read his mind—and, easier, his emotions. Something was up. "Tell me."

"Nothing, I'm—"

"Hey. It's me. The baby who was imprinted on you at my birth, okay?"

"I'm scared. Worried about my brain. I might have post-Covid dementia."

"What?!" She was shocked. "Wait. I've never seen any—"

"I know, it's scary. Just listen, Doc, okay?" She nodded. "Names!

I'm having a lot of trouble dredging up names—last night Miranda was talking about a good friend of ours and for the life of me I couldn't recall her name. I kept thinking Jackie, but I knew it wasn't it. Turned out that it was 'Frankie.' I could almost *see* my brain going, like my 'search' memory went up the synapses to 'two syllables, last one is "ie"' and got stuck on *Jack*ie, and never got to *Frank*ie. And words. I'll be talking and slam into the 'right' word and can't find it, on the tip of my tongue, and to cover up, I use a synonym. I also can't find my keys or my other stuff; it's scary. Can we set aside the Covid now, and cure the dementia first?"

She smiled, nodding.

"The worst is forgetting—lights and keys and where I put stuff— in the broiler, or on the stove so the boiling eggs explode and hit the ceiling?" He stopped. "I used to have a great memory. Now? I get a phone number and when I go to dial it—I mean punch it in—I realize I've forgotten it!"

"And you weren't like this before the Covid?"

"Ask Miranda. She's at her wits' end. She's been really busy with the new book—researching, talking to people on Zoom—so at breakfast when we meet, we tell each other what we have to do that day. And I mostly forget it. So then I write it down, but I forget where I wrote it, or just forget to look!"

"Have you told her how worried you are?"

"Sure. But I don't think it's sinking in."

"Listen, Orvy. You're just out of a hellish, sensory-deprived experience. For almost a year! And then, a death-defying romance with the worst virus ever? Of course there'll be post-Covid healing. We'll keep an eye on it, okay?"

"Sorry—you've got enough on your plate, kid. But you should be aware that I'm feeling I've lost it, that sharpness—maybe it's long-haul Covid?"

"I hear you, hon, loud and clear. Your brain and body may need more time to heal whatever's going on. It's probably transient, residual inflammation, now calming down, healing itself. You are, right now, clearly here with me and—"

"I know, I know. Sorry, really." He shook his head. "Honey, I'm scared."

She paused, and then nodded. "I know, dear, really I *know*. How could you not be? Look, I'm sorry, but I *have* to go to the team meeting—a big one."

"Bad?"

"Worse than ever. You and me will keep talking this out." She put her hand on his arm, and then his cheek, holding his gaze, joining him in his dread. Dry-eyed fear.

"I promise, Orvy, you and I will take this seriously. We'll get the data, talk to the experts. You've had a real trauma, for sure. *I will be with you, all the way.*" She smiled. "As you've always said, 'the body has an incredible ability to heal.' So we'll do a max dose of 'tincture of time,' okay?"

His mentor Bill Starbuck's words, which he had passed on to Amy.

He smiled back at her. "Yes!" he said. "And looking at you right now, I believe it, all of it. I'm grateful, and I'm lucky. Thanks for reminding me of all this—good doctoring. Umm, what'd you say your name is?" They laughed. He took her hand, squeezed it, felt the solidness of the bones, and then the pliancy of the skin. A kind of lesson. "Love you, kid."

"Love you too," she said, holding back tears. "With all my heart."

———

While Amy was up at six, dog walking with Razina, Roy was in the ICU, at his wits' end.

He had been there since five, dealing with a horrific case of a dying son on a ventilator. Except his mother would not let him die. It was pure torment.

It triggered in a caretaker "the Big Rage," rage caused by dealing with patients who didn't believe in masks and distancing. It had gotten worse than ever.

It's simple, Roy thought. *We do everything, literally killing ourselves for our patients. All of us sworn to that calling by the Hippocratic oath no matter what—and they trash it all. After all, it's in our nation's blood: the Declaration of Independence, not the Declaration of Interdependence. Nurses, mostly women, are being treated the worst. Naturally most of them are enraged. (Although some, like saints, are able to feel sorrow.) Families of the patients are going wild. Screaming at any and all of the health-care workers, spitting abuse. Doctors, nurses, invaluable respiratory technicians, cleaners, and aides, whose very jobs are to guide their loved ones through, to life—all are enemies; harassed, disbelieved, threatened. Whipped to a frenzy on Fox and Facebook, attacking us, whose job is to guide their loved ones through, to live.*

And so for all health-care workers, it had gotten perilous. As some great American had said to Roy early that morning: "You *chose* this, Doc. *Suck it up!*"

Oh, sure, once in a while, upon their deathbed, a patient— almost always a male—would get a message to his family: "I was wrong. It's not fake. Wear a mask. Don't hug anyone. I love you."

The rage. Doctors and nurses and techs risking their lives at a toxic workplace to save people, and the people happily risking nothing? Doing nothing to help save themselves and others, not even a little piece of cloth over their noses and mouths.

Rage and peril. The only hope? The vaccine. It couldn't come soon enough.

Now Roy was in a real tight spot.

The patient was John Dozier, a 61-year-old guy on the vent who was dying faster than they could keep him alive. He was a longtime worker in the Columbia Pocketbook Factory, before it was turned into yet another bank. He caught Covid at a huge presidential rally in Maine, and a thousand others had started a third wave all over New England. John Dozier's mother, Doreen, who was immunosuppressed, was convinced that he was dying because Roy "didn't clean his ventilator." Roy tried for hours to get what she meant—she gave no explanation. Her six adult children agreed to transition their dad to comfort care; his wife wanted another opinion. And a second. A third. Fourth. Fifth. Two intensivists, one ID—infectious diseases doc—one pulmonologist, and, in the Christmas spirit, a palliative doc in a pear tree.

Doreen wanted still another opinion. She wanted to know why Roy didn't treat him with Big Mac's horse deworming drug, and a dose of vitamin C so high that Roy didn't think there was enough C in the entire city to get it.

Now Roy was due elsewhere. The team's "special meeting" was about to start, on what to do about this new wave's threat to good care.

"Laws of the House of God, Number 13," a familiar voice said. "'The delivery of medical care is to do as much nothing as possible.'"

What?

"You heard me."

And there he was, about ten feet above Roy in this high-ceilinged wing of the old hospital, not holding on to anything, but once again floating easily, a little this way, a little that, eating a Katz's kosher salami. He took a big bite and chewed, relishing the meat and the floating like a kid on a tether. He was wearing a long white lab coat, immaculate—but for stains of salami grease and mustard and Russian dressing. And a woman's red pillbox hat.

"Fats! I'm glad to see you!"

"I wish I could see me too. No mirrors up here. Vanity is verboten. No scales, though."

"Up? Is there really an 'up'?"

"Y'think death stops gravity?"

"What's with the lab coat? Are you doing research now?"

"Yop." Another bite, a chomping, a swallowing, a wiping of a glob of Russian.

"I bet you're working on the vaccine?"

"Of course! What else would I do in this mess? *Cheeze*. I'm with Pfizer, West Coast. And in this gig get this: I shouldn't tell you, but c'mere c'mere listen: I'm a woman! Same IQ and I got a cool zaftig body with my same old brain—!"

A sudden clap of thunder near him—he went to the ground, flat on his big gut, bouncing on the ground in sudden explosions and sparks, and then stopped.

"Sheesh," he said, shaking himself as he floated up again to his tree, went on.

"It's a tough gig—most of 'em don't believe in the power of heaven. I have to titrate my inspiration. We might get interrupted by a call, and I'll have to take it. *But*." He seemed to straighten up, push out his chest, grit his teeth as if for a war. "Roy, I failed real bad in Man's 4th Best Hospital, failed real bad with all of you, and with medicine, and—"

"Hey, give yourself a break, Fats, you did all you—"

"Up here, kid, we don't 'get breaks,' we try to *explore* so our fear or guilt or anger, well, if we stay with it, we're forced to face it, and it *softens*, and—supposedly, 'cause I'm not there yet—we come to understand that it's not a defect in us, it's just, well, *human*. Not *my* anger, just *anger*. Not *my* guilt, *just* guilt. *Just* human. Not valid currency in heaven. But I'm nowhere near that yet!" He paused. "Hey, I don't mean to pontificate, or rabbittanize. Sorry."

"No, no—it's great to hear it, and Berry will—"

"But!" Fats took a few breaths, each intake making him rise several inches, and out breath bringing him back down—as if breathing helium. "I'm *still* working to put the human back into medicine. And one day I came across an old doc—as old as me, and he was at a play—remember plays?"

"I do. I grew up with real live plays, just like you, right?"

"Yeah. Him and me got talking about my lifelong-and-after quest to put the human back into medicine?"

"We're still trying, here."

"Yeah, I know. Goodgood." He smiled. "So this doc was at a play, and suddenly one of the actors fell down onstage, and was lying there. A hush. And the doc says to me, 'And did the call go out to the audience, "Is there an insurance executive in the House?"'"

We both laughed.

"Private health insurance is killing us all—doctors, patients. And all we gotta do is"—he seemed to unroll the words in the air, like a banner, or a commandment—"stick together, squeeze the money out of the sick insurance machine, and put the human back into medicine."

"Beautiful, Fats."

"Yeah. It'll work. It's the only thing in heaven and hell that will."

"*Hell?* There really is a hell?"

"Who knows. Still under debate. I mean who the heaven cares!"

Roy nodded.

"Whatwhatwhat?" Fats said. "I didn't hear that."

"Oh, I just nodded."

Fats sighed. "This damn audio! Can y'hear me? Unmute. Say something."

"Yes. Testing testing."

"Got it. But listen up, Basch. Y'wanna get *through* to this woman, okay? She's suffering a *lot*! Sit down with her, face-to-face, at her level.

Tell her something personal about yourself, about, maybe, umm . . . ah yes, say, 'Doreen, if it were my own daughter in that hospital bed, I would let her go.' And wait. Give her time, 'cause she's got a lotta grief to unwind, and it's gonna take a while, maybe sixty of your seconds, to respond."

"Not *your* sixty seconds?"

"Ever hear of eternity? No rush. Do it."

Suddenly from behind Fats there was a blast of terrible grinding, like stones being crushed to dust. Not from the hospital but behind him, getting louder coming toward him.

"*Connect!*" Fats shouted, then he swooped and cried out, "But y'gotta *mean* it, as if she were your own daughter. Whoop-si-doodle!" Gone.

Shaking his head, thinking again he himself was going nuts, Roy sat down with Doreen, eye to eye. He thought of his daughter, Spring, found a place of good doctor sense, and said what Fats suggested, and meaning it: "What I know as a parent is, you're only human, and we humans make mistakes." And waited.

She opened her eyes wide. Then opened her pocketbook, tried to find something in it, found a blue hankie, blew her nose several times. Folding it back up and snapping the pocketbook shut, she let out what had been killing her all this time.

She told him the last conversation she had with her son was a terrible fight, before he went into the hospital. The fight had ended with them both telling each other, "May God strike you dead!" Before he was intubated, he had called and pleaded with her to forgive him but she didn't realize how sick he was and refused to talk to him.

"I didn't know—he was going to die—I refused . . ." She tried again to go on, but cries, one after another, wrenched her, back and forth, sobs and shaking tears. On and on.

Roy understood why she had felt so responsible. And then her behavior and clinging to every tiny thing suddenly made sense. After a while, she flushed pink, her lips relaxed. She sighed.

They sat together in silence. Her guilt finally eased, palpably. And then she agreed to comfort care.

Roy arranged for her to bring in the family. Later tonight John would die, surrounded by his mother and the rest of the family.

Sometime later, Roy realized that what they had really talked about was laying down a pathway for walking through her grief, her suffering. At least he hoped so.

18

"I'm going to make a change today," Amy was saying in the team gathering in the on-call room. "From now on we have a change of leaders."

Gasps. Was she quitting?

"Starting today, I *and* Shump will lead the group together, as co-chief intensivists, equal in every aspect. *Every aspect.* Bringing together our two different strengths." Amy smiled at Shump. "Seamlessly, right?"

"It won't be easy," said Shump. "But that's what'll make it work. Anybody trying to come between us, against *us*?" Her blue eyes flashed. "Not happening!"

Someone in the group started clapping, and shouts of affirmation and, even in all the depression, joy. The two policemen were in the back—standing there leaning against the wall, legs crossed like the front wheels of two parked bicycles, arms like handlebars—and let out piercing high whistles like sirens.

"Great, great," Amy was saying now, to the wild cheering of the announcement of this new two-woman team. "Why did we decide this? It is exactly what we need, in this hell. For forever, nurses have been second-class citizens in medicine. No more. I'm changing that. It's sending a message to all of Kush Kare—and other places. *Not here, not now, not with me, and not by this team.*"

More applause. "Shump?"

"Thanks, dear. *Well!*" Beaming, she looked around the room. "First, thanks, Amy. You're the greatest person I've ever worked with. And all of you have seen us work together, in mutual admiration of our guts, smarts, and caring respect, right?"

"Right" flew back and forth around the table.

"Under horrible conditions, we all have done incredibly well so far! It's hard to believe how long I've been working in health care in Columbia. I started out as dental hygienist to Roy's dad, remember?"

"You held my hand for the Novocain," he interjected, "the only way I got through."

"And somehow I got through nursing school. A few years ago, when Natasha and I wanted to get our master's degrees in business, Henry Schooner—on the hospital board when it was Columbia Hospital, and now on the KK board—financed and gifted money to send both of us to Harvard Business School for two years."

Henry? Murmurs around the room. No one had known this.

"What a blessing that man is—a *real* friend of our mission. And now this? The hardest time in all our lives. How do we get through?" She paused, swept her eyes over the group, hesitating for a moment at each. "We do it *together.* In this shared power, if Amy or I see someone being stupid, or cruel?" She wagged a finger, shook her bright red hair, and said, "Momma's comin'—look out!"

Everyone laughed.

"So many nurses are hanging by a thread. At one moment, it's enraging; at another, heartbreaking. We—all of us—are tired. We health-care workers are supposed to stick to our work, not get involved in the bigger picture of the health-care system. No more."

She looked at her watch.

"This is a new paradigm, starting with the two of us. Amy got it from Berry, Roy's wife. Power-with. Not power-*over*, power-*with*! Not power alone from up on high, power with others, mutually. Not the power of the self reigning *over* others, but the power of good connection *with* others. With everyone in this room! And if we can do it, it'll spread! Forgive me, it'll go viral." She paused. "Just one thing that I want you to understand about me—and Amy too—and I would guess about all of us." With a ferocious twinkle in her eyes, she said, *"None of this is going to be solved by Mr. Kush giving us cookies and candy on the night shift!"*

Cheers! And then, because there had rarely been anything like cheers in the room since the virus had struck, it kept going, louder and louder until laughter took over, and then relief, and hope. The rest of the meeting rode on a rare sense: *Yes, this is right. This helps.*

"Okay," said Shump. "Before we go around and check in, we want to tell you about a great opportunity that has come up."

But then her phone chirped with a video call alert. She punched it on, put it on speaker.

"It's me! Henry Schooner. Open your laptop, so everybody can see me."

She did, and somehow there he was, standing in a hall of Congress, in suit and tie and smile. She turned the screen to the group, and asked, "Henry?"

"Congratulations," he cried, "to my dear old high school friend Shump, for three whole great Columbia Bluehawk years and best wishes. But before you take the job for good, I could really use you down here!"

"Sorry, Henry," Shump said. "It would be too *easy* there, compared to this."

"Roger! I'm just finished with MSNBC and they're doing me a quick favor, getting this on video for you and me and the team."

At that moment the door opened and a huge bunch of red roses, so tall that it seemed to be floating in, rather than carried by a very small and thus invisible man, was put on the table. They were hothouse perfect.

"How did you know about this?" Amy said. "I thought it was totally secret."

"That's how I know! What you two are doing is astonishing. Two women, a doctor and a nurse, together? Rarely happens. I mean a *two-woman* team taking over *the* largest and most intensed-out intensivist practice for miles and miles around, and doing it right!" He paused. "Y'like the flowers? Addressed to both of you!"

"Lovely," Amy said.

"Thanks so much, Henry," Shump echoed.

"All good," Henry went on. "So I've gotta go, but as senior board member of the Columbia Hospital Board slash KK, I have raised the monies, whose interest will pay for not one but *two* full-time chief intensivists, in perpetuity!"

"What?" Amy said. The others were hushed—what the hell?

"Yes! You two are now endowed, good to go, for as long as you want, and it goes on *in stasis*, and I—" He ducked out of the TV picture, said something like "*No no no* on the goddamn filibuster!" And then he appeared again and said, sharply, "Gotta go and save the world! Congrats to all of you, mercy workers in this great American war." Gone.

"Ooohh-kay!" said Amy. "Shump? Go on. Good news, for a change."

"From the beginning of the pandemic, we've had trouble keeping up with the things we need to work—never being able to predict the next wave. About a month ago, it got way bad again. We started to run out of what we need to do our jobs right—protective gear, machines that work, cleanup crews. Suddenly now it's worse. But now, *at the same time*, KK opened the doors again to the surgeons to do 'necessary elective' surgery, high paying, far beyond what we bring in. No money to guarantee our safety. We *improvise*, and they're making fortunes in normal *colonoscopies*? How the *hell* did they get the regulatory okay to open up again, *while the numbers of Covid are still increasing every day, going off the charts—and we need help desperately?*"

All nodded.

"Why? Well, that's my priority now. I'm working on finding out. But our *worst* intensivist issue, our life-and-death issue, is that *we need to be able to be prepared in advance*. Here's the deal: number one, we need to know when a surge is coming. Number two, we *must* have the equipment and safety gowns and masks to deal with it!" She was on fire. "*Enough is enough! I'm getting this done. Period.*"

She paused, nodding. The others nodded back.

"Last night I called a good friend from high school, who shall remain nameless. I'd happened to see his father's name on our intake form—rule out Covid. They waited four hours to be seen, luckily negative. My friend is the number two hospital accountant, now working from home. Being a local, he's not happy with what Kush has—his word—'*wrought*.' He's been depressed, feeling alone in this—and he was glad to hear a human voice, especially mine." She paused. "So I said we docs are desperately concerned about the lack of communication surrounding Covid, for *surge planning in advance*. Now, every surge blasts in without warning, we're underwater, and scrambling. Like right now—and soon more. We're left in the dark with current Covid numbers but without knowing how these are *trending* we are unable to surge-plan. It's killing us and patients. He was shocked. He said, 'Unable to plan? Not good. I'm sure I can find the data, probably right under my nose. And I'd love to help you out, Shump. Want me to help?' I said, '*Would we? Yes!*' He said, 'No problem. I'll get back to you today. You keep that team of yours safe!'"

She looked around. Everyone got it. *The numbers guy will get us the data.*

"Ohhh-kay!" said Shump. "Suddenly Amy and I have lots to do today and tonight, so for today's check-in let's do a lightning round, just the crucial stuff."

Nods.

"Go!"

The team responded heartily, "Great job," and "We're on our way," with Hyper saying, "If you find bags of money lyin' around—I'm a little short this week."

"Ah money," said Shump. "Two rules we learned at business school? 'Follow the money' and 'Nobody ever got fired for making too *much* money.'"

Sev raised his hand, which wobbled as if it had a computer mind of its own.

"Yes, Sev?"

"I don't have anything to say. Thank you."

"The policemen? Brief! Lightning!"

"Forst," said Gilheeny, "in fabled lightning, the equivalent of brief flashes—"

"*Stop. Focus.* Count slowly to three, and then—like lightning!"

He stopped, widened his eyes, closed his eyes, opened again. "We cops have been awarded *the* contract with Kush, from now on, to be the chiefs of security, with reign over all others." He stopped. And stayed stopped. A first.

"But, dear policemen," said Shump, "this is too brief. You, then, Quick."

"Agreed," Gilheeny went on. "We drove one Humvee out to Spook Rock, and while my loyal thin man gave tours for Kush kids and grown-ups, I lathered up the bumbling boss Kush with a pro-sized slide deck of our previous merit, a fantasy CV with solid-gold payments from other household names—so household they couldn't be contacted for references. At first all were suspicious—"

"Because," said Quick, "we were not slick. But the clincher? The first year of security is for free."

"They balked at this," said the red-faced giant. "We explained we had a yearlong generous gift from a 'Household Name' who suffered a terrible breach, and we arrested the culprits and returned the diamonds! Who wouldn't take that deal?"

"Why, no one wouldn't," said Quick. "No one wouldn't at all! And the more the money, the more worry to keep it. Big money is the most fearful."

Gilheeny glanced at his loaded-up watch. "In being loyal policemen to the skilled and honest medicos, the last in Man's 4th Hospital. Always remember: *We are with you in whatever you are doing in the name of health and kindnesses.*"

"For wealth management is a grand gig!" said Quick.

"Great!" said Shump. "We're going to need all the security y'got. Next?"

"I'll go," said Eddie. "Totally great, you two women together." He squirmed in his chair, gritted his teeth. "Well . . . my wife . . . we'd been having a bad ride for a while, and that was part of my signing up here. But things have changed. Now, when I talk to her, we're doing a lot better. And I've picked up a new law dealing with patients. I'm a bit better too, right?"

All around the table were startled for a moment—Eddie never asked for anything.

"Hey, I'm *dyin'* here! Say 'yes' even if you don't think yes and—"

A chorus of "Yes!" came back at him.

"Berry. Just listening to her over all these years, from House to Man's 4th, has helped me through this. One thing she said, 'With a hard patient, try to find the *emotional distance* where you can sense some empathy for them.'" He paused and shook his head. "For a while I was thinking of leaving. But now I'm here for the duration. My wife said last week, 'You actually sound good, Eddie, it's okay to stay, because you're opened up and telling me about it.'" He shook his head. "But it's gotten even more dangerous for the basketmakers. I'm followed, so I stay away. If just one of those bigots finds out where he and the others are?" He sighed. "Now, this ride with all of you, with the shared women at the top? I'm all in for as long as I'm needed. Even for . . . never mind."

"Go ahead, we can take it," said Hooper.

"Nah, it was *old* Eddie, having to do with planning assassinations."

Shock. Did he mean it?

"I'll never take action. It would screw up our 'we.' A hellish good 'we' right now, right? Lemme hear it, *right?*"

"Rights" shot around the table. The air cleared.

"Goodgood, Eat!" said Shump. "Hooper?"

Hyper stopped rocking. "Thanks, Eat. Wife, kids, grandkids, asking for me. Youngest asked, 'Is Grampie dead?' Family does *not* like it."

He stopped, still. Silence, the longest ever heard from him. A frozen body. Was he going to explode?

Then he blinked, rocked. "Okay, I'm burnt out from Covid, and things're bad at home. Plane trips are killers. *But!* We're doing something great here, greater now with the new daring duo. Soooo . . . I'm in. And they say we might get the vaccine in late December? Everybody will get vaccinated, we kill the Covid, I fly away to LA and solve fat. . . ." He trailed off. "I'm done."

"Binni?" said Shump. "Then Roy."

"I'm flat-out living a miracle!" Binni said. "I'm in love, with two women at quite the same time: Amy, and at home my twelve-year-old daughter, Razina. She's spending a lot of time with a girl who is a big sister she never had—Eleanor, Amy's niece. She's part of Orvy's crazy-happy family—and she loves the huge dog, Ben. She's *thriving!* I, terrified of dogs, love this dog too. Thanks, Amy and Shump, for slowing down my patient care. The stem cell infusion will be in broad distribution *soon*, same time as the vaccine!"

The group was stunned—he'd come that far so soon? They started clapping.

"My work for Moderna is all online, now tweaking the vaccine against the next mutation. It's a chance of a lifetime." He paused. "I was never a popular kid. Now, I have all of you, I love all of you and—" His dimple deepened. He was choked up. Searched for a tissue, failed. Others were offered, he gave out tremendous blasts, everybody laughed, and waving to the group as if he were leaving, he smiled.

And then out came a loud affirmation of the little guy doing bigger things than any of them, louder and louder around the small room, echoing as if in that moment all humans had awakened, off ventilators, and were yelling with joy.

"Okay, Roy," said Shump, "you're last."

"Bravo, you two women! Seeing our old, good, deep, well . . . love, makes me think of the Fat Man. He tried his best to make our Man's 4th Clinic work. He said, often, 'I'm doing this to show how to put the human back into medicine.' Remember?"

Hyper, Eddie, and Sev nodded.

"We didn't make it. But . . ." He looked around at each person. "This, right here, right now, *is the perfect time and place to do it*. To put the human back in health care. Starting now, on a smaller scale. All the pieces are in place. Yes, we rage, and get depressed to death, but here, now, we've gotten to the *mutual*, a jewel of a '*we*.' If we can turn it around here, we can do it anywhere. Let's keep that higher purpose in mind." He paused. "Berry would say: 'Be aware of the suffering. In patients, doctors, and nurses, stay with that awareness, and it will shift to sorrow, and sorrow will heal.'"

At that, there was a sense of all having held a breath tightly and too long, and now was the time, together, to let the breath out.

"And let's remember," Roy said, "Fats made it clear as day that *in order to put the human back into medicine, we have to squeeze the money out. Right?*"

"Rights," and nods.

"But how do we do that?" asked Sev.

"We keep on doing this," Roy said. "Right here. As long as we stick together, the Kushes of the world don't stand a chance."

The team walked out feeling lighter, lifted by the possible.

———

That night at nine o'clock Amy, Shump, and Sev, using the policemen's master security keys, entered a small "Restricted Access" room next to the President's suite. The room was high-ceilinged and spacious, with two small windows. From another era, perhaps a decade after the Civil War, when the hospital was built. It was uncluttered, with labeled file drawers, much in computer-talk or code. Now musty, needing dusting. The accountants had been working from home for almost nine months.

Shump told her classmate that her team had been left in the dark, with no accurate projections of Covid numbers that would be coming into the intensivists. This left them unable to plan. This was the cause of his father's many-hour wait to be seen in Emergency. The classmate jumped at the chance to help. But to avoid being implicated, he could not be on the premises. He would get to her, securely, the passwords to the Covid dashboard computers. He had paused, and then said pointedly, "The *two* designated computers, Epic and Zetz."

"Why two?" Amy asked.

"You'll see," he'd said. "You will see."

Now, Sev easily got into Epic, found the Covid dashboard with all the data on the emergency Covid numbers from the first wave to the present. He started transferring the data to his thumb drive, timing it. He took a Magic Marker and labeled the thumb drive "EPIC."

Then he went to the other computer, Zetz. "It's Yiddish," he said, "meaning 'a blow' or a 'punch.'" He pointed to a hand-printed sign across the top part of the screen's frame: **I'LL GIVE YOU SUCH A ZETZ THAT YOU'LL NEVER FORGET!**

Sev found in Zetz the same Covid dashboard as Epic, seeming to have similar data. He stuck in his thumb stick. As he watched and waited, he looked puzzled.

"Okay, we're done," he said, pulling out the thumb stick. "But something doesn't make sense. The Zetz is known to be slower, but this is nuts; it took three times as long." He stared at it. "It also used a lot more RAM?" He marked the thumb stick with the Magic Marker. "Weird."

"Why?" asked Amy. "Why would the same data take more RAM?"

A key in the door. A turn of the key. A *snap!* of a bolt shooting back.

"Ohhh shit," Sev whispered.

Creaking from the door.

Everybody froze.

Light from the corridor behind the person, impossible to see who it was.

"I *thought* I heard something down here," said a woman's voice, a voice all of them knew. "What's up?"

Nurse Natasha.

"Oh God!" cried Amy. "You scared the hell out of me."

"Sorry. Hi, Shump, Sev. What's up?"

"Tell y'later," Shump said. "We're outta here."

Sev wagged his second thumb stick and said, to no one, "*Why two? Why indeed!*"

19

"You won't believe this," said Amy.

It was eight o'clock the next evening at Orville's house, and she, Shump, and Sev were telling Orville and Miranda, Roy and Berry, and Henry Schooner what they had found.

"I have all of it on these thumb sticks," said Sev, holding them up in his hand. "Amy has a copy, and a third is backed up on my crypt-toed hard drive. One thing I do know is numbers."

For safety and secrecy, they were meeting in person, celebrating a happy masked reunion outside the hospital, now that Orville was safe and sound at home. Henry Schooner, always looking at an action from all sides as well as top and bottom, had "just happened to be taking my nightly constitutional and dropped in on my old best friend in Columbia, now that he's beaten Covid, to say hello."

Actually, Miranda had called Schooner's wife, Nelda Jo, to ask him to come.

They were all in the most secluded and "safe" room in the house, Orvy's large office, overlooking the massive copper beech, the larch, and the Leyland cypresses. Behind the trees was a high large fence, all around the sheltered backyard, so that no one could look into the house.

"As I told everyone but Henry," Amy went on, "we found something fishy." She looked at a sheet of notes. "They're maintaining two different Covid lists. One list is in Epic, the forward-facing list *that everyone sees*. This list only includes patients in active isolation for Covid. Our infection prevention department pushes like crazy to get people off of isolation, now we know why: so that they can be removed from the list. Once patients are off this list, they are no longer counted as 'active Covid' infection, and therefore no longer counted toward the staffing, PPE, et cetera needed for Covid. These patients are still sick as hell, but the administration doesn't count them, so we don't get the things and people we need to care for them."

Amy paused, to let this sink in.

"Sounds ominous, Amy," said Schooner. "And the second list? The Zetz."

"The second list, the backroom or secret list, so to speak, *has the real numbers*. These are the patients still being treated for Covid, *but no longer on isolation*. The numbers on this list are much higher, and had they been made public, would have shown that the hospital was reopening elective services and neglecting Covid patients and staff, in order to prioritize money over people."

"*Oy*," said Schooner, puffing a terrific cigar. He sighed. "Continue."

"The first ledger, which we record as we go, is on Epic, the electronic medical record, that all of us see on our computers. That ledger is accurate, the *true* number of what we know is really going on. But on Zetz, large numbers of Covid patients were *deleted*."

"They cook the books?" said Schooner.

"Yes."

"And why?"

"Money," Amy said. "They can show the cooked book to the

regulatory guys. It shows, falsely, that *Covid cases are falling.* That makes money in two ways. First, they can show that our emergency resources—nurses, respiratory and other techs, PPE clothing, cleaning supplies—even ice trucks for the bodies—can be cut further from our budget in Emergency and the ICU. Second, they show the regulatory commissions that, since Covid cases are falling, it's time to allow the doctors who are the 'cash cows' to ramp up again. Sure, restarting procedures puts even more strain on the Intensive Care Unit by diverting resources away from us and adding patients that wind up having procedural complications. But elective surgeries also bring in anesthesia, MRI, and other scans, i.e., more money, *and* get the hospital big insurance payments for the procedures they've been missing for most of a whole year. Then the traders go, 'Buy KK!' Investors pour in. The stock goes up."

"Okay," said Schooner, "this is important. Do you have proof to substantiate that they have actually sent out these *bogus numbers* to anyone?"

"No. Sev and I looked, hard, and found nothing."

"Unfortunately," Henry said, "if it's just an internal document, we can't make anything of it."

"Yet," said Orvy.

"Exactly," Henry said, nodding. "So what *can* we do?"

"Over to you, Shump," Amy said.

"Right. What we *do* know is that they are compiling false data. If the investors and markets see that KK's flagship hospital *seems* to be moving toward fiscal health again, and they know they'll see those big-insurance payments again, those kidneys and prostates and colonoscopies, *all* these lucrative ones, what will the traders do? They'll buy KK futures. They'll think it's a turnaround. All during Covid, they have been considering selling their investment in KK—'going short' on it, or 'shorting it.' Going short would be a disaster now, start a stampede—ending in bankruptcy. KK would have to close the hospital and sell it. Use the buildings for upscale condos or whatever. Just last year another private equity fund 'flipped' Hahnemann Hospital in Philadelphia, destroying the only large hospital to treat the poor—*as well as the medical school*! A *teaching* hospital! They actually demolished them all for *condos*, okay? Made a fortune." She paused. "But if KK could say that they are doing *more* procedures of all kinds, *more* operations? That's a lot of money coming in. Go online, look at the smiles on the KK board photo—all in surgical garb. 'With our *healthy* outlook at KK, and our regulatory easing, we take these monies to be self-evident.' If you're a trader playing in the private equity space, you can bet your bottom dollar it'll soar. The word on the street is: 'Go long!'"

"Meanwhile," said Roy, "we docs and nurses and respiratory techs in the *real* world have been barely surviving for all these months, barely able to do our work. We're providing a level of care that we can just barely live with. And no help is coming. The poor patients!"

"And all this *mishegas*, Henry," said Orvy, "is just for cash. To hell with care for folks who are suffering, and in pain."

Nods all around. A sense of doom.

"It is astonishing," said Shump. "Given Jason Kush and the entwined other Kushes, of *course* they'd try to do all of this. But there's a weak point at their core. I keep track of the market trending averages, especially, of course, hospital indices, and bond futures. KK is totally dependent on the market to stay alive. And the market people are just like *the Kushes*." She let this sink in. "If Wall Street ever saw the real data, they'd sell off in a New York minute, and the private equity market will follow. KK's weak point is their being at the mercy of people *just like them*, just as greedy. And that's the way we can bring them down."

"Got it," said Schooner with a smile.

The group fell quiet.

"The Kushes *crave* money," Berry said, "and the ego is insatiable. In fact the Buddha said there are 'three poisons' in human life, which can only lead to suffering: craving, hatred, and delusion. A life of creating chaos and harm. Sounds like the Kushes, right?"

Nods all around.

"The good news," she went on, "is that they're poisoning themselves. Their world is teetering, but if we can find a strong, clever challenge by all of us and others together, they will start to suffer terribly, and crash, implode. Guaranteed." She smiled. "One day the Buddha was walking with his monks, a beautiful day, and a farmer comes up, crazed: 'Have y'seen my cows?!' The Buddha asks his monks if they'd seen his cows. They say 'No.' The farmer runs off, screaming, 'My cows! My cows!' The Buddha looks at his monks, and says, 'Aren't you glad you don't have cows?'"

"Berry!" said Schooner. "Heard a lot about you. Take the spiritual road—the only way that'll save us. Sounds like you've spent time squeezing politicians!"

"Great, Berry," said Amy. "And there's something else we found. Shump?"

"A 'for your eyes only' memo from Jason Kush himself. Probably sent out only to the top level. It says that when the vaccines come out—maybe as soon as January—they will be available *only* to Kush executives and administrators, and to 'high throughput billing employees, in particular surgeons, anesthesia, pharmacy.' *Not* for us, the ones in the trenches."

"Not going first to the first responders?" Henry asked.

"Right."

"Are you sure?"

"Absolutely," said Amy. "Sev's got photos on his phone."

"The Kushes are such solipsistic knuckleheads," Sev said, "they think their expensive data firewall can't be hacked? I mean I have to

admit it took me a long, long, *long* time to crack it and download it."
He giggled. "A whole sixty-four seconds."

"Whoa! Son, you are fast! How'd you like a job in the government?"

"Talk to my agent," Sev cracked.

"You have an agent?" said Roy.

"*Tomorrow* I will."

Schooner laughed. "Guys and gals, I give you my word that when that vaccine is first available, it goes first to all of you on the front lines. Even before me."

"So," Amy said, "what are we going to do about all this?"

"What do you want?" Schooner asked.

"I think I speak for all of us," Amy said, looking at the others, who nodded. "We want Kush out. Totally out."

"How do we do that?" Schooner asked.

"Shump," said Amy, "what about threatening a nurses' strike? Or even—a nurses' and doctors' strike? Doctors and nurses *together* would get incredible attention. The nurses' union never loses, right? The hospitals *always* settle, mostly before the walkout?"

"Yes, so far," Shump said. "But this is different. In the midst of the worst pandemic ever, and we nurses threaten to *walk out*? We're already incredibly short of care. We'd be risking patients' lives." She paused, sighed. "If we did it now, imagine the attack by Kush Kare? We always have to be on the patients' side. Plus, the Columbians wouldn't stand for a strike—the wackos would get even more dangerous. It would just make things worse."

"Agreed," Amy said. "But we've got to do something fast. We're *dying*."

Silence, and a sense of doom.

"How 'bout we buy the hospital," Shump said. "Somehow raise the money and run it ourselves? Get rid of the middleman—who, in terms of medicine, doesn't know his ass from his elbow."

Everyone looked around at every other one, as if just waking up.

"Raise a huge amount of money in a short time?" Orvy said. "Doubtful."

"Run it yourselves?" Schooner said. "Run it yourselves . . ." He drifted off, puffed his cigar, blew a smoke ring, and then blew a second stream out that neatly speared the first. He nodded slowly, until his cigar creation had vanished. "Run it yourselves is absolutely what you can do. But there's no need to buy it."

"What do you mean?" asked Amy.

"I believe you can get it for free."

Everyone was stunned, looking to each other around the table.

"Are you serious?" Amy asked.

"Totally." Suddenly Henry's pink face was all smiles. "Given their financial difficulties, KK may want out. We want control. All of you are burnt-out—patients are dying. This has got to happen fast, real fast. Got it. I haven't been chair of Ways and Means for nothing. *We will win this fight.* The only thing that could make us lose is if we don't consider every possible obstacle in advance. And that's my forte."

"What can we do to start?" Shump asked.

"I've already started," he said. "You go ahead on the ground here, do whatever you want, with two caveats: *yes*, galvanize; *no*, don't piss off the Columbians. Got it?"

He looked from one to the others, and all nodded. "Other ideas?"

"In the House of God," Roy said, "we used Law Number 13: 'The delivery of medical care is to do as much nothing as possible.'"

"Yeah, I've heard of that somewhere," said Henry. "I heard of that. But y'think it'll work here, Roy, with all the treatments you're trying in order to save them, and with all the breakages?"

"The key is 'as possible,'" Roy replied. "With Covid, we go all out, in every way we know how. That's the *particular humane possible*, okay? Never fails. But we have to do nothing *intensely*. And we have to be *deft*. It's hard to balance the right amount of nothing, but I can help with that. All of us House of Godders became expert with 'as possible.'"

"And even with Covid," Orvy said, "we can do what old Dr. Starbuck taught me: the tincture of time. Do everything to keep 'em alive, and let the divinity heal."

Roy looked out the window into the dark. In a soft gold beam of a lamp that he knew wasn't really there was the Fat Man, wearing a spacious, flowing Indian sari, eyes closed, sitting cross-legged on a meditation cushion set in midair. He was smiling beatifically—a guru, of sorts. As Roy watched, Fats opened his eyes.

"Hey, Roy, you red-hot, the *least* you could do after all these years since you stole my list of laws would be to credit me. Now, *just this once*? Tell 'em!"

Looking out the window at Fats, Roy went on. "A great doctor named the Fat Man was the one who coined Law Number 13."

The Fat Man beamed, put his two palms together under his chin, and nodded in gratitude and benediction, and then, like a guru who was late for another guru gig, he snatched up his cushion, put it under his arm, and flew away.

———

Dear Highly Valued KK Health Kare Team:

Great work! Great Holiday Spirit! Now it's our ten-day fiscal countdown/closeout to the great New Year! Happy all! Great Billing needs your Great Attention! The max billing and the max money. So let's all keep billing together or we'll all get billing separately. In Great Appreciation for all you've done so well! Happy Holidays, Happy Kush Kare.

Warmly,
Jason Kush, the Kush Family, and Fiscal Kare Team

In the photo on the holiday card that all employees received, the Kushes were dressed in high-formal penguin black. Jason Kush, front and center, was astonishingly short.

Roy was on night call, about four a.m. It was a rare moment; he was sitting in the call suite, doing nothing! Marvelously quiet. Only really sick Columbians would come in at this time of the morning, and on this particular night. The Columbia weatherman forecast "a winter throwback to summer—clear calm skies, upper fifties." Long-living citizens knew that this raised the odds of the horrific, and in late evening a terrible series of squalls hit, hard, low to the ground, rocking cars and forcing them to pull over and wait it out. It was a long wait. The emergency phone rang. Roy picked up.

"This is Michael Rocha, New York State Police. You the doc on call?"

"Yeah, Roy Basch, Mike—I remember you."

"Yeah, you too, Doc. We're bringing a young woman in . . . It's, well . . ." He couldn't talk for a moment. Roy went on full alert. ". . . awful. I'm glad we got *you*. This storm was a total whiteout, for hours. We got a call from an elderly woman in the woods near Red Rock, a car stuck in the snow way out near New Lebanon. Emergency lights on." He cleared his throat. "Bringing in a young woman who miscarried by the side of the road. In shock, can't talk, lost a lot of blood. I mean, this is the worst." He choked up again. "Sorry. So the car was half-buried, lights on, engine on. The back door on the passenger's side was unlocked. We opened the door slowly and caught a body that had been leaning against it. And there was a newborn baby, a lot of blood, still attached by the cord. It was dead. Driver's license says her name's Desiree Hemming, twenty-six, lives not far from your hospital, outside of Claverack. Husband a Navy SEAL, somewhere in the Middle East. Friend listed as second emergency contact. Clearly she was in trouble, in labor—but why'd she drive away from Kush, alone, and head toward Albany Hospital?"

"Kush doesn't do deliveries, long story."

"Her phone was in her hand—must have fallen into the big dead spot out there."

"Let's keep her from dying." He peppered Mike with questions about her vital signs: breathing, cardiac, blood pressure.

"I did it all. I'm certified. She's lost a lot of blood, she's hypothermic—eighty-nine. We're trying to keep her warm—heat on full, and right now I'm sitting with her in the cruiser's back seat with my big winter coat around her, and the baby. Should I cut the cord?"

"Nope. Just get in here, *stat*. And hey, you've done . . ." Roy's voice caught in his throat. ". . . great, man, great. And if you reach the friend you mentioned, tell her to call me direct. We need to find her soldier husband."

When Desiree came in she was pale as death. Temperature 85, blood pressure 55, unconscious. The greatest risk would be infection and septic shock. Roy first clamped off and cut the cord. Next he needed to deliver the likely infected placenta—something he hadn't done for years.

Luckily the nurse on call, Carter Heyward, was qualified in obstetrics. "Next thing," she said, "I suggest a shot of a pressor—adrenaline'll do—raise BP, constrict the bleeding, and maybe make the placenta delivery go faster."

It worked on the delivery. But the blood pressure and other vital signs were not moving.

The sun came up, unperturbed. The team was mostly in. Roy and Carter presented the case, and Roy said, "All of us know that the big devil in front of us is septic shock. I say we put her on the top floor, with Natasha. What do you think?"

They all thought that was the right place for her. They walked out of the morning meeting as if to a funeral.

———

The two beds were almost always empty, but now, Roy and Eddie each had a patient on the ward.

They were sitting with Natasha at the nurses' station enjoying fresh-squeezed orange juice and warm chocolate croissants. Eddie had been seeing his patient diligently for a few days now—Simon, the 34-year-old son of Eddie's dear friend the chief of the basketmakers, had caught Covid. After attending Roeliff Jansen School in Copake, he had left the village, gotten a scholarship to Baruch College in the Big Apple, graduating in business. He was married to an Anglo woman, a court judge in Columbia, and lived in the New Yorkers' neighborhood, near Orvy. Two days ago, Simon had been put on a ventilator. The bad news was the Covid; the good was that he had not transmitted it to anyone in the little hamlet in the mountains above Copake. His father and mother came to see him every day. Standing on the other side of the glass.

"So how you doin', Eddie?" asked Roy.

"How'm I doin'?" Eddie replied. "No suicide yet."

"Unless this is heaven," said Roy.

"Don't push it, okay?" He turned to Natasha. "Is the chief still here?"

"No, Gilheeny and Quick happened to see him leave, I think about one a.m."

"Damn! I was so busy yesterday I didn't get to see him. I miss him!"

"Can I ask," said Natasha, "why're you so in love with him?"

"Easy. He's the best! I never had a father, really. So my mother took over as father, and kind of forgot to do my mother. A mess."

"Hmm," said Roy. "You'd think you'd look for a *mother* figure, not a father."

"The chief's a good mother, and so's my wife. She's a good father and mother both. God, I miss her! I gotta get outta here and get back to her. Maybe soon?"

"Yeah. But meanwhile you've got all of us. Good, good friends, Eddie, right?"

"*Very*," he said. "The House, Man's 4th, and now this? Amazing, eh?"

"Totally."

The respiratory tech arrived. Roy and Eddie left to see their patients, Natasha following. There was no change in the chief's son, so Eddie soon left.

Desiree Hemming, Roy's patient, was one of the saddest cases anyone had seen, even the whole long Covid year. Before he went to see her, he had sat at the computer and brought up her latest numbers. Ever since she'd come in, they were terrible. But at least her "patient history" had been filled out.

Desiree was married to Joe, her high school sweetheart, a magnet for friends. He'd been overseas for several months. They had always been a kind of "star" couple, known for their energy and fun and the ability to cultivate longtime friends. Their house was out in the country in Columbiaville, on a stream that emptied into the Hudson. Neither family lived nearby. Everyone who'd met the young couple thought the world of them—they had come from North Carolina to take care of Joe's aging aunt until she had to go into assisted living. Desiree loved dogs and had a knack for caring for strays, which recently had led to her dream job at Doggone Good Dog Care and volunteering at the award-winning Columbia Animal Rescue. As usual in our fractured and fractious country, dogs had a better safety net than humans.

She had found out she was pregnant with their first child shortly before Joe left. He too had been ecstatic. But lately he'd been hard to reach. The pregnancy had gone well, and she was getting close to delivering. Since all Kush Kares had gotten rid of obstetrics, she had gotten her prenatal care 40 miles north at the Veterans Administration Hospital on the far side of Albany. Her baby girl would be delivered there. They'd decided to call her Sarah, after his grandmother. Her routine exams and numbers were normal. The due date was upon her.

Sometime late that night her water broke. Roy learned later that Dez, as she was called, had previously arranged for a friend to drive her. But there had been a breakage. She couldn't get in touch with her. It would turn out that her friend had gotten a bad sore throat, headache, and high fever, and, panicking that it could be Covid, went to stay at her cousin's house—not realizing that her cell phone was out of range in that part of Kinderhook County. So Dez, feeling good, figured she could drive to Albany. She grabbed her "delivery" suitcase and—according to a woman walking her dog—left at about midnight.

Her car had been found 20 miles north of Columbia, at four a.m. It was snowed in on the side of a two-lane road, a shortcut that would link up with the highway to Albany. Clearly she'd gotten really lost, caught in the freezing blizzard. Sprawled in the back seat of the car, delirious, bleeding, baby dead.

When Desiree, half-frozen, reached the hospital, she rapidly developed a high fever and sepsis. Pre-antibiotics, "puerperal fever" killed at will. Still today, sepsis, no matter the cause, was a dire diagnosis. Dez was hovering at death's door. The story was so horrible, the whole hospital clicked into top gear, going flat out for her care.

Now, a week later, Roy finished checking her chart and went in to examine her carefully. Despite meticulous care, septic shock is hell to treat. Even with perfect clarity of the pathogen and metrics and research, with the best care, death tolls are high. Roy, sitting next to her, was nagged by a little voice that seemed to mock him: *All your docs' sophistication, yet death often wins.*

Touched, he did a bit more: smoothing out, tucking in, making sure she was as comfortable as possible. Despite being sick as hell, sedated she had a certain quiet. He thought of Spring, his and Berry's daughter of about the same age.

The drugs now were bringing a regular sleep. He sensed the deep peace of a child's sleep. But oh, when she awakens—if she awakens—the horror that will face her, *her whole life*. The worst phone call that she could make to her beloved, or that he will ever get. The explosion of a man's tears. A soldier's tears. Shock. If she does, if she makes it. The body of their baby is in a cold place. Tears came to his eyes. He said a prayer, wiped his eyes, and left.

The *Crier* headline about the case was somber, with no breakages:

Tragic Birth and Death: No Obstetrics at Kush Kare

20

It started modestly enough.

Pam Hamlet had been a long-serving nurse before Kush Kare took over her hospital. She had retired a bit earlier than planned.

After that, Pam had happily lived her married and mother-of-three life in the county in a restored 1750 Dutch house, on land bordering Bell's Pond. Ten years widowed from the Hamlet family business—Whale Gas and Oil—she had "nursed" her beloved Columbia and Kinderhook County. If there was a need in the city or farmland, a good deed to be done, the first call was to Pam. When Covid hit, she realized hunger would be a great danger to the poor, in city and county. Americans *starving*? Of course. So she spearheaded two "Columbia Cares Food Pantries," organizing a crack team that had kept those with no money or job from starving.

It now ran itself, so successful that she was bored. Her children couldn't visit except on Zoom. She and her spaniels were itchy—she needed a project. And so in the depressing gray slough between Christmas and New Year's, she had arranged to visit Shump, her old high school and nursing school friend and right-hand woman when she was in charge of the nurses at Whale City Hospital.

Pam, like all the faithful who read the *Crier*, was following the difficulties of the nurses and was horrified by the baby's death in a ditch. Something had to be done. In fact the *Crier* had clicked into clear, sharp reporting, first to break the news that Representative Henry Schooner had located Desiree's husband, a Navy SEAL on a secret mission who was on his way back as soon as possible.

"I'm going *bananas*," she said to Shump. "Between Big Mac screeching and one more Zoom with my friends in little boxes on the screen, I'll die."

"I haven't had time to peel and eat a banana in six months," Shump replied.

"When's the last we saw each other? Three months?"

"At least."

"I'm ready for another project. I know you're flat out, but I'm free. I want to come in and see exactly what's going on, and I want to help. Can you get me full protective PPE so I can shadow you? And I'd like to see the rich-guy helicopter ward, and Natasha. The girl whose baby died is there? Septic shock? Horrific. I'd love to help—anything I can do. Fact is, I miss nursing, imagine?"

"Bless you! Come tomorrow at noon. The parking lot will be full—what's your license plate?" She gave it. "I'll send our two dear policemen, one to park your car, and the other to get you through the crowd to the back entrance."

"The crowd?"

"Between the patients waiting to be seen and the 'Save Desiree' women protesting against KK for cutting obstetrics, it's a circus." As if on cue, there was screaming in the background. "Gotta hop!"

The next day Pam was able to drive up the hill only halfway to the entrance, where she ran into a crowd of dozens. One part of it was packed tightly together—most not masked—at the mouth of Emergency, waiting to get in. The other part, 20 or so and mostly women—with masks—carried signs calling out Kush Kare for canceling obstetrics. Signs like "KKare Kills Babies and Moms!" and "Save Our Desiree!"

Even through their masks they were loud, chanting:

"Hey, hey, Jason K, how many babies have you killed today?"

Pam was stuck, with no way through.

Suddenly she heard a mechanical roar and ear-splitting sound of a big machine and a jagged siren and flashing, harsh, crazed spotlights coming from a wide roadway to the side of the entrance. Then a sudden, scary silence. *What was going on?* All sound stopped. A Humvee pulled up alongside Pam's car. A tall, thin, sallow man in a policeman's uniform jumped out.

"Hello, dear Pam!" he cried over the insane Hummer thunder. "I'm Officer Quick and within that desert-tan monster of USA slash Afghan armaments. And up on top, just popping up out of his lair and waving, is Sergeant Gilheeny!"

Gilheeny waved. His fat, pink face graced her with a broad smile. She waved back.

"The plan," Quick shouted to her, "is that you get out, I park your car. You get in the Humvee, which will go back up and around on the service road to the entrance where you will meet our phenom—and your Shump. Mask up." She did. "The extreme viral-load transmission danger of your walking through the Covid-packed crowd—liberated into freedom from masks—is fierce. No need to sacrifice yourself to the fasci-shitzers. Ready?"

He escorted her the few steps to the Humvee. Gilheeny, huge and fat, with the delicacy of a dancing Falstaff, climbed down from the top and opened the door over the wheel bed and helped her up and in, and they were off, the siren silencing all dissent. At the Deliveries entrance he parked, helped her out, unlocked the door and showed her inside, where a homemade wooden sign proclaimed:

WELCOME TO THE HELL OF THE INTENSIVISTS. RELAX.

Gilheeny walked her to the meeting and changing rooms, fitted her with brand-new PPE—embossed with "Thanks to Our Rep. H. Schooner, Esq."—walked her to a curtained examining space, and loudly identified the person hunched over a patient as "the Great God Shump!"

Another moonwalk-suit-clad person straightened up, recognized Pam, and gave a muffled scream of joy, and a high five.

"Just who I need," said Shump, gesturing to the patient. "None of us knows what's going on here. Name is Pedro Arbenz. Sixty-eight-year-old migrant with family, staying here after harvest rather than going back to Guatemala—he's undocumented. Seems to be living on hunting skills, out in the woods and fields. Could be Covid—but nobody in his family has any symptoms. Fever, cough, lethargy, hypostatic—blacked out and fell in front of his wife. Lungs have some rales and rattles. Labs are normal. Nobody knows what this guy's got."

"Shall I take a look?"

"Be my guest. But my *fast* guest?"

"Two minutes tops. Got my trusted old flashlight." Suddenly she was quickly scanning every inch of skin, even flashing open the KK johnny to expose the groin. And there, at the level of a testicle, was a small bite mark with a faint jagged ring. "Okay, Nurse Shump, I'd bet this is your diagnosis."

Shump looked closely and said, "Lyme?"

"Maybe. But the location is weird. I'll ask him if he breeds rabbits. *Conejos?*"

"Si si, yes yes. Muchos conejos."

"Could be tularemia. Serious, can be deadly. Hardest to diagnose of any tick-borne disease—can mimic anything. Especially when you're totally overwhelmed."

"Nice. Forgotten what a great nurse you are. Forgotten men's groins too."

"It's like riding a bike—y'never forget. These little hints keep our balance."

"I hope you won't mind, but I want to have lunch upstairs with Natasha—you've met her, right? Something important to discuss."

"Sure. She's dynamite."

"Just let me chart the antibiotics for Arbenz."

On the ride up in the elevator, Pam said, "Y'know what? I have a confession to make. I love this! I love this work! All those years, so many good memories—when nurses and doctors all worked together. It was run by doctors, yes—a stiff patriarchy of course—but it wasn't run for money. It was nonprofit, remember those days? It had spirit."

"Instead of pigs at the trough, killing off care."

"Which is why I quit."

"It's why we all want to quit—yesterday. Team spirit's down. Pam, *this can't go on*. It has never been like this. We are down. Ground zero. *But*. We've got a plan. After lunch, we can look in on poor Desiree—Amy's up there with her now, and she'll stay for lunch too. Dez has finally turned the corner—physically. We can only imagine her depression."

———

"Let me get this straight," said a startled Pam, at lunch. "We could *own* it?"

They had talked animatedly through a marvelous lunch in the private dining room, which looked out over the town and then across the Hudson and up higher to the Catskills, its waves of crystal-blue ridges wavering in the sunlight and walking south toward New York City, north toward Albany.

The local weatherman had predicted freezing snow all day. It was clear and 68, a record breakage.

"Yes," Shump answered, "Henry said that if he and the rest of us played our cards right, the Kushes would wind up *giving* the hospital to us."

"Give?" said Pam. "Those shits have never *given* anything to anyone."

"That was our first take on it too," said Natasha, "and he didn't say how. But Henry's *never* lost anything in the battles he takes on for Columbia—except the General Worth Hotel—but he learned his lesson on that one. Right, Amy?"

"Yes. In 1980 he got conned by my father. The Worth was a grand place, a hundred years old at least. It was broken, in disrepair, and it was either rescue it and begin the Columbia renaissance, or build a Price Chopper store. Orville and I tried to save it, but behind our backs they demolished it. Schooner learned his lesson. After that, he became the leader in preserving the town."

Natasha nodded. "He said we should go ahead and do what we thought best while he focused on Washington, his 'Ways and Means'—money. All top secret, for only us, Orvy, Miranda, Roy, and Berry."

"Well, I didn't expect this!" said Pam. "I'm all in! I gave my heart to this place for forty years. With KK, forty days. What are *our* ways and means?"

"First we thought of a nurses' strike," said Shump. "But to *walk out on our patients* in the middle of winter, the holiday season, for more *money*? Sounds like Kush himself. So now we've been trying to think of any kind of pressure we can put on KK without hurting patients. But we are royally stuck."

"We can't wait for Henry," said Natasha. "We've got to do something to help ourselves."

There was a long silence, a sense of tightness, even smallness.

"I've got a crazy idea," said Pam. "I'm thinking about what I did today. I called up to meet Shump, walked in and put on 'my' PPE, and saw a patient. For all anyone knew I was a new nurse. I examined him, diagnosed him, and treated it."

"Yes, and?" said Natasha.

"I'm still a registered nurse. I did my job because I wanted to help—I love nursing! And with this patient I had a good result. And did I get *paid*?"

Looks all around, and then some "Oh my Gods!" and "Holy shit!"

"You're saying," said Shump, "we could get nurses to come in and work, without pay?"

"I can tell you for sure that right now, as we speak, there are a lot of good nurses sitting on the sidelines, wanting to work."

"But they'd never work for the Kushes!" said Amy. "And for free?"

"For helping, for service, for saving lives, for the oath we took."

"Maybe," said Natasha, eyes wide. "If they could do it on *their* schedule, for however many hours a week they want to. I bet we could get enough nurses so that no one of them will be blasted with more work than they want."

"But what if they really need money?" Amy asked.

"Well," said Pam, "some have partners who earn enough. Others left KK because the ratios of nurse to patient made it impossible to treat patients safely, and got travel nurse jobs all over America, making up to *3,000 dollars a week*! And under those conditions they were honing their skill set on Covid, and for the most part, avoiding burnout. Many of them put money in the bank, came home, rested. But some are now getting bored. Most of their partners are still working from home, and able to watch the kids. A lot of nurses *hated* Kush K before Desiree. And now just about everyone in the city and county hates Kush even more. Not only are there protests every evening at five in front of the hospital, but people have even shown up way out in Spook Rock, picketing at the armed gatehouse leading to the road to the Kush mansion. This is the *forme fruste* of all bad hospitals—an incomplete example of a bad disease."

"And y'know what?" said Shump. "They, and we, want better for our town."

There was a moment of quiet, as all of this sank in.

"But how would this put pressure on KK?" asked Natasha.

"Simple," said Pam. "The *Crier* will pump this out like crazy—and the New Yorkers will take it up from there. It'll be a wildfire. Squeaky-clean try to heal us compared to dirty-money Kushes—and don't forget, their other hospitals are just as hated as ours, ripe to explode. Nurses have a tremendous national footprint—and I know the leaders. Think about it: nurses, donating their time, in the most dangerous pandemic, for free?"

"Beautiful," said Amy. "It's simple. This is just what we need to expose and crystallize the hatred of all Kushes. All over the franchise."

"But when KK finds out and won't let them in?" said Shump.

"If the new nurses aren't on any payroll, they'll have no records," said Shump. "The Kushes won't even *know* for a long time. One nurse to them is the same as any other."

"And we'll be skillful, deft," said Natasha. "And *flexible*, both in days and lengths of shift, half time, quarter time, nights—whatever! We can find a place and time for anyone! Chances are, KK won't even *notice*. First of all, we've now got the A-team—the best educated and most experienced of any health-care practice for miles around. They're gutless weenies, scared to engage us except on the internet, not face-to-face. None of them have ever come inside Emergency. They know that the worst thing for them would be talking to any of us intensivists. They and their goon squads in Security *never* come, unless called. In fact, just yesterday in a memo they made it official:

the *only* Security that we intensivists will use from now on are Gilheeny and Quick, and a third policeman who's just joined, from Boston. They are the new bosses. And I have strong evidence that even some of the KK Security has flipped, secretly helping us. I mean almost all of 'em were our classmates! Are they going to cheer for KK, or for the Old Blue and Gold? Go, Bluehawks!"

Cheers, laughs, screams.

Shump went on. "We'll tailor the 'volunteer' nurses' schedule to their life. Make their work flexible, to suit them. Make it easy to change schedules—even on a same-day basis. Obsessives can work 'long' shifts. If suddenly needed at home, fine. And a whole army of nurse insomniacs would take the night shifts."

"I love it," said Natasha. "A lot of us might work a little, and a little of us might work a lot. And guess what? The holy grail: less stress."

"Forgive me," Pam said, "but that flexibility is going to need a giant, adaptive computer program. Able to change schedules quickly—with no mistakes."

"No problem," said Amy. "One doc on our team is the world's second-best designer of medical computer everything—he eats pixels and drinks code."

"Ah yes," said Natasha. "That cute little shy doctor guy, always shuffling his feet. Sev?"

"Sev he is. Loves challenges. Can do anything. Even hack KK, if we need."

"Eventually," said Pam, "they'll find us out. But if they try to shut us down, the media will kill them. My daughter-in-law is editor of the *Crier*."

A long silence, everyone looking to everyone.

"Can't you just hear the conversations?" said Amy. "'Well, Miss Pam, if you keep doing this, we'll fire you!' 'You can't fire me, because you never hired me.'"

"Great!" said Natasha. "And with Henry with us, national news'll kill them."

"We need a name," said Shump. "Every movement needs a name. What do we call it?"

"Well," said Pam, "thinking about 'strikes,' how 'bout this?" She spread her hands as if unfurling a banner and said, "The Reverse Strike: Not a Walkout for Money, a Walk-In to Heal."

Silence. Then "wows," nods, and smiles. "This reminds me," Amy said, "of when I was just starting out in practice in California. My uncle Orville told me about a nurse friend of his who'd taken a break from working at Whale City. She'd gone off to serve in a leper colony in India for two years. When she returned, Orvy said to her, 'I couldn't do that for a million dollars.' And she said, 'Neither could I.'"

21

They had started sketching the nuts and bolts of who does what and with whom when Natasha's phone let out with Mozart, her ringtone. She glanced at it, raised a finger to all, put it on speaker.

"Hi, Henry."

"I'm in a copter with Desiree's husband, Joe umm . . . Something. Also, we got Vice Admiral General David Thorne, and a Pentagon PR infant with video. Touchdown in ten minutes. Your security guys are on the way upstairs, Gilheeny and Quick, and so's the *Crier*'s editor, Lisa Cohen—good kid. She'll ring the bell in two minutes. Desiree's doctor, Roy Basch too—get him at her bedside showing confidence. Got a call this morning that she's turned the corner, but she could still relapse, has to stay a while?"

"Yes," said Natasha. "It's still a tricky time. And starting to let it all sink in. But we cleaned her up really well this morning, in case you—"

"Dynamite! Great work. Her husband Joe . . . um, Something, will stay in the suite next to her. Everybody will wear masks when we go into her room and at the presser in the board room. Shows what side we're on. Any news on your end?"

"Pam Hamlet's joined us—the team had a great meeting. Lining up nurses to work for free, volunteers."

"Yeah, I heard all about it! Genius, Pam!"

"It looks good for a rollout in a day or two," Natasha went on. "As soon as Sev the computer maven gets online, we're good to go. It's going to work."

"Always does, Tasha, with you and me. I oughta get you on those Kushes! That bastard Jason Kush won't return calls, the last one threatening a criminal subpoena from my Ways and Means." He sighed. "And what a great idea, Pam, to work for free? Dynamite!"

"And I hear you're getting Kush to give us the hospital for free too?"

"You bet. Like the Veterans Administration. Free hospitals. When my boy got all shot up in Iraq—in the brain, imagine? Where'd we take 'im? To the VA in Texas. Amazing place! Was gonna die. Took a year, but full recovery. All for free! Hey, Larry! Make a note: 'Get Ways and Means to do free VA-style national health care for all those who need.'" The copter jumped, as if the pilot couldn't wait. Then he said, "Starting descent. *Ciao.*"

Henry Schooner, clearly, had gone all impresario. Desiree was prepared: showered, hair styled, lipstick. Wearing a crisp off-white johnny, with a gold insignia: "U.S. ARMY WIFE." Roy and Natasha wore starched, pressed whites, each holding its creases as if made of metal.

The camera rolled. They chatted for a moment. Natasha told Desiree she was almost out of danger, and that she had a visitor. She turned toward the door.

Joe, in snappy uniform of bars and ribbons, stopped, stunned—amazed at seeing her look so beautiful and alive. She saw him, screamed, burst into tears, started shaking all over, and with a shout that was cut off by his explosion of tears he rushed to her and took her in his arms, and they just cried together as hard as anyone had ever seen. They held each other tight, for a long time, and then at arm's length they gazed deeply at each other. Then still hand in hand, Joe sat on the bed staring at her and shaking his head in disbelief that the day before he'd been running around doing some really dangerous secret shit in a cave until they found him and yanked him away and now he was all cleaned up and with her, each taking in the other, in love. But suddenly, as his eyes fell on a little pink bear on the pillow, and her eyes followed, they stopped. A look of terror came to their eyes. Their baby.

To all, it seemed that time itself, mortally wounded, stopped.

And then Henry came in, in perfect lighting and, sensing the terror—and maybe needing things on the brighter side—took each of their hands in his hands and held them for what seemed a long time. Finally he said, "Shall we have a silent prayer?" They nodded, all lowered their heads, closed their eyes. "Amen," he said. Giving each hand a squeeze, he smiled.

"Thank you, sir," said Joe.

"Yes," said Desiree. "Thanks."

Henry sat holding both their hands, with Natasha and Roy in the background, while the Navy camera rolled and the *Crier* shot stills. A grand paterfamilias, he smiled and wiped away tears and shook his head at the fact of the miracle reunion. The *Crier* interviewed them briefly. Desiree was shy, but Joe was not—he was too raw—and clearly he had been told everything that had happened to kill his baby and almost his wife.

He thanked everyone, especially the doctors and nurses and Representative Schooner, who had arranged everything—finding him "literally under a rock" and "extracting" him and rushing him back home.

"To make this happy miracle. But it should never have happened.

I've been briefed on Kush Kare Incorporated. When they bought our *wonderful* Whale City Community Hospital, the first thing they did was kill obstetrics. So now people have to drive forty miles to have their babies. And *my* . . ." He paused, his face contorted to prevent his breaking down again, but failed. To see a man, a soldier, a warrior trying to control himself and not being able to, shaking with grief, was wrenching. "Sorry." He blew his nose. "Our daughter—Sarah was her name—*is* her name—we call her after Dez's mom—would be alive today, and my wife not traumatized. On the long flight back I had time to think. To not offer births? It should be a *crime*. I address these words to the President of Kush Kare, Jason Kush." He seemed to straighten his backbone, lift his chin, gather himself, a good soldier full of, well, *purpose*:

"Bring back obstetrics, before another baby dies." He paused. "Or else!"

Henry Schooner nodded and faced the camera. And paused. He always started with a silence, which somehow always seemed to blossom into a version of a sacred silence. *Still* he paused. When he spoke, that *voice* came out, in his arresting tone, deep and yet light, full of gravitas, and from a height of power.

"Like all of you, we thank God for reuniting these great young patriots. We are filled with sorrow and anger. And thank God for the superb healing that our doctors and nurses and other medical staff performed, saving this young woman's life. They are the best. But the sad truth is that the owners of this for-profit hospital, one of its chain, is listed by the money changers as quote 'private equity' and, well, KK's crazed quest for profit played a crucial part in ending their baby's life. The fact is, their new policy when they bought the wonderful old hospital was to get rid of deliveries. They closed up obstetrics in all of their dozens of hospitals all over America. Well, folks, this is not my *American* hospital, nor yours. To not deliver *babies*? Because it's not profitable? It's a money-driven abomination."

He wiped his forehead.

"And so I pledge, as chairman of the Ways and Means Committee of the great United States Congress, to leave no stone unturned to find out what culpability the Kushes bear, and *bring them to justice*. I'm hereby sponsoring a law, Sarah's Law, to *Bring Back Births!* in every licensed hospital in the great United States of America." He was stern-faced, eyes in a squint, dead serious. "We can't bring Sarah back, but we can see that *it never happens again*. So help me God."

A short and powerful video, featuring Henry and Joe and Desiree, and the doctors and nurses and a few techs, would be seen all over America.

The *Crier's* front page story?

Safe Home by Hero, Danger in Kush Kare

With Sev pulling an all-nighter, the others of the team got everything ready to launch the "Reverse Strike."

The usual "KK Security" guys, chosen for their "bouncer" mentality, had always been scared and reluctant to go anywhere near the entrance or inside Emergency. They were afraid that they would get into hassles with the tight and battle-tested group of nurses, respiratory techs, and others—and the newly empowered policemen. And they feared getting infected, so that one day you're a tough, strong dude and then overnight you start coughing your lungs out, headed for a ventilator.

Amy and Shump and the others had formed a mutual admiration society with the policemen—not only Gilheeny and Quick but also the new addition from Boston, a third policeman named James Barnacle O'Toole. Tall and handsome and seeming older, he said little and did much to herd the other two. Soon the three were everywhere, helping, and with minimal protective gear would go wherever they were needed. The Humvee controlled the battlegrounds of parking and protest.

And a new five-o'clock protest was back.

"Hey Hey, Jason K. How Many Babies Have You Killed Today."

By Christmas, the Reverse Strike was working almost seamlessly. The Kush-run scheduling app was out of Lewis Carroll and Alice. It was a sick perfection, so that if you were trying to change your shift, you fell down a rabbit hole of horrors, until you gave up. Sev's scheduling app was up and running in two days and, unlike KK's, was simple and never broke down. Suddenly there was new energy in the air, even hope. With one nurse now taking care of a reasonable five patients, nurses blossomed. Old friends came back to work, new friends came from all over. Nurses are typically a friend-making "relational" tribe who actually *like* people and like *helping* people heal. Overload and stress had killed that. But now they could show their kindness and compassion to their patients and colleagues—and also at home.

In the past, KK was cheap on PPE, forcing nurses to wear the same life-protective mask for a whole week before changing. Now nurses had PPE and equipment via Schooner's ongoing secret supply chain—a huge sigh of relief. And the "high" of it all, clean as a whistle, was just doing service to relieve pain and suffering. Energy flowed into them—and then out to care. It was humane, imagine? They worked when they had the energy, and stayed home when not. Reminding them, and clarifying to all who witnessed them working, what good care could be. Nurses and doctors and other health-care workers spread a sense of "each is valued" and "we're all in it together"—even trash handlers suddenly liked coming in to work.

Taking care of sick and suffering people, now, was once again "a healing art."

Knowing that they could work as much or as little as they wanted and change hours quickly if a child got sick or a partner went nuts—well, it was heaven. Linked together by their shared respect, they were lifted up out of the raw isolation of the pandemic. Mutual connections arose, even through all levels of workers. Kindnesses at work, the underpinning of our healing art.

Doing good work, seeing old friends and making new ones, with their hours tailored to their *lives*, made volunteering their time rewarding. Soon there were so many applications, there were waiting lists.

Of course they still got overwhelmed by the horror, but never by the work.

Sometimes, even, the job morphed into a kind of elegance.

Some of the KK security couldn't help but notice that behind that emergency door something funny was going on. The usual nurses whom they knew were keeping their usual shifts. But there was a much larger group of nurses they'd never seen before, who had irregular hours and lengths of stay inside—sometimes as little as two or three hours. They reported this to the bosses.

22

A few days later, Amy, Roy, Hyper, Eat My Dust, Shump, and Natasha were sitting in the doctors' and nurses' room, a homey, lived-in-during-a-pandemic feel, with empty food cartons and lots of half-eaten cakes and cookies and fruit and, on the wall, inspirations for their daily work:

ISOLATION IS DEADLY; CONNECTION HEALS—
STICK TOGETHER, NO MATTER WHAT.
WITHOUT HEALTH-CARE WORKERS,
THERE'S NO HEALTH CARE.
PUT THE HUMAN BACK IN MEDICINE.

"Jason Kush himself says y'can't do this," said Kenneth S. Miller Jr., director, Kare 4 Safety. He was speaking on Zoom, from an undisclosed location that looked like an underground bunker. "You can't hire nurses and not pay them. We deem this fiscally unsound. Stop it."

Amy said, "The new nurses won't work for money; they get paid in patients' gratitude."

"How touching. We deal only in money. We will not pay. Fire them all."

"No one can fire them," said Roy.

"Why not?"

"Because they were not hired," Roy replied. "If they're not hired, they can't be fired. By you or us or anybody else."

"Very funny. We know what you're up to. This is a disguised strike! Classic hatred of owners. You can't do this. They are not employed by Team KK."

"Oh boy!" said Eat My Dust, looking around the table. "Why did all of you stop me from strangling him the first time we met him?"

The team took this as rhetorical and said nothing.

"Listen carefully," said Shump. "A strike is when you stop working, to fight for more money. But these nurses started to work here for no money. It's a *reverse* strike. Go look at the banners the people are putting up all over your building: 'Support the Reverse Strike.' 'Not walking *out* for money, walking *in* to heal.' It's new, it's sexy, it's hot, and it works. You might want to try it, Kenneth. A lot of no money to be made. Join us."

"Funny joke. You haven't got a chance in hell."

"More a chance than you," said Hyper. "'We kill babies' is not good advertising. You're—all of you are—going down the skids, to bankruptcy."

"Think candy stripers," Amy said. "We have attracted volunteers, altruistic nurses who are, in fact, registered workers, *donating* time. Like when I was a girl, in this very hospital I was a candy striper. We donated our time to help take care of patients' needs. For free! Nobody ever kicked me out. That's what we're doing—not for cash, but to serve."

"And as you know, Junior KK Man," said Eddie, "once you *pay* 'em, you get into a lot of crap, regulations, benefits—you hate that, right?"

Kenneth Miller did allow that he hated crap.

"We're purists," Eddie summed up grandly. "Crap-free. Free is easy."

Kenneth sat silently, puzzled. "So we can't force them to take our pay, correct?"

"Correct," said Shump.

"Suppose you fuck up. Suppose one of your nurses fucks up and—"

"*Excuse me?*" said Shump. "*Shame on you!* We will not be spoken to in that manner. Apologize, or we hang up."

He squirmed in his chair and grimaced, as if his dad had smacked him a hard one across his face. "Okay, reboot." He twisted his face into a series of advanced scowls, then quickly muttered, "I apologize." Squinting, teeth gritted, he went on, "Suppose one of your nurses, um . . . makes a mistake? And gets *sued*? Guess who pays? Us! We are liable! Just to allow your new nurses to work there, we have huge liability that would hurt the bottom line and fiscal trend up. Who pays? *We* pay!"

"Awww right, baby!" said Eat My Dust. "Kenny, now you are *talkin'*!"

"Sign us up!" said Hyper, rocking harder.

"Why, Kenneth," said Shump, "that's quite interesting! I myself would not like to get sued, but I'd love to see you sued all the way up to your miniature testicles."

He went white. He wanted to hang up but he had not "solved the problem" he had been trusted with by the higher-ups.

"Do you know," said Natasha, breaking the silence, "that there *never used to be* anything like quote 'insurance.' For the first fifteen hundred years of modern civilization, if there was a calamity in a town or city, neighbors and leaders used to *help each other out*. But then, in the alleged Italian Renaissance, the Medici princes came in—they were bankers, Ken, money men like you—they created insurance. That was the moment when 'help thy neighbor' pretty much died. The choice is always simple: *self*, or *care for*, right?"

Ken did not aver that she was right. He looked like a dog in pain.

"The Old Testament was 'an eye for an eye,'" Natasha went on, "but Gandhi said, 'An eye for an eye, and the whole world goes blind.' And Jesus? 'Love they neighbor as thyself'?—he chased the money changers out of the temple."

"I know you want to get off this call," said Shump, "Let me speak for our group. Tell your pal Jason Kush, quote: 'You and yours are on the wrong side of this history. *You . . . will . . . go . . . down.*'"

————

But as the dead time nearing the New Year slogged on, Jason Kush never replied to any attempt to contact him. Henry Schooner used the ordinary channels, and the dirty channels. Nothing.

The only reply Kush had made was through his son, Jason Jr.: "My father says, 'I never deal with the *chazerai*. Cease and desist. Or else.'"

Henry Schooner went to Orvy for translation of *chazerai*.

"The underclass," Orvy said, "the garbage, the badly informed. The stupid, the dirty, the poor, the *lumpen*. Goyish peasants. Get it?"

"Are you kiddin'?" Henry said. "Insulting my upbringing, with no mother and only one parent in the picture and look where I am today?"

"It's the price you pay, Henry," Orvy said. "He's jealous of you."

"He'd be jealous *dead*, by me if it were legal," said Henry. "Give no quarter. Buckle up."

Meanwhile, the Reverse Strike worked. Each of the new workers had choice, to work or not? When? How much? They were not killed with work and had safe PPE, and as soon as you walked through that door you could feel the hope and excitement. Good care increased, suffering was less. Simply put: it was a good place to work, and it was clearly doing good.

The two patients on the top floor—the Chief's son, under meticulous care by Eddie, and Desiree by Roy, continued their recoveries. The Chief's son went home. Because of threats, he was wheeled out and into his father's Toyota in the dead of night—a sweet save! Desiree was getting ready to leave as well. Eddie was still a target, from his Facebook posts, and had to move to an undisclosed location with the three policemen.

When the chief's son was discharged, Eddie went crazy happy. "Now I gotta think of Naidoo," Eddie said to the group. "Gotta get back to her in Napa. All she's had are fires and floods, floods and fires." He considered. "Why can't we get the floods *with* the fires, huh?"

A shiver went through the group—*no Eddie?*

"Don't worry, I'm not a quitter." He paused, sighed. "But I realized I'm getting a little old for this frontline stuff. My seventieth birthday was portentous. After seventy, it rounds up to *death*."

Roy was also happy. Desiree had had another mild attack of sepsis, swiftly met by Binni with a tailored new stem cell infusion.

Binni was amazing, always available, mostly curative—and always happy. He somehow managed to be everywhere patients were really sick, always with a constant glow and a newly specific stem cell line, boosting his monoclonal antibody treatment. When Desiree had had that other septic attack, he had snapped her out of it overnight.

She was finally ready to leave. A date was set. December 28.

Her story had rocked America. After the first short video with Henry Schooner and her husband Joe talking, she had not given any interviews. Which made the press hungrier. Henry and Natasha were secretly about to roll out interviews when it would help most.

Far and wide, Kush Kare was reviled—and it denied comment.

But Schooner heard that in polls the Kush Kare Private Equity Fund had gone "name-brand negative."

————

"Sorry to bother you, Amy," said Binni's second ex-wife, in a voice-mail. "I want to talk to Binni, I've tried e-mail and phone calls, but he's not getting back to me. And it's important, about Razina. Would you be so kind, Amy, as to get him to call me? *Stat*, as you say?"

It was shortly after six, a crisp bright December day. She got the message when she woke up and was startled but not surprised; Binni had been working for Moderna as if possessed, making tweaks for the vaccine rollout in a few days. She had barely seen him.

The Presbyterian Church had just rung out 13. Amy was still floating high on two miracles—Desiree's life, and the Reverse Strike. And Razina was flourishing. A rare, blossoming, full life in the midst of the deadly pandemic.

Raz had become a vital part of the extended Rose family pandemic pod, spending more and more time at the house. Miranda was helping Raz with her online schooling. Eleanor and Raz had become close—Ellie's laser focus on her whales was helping the younger girl to find a sense of purpose. Orvy, of course, was a grand grandpa, one that Raz had never had. And, of course, her God, Ben. And now here Raz came, rushing out to catch up for the first walk of the day. Amy handed the leash to her, and called Binni.

"Hey," he said, clearly wide awake but already distracted by his work.

"Your ex left a message for me, to get you to answer her message to you."

"Yes, she's been calling. Left a long message. I'll call sometime today. But I'm flat out on a crucial point—"

"Two things, dear: one, call her right back; two, after you hang up with her, I need face time with you, *stat*. In person, here."

He showed up in 20 minutes. She hadn't seen him in days—he was working intensively at home. When he arrived, Razina was bringing Ben back from his grand tour, gathering himself for another stolid day.

"Hi, Dad," said Raz, with a look of surprise. "What are you doing here?"

"I wanted to see you and Amy."

"Okay, but I've got to feed Ben and then groom him, maybe an hour, okay?

"I'll try."

She went inside. They sat on a bench. Neither noticed the outside weather. To her he looked strung out. His eyes were red-rimmed, and his charming dimples framing his pursed lips were gone. All seemed to her, all at once, that his face had gone flat—a failure of something vital, collapsing inside. Not *with* her.

"What did your ex want?"

"She was worried about why, when she calls, Raz is almost always at the Rose house, not with me. She asked if Raz was living there, which would violate our agreement. She's supposed to live with me. I said she stays over sometimes because she's crazy about Eleanor, and I go over there all the time. So no big deal. She wanted a schedule of how much Raz stays there, and I said I'd gladly provide it. Case closed."

"When was the last time you saw Raz?"

He paused. "I don't know, it's all a kind of blur now, with the rollout." He brightened. "I discovered a new carbohydrate coat for protecting the RNA when it's injected—a perfect adjutant! Lots more work, but the payback is extended—"

"I asked 'when'?"

He stopped, trying to think. "You know I'm bad on dates. Two days?"

"Four. Your daughter keeps track." He looked down. "And the

last time she slept at your place?" He shrugged. "Eight nights. Over a week."

He looked up and spoke quickly. "She loves it at your house—with my working so hard, staring at my screen all day and half the night—better than being with me. It's for a great cause and—"

"Yes! The work is great! But she's picking up that you don't *see* her. Distracted by work."

"Yes yes, but she loves it here—much more than with me—"

"But that wasn't the deal with your ex! If she knew that her daughter's settling in happily in *another family*? She'll pull the plug on you, and on Raz."

"I doubt that—she's in a tough job, has another guy who doesn't want Raz—"

"You want to try it? Risk losing custody?"

He was stunned. "I never thought of that. I get so engrossed helping others, I . . . neglect her."

"And me."

"What?"

"You're putting your work first. She and I have become less vital to you."

He was stunned. "Of *course* you are vital to me. It's just that right now . . ."

"Forgive me if I take a chance on this, okay?" Suddenly he looked scared. "I'd bet that this is why you've gone through two wives already. When the science—beautiful and lifesaving—your science is more important than your partner, and your daughter."

"But I picture her having a great time with the Roses—they're so free, they have *you* there, a dog as big as a cow—much more than—"

"You'll lose her. You really will lose your daugh—"

"No! The law is—"

"Not by the law. You'll lose her love because of *you*, not the law. It's starting."

He looked as if he'd been shot. Eyes wide, getting it. He blinked, startled.

"You probably can arrange time to be with Raz more. But I don't know if right now even when you're with her, you're not really *with her*."

"Oh God!" He paused. "And . . . so what about us? I do love you, Amy, terribly."

"Yes, I know. I love you too. And I know how terribly you sometimes do it!"

"Like right what I'm doing now?" he said morosely.

"*No!*" She took his hand. "Listen very carefully. Right now is *not* terrible. This, now, is *better*!"

"I want to be a good man for you, and a good dad. Can you help me?"

I've been here before. As with other men, it's here that it falls apart. Take care. She paused, then said, "*We. We* can give it a try. Now, with the focus moving to the vaccine *marketing*, maybe you can ease off a little? Make time for Raz. And me?" He nodded. "And join in, with more time, with all of us at the Roses'. If not, you'll miss the boat."

"Yes, yes!" He softened, body letting go, down into the hard slatted bench.

"How did you leave it with your ex?"

"She wants my plan for Raz, here. Wants it today. Where and when and why she's with whom. I said okay. But I have no idea how to do it!"

"She wants structure. Not your working 24/7 on the vaccine, but working on being a dad." He nodded. She went on. "What have you told her about me?"

"I've described you. She's glad I have a woman friend like you."

"Okay, tell her if she wants to talk with me, I'm available."

———————

On the day of Desiree's discharge, a crowd was there to celebrate. December 28 was mercifully crisp, not freezing, clear as a bell. The sun was going down fast, leaving behind a languorous, gold glow. The media, local and national, were all there, some on foot near the doorway, some in network vans that had buckets for better coverage.

To keep order, the three policemen had somehow purloined a second Humvee, operated by the tall chief, James Barnacle O'Toole. He was parked on a slight knoll at the back of the crowd, to have a panoramic view of any disturbance. The other two, at the entrance: Gilheeny in the turret, and Quick in a bucket high up at the end of a crane reaching up to the façade high above the doors.

The high school band was playing. Festive. Underlaid with rage.

There were a lot of citizens, and no signs—what could one say? A rare crowd—all gathered around her suffering, with a sense of kindness, and hope. Columbians showing their better sides, yes. Freeman Bell—the choirmaster at the Whale City Catholic School—was guiding the students in soothing and inspirational songs, "You'll Never Walk Alone" and "Nearer, My God, to Thee"—hitting perfectly the high tenor notes that are often broken.

Right on time, there was silence. Out people came. First, the nurses and doctors and respiratory techs and housekeeping and other employees. They formed two lines, one on either side.

The cheers built to a thunder.

And then a hush.

Desiree looked worn and thin, small in a large, sparkly wheelchair decked with sequins shining in the bright, low December sun, pushed by her tall, handsome husband, Joe, in the crisp-as-the-day uniform of the Navy SEALs, known to almost all because of the

Crier's daily photos and captions. All in the crowd were wearing masks. Mandatory. A first.

On one side of the wheelchair was Roy and on the other side was His Honor, chairman of the Ways and Means Committee, the most beloved politician in the region, Henry Schooner. On his arm was his gorgeous wife, Nelda Jo. Both wore serious black suits, signaling the mourning. It recalled to many in the crowd the Schooners' own son, who had returned in horrible shape from one of those wars lasting so long that you had to try to remember why in hell it had begun. At great price.

Behind them came Dr. Orville Rose and Miranda.

The group stopped. A microphone was readied.

Orville stepped up to the mic, Miranda at his side. After being town doctor for five decades, nearly everyone in the crowd had either gone to him or had a friend or relative who'd gone to him. Almost everyone knew Miranda—from her decades of loving work to "rehabilitate" Columbia's historical record, which had become core to rebuilding the town and county. The other health-care teams fell in behind him and Schooner. No one from the Kushes came or sent notes.

Many hadn't seen Orvy in a year but on Zoom. He looked good, and as he stood behind the podium and the crowd saw who it was, cheers went up and a round of applause and more and more—and he blushed.

"I will be brief. This is a sad and happy day. These two are now back together, and healing, in body and soul. Their grief will be harsh, but with all our help it will start to move toward sorrow, toward healing. The great doctors, nurses, techs, and everyone else deserve tremendous applause!"

Loud and happy, it went on for a long time.

Henry Schooner, wearing a black mask, advanced to the podium, and took the mask off.

"What a guy," Henry thundered. "Dr. Orville Rose! How lucky can we get!"

Cheers and applause. Then Henry stood up straighter, the soldier that he had been in Vietnam. He looked to Joe and Dez.

"My fellow Americans. What a day! These nurses, doctors, techs, and all the others who diligently *cared* for this wonderful woman— give 'em another hand!"

They did.

"*Diligently* cared. And how hard they worked to save her life!" Again he paused. "I completely agree with Orville. They saved her life in her escape from a dire illness . . ." A longer pause. He seemed to be struggling, even holding back tears, and enunciating by tapping on the podium—picked up by the mics like nails in a coffin—he repeated slowly and carefully so the words were clear and loud with each tap. ". . . *a dire illness that could have been prevented.* How? Simple, as simple as it gets. If we had a hospital here that would *welcome* any and all birth within its walls, not force her to travel alone in a storm *all the thirty-four miles to the nearest obstetricians in Albany*! To lose her baby and almost die in a cold car on the side of a road, alone?" He let this sink in, and with his chin firm and high, said, "God bless Joe and Desiree and all of you. And God bless our troops!"

It was astonishing. Clearly from his soul. He stood there in silence looking over the crowd and then up to the light falling over the west in the darkened sky, his words echoing.

Everyone went wild. The cameras rolled. The crowd was led in singing "Amazing Grace."

It was full dark. Joe and Dez and Orvy and the medical workers were talking to the Schooners and members of the audience when suddenly in the dark, an intense light beamed from the Humvee parked near the front entrance. It was focused up to a tarp high on the façade. Quick released a switch, and the tarp dropped, revealing a billboard-sized glittering sign that seemed chiseled with permanence into the façade, in large, clear letters demanding:

SHORT KUSH

In the greater world, most people would have no idea what that message meant.

But "money men" would know.

And one strange and astute man, a money man, did know. He was an aging recluse, an ascetic in a house in Napa, California, protected by walls and vineyards and sophisticated security. Not known by name, he worked behind several levels of tight, untraceable "dark money." He was the majority investor in Kush Kare Hospitals. But he had taken no board seat or other connection with KK. His personal brokers of his dark money assured total privacy.

Besides money, his passion was llamas. With no real family, all his life now had devolved into three beautiful, long-necked, enigmatic, and cantankerous llamas—who loved only him. For years he had tried to breed his signature llama, and Roxie was she. But that morning she was gone, somehow gotten through a fence. Or stolen in a ransom plot. A search party had gone out, but by noon, nothing.

"How the hell can you not find a llama?" he shouted at his workers. "Find her or you're fired!"

Anger turned to fear. Was she gone? If not stolen, hit by a car? Dead at the side of a road? He was startled to find he could not catch his breath, felt too heavy in his chest to move. He whispered to himself, "Her death would be my death."

Upset and raging at the unfair world, he soothed himself a little by routine: sitting down as usual at his four-at-once Bloomberg business terminals. He chanced upon a rare "human interest story" about Kush Kare. The human interest was of a dead baby. Dead on the side of a road in the dark. Because there was no local hospital within miles that had obstetrics because Kush had canceled them. All at once he felt bad, really bad, as if all of his strength had been drained out of his own body, leaving him for dead. He was in pain, suffering. What to do?

Given his fierce religious studies that emphasized coincidence as fate, the sign on the building façade seemed to be a, well, more than a sign, but a *sign*. An inside voice, which had always helped him out, whispered: *Rid thyself of KK.*

He contacted his two trusted dark-money brokers at the same time, in code. They had always known how to do these things legally. Or at least, without ever getting caught. They were meticulous, choreographing buys and sells on the edges of nano-shivers of seconds.

He was brief. "Number one broker, sell all my Kush. Number two broker, short all Kush. Please repeat this to me?" They did.

Click.

He breathed out—realizing he'd been holding it. He doubled down on the search for Roxie.

Two days later, Jason Kush himself called Henry Schooner.

"I want to sell Kush Hospital Columbia. I've heard that your emergency doctor buddies want to buy it. Tell 'em to make me a quick offer. If I don't hear by tomorrow at nine, I flip it and make it into lovely luxury condos all with very nice views."

"As you know," Henry said, "because of my position I can have no part in this."

"Don't gimme that. What's their first offer?"

"Not sure. But the figure I've heard is also their *last* offer."

"What is it?"

"Zero. The rumor is zero."

"You're joking," said Kush.

"You're not laughing, because it's true. They said that Kush may not even be worth that much. The tush of Kush is hurting, bad."

"You fucker! Wait 'til Congress hears your part in this!"

"Fine. For the record, all I've done here, as a resident of Columbia and with their permission, is, when asked, to state their offer. Zero. Call them."

Silence.

"Why not just give this to them," Schooner went on, "give it to our town, for free! Imagine—you could be seen as a great benefactor."

"Fuck that."

Long silence. Then nose blowing.

"Who the hell do I call? Who's the boss?"

"A couple of angels. Natasha O'Brien and Leatrice Shumpsky. Nurses. Call them."

"Me? Negotiate with *nurses?*"

"Yes."

"Which one's the boss?"

"Yes."

"No no no—which *one* is the boss?"

"Both," said Schooner.

"Oh Jesus! Women's *equality* blahblahblah."

"No. Not equality. *Mutuality.*"

"What? What the hell does *that* mean?"

Silence.

"You wouldn't understand," Henry went on. "They're sharp. Trained at the Harvard Business School. Where did you train?"

"On the front lives—I mean *lines*. Nuts and bolts, in the jungle. Borough Park."

"It shows. Just so you know, they're angels, two angels who love healing people." He paused, and then went on. "I've taped this whole call, Mr. Jason Kush, because I'm sure that you have done so on your end. God bless you and God bless America. And as our President Biden says, 'God bless our troops.'"

———

A few days later, with no phone call to the nurses, someone leaked to the *Crier* what was going on. The headline the next day?

Kush Kare Krashes:
Donates Us Back Our Hospital

The article detailed how KK was "going down the toilet in the markets," and that one option being explored—"before the toilet is flushed"—was to make a gift to the town. This news—after the nurses' Reverse Strike and the senseless death of Baby Sarah—exploded all through Kinderhook County. The demonstrations took off.

The next day there were maybe a hundred Columbians, the day after, almost two. The people were of every race and power—almost all had come to more or less hate Kush Kare. Signs were made, some put up on the front wall by the policemen. The people settled on a couple of slogans that told the story, chanting:

"Take Back Our Hospital!"

"To Save Us All—Docs, Nurses, Patients!"

"Our Hospital, Not Your Profit!"

"Bring Back Obstetrics!"

And even, "Our Hospital Needs a Veterinarian!"

All kinds of people came together. Most had seen, in the Kush regime, the care and healing go down, while the bills had gone up. And the bills had become ever more impossible to understand. The harder you tried to follow instructions to understand your bill, the more obfuscated it got. Many good Columbians knew someone who worked clerically at KK in the "Billing Building" and realized that it was a zoo. The workers were doing their best, but they too were getting squeezed and screwed—impossible work and low pay. The crowd wanted good medical care. Mostly they knew when it was good, and when it was not. And almost all—from the least educated to the most—knew two true things: the goal of KK was taking their money; and the doctors and nurses and other employees were just as trapped and pissed off as anyone.

The crowds of Columbians and media got larger and larger—one day even about a thousand people.

Chants were refined and winnowed down to the best, and megaphones improved, so the words bounced back off the scalloped front façade so loud and clear that they seemed to blanket the little town, then jump the Hudson to echo back off the Catskills:

"NOT *THEIR* HOSPITAL, *OUR* HOSPITAL!

"NOT *THEIR* HOSPITAL, *our* hospital . . .

"Not *their . . . ours . . .* "

———

The people won.

23

The story of Baby Sarah and Desiree had gone national, with Joe and Desiree doing short, selected appearances. Book deals had been offered. Bottom line, almost all of us Columbians wanted the Kushes to get themselves the hell out of our lives, period.

With fierce pressure on KK from Henry Schooner, the deadline for the signed deal between the Kushes and our town—represented by Shump and Natasha—was five p.m. on Thursday, December 31. As the day went lazily on, everyone on the team was on edge. For all of us in Columbia, our faith in the Kushes keeping their word was almost zero.

The *Crier* was late—hours late. Finally it arrived on our doorsteps.

The front-page headlines proclaimed:

IT'S OUR HOSPITAL!
KUSH KARE CRASHES
TWO NURSE-BOSSES SIGN DEAL

————

All over town and county, the celebration was a dynamite, off-the-charts party. It was as if the whole shitty, hard, plague-year misery and death had—not been worth it, of course, but, well, had created something that was sure to be better, maybe even a beacon of good medicine and health care in all of America. Maybe, even, it had to get so bad, so drowning in money and fraud, that the good would arise. The rotten institution had collapsed under the weight of its own contradictions. With a little help from their enemies on how *not* to do it, the nurses, doctors, and others were free to do their *calling*: give good care.

Kush transferred the hospital to a duly-formed entity of us citizens. From this time on, it would be our hospital. The words used? *In perpetuity.*

————

What a great celebration at Orvy and Miranda's!

The ecstatic core team was mostly on Zoom, on a giant screen that Eleanor had bought as a gift to her parents, but also to watch animal protection documentaries and to examine and categorize her own drone video data of the whales off Ecuador. She was chafing to get back there and finish. On this big new screen you could clearly see two mother humpback whales shepherding their newly born calves in the tropical waters—teaching them how to breathe, and mimic how to flip a flipper—a dance of hope.

Roy and Berry had planned to come to the celebration in person, but their daughter, Spring, had surprised them, coming from New York to announce that she, after a long relationship, was engaged to marry her guy—a great kid. They would be leaving first thing in the morning to tell his parents, who lived in northern Vermont. They would join by Zoom if they could.

The first to speak were the two heroes, Natasha and Shump. For several days and nights they had worked on terms to get the hospital for free.

"We spent a ton of time writing the contract," Shump said. "It's rock-solid. No one, but no one, breaks this baby."

Cheers.

"Great job!" said Orville. "But you two look like you've been hit by a truck—you okay?"

"Not just any truck," said Shump, "a garbage truck. But we got everything we asked for. All free and clear and with no debt."

"Turns out they're not only in trouble here in Columbia," said Natasha, "but all across America. For some reason the stock took a helluva nosedive recently. It's still ripping through the chain of all the other KK hospitals. Big trouble."

"From your mouth to God's ears," said Amy. "The death of Kush here is a new life for us, not just us workers and patients, but health care itself."

"Oh," said Shump, "I forgot—comic relief? During our negotiations, Kush Sr. was so obnoxious that his lawyer lost his cool and said in front of everybody that if he didn't shut the hell up he'd walk out. A lawyer, walking away from big money? Our lawyer, Theo Geiger, said he'd never seen anything like it." She shook her head. "Anyway, friends, we won, big. Annnnd . . ." She yawned. "After twelve hours straight today with the Kushes, I need five hours of hot shower to return to all that's clean and good in the world, so I'll hang up. Love you all, we did good." She left the Zoom.

"I just want to say," Natasha put in, "I'm so happy I could cry. Yes, we all did a good, good thing in the world. And now for a celebration with my husband—if he remembers who I am?" With a wave she too vanished.

Cheers all around, including from the three policemen watching the screen from the porch. They had been guarding the house, just in case. The Humvee right in front was a further warning to, in Gilheeny's accent, "Don't try nuthin' fooney."

In the wake of the presidential election, when the Big Mac was buried by Biden in a landslide of the popular vote, and definitively lost the electoral count, he'd started the Big Lie—that the election had been stolen—and was still not conceding.

Our country was even more fractured than ever. The city of Columbia had gone Democratic; Kinderhook County, Republican. The Big Mac's citizen army was restless. Scary, even dangerous. In the last few days rumors spread on the internet that armed militias were gathering, planning to right the wrong of the "stolen" election. Things were more and more tense all over America.

But in Columbia, hurrahs for the three policemen. Everyone at the party breathed easier that they and their cute Humvee were present. Cute, yes, because they'd allowed New York artists to cover the machine of war, turret to tread, in art. Some were faithful to reality, others—two nude Columbians entwined—not so much.

The cops had commandeered the front porch, bringing cushy chairs under a summer umbrella that read: *Work is the curse a' the drinkin' man*. Orvy had located bottles of Dublin's spirits: Jameson whisky and six-packs of Guinness.

A high point for all those at the party was seeing Eat My Dust Eddie. There he was on-screen on Zoom from the basketmaker chief's house high up in the woods of the Taconic Range. The chief and his son, now doing well, were at the kitchen table, where Eddie was saying good-bye to the tribe. At sunrise he'd fly back to his beloved Naidoo.

"This has been a great trip, all of it," Eddie said. "A lot of you thought I was a real, um, basket case, and you were right! Turns out that this time with all of you, for all the hellish months, has helped my marriage. Naidoo's anxious for me to come home. So this is so long. I love you all. *Really.* And—" He snatched his red motorcycle bandanna from his head but before he could bring it over to hide his nose and eyes he was weeping, nodding, crying out, "Love you all I mean I . . . just . . . love . . . you . . . all!" And then he froze, trying to hold back his body-shaking sobs. Finally he pushed through, half crying and half shouting, "This is probably the last time we see each other for a long time and maybe forever, so I just wanna say that it's been a helluva ride since the House of God to this, *for what we did all these months of hell, doin' so much good*? On fire! What we did together was the best! It was beau . . ." Tears came. He searched for his bandanna, and blew his nose, trying to get words out. "With . . . I mean with a love for all you great docs and nurses and people doin' together *the best thing in my whole life.*" And then he was gone.

Hyper Hooper was at the airport, waiting for the last flight to California that night.

"Hey, guys, I caught the same disease as hit me hard in the House all that time ago—MOR, man, Marriage on the Rocks. Gotta rescue it again, and play more with the grandkids. So long and always remember Hyper Laws: Stay Hyper, it's the best defense; and low-fat, low-carb, pomegranate shakes." Gone.

Shortly before nine, with Roy and Berry on Zoom and the family Rose and Binni and his daughter still celebrating together, who should appear in person but Henry Schooner, dressed perfectly to "relax in style," but of a former time, almost as if he were just coming back from tennis on a private court in the Gatsby Hamptons: white flannel trousers, creased sharply, a faded blue "work shirt" with pockets, a zip-up red jacket, unzipped, and collar up and with an insignia of a flag wrapped around a sheaf of grain and a musket, and the words: "Ways and Means, H. X. Schooner, Chair."

"Hope I'm not interrupting," he said.

"Ladies and gentlemen!" Orvy said. "Welcome my dear old friend, who made it possible for certain parties to *give the hospital to us for free*. Our hospital. To a great American, a great friend to me for all my life, Henry!"

"Thank you, thank you. I did what I could, because this town is in my bones, and because of my admiration for all of you but especially for my good doctor Orville Rose!" He led the applause. "And hey, what better place to be right now, than right here about to see a remarkable moment in our nation's hard walk to home, our soon-to-be President. Hey look! On the TV? There he is!"

President-elect Biden and his wife were at one end of the Reflecting Pool, facing the Lincoln Memorial at the other. In his stone shelter was that huge, astonishing person who tried to "bind up the nation's wounds." Biden motioned with his hand. Lights came up to reveal 400,000 small American flags lining the pool, far and wide. *Each flag a Covid death*. All in just eight months. What a waste.

The silence in the house was sober, and then uplifting. Biden had one message: "*We will stop this suffering. Together we can heal.*"

Breathtaking.

"This, now," said Miranda, "is hope. Real hope, yes?"

"You bet," said Schooner. "I've known Joe for decades. He's like us, a good man, an ordinary man. He's walked his family through hell, and survived. Lotta hope. But stay tuned. We may have to get through hell, first."

"What do you mean?" Amy asked.

"Can't tell you, but we're workin' on it, to blunt it when it comes." He yawned—a rarity—and said, "Thanks muchly. Gotta go—"

"Wait, please, sir—I have a new announcement, of hope!" said Binni, jumping up from his chair. "The trial results of the Moderna vaccine are already showing its power. The FDA will okay *full national rollout* starting in late January. We'll beat back Covid!"

Everyone was stunned, silent. Then all were shouting at once.

Binni answered all the questions—mainly that it was safe, and it worked.

"And everyone will want it!" he went on. "Surely *surely* we'll never see another four hundred thousand deaths in America from Covid."

"Remarkable," said Orville. "So fast? And totally safe?"

"*Totally.* RNA-based, safe, *and* cheap. We just need to get to herd immunity, seventy-three percent inoculated and we're done! Friends, this is *real hope*! Surely surely *surely* this will happen! Just a little prick in the deltoid, done! *Everyone* will want it!" He glowed. "Surely this will happen!"

"Greatgreat," said Henry. "Call me if you need me." He yawned. "Been a long day. God bless." He waved as he walked out, and stumbled a bit, catching himself, then continued out. He could be seen on the porch chatting happily with the policemen, and all burst out laughing. He walked away into the park, threading the path toward his house, a Guinness in his hand.

Orville looked at Miranda, wondering if he should say something about how hard it is to change a person or two—much less a whole country? Seventy-three percent of *this* whole country? And Schooner had told them that the Big Mac had done nothing—*absolutely nothing*—to organize the distribution of the vaccine. He had delegated total responsibility for this national rollout to his son-in-law, a sepulchral child who knew nothing of such things and cared less. The new President would be starting from zero.

Miranda could sense what Orvy was thinking of saying, and gave a slight shake of her head, a warning, whispered: "*Only if you are kind, and positive.*"

He nodded, and took a deep breath in, and out. "Great, Binni. And in such a short time! I'm sure it'll be fast, but it won't be easy. All of us have been up against the Covid deniers all this time—we know it's tough. Real tough. And we're a *blue* state. Imagine a *red*?

Even here, out in the county. But I'm optimistic too. And no matter what happens, however frustrated we all get, what we're doing, right here right now, is redemptive. An incredible, invaluable spirit. The message from the universe a few months ago was that we had been called to meet here at this moment, at great risk to our own lives. And so we worked together to find hope—even when it seemed hopeless. Even more, we have *given* hope, all of our hope, to others—even when it got shredded. We've ridden the waves, the rising and falling of hope, and we never let go of holding to the good, the true, and, mostly, to our kindness. Our hope will probably rise and fall as we go on. But that's the thing about hope—we know this from our patients, right? Hope rises. You ever felt that?"

Nods, and smiles of understanding.

"I mean isn't that the damnedest thing? Hope rises."

"I hope it does," Amy said, "but sometimes, you know . . ."

"Of course, but think how we survived these nine months? When one of us was hopeless, another just happened to be there, with a little extra hope. How many times have we been in that dance, treating Covid? Our solid 'we' saved us, time and again. There's no end of that. *Surely.*"

The silence was one of invited inspiration. Facing the hopeless, back to hope?

"Wonderful, Orvy," said Berry. "Roy and I have to leave. Shall I offer up a Buddhist prayer?" Nods all around. "It's called *Metta Sutta.* On loving-kindness."

> *Let none deceive another or despise any other being in any*
> *state.*
> *Let none through anger or ill-will wish harm upon another.*
> *Even as a mother protects with her life her child, her only*
> *child,*
> *So with a boundless heart should one cherish all living beings,*

Radiating kindness over the entire world, spreading upward
  to the skies,
And downward to the depths, outward and unbounded, freed
  from hatred and ill-will.
Whether standing or walking, seated or lying down, free from
  drowsiness.

She paused, and smiled before finishing the prayer with:

May all beings be free from suffering and the root of suffering.
May all beings see with the eyes of loving-kindness.
This is said to be the sublime abiding.

After shouting "Happy New Year," everyone had gone to bed except Amy and Orvy and Ben. Uncle and niece sat together at one end of the long cherry table that could seat 12, and in a pinch 15. Happy and tired, coming down fast from the excitement. Ben was happy too.

"God you look gorgeous!" said Orvy to Amy. "You're glowing! Winning is good for you!"

"And you too," Amy said. "What the hell did we do?"

"Oh, nothing much, just changed this little town of breakages, for a little moment in time anyway, to a little town of healing. Here's to us!"

"And Ben!" said Amy.

Out of the mass of dark black fur on the floor came the bright red of a tongue and gums and jowls, the best he could do to smile.

Orvy drained the last champagne. Amy felt tired, body and mind, and yawned widely, once, twice. Orvy caught it, and joined her, yawning.

"Suffering," Orville said. "Weird that we don't use that word in medicine, isn't it? It seems to me that if you ask a patient, 'What is your suffering,' you open things up a lot more, instead of asking: 'What brought you here today?'"

"Which often brings the answer," Amy said, "'The number six bus.'"

"Exactly. Everybody suffers, doctors too. It would connect us better."

Amy started to yawn, but stifled it. "Berry's a real spirit. I love 'er."

"It's all so chancy. We think we're in control of our lives, but we have no idea of how our lives will go. Chance or fate, all based on the flicker of a butterfly's wing."

"Yes. Big yes."

"Remember when Miranda and I broke up—you were what? Fourteen?" She nodded. "I'd fulfilled my mother's crazy will to live in this house for a year and thirteen days continuously in order to get her bequest—the house and the Chrysler and a million bucks. I'd chosen to leave town, go back to Rome and Celestina. I was sitting on the train, leaving."

"Yes, I remember. My mom and I and Miranda and Cray were there too, sending you off, watching the train leave. We turned around and started walking away and heard a shout to us—you'd jumped out of the other side of the train and you were running toward us, and we ran too—even Miranda, limping! You never told me what made you change your mind, how that had happened, really."

"Y'think you're old enough now?"

She laughed. "No, but I'm humoring you before I go to bed."

He laughed, and then caught her eye, and they laughed harder, together.

Amy asked, "Did you know then that Miranda was pregnant with Eleanor?"

"No. She didn't want that to be the reason that I stayed."

"Really? How . . . honorable. Why did you decide to get off the train?"

"*I* didn't. I heard a voice: *Don't spread more suffering around. Whatever you do, don't spread more suffering around.* And so I jumped off the train and you all were walking away, heads down in sorrow, and I shouted, '*Hey I'm here! Wait!*'"

"*That* I remember. You started running with your bags and we started running—even Miranda, limping along—and it was one of the most joyous moments of my life—up there with your not dying from Covid."

"I'm telling you this, now, because I'm thinking of us both being doctors, good doctors, carrying it on: for me learning from old Bill Starbuck—and he learning from the gun-slinging 19th-century doctor hanging on the office wall—and then you, at fourteen, asking if you could hang around with me on my rounds and in the office—learning from me, I from you. *Good* connections are always mutual. And now you, showing the young docs."

"Yes. In this warp-speed time, our lineage and—" A huge yawn was starting to bloom, and she didn't want it to interrupt this, tried to stop, but couldn't. "Sorry, Orv—" A huge yawn. He yawned too. They laughed.

Orvy said, "I shall be brief."

"There's a first time for everything, Doc."

He smiled. "*Don't spread more suffering around.* And what I realized, in all these years, is that everyone suffers—it's not optional. Big suffering, little suffering, we all suffer. It's not the suffering, it's how we walk through it. If we walk through our suffering alone—especially men—'stand tall,' 'tough it out,' 'draw a line in the sand,' we will suffer more, and spread more suffering around. But if we walk through suffering with another, or others—and that's where *we* come in, we *doctors*, it's our job! We are there at the most suffering moments in people's lives, it's what we signed up for, it's our job, and *our gift*, to be there with them in their suffering—we will *not* spread more suffering around, and if we're lucky, we'll heal. Heal others, *and* heal ourselves. The word goes both ways. Our spirit." He paused, eyes glittering.

"Beautiful."

He took a deep breath. "I never told you much about my relationship with my mother. Difficult, at best. When I came back to Columbia after her death, and was forced to stay here, I started getting letters from her, mailed throughout the year by someone she'd given them to. They were horrible, accusatory, resentful mostly—that I had abandoned her in her plight when she had a brain operation on an acoustic neuroma that cut the facial nerve, spoiling her beauty. She accused me of running away from her. It was true. But the last letter was different, short." He took a breath.

"In that last letter she wrote to me, 'I've finally realized that you were not running *from* me, but running *for* me.'"

Tears came to his eyes, but he kept looking at Amy. He and she, uncle and niece, doctor to doctor, and in all the other ways they were tight together right there, right then. Still holding each other's eyes. Both felt tears come, of love, of joy. And of a profound sense of being part of the spirit of the place.

24

The next morning, the first day of the New Year. The new weather-woman, relocating from Manhattan, had predicted a record warm, sunny day for Columbians. She was right. Amy and Binni stepped out of the house to poop and pee Ben. The Presbyterian church rang out 13. Her Fitbit read 06:43 Friday, January 1, 2021. Glowing from last night's news and party, she smiled.

"Ohh, what a hangover," Binni said, brown eyes like slits, cheeks clenched up. "Did you really need *me* to poop Ben? Isn't that Razina's job?"

"You've been gone for three weeks straight. Razina was asleep too. And I've got something to talk with you about in private."

"Couldn't it wait 'til after coffee?"

"It won't take long." She looked at Ben. "Okay, Ben, hurry up."

In three giant plodding steps, nose down, he happened to find a delicious urinal on the ground and peed, and peed, and, well, peed.

"Ah, I wish I had a bladder like that," Binni said. "If I'd had a bladder like that I would have made something of my life."

"And now you have anyway! I'm so proud! I could love you just for that."

"Not for anything else?!"

"We'll see." She paused, finding it hard to jump in. She looked at him closely, his hand kneading his brow as if it could bake some life into him. He coughed a few times. Then, shading her eyes from the profound slant of winter sun, thought, *This is not promising. Now or never.*

"I'm pregnant."

He turned to her, eyes wide, astonished. "But I . . . I . . . The pill . . . What happened?"

"I've been taking the pill religiously. I've gone over and over this—I don't understand it either. The only thing—*maybe*—is that in the chaos of the pandemic, I forgot sometime? I don't know."

"Oh my. Oh my oh my." He blinked, and blinked. "Now what?"

"After all these years, *you* did it. And that, Binni, is amazing! I mean a vaccine to save the world is one thing, but to save my deep wish is another. Helluva job, you."

"I . . . I . . . well, thanks." He cradled his cheeks between his hands. "Ohhhh. I . . . I'm speechless, so many questions . . ."

"Four months pregnant—all going well! And it's a boy."

"Four . . . a boy . . ." Still clutching his face in his hands, peering out at her as if from a bunker. "A boy?" His face turned from light brown to dark red, and he tried not to cry but couldn't stop.

Is he weeping for joy, or feeling trapped? I've never seen him like this. His work has always come first—he's at the top of the heap now—is he afraid he'll lose what he's always aimed for? And another child, taking him away from his science, and bringing him another disappointed wife to deal with?

She opened her arms to him, and he kind of fell into her chest.

"Why . . . why didn't you tell me sooner?"

"I wanted to be sure. And I wanted you with me. Are you . . . mad?"

"Mad?"

"I've never seen you like this."

"I'm over the moon with joy!" He started crying again, great heaving sobs, and she quieted him, smiling, and she rocked him—yes, like a baby.

"Thank God, my love," she said. "I'm so relieved that—"

"Hey, Ben!" Raz shouted from the porch. "Amy, why didn't you wake me up?"

Ben lit up. A yearning whine, a thundering "wrOOF!" Raz was running toward them. Seeing her father wiping tears away, she stopped still.

"What's wrong?"

"These are tears of happiness, Razina. More happy than I've been in years."

"Your experiments worked!"

"Yes, especially one that no one else has heard about yet, except Amy."

"Tell me and Ben later." She hugged Ben, and then grabbed his leash. "I feed him and walk him and poop him—and love him as much as anyone on earth. Sorry, Dad, but it's true!"

"All he did so far was pee," said Amy. "Why don't you feed him, come back out and poop him, okay?"

"C'mon, Ben—y'can't *really* rely on these guys. They don't know that"—she pointed her finger at them—"the one thing dogs need is *routine.*"

Ben, clearly upset by Binni's tears, resisted Raz.

Amy said, "Ben, it's okay. Go!" He left with his newest favorite human.

"I'm so happy," Binni said, "but I'm, well, I'm not that good at it."

"You're good at *me.*"

"But . . . but I'm zero-for-two wives so far. It seems that when I go all in, I lose myself, and turn into my work, and then it's over."

"I know, hon, I've seen it." She touched his hand. "But haven't you ever been in a really *good* relationship, where you feel *more* yourself—able to do your best in everything, love and work?"

He considered this. "With you, yes, yes—and Razina sometimes." He paused. "You mean, in love we can do more? In the lab, and as a good dad, and be loving even more?"

"Yes."

"Yes!" He seemed startled at this. "In love, I'm *more* myself?" She nodded. "Not a capped variable, but an expanding one? A paradigm shift, like Schrödinger and his cat, quantum relationships?"

"You lost me."

"Sorry. But I've been such a failure, in two tries! A bumbler in love."

"Guess what? Me too! At least you *tried* marriage, I never got that far! So I'm a bigger bumbler." They laughed. He took her hands. She said, "One thing I've learned, though, is *how to bumble.* It's not just that we do the right thing with love all the time, we always have disconnects. The key thing is what we do *next.* If we can just hang in, hold the fact, especially at hard times, that love is still somewhere, our bumbling 'we' is still there—we can move on, or remember, that the love didn't go anywhere, it's still there. Back on track. Better, even." She smiled. "Like we're doing now, right?"

"Right."

They both fell silent.

"Hey! Hey you lovers!" Raz was coming back outside. "Gonna poop him! Then I'll come back."

"Go for it!" she said, and turned to Binni. "I didn't get to tell you that at one of the rallies to take over the hospital, a young couple came up to me, and they'd changed so much I didn't recognize them—they'd grown up. I'd met them when I went out to a run-down house out in the county for an emergency delivery?"

He nodded.

"The girl was going to die unless I got the baby out. To do so, I had to reach in and break both clavicles, and—"

"You broke the clavi—"

"I'd seen it done a few times before, in Africa, and in the Navajo nation. At the rally, she was holding her baby, as healthy and happy a baby as you could wish. And strangely, I thought of you."

"Really?"

"Yes. I knew you knew we were in love, and growing that love, but maybe about to drop it. And I decided that *I wanted to be with you*. I mean, with a few crucial adjustments, but yes, with you." She smiled at him.

"But how does that pertain to this?"

"Because broken clavicles heal stronger."

His brown eyes flooded with tears. "I . . . I . . . can only bumble. I say yes."

They hugged, pure joy, for a long time.

Ben and Raz had started walking back toward the bench.

"Shall we tell them now?" asked Binni.

"Fine with me. You?"

"Yes."

Razina and Ben were very happy.

They walked across the park and up the stairs of the welcoming house, hand in hand.

And Amy was suddenly aware of feeling part of something else, part of something at the heart of the universe, a universal law of love.

25

Berry and Roy, shortly after dawn of New Year's Day, stood on the front porch waving good-bye to their daughter Spring, and Denis.

Their waving good-byes were shadowed, a last connection with the thread of their family of three. No more. Now Berry and Roy turned toward each other. Each seeing the sadness in the other—and their own reflection again. They hugged, hard, shuddering with love and loss and care for the kids, kids no longer. Great sadness and great joy. Life as that butterfly's wing.

Luckily, Denis was a good choice—from the start they had liked him and grew to love him as she did, and welcomed him into the family. They'd met the night when Roy had fallen off the mountain in Costa Rica headfirst. Battered and bloodied but okay. Denis helped Spring make arrangements to fly down right away—and came with her. A treasure.

Spring's Volvo two-door sporty car vanished down toward the Rip Van Winkle Bridge. Roy and Berry looked at each other again, and both burst out crying, hugging. This outburst didn't last—joy had crept in on its soft feet—with wiping of eyes, and laughter and headshaking. It was the most anyone would want for their child—a good prop in the revolution of aging parents. Especially for a child adopted from a Chinese orphanage at four months.

"More coffee?" Berry asked. "It's warm enough to stay out here."

"Yeah." He took off his sweater. "January one and it must be fifty."

"Breakage." She went inside.

Roy stared west at the Catskills, the rising sun behind on his back. He sat down motionless in the warmth and spectacle of the morning—but the future once again felt bad. *She's gone! The love of our lives, in love and happy, and I'm glad for her. Happy that he's a great kid but, well . . . it is sad. And hell, I've been wondering what I'm going to do with my life now that the third wave Covid is dying off. Sad!*

"It is sad!" said a familiar voice, trembling with grief.

Startled, Roy looked around. Nothing.

"The hardest thing for a dad or mom," the voice said, "is to see the next generation come along and grab your kid—especially, for a dad, *your girl?* An ache in the heart that, Roy G. Basch, y'might not be able to bear."

"Fats?" he cried out.

"Roy?"

"Roy!"

"Fats!" And there he was, bobbing up and down slowly just above a low limb of their 20-foot-tall dogwood, now naked of its white-rose blossoms, eye to eye with him.

He was wearing a voluminous Renaissance gown and a floopy violet hat that looked like a fat pizza collapsed on his head, with a wilting red rose standing straight up like one of those wavy old antennas, maybe a connection to the internet?

"Why the hell are you dressed up like the Borgias?"

"Ooops. Wrong century." He settled on a low bare branch, and in a trice he was in his usual doctor garb: fat shoes, fat trousers straining to contain the plump thighs, long white doctor's coat skimming the branch, and shiny stethoscope cavalierly encircling that size 19 neck. "Man, seeing her leave here with her beloved is . . ." He broke up, weeping—a monogrammed "FM" hankie appeared in the air and he grabbed it and made for that Jewish nose that started out high up striving, rising out until, as if recalling its tormented ancestors, made a sharp dive down toward his lips. Two walloping nose blasts.

Roy started crying too. They blew their noses—Fats' trombone, Roy's trumpet.

"Yes," Fats said, "a heartache to have her go—a little death, but a benediction too."

"It brings back when Cinnamon died. I'm still not over him."

"There's nothin' like a dog! Dogs affirm God. When Chubby died? Ugh!"

"Speaking of death, do you forgive me, *really*?" Roy asked.

"What?!" He fell off the limb, but floated. "Forgive what?"

"In Man's 4th, Chuck and me letting you take the elevator up to become President of the hospital—"

"Are you bananas? If I couldn't stop myself, you think *you* coulda? Nuthin' coulda! I woulda died in six months, max. My heart woulda attacked me! Gone."

"Promise?" Roy smiled.

"Cross my heart and hope to die." He paused. "But I already did. That's the great thing up here: no worry about dying. No PSAs, no colonoscopies! And above all, no need to diet, or work out! *Perfetto!* The root of pain is time."

"Thanks."

"So now, Basch, what are you going to do next? Y'gonna write more?"

Roy was startled. Berry had always said that as much he and

others—and even she—loved Fats, he almost never *asked* anybody anything. He just *told* people—mostly by talking, talking, talking, and his laws and laughs. She said, "He doesn't get to mutual."

"Thanks for asking," Roy said to him.

"Yeah, I learned to do more of that 'asking' up here," he said, as if he could read Roy's mind. "Tell Berry that I'm learning in a Post-Mortem Men's Group: 'How to Get to Mutual.' It's a real *small* group. Really hard. Makes you a caring man!" He beamed, really beamed. "So? Write another novel?"

"This one's the last."

"Nah. Keep writing about putting the human in health care, and squeezing the money out." His face turned pensive, and serious. "Of course, things have changed since *The House of God* in what, 1973?" Roy nodded. "Yeah, Nixon! Shit, fifty years ago! And then *Mount Misery* and *Man's 4th Best Hospital*."

"Yeah. And now, with this new one?" He paused, astonished. "Nineteen seventy-three to 2023? *Fifty years* of American medicine?"

"A quartet!" said Fats. They laughed. "Okay, y'gotta get online, big-time. Start a podcast. Also, do high-paying personal appearances before live audiences—if the Covid ever ends and—oops, gotta hop."

"Why? Wait! I can't do anything—um, expansive—without you."

"You think I'm goin' someplace *else*? I'll *always* be here. It's not like the *living*—they can't make that 'always' claim, right?" He shook his head. "Cheaters. A whole human life making promises they can't keep!"

"You got a point there, Fats."

"Much more sensible, what I got now."

"But I don't have any control over when I see you—you pop up at random and—"

"*Random?!* Y'think, after all this, that there's a *random*? Sheesh!"

"And what about in our dreams, and—"

"Uh-oh! Berry'll be here in twelve seconds. Gotta hop!"

SAMUEL SHEM

"Why don't you want to see her?"

"Not now. It would jangle the flow. Bye. 'Til we meet again. I love you!"

In another trice he was wearing an old-time pilot outfit with a lavender scarf and leather goggles and pretended to turn on the invisible motor and the imagined plane itself. Waving gaily he said, "*Ciao,* Roy G. Basch, MD, *ciao ciao* and think Tulsa!"

"*Tulsa?* What do you mean 'Tulsa'?"

But he was gone, and Berry was walking out with the coffee.

"How was he?" Berry asked.

"You saw him?"

"No, but unless you've gone crazy, you're not talking to anyone *else* who isn't alive as if they were."

"He loves you, y'know. Listens hard when I talk about you. He says to tell you he's in a men's group, working on 'asking'—not just 'telling.' It's called something like 'Getting to Mutual in the Post-Mortem World.'"

She laughed. "And how's it going for him?"

"Says it's helping. Believe it or not, just now he actually did *ask* about me? First time ever. Asked what I was doing next."

"Amazing!"

"Sounds right. But he said to 'remember Tulsa,' and I don't know what he meant."

Berry responded, "For two years after *The House* came out, you refused all appearances—you were a purist. Then you got a letter, something like: 'I'm alone on call all night at a Veteran's Hospital in Tulsa, and if it weren't for your book I'd kill myself.'"

"Ohhh, yeah!"

"That's when you started getting out to audiences, talking about putting the human back into medicine."

They fell silent. The weird January breeze wafted over them, really wafted.

"Fats said I should start getting out there again. Maybe he's right?"

"Maybe *more* than maybe."

Their eyes met, and held.

All these decades and now, all this burden of age—hearing, sight, touch, joints, going to doctors—all at once there's this old zing of not just love but first love and 50 years later love, and brand-new love, in her Buddhist spirit: loving-kindness.

"I have such gratitude for you!" he said. "You're a gift."

"And you."

"Annnd . . ." He smiled. "I want to ask about your Zoom meeting today—it starts soon, doesn't it?" Startled, she nodded. "Teaching Buddhists all over the world? A 'New Year' day of mindfulness?"

"Oh my God, you remembered, and actually asked? There's hope!"

He laughed. "I mean it. Tell me what you'll be doing?"

"It's new this year. I'm leading a world group in focused Buddhist practice—from Australia to the Netherlands, Japan to Germany, India to Africa—it's astonishing! Encircling the planet! Teaching teachers how we can go from our own spiritual practice to taking action out in the world. We'll be meeting for the next eighteen months."

"Taking the Buddha's 'right action' out into the world?"

"Yes. Asking how we can live with awareness and compassion in these horrific times. Covid, climate, the right-wing takeovers here and all over—and, for God's sake, *race*! The challenges are big, real and big. And the only thing we can focus on, in practice together, is the challenge of 'How do we live in this world now?'—right here and now, in all the defiled nows. We will not be getting back to safety, no way. This is not a path to safety. It will be risky, working with the suffering, together, learning how to walk through the suffering to practical ways not to just live, but to help others, and resist. It will be about the world *now*. And how we can take risks on whatever ground we stand on, wherever we live. No return to safety. Holding the hope, the suffering, walking through it *together, we will act.*" She smiled, and said lightly, "That's all. Easy, huh?"

"It's wonderful, kid. Makes my work seem trivial."

"Have you lost your mind?"

"Just my memory."

"You do medicine, and I do spirit—and we're all set."

They laughed, together. And then silence. Her eyes were shining.

What a long time it's been, this laughing, hard, together. This new focus. No search for safety, no, none. Go for it in any way you can.

"Y'know what I realized when I went over the list of the participants for today?" Berry asked, shaking her head. "Every single person in this new worldwide group is *at least* a generation younger than me. I'm finally a matriarch—hoping for a grandchild while I still have my spunk! A couple of new generations have already come around. But I can share, and teach, and help to grow them."

"I'm with you, totally. Almost everyone in medicine is hurting, doctors, nurses, all the others. Working in the money-driven hell-realms of American care. We're all suffering terribly. Covid has lit it all up for all to see. The risks to our bodies, minds, and spirit are profound. Killing ourselves, acting normal. The poor and people of color dying in droves."

He paused, scanning the trees for Fats. Nothing. He went on. "We do miracles every single day, but we haven't been able to get a place safe to work in, body and spirit. *One in five health-care workers have quit. Many of us died.* At the start of Covid, we did the most important thing, for us and our patients: *we stuck together.* We. But it became a very hard thing to do. We ran into the Big American Self, killing off the American Dream—because it was only a solo dream, in darkness, not really with others—not lasting into the day. Hatred and money killed it." He smiled at her. "As the Buddha said, it's the

Three Defilements: greed, hatred, delusion. The roots of suffering, right?"

"Yes," she said. "So when you go out there and do what Fats suggested, what would you say to the next generations?" She smiled. "I'll pretend I'm one of them."

He looked down over the deck, down to the flat land before the river.

"Now we turn our sight to you, the next generations. This isn't our fight anymore, at least not on the front line. But it breaks our heart to see you this way. It's your fight, and we have your backs. *We have faith in you. Stick together. Lean on us. Count on us, call on us, and we'll be there with you.*"

As he went on, it was as if he were reading from writing in the sky.

"All of you have made it as doctors and nurses, all you need from us now is inspiration. We promise we will help, with that. It will be hell. But listen, take this in deeply: these things can change like lightning, and with *lightening.* Sometime, maybe when you are down, your dark sky may lighten, and in that moment you may glimpse a beloved person: a love or a wild, kind teacher or family member or, as I did, a fat man. And in that sudden, strange awareness you can count on one thing above all else, for sure."

He smiled at Berry.

"Our job is to reveal and heal. We all, together, have the power to lift you, and your caring, up! It is a rising time." He paused.

Berry nodded, reached out, took his hand, gently, and smiled.

He finished, "We wish you all well."